MW01058433

LAST
WINTER

CARRIE
MAC

RANDOM HOUSE CANADA

PUBLISHED BY RANDOM HOUSE CANADA

www.penguinrandomhouse.ca

LIBRARY AND ARCHIVES CANADA CATALOGUING IN PUBLICATION

Title: Last winter / Carrie Mac.
Names: Mac, Carrie, 1975- author.
Identifiers: Canadiana (print) 2022024085X | Canadiana (ebook) 20220240876 |
ISBN 9781039005198 (softcover) | ISBN 9781039005204 (EPUB)
Subjects: LCGFT: Novels.
Classification: LCC PS8625.A23 L37 2023 | DDC C813/.6—dc23

Text design: Jennifer Griffiths
Cover design: Jennifer Griffiths
Image credits: aaaaimages / Getty Images

Printed in Canada

10 9 8 7 6 5 4 3 2 1

Penguin
Random House
RANDOM HOUSE CANADA

For Annabel Lyon

I wish great welcome to the snow,
Whatever its severe and comfortless and beautiful meaning.
—MARY OLIVER

BEFORE

The people of the town would look back at those autumn weeks when they were waiting for the first snow, when the trees were leafless and the roads were dusty with salt. At some point the street lights began to stay on for the children's walks to school. They'd reach back further and find the warm zephyrs of late summer evenings. People take pictures of those moments, their children around the fire in stretched-out swimsuits and bare feet, dirty fingers pulling apart charred marshmallows. Brand new school supplies tucked in a new backpack. Newly too-small jeans and dresses taken to the thrift store to make way for fresh clothes, washed and folded, except for the chosen outfit. First-day-of-school photos, all the siblings with their hair wet-combed. It's time to put away sprinklers, and sun hats and sandals. Then piles of crisp orange leaves dot the lawns of the town, and horses graze in misty fields up the valley. Mothers take pictures of Halloween costumes, of hockey stars and wizards and little ducks. The fathers walk the little ones around with their plastic pumpkin buckets.

The parents of the five dead children would've put away their summer clothes; brought the warmer pyjamas to the front of the drawers. Carried the citronella candles and the patio cushions to the garage. Noticed the mornings getting cooler, and the mother bear with her twins daring to come into town to feast on the windfalls from the crabapple trees that lined the main road. Maybe they would look back on those ordinary things and find some kind of comfort.

The snow came, and the cold hardened the ice on the lake until it was safe to skate on. That first night of skating there was a bonfire, like every year. The kids tore around beyond the glow of the fire, laughing and shouting in the half dark. There were three truckloads of wood. The tips of the flames touched the low-slung stars. Cans of beer poked out of the pile of snow left after ploughing the lot. Whiskey and vodka and coolers too. Most of the vehicles had their stereos set to Mountain FM, but not obnoxiously loud. A set of moms heated up hot chocolate in a canning pot big enough to bathe the babies, who sat roly-poly in their snowsuits, eating snow. The older children, including all the ones who would perish in the avalanche, stood in line with rosy cheeks for a ladle of hot chocolate topped with little marshmallows and whipped cream from a can. Ordinary things. Perfect treasures.

Ten days after the avalanche, and it had already fallen out of the national news cycle. Even locally, it had been bumped by a controversy involving the Land Use Commission and by the discovery of a bear's carcass with the paws removed. No one beyond the mountain passes on all sides seemed to want to talk about the five dead children anymore. People still talked about it all the time in the snowed-in valley of Casper, where the sun gave up early each day and everyone knew at least one of the families involved.

With the exception of the young RCMP officer, Constable Simard, who stood in front of Fiona now. He'd transferred to Casper just at the new year, and did not know anyone involved in the avalanche, although he was quick to tell Fiona that he'd bought a pair of snowshoes and a ski jacket from Gus's store, shortly before the tragedy.

"When did you notice she was gone?" His French-Canadian accent was thick.

"I'm not sure," Fiona said to the photo she clutched of Ruby, the one from the school play about the big bang. Ruby, then six, played a very small, hot mix of fundamental forces, containing no stars or atoms. She was nine now, and she'd hardly changed a bit, except in height.

Fiona had not thought of her daughter at all during the night, and not for the better part of the day before. It might've even been since that previous morning. Or maybe noon.

On stage, Ruby's one job was to crouch until given her cue to explode. She didn't have to yell, of course, because she didn't ever speak at school. The school was supportive, and the kids always appeared to be too, but Fiona knew they made fun of her, even if Ruby didn't tell her about it. The other kids yelled *Bang!* in her place, obviously happy to do it. Those children were gone now. Except Liam. Now Ruby was gone too.

Constable Simard sat down on the couch, leaning forward with a notebook on his knee. His feet were impossibly large, entombed in shiny black boots, damp with melted snow. "Focus, Mrs. Tenner. The last time you saw her. Think of what you were doing. Sometimes that helps."

Another officer stood behind Fiona's chair, casting a shadow over her and the coffee table.

Ruby's father, Gus, had snapped that photo of her just before curtain call. He took it from a distance, but Ruby was looking right at him, under the one backstage light. She was a sinewy flame against the shadows of the other children getting in line behind her. Her face was supposed to be painted to match her costume, but she'd refused any paint at the last minute.

Gus's best friend, Mike, appeared at the bottom of the stairs. Fiona hadn't noticed him go up. She'd called him immediately after she realized Ruby hadn't slept in her bed. He got there before the cops did, even though the station was much closer. Mike took her hand and placed several pills there before folding her fingers closed over them.

"It was yesterday," Fiona admitted. "After my friend left. Willy's car came around noon. Then Sarah stopped by." She glanced up at Mike. "I remember now. It was after that. Ruby was with Liam. At the door. They'd come back from somewhere. She must've left again, later."

"Who's Liam?" Constable Simard said.

"Mike's son," the other cop offered before Mike could. His name was Arnold, Fiona knew, but she couldn't remember if that was his first name or his last, and she couldn't read the name on his jacket since he was behind her.

"He's nine." Mike scratched his beard. "They're in school together."

The only other child to survive the field trip.

"What did you put in her hand?" Arnold asked as Mike handed Fiona her mug of tea, which had gone cold almost immediately in the freezing house. Each time someone spoke, it was marked by a puff of icy white.

"Pills," Mike said.

"What are they for?"

"I don't need them." Fiona tightened her fist. "I'm fine."

"She has a mental illness," Mike said. "Bipolar disorder."

"I'm fine," Fiona whispered.

"Want some water instead of that cold tea?" Constable Simard said.

"I don't take medication in the morning." Fiona kept her fist closed, her eyes fixed on Simard as he nodded at Arnold, who put his hand to his radio as he left the room. She heard him in the kitchen, but she couldn't make out what he was saying.

"Let's move on so that we get this out to the searchers." He made another note. "Where were Ruby and Liam all day yesterday?"

"I don't know," Fiona said.

Constable Simard glanced up at Mike.

"They're kids," Mike said. "They take off. They know what they're doing. Especially our kids."

Liam hadn't come inside, Fiona remembered. He'd said something to Ruby. *Goodbye,* maybe. *See you tomorrow.* Fiona tried to hear him now, but she couldn't, not over the sound of the radio squawking in the other room and the search helicopter in the distance. How wretched it was to hear that helicopter again, after days and days of it when the children and Gus were missing.

She squeezed her eyes shut, trying to remember. She hadn't got off the couch, but she had sat up to yell at the two of them. *In or out, shut the door!* Ruby was wearing her pyjamas with snowboarding bunnies all over them, the ratty hems stuffed into her winter boots. Over them, her glaringly orange parka, the hood covering her blond hair, matted at the back because she hadn't brushed it since the memorial. She had her filthy backpack too, hung low from her shoulders, greasy with Gus's sweat from the years he'd used it before he gave it to Ruby. *Don't stand in the door like that.* That had come out as more of a whisper, the words slurred. She was stoned. Still drunk. Sleepy. *I don't care, in or out. Shut the door.*

"What were you doing, Fiona?" Simard said. "Picking up her toys? Doing laundry? Having coffee with a friend?" This was a housewife's inventory, made exotic by his accent and his big brown eyes. This was a list of things Fiona had not done since at least the last time the police came to her home. "What was she wearing? Was her hair in pigtails? Braids? Painted nails?"

"Her hair is too short for plaits." Fiona closed her eyes and bent to kiss Ruby's head. She breathed in, hands cupping her daughter's temples.

"Mrs. Tenner?"

Fiona kept her eyes shut, her hands up. Inhaling.

"You'd call it a pixie cut, I guess." Mike said. "Blond. Lighter than it looks in that picture. The one I gave you from my phone is from just a couple of days ago. No nail polish."

Not a pixie cut. Just a shag, like Gus had when he was little. Fiona wanted to show them that picture of six-year-old Gus on his BMX bike. The one on the wall by the wood stove, but she found that she did not have the energy to get up and take it off the nail and hand it to the officer, to show him that Gus was still here, in Ruby. Not a pixie cut. A boy's cut. Ruby and Gus, twins separated by thirty-one years. Ruby did not display even one splash of Fiona, whose hair and eyes were dark. Gus and Ruby were pink to Fiona's creamy complexion, freckled to her not.

"Mrs. Tenner, open your eyes, please." Simard was beginning to sound less like a kind television version of a francophone RCMP officer now, and more like an irritated cop. "I do not need to remind you that time is not on our side."

"I'm sorry." Fiona opened her eyes. "I don't know how to do this." She would be out there looking for Ruby herself, but she could not move her limbs, frozen and drained from the cold inside the house and the cold white winter outside it, with drifts of snow over her head and no idea of where to start.

"What was she wearing?"

"Didn't I say?"

"You said you weren't sure," Mike said.

Ruby had been home to see Willy off. She'd gone up to her room after that. Then she'd gone out. Fiona remembered that now, because she'd asked Ruby to make a fire in the stove before she went, but there was no firewood in the house. The cord of wood had shifted in the weeks before Christmas and had threatened to topple every time Gus loaded up the wheelbarrow. Fiona supposed it was her job now that he was gone, but she simply had not done it.

When Ruby came back with Liam, thin midday light leaked through the living room windows, all of which were frosted on the inside because the furnace had stopped working weeks ago and the remaining fire in the wood stove had burned down to ash. The light was already headed for its daily refuge behind the mountain and the living room was dark. Liam leaned in from the outside, his mittened hand on the doorknob. Ruby was wearing her ski mitts too. Neon orange to match her parka. Liam wore his puffy green jacket, a patched-up hand-me-down from his older brother, Luke. Liam handed Ruby something yellow, which she slipped into her pocket. She said something to him, no more than one word. Snow drifted in on a low, thin eddy.

One more word than she'd said to her mother for as long as Fiona could remember. *Shut the door, shut the door, shut the door.*

"Ruby said something. Just one word, I think."

"She did?" Mike said.

"What did she say?" Constable Simard readied his pen.

"I don't know." Fiona shook her head. "What she *said* isn't the point."

"She's selectively mute," Mike said.

Shut the door. She remembered not caring that Ruby said something, just wanting her to shut the door. That was the first time she had not felt that scrambling sensation in her gut whenever Ruby spoke to someone who wasn't her. This alarmed her nearly as much as not knowing where Ruby was. Fiona squeezed the pills in her fist so hard she felt the capsules crush. Just as she could not make her limbs move with purpose, she could not make herself take the pills, even if they might set the world back on its axis enough for her to regain her footing.

"This must be very, very hard." Simard's expression softened. "We'll ask Liam what she said."

Fiona remembered lying on the couch under a down quilt and Gus's warmest sleeping bag, unzipped and smelling of him. A book lay open on the floor beside her, one of the five novels her best friend, Willy, sent her from the *Guardian* top twenty of the year. Each exhalation was a suspended mark in the cold. Her fingers were still cold inside possum-down gloves and fleece mitts overtop. With Gus's black toque pulled down over her ears, her head was warm, but her feet were not quite, even in two pairs of thick wool socks. She'd started the day with the scarf Gus helped Ruby knit for her for Christmas. Wonky pink-and-purple stripes, an endearing and very soft caterpillar. Then she added the one Willy brought for her from Liberty's of London, a large square with paisley swirls of peacock blues and greens. Fiona's colours, and so soft. She'd taken both scarves off at some point. Her fingers drifted to her neck now. The one from Willy was folded in tissue in the Liberty box, packed in her luggage at the bottom of the stairs. But where was the one from Ruby and Gus?

"Liam left. I heard the door close." Then a thump as Ruby let her backpack drop. Two more thumps as she kicked off her boots.

Ruby walked past her, into the kitchen. *Ruby?* She turned and came back, then leaned over the couch to kiss Fiona on the forehead. Ruby picked up an end of the striped scarf and let it drop with a smile.

"She went to the fridge." It was full of sympathy bounty from the townsfolk—casseroles and containers of soup, trays of deli meats and cheese cubes and jumbles of olives, a platter of salmon pâté sandwiches, a bowl of quinoa pilaf dotted with red peppers and artichokes—what did Ruby pick? From all of that, what did she pick?

She'd heard a jar set down on the counter, then another jar, a loaf of bread, rustling as she slid a piece out of the bag. A cupboard door, a plate, the cutlery drawer clanking open, clanking shut. "She made a peanut butter and jam sandwich." Was it the blackberry jam? Or the crabapple jelly? Or the peach jam, or the strawberry jam? Or one of the other jams that lined the counter now, part of the endless train of bags and baskets and boxes and any other way that well-meaning—or hateful—neighbours could deliver food, as if that's what she needed, as if any of them genuinely wanted to help her. This was for Ruby. Not her. Whoever was in charge was simply taking pity on a child. Dropping off the same meals they'd organized for the other grieving families. Battalions of support, surely, so that each of the deserving families got a dozen burritos, two lasagnas, butter chicken with rice in a separate container, pot pies, old yogurt tubs filled with chili or stew or dal. She can imagine them stumbling at her name. *Think of the child. Let's do it if only for that poor child.* A child needs to eat. *That poor child needs to eat. She was so tiny before and now she's just wasting away.*

Somewhere out there, in the snow.

Her child, silent and small, in the snow.

If Fiona stayed with that thought for even a few seconds, she began to slowly pull away from earth, in danger of becoming breathless and frozen in outer space before shattering into a million shards that would float for eternity.

"That means it was lunchtime," Fiona said. "Or middle of the day, anyway. Ruby only eats peanut butter and jam sandwiches for lunch. She offered me an orange."

Arnold was back. "She called out from the kitchen?"

Simard glanced at him. "She doesn't talk."

"She does, though," Fiona said. "She can."

"That's why it's called selective mutism," Mike said.

"She came in here with it in her hands," Fiona said. "Cupped like this." Fiona did the same. The pills were gone. She did not know if she'd taken them or let them fall into the mess of blankets on the couch. "She offered it to me."

"Good, good." The cop leaned forward. "What did you say?"

"Did you take the pills?" Mike interrupted.

Four capsules of lithium, one each of lamotrigine and divalproex, and one *as needed* quetiapine pill added for good measure. Fiona glanced down and spotted them wedged between the couch cushions. She rearranged the blanket over her hand and slid them down farther. She'd already taken quetiapine and lorazepam, and vaped weed at some point in the night when she got up to go to the bathroom, the toilet like a ring of ice, when she had no idea that her daughter was out there, heading for the mountain, no doubt. She'd told the police that, and the search and rescue captain who came by. They all said there was no way Ruby would make it that far. But they flew the helicopter over Tiffen Lake anyway, looking for her parka from above. Fiona squeezed her eyes shut. The quetiapine was tar on her brain, sticking things into dark corners, not letting her think clearly. She did know that, of any child, Ruby was the one who would be okay out there, perhaps more so than here at home with her.

"I took the orange." Fiona straightened and reached for her cigarettes, a negotiation with heaviness. She took one out and held it between her stiff fingers. "And I ate it." Peeling it, then coaxing apart the pieces, slipping them into her mouth one by one, while Ruby stood there. No one will ever know how hard it was to eat those dripping wedges, when all she wanted to do was throw that orange through the window and never eat again. It was Gus who taught her to say yes to Ruby as often as she could, because then maybe she would talk to them. *It's not spoiling her,* he said. *It's just showing her that we're on her side. More than anyone else.*

Though she could still smell the oils of the rind on her fingers, Fiona was not entirely sure she had eaten the orange. Maybe she'd said no. The quetiapine tar made her look back at that orange in her hands and doubt it. Maybe she'd thrown it through the window after all. She ripped a match from the book perched on the thick glass rim of the heavy jade-green ashtray. The sulphur flare stung her nose, then came the quiet crackle as her cigarette caught. Inhale. Tighten. Exhale. She had eaten the orange. There was no broken window.

"Ruby will be okay," she said.

"Of course she will."

Fiona knew that Simard didn't believe it and had only said it—and so quickly—because he needed to believe it. She looked up at Mike, who was nodding. He met her gaze and kept nodding. He knew that Fiona was right. Just because Ruby was not here did not mean she was in danger, or at least not like most kids her age would be in the same circumstances. Time would be the true abductor here, though, the one who could actually steal her away.

Inhale. Hold the smoke. Feel the burn in your lungs like a punishment. Exhale. Do not think of the vast expanse of wilderness between this couch and the avalanche site.

Fiona closed her eyes and saw that tiny moving smudge of bright orange against the snow. Ruby was the child who could get there. She might even be the kind to find her father, dead or alive. But was she the child who could make her way back?

Ruby packed after she got her mother to eat an orange. She used the bright-red backpack her father gave her for her seventh birthday, his old one that she'd wanted so much, the one he wore when he went snowboarding. Small for him, and still too big for her. He'd filled it with enough gear to keep her safe in the backcountry for twenty-four hours. In it she put the folding shovel he gave her for Christmas—this would be essential—her first aid kit, four hand warmer packets, an emergency bivvy, three of the homemade granola bars someone had left in a grocery bag hanging on the front door, each wrapped in waxed paper with a band of tape around it and the flavour written on it. CHERRY ALMOND. CHOCOLATE PECAN. PUMPKIN SPICE. An emergency candle, waterproof matches, spare base layers, gloves, a headlamp, ten feet of paracord carefully coiled and cinched at the middle, Luke's bright-yellow GPS that Liam had given her earlier. He'd told her how to use it, but she wasn't sure if she could figure it out without her dad. She strapped her new snowshoes to the outside, like her father did with his, and hung her avalanche transceiver around her neck.

Liam met her at the end of his street and gave her a piece of paper, folded and folded and folded.

"Don't lose it," he said as she tucked it into her pocket. He stuck his hand in and grabbed it back, then put it in her chest pocket, the one that zipped shut.

The two of them made their way to her snow cave, which was about halfway between her house and the gas station. She dropped her pack there, then checked on the rabbit warren she and her dad carved into the wall after they built the cave. The three little plastic rabbits were still asleep in their nest of down, salvaged from a sleeping bag that had gotten too close to a campfire. The members of the wooden peg family were in three separate rooms. Her dad was with the rabbits. Her mother was in the living room, reading a book beside the fireplace with its orange-and-yellow Cellophane flames. Ruby was in the kitchen, in front of a tiny apple pie eraser that actually smelled of cinnamon and apple. Ruby figured she could use another of herself that night, so she put the wooden peg doll in her pocket that already had the rabbit with the hole in its back and an energy bar she was saving for her dad.

"Don't lose that either," Liam said. "That would be the worst luck ever."

As if it wasn't already.

The sky was indigo blue when she came back for her pack later that day. Mount Casper rose up behind the town, the glassy cliffs awash in the last light of dusk. Wisps of cloud caught on the jagged rocks; above the treeline was nothing but white upon white upon white, in dips and swells, a frozen ocean, a picture of terrifying, tremulous cold.

Ruby cut through the forest and came out by the gas station on the highway. A few cars passed, and then a truck with studded tires crunched into the gas station and up to the pumps. It was Mike's. He parked the nozzle in the gas tank and went inside while it filled. The store was so bright, it was like watching a movie about a store. Mike grabbed a coffee from the machine. Cherise, the cashier, waved away his money. He was talking, and she was talking. They were just having a conversation.

Normal stuff. No one was panicking. Mike wasn't worried, which meant no one was searching for her yet. They both looked sad, though. Mike always looked sad now. Everyone in town did. Maybe they would forever.

When Mike drove away, Ruby waited for another few minutes—two more trucks, another car, a semi-truck heading north—and then she darted across the highway just past where the street lights stopped. She skirted the gas station, staying in the shadows, until she was directly across from Cherise's car. Ruby pulled out the piece of paper with Liam's writing on it. He'd written down her licence plate number. *You have to be sure that you get into the right car,* he said. *Because if you don't, you might end up in Lil'wat, and that would be bad.*

Or Vancouver, Ruby said. That would be worse.

It was unlocked, just like it had been when she and Liam checked earlier, but it was still a relief. Ruby pushed her pack onto the floor and crouched behind the driver's seat. The cashier's shift ended at seven o'clock. That was only half an hour or so, right? Ruby didn't have a watch. She didn't like anything on her wrists. She did wish she had one now, though. Or a phone. The GPS had the time, but it was buried in her pack.

It seemed a lot longer than half an hour, but Ruby finally heard Cherise shout goodbye to the guy who replaced her, then the heavy clang of the back door of the building slamming shut. Seconds later, she heard the metallic rattle of the chain on the garbage bin and then the lid squeaking as it was lifted. The hollow *thunk* of a bag of garbage landing inside an empty bin. The lid banged shut, the chain rattled again, and then Cherise opened the driver's-side door. Ruby held her breath. She was crouched in a tight ball, her face pressed to the dirty carpet scattered with Cheerios, her knees digging into the hard plastic lines of the carpet protector that was half slid up under the front seat. The car shifted with Cherise's weight. She was fat. Not just a bit fat, really fat. Shane called her Dumptruck even though her name was Cherise, which was cherry in French, and so maybe the prettiest name ever. The other kids called her Dumptruck too, only because Shane did, and he was the boss of things like that. Although now that he was dead, was he still the worst bully ever? Did that change?

You can call her whatever you want, Liam said after Ruby shot him a stern look when he called her that. *It doesn't matter what her name is, so long as she gets in her car and drives all the way home. If she goes somewhere else, you'll freeze if you stay in the car, and if you get out and you don't know where you are, you might end up knocking on someone's door and then the whole plan will be ruined. You better hope she doesn't go to her friend's house and play Monopoly. That's a really, really long game. Or Dungeons and Dragons. That takes Luke all night, most times.*

The engine turned over. Once, twice, and then it caught. The stereo blasted a commercial for the new indoor wave pool in Whistler, an ad for the Tandoori place in Creekside. Then a song came on. Ruby knew it. It was by Snow Patrol, and it made her think of her father, even if she didn't want to think of him right then. Besides, Gus hated this song. He said it was whiny and stupid and overplayed. He called Mountain FM once and told them so, and sometimes the station still played that call. *Even the famous Gus Tenner hates Snow Patrol! Listen to this, folks, have a listen. It's funny.* Whenever they played the call, Ruby listened so hard that her ears ached. She had been in the truck with him when he phoned in. *I hate this song so much,* he said to her. *I'm going to call them and tell them so.* He held the phone to his ear while he drove, and when DJ Half-Pipe picked up, he told him who he was, and then he was laughing and telling the DJ how much he hated the song and that for every time they were going to play it—but didn't—to let him know and he would donate five dollars to Lifts for Gifts, a charity that brought Christmas presents to the kids who lived in the communities up the Lil'wat valley. She bet he gave them a hundred dollars. Or more. That stupid song.

The fan was turned up high and hot dry air filled the car as Cherise drove along the highway. Ruby was too hot in her layers. She pulled her scarf away from her neck, but that didn't help much. She was drowsy. Queasy, too. Three songs later, the car turned the sharp corner into the reserve and then another sharp turn out onto Tiffen Lake Road. Two and a half more songs and Ruby was asleep. She didn't wake until the car bumped along a long, snow-covered dirt driveway. For a moment she had no idea where she was, but then she remembered. Mostly, she wanted to go back to sleep. But she didn't either, because even more mostly, she wanted to find her father.

Cherise parked and reached across to the passenger seat for her purse. She got out and shut the door and took another minute to plug in the block heater, and then she crunched across the snow and up a few creaking steps. She kicked the snow off her boots and went inside.

Ruby waited a little while—was it long enough?—before she uncurled. Her legs were numb and tingling, and her feet were concrete in her boots. She wriggled around the dirty baby seat and sat in the middle, where she could just see over the dash and out the window. Ruby knew that Cherise would go straight home, and she had. She wished she could tell Liam he'd made a big deal for no reason.

The car was parked beside a truck, both nosed up to a single-wide trailer. A swing set stuck up out of a snowbank on one side of the trailer, beside a drift-filled plastic playhouse with pink shutters and a little green roof capped with an icy crust.

The curtains were drawn in the living room, but they were thin enough that the pale glow of the TV shimmered onto the snow. There was no curtain in the small kitchen window. Ruby could see Cherise's mother standing there, still in her uniform from the grocery store with her name tag on her pocket. She glanced up, down, up—washing dishes? She turned away and then disappeared. When Ruby eased the car door open, the overhead light popped on, so she quickly threw her pack onto the snow and slid out after it, pushing the door closed gently, extinguishing the light. She carried the pack in her arms until she was around the back of the trailer and in the dark. She put on her snowshoes and settled her pack on her back, snapping together all the clips and adjusting the straps like her dad taught her. *You want to carry the weight on your hips, Rabbit. Not your shoulders.*

She turned to look at the trailer one last time before she set off into the forest, past cordwood neatly stacked under a tarp, and an empty rabbit hutch under the cover of corrugated plastic, bowed beneath the weight of the snow. A dirty, white, trampled-down patch stretched out from the tiny back porch, a half-circle of it illuminated by a light hanging above the door. A plastic toboggan with a yellow rope. A ride-on toy car with two wheels missing and wide eyes for headlights and a big grin for a grille. One dark window, another one barely lit. A small face above the sill. Ruby froze. Cherise's toddler looked out at her. She had little brown pigtails above each ear and a soother in her mouth. Ruby relaxed and waved. She wasn't worried about a little baby.

Smoke drifted up from the chimney and into a black sky where the stars sparkled in their places. She hadn't brought her star guide, but she knew Ursa Major, and the North Star. And Orion's Belt, when her dad helped her find it. Ruby looked up for a long time, hoping for a shooting star, because that would be very good luck, and she wished she could be especially lucky right now. But there were no shooting stars, so she picked the brightest star and wished upon it. She pulled the little plastic rabbit from her pocket. It had broken off the key chain, but it still had the tiny hole on its back where her father had screwed in the little eyelet. She glanced up at the sky again, and there it was, a thin, bright streak across the sky. She held the plastic rabbit in her palm and made a double wish, one on the star, and one on the rabbit. Two times lucky was better than one. She dug the peg doll of herself out and made a wish on that too. All the luck was the best kind. As she plodded into the dark of the forest, she was thankful that she was already halfway up the mountain. Thank you, Cherise's house. Thank you, Cherise's car. Thank you, Cherise.

Liam might not be one hundred percent wrong about her father being dead. He could be right. Her father *could* be dead. She would be stupid if she thought he was alive for sure. She wasn't stupid. But everyone who said he was dead for sure thought they knew everything, when they couldn't know. Her father might be dead. He really, actually *might* be. But he might *not* be, too. If anyone could survive like one of those crazy, impossible wilderness survival stories that she and her dad watched on TV, then it was him. Even if he lost his nose and toes to frostbite. Even if he had a broken leg and had to make crutches from branches and strap his leg to another branch with cedar strips. Even if he had two broken legs and was dragging himself along like a rabbit that had been caught in one of those terrible snap-fang traps and gnawed itself free.

Either way, she was going up there, and she would find him, and she would bring him home. And if he didn't want to come home because all of his friends had stopped looking for him and he and her mother only made each other mad, she'd live up there with him, just the two of them in a lean-to near a stream. Food might be a really big problem, but they'd come up with something.

Ruby needed to find him *tonight*, before her mother took her to England. Either she was going to stay up on the mountain with him, or he needed to come home right now and get healed up so he could go back to work and fix the furnace and make her grilled cheese sandwiches and tomato soup served in her favourite mug. He needed to re-stack the wood so it wouldn't fall over. She'd help him. Mostly, though, he needed to be home, waiting for Ruby to come back from England, because if he wasn't there to miss her and want her to come back, she could be stuck in England forever. If he wasn't there waiting, her mother might just not bring her home at all.

The secret in her heart was that if she couldn't find her dad, she would never leave the valley ever again. She would grow up to be a teenager and an adult and an old woman, and then she would die, but unless her father came down from the mountain, she would never leave Casper.

DECEMBER 20

When Fiona got dressed for Gus's birthday party, she put on the chandelier earrings she'd worn when they first met. That was the only fancy thing, because party attire in Casper was no different from attire for grocery shopping, or picking up your children from school, or going for a run or a date or a meeting with a lawyer. The earrings, though—Gus would remember those. And when he did, he would pull her to him in a way he had not done in a very long time, at which point she could lean in to him, and take him to a dark corner. And then, perhaps, something would shift, and they could start looking at each other like they loved each other and were not just two crows circling the shiny treasure that was Ruby.

It would take a strong talisman, and these earrings were that.

Fiona had spent the day in her pyjamas, putting together canapés and assembling a chocolate fountain with a tray of pound cake cut into squares and slices of apple and pear and banana. Ruby helped her for a little while, slicing the bananas before Fiona could tell her it was too early, and then disappearing out the back door for the rest of the afternoon. The bananas browned, of course, and so Fiona peeled the rounds and put them in the freezer for banana bread or smoothies. She'd cut the remaining two bananas at the last minute.

Gus closed up the shop and brought home enough alcohol to stock a pub for a week. He'd found Ruby on the way home, so she helped him carry it in. The two of them went to build a bonfire in the firepit, which is when Fiona retreated upstairs. She didn't like greeting guests at the door, so she had a long bath, and wasn't out when the first people arrived. Mike and Sarah, with Liam and Luke, and Luke's girlfriend, Aubrey. Fiona especially did not want to open the door to them. Not tonight, when she was going to try to pull Gus back to her.

Even though it was barely seven o'clock when she descended the stairs unnoticed, the party was in full swing, the way that small towns do parties early. She began collecting balled-up napkins and empty red plastic party cups. People said hello to her, patted her shoulder as she passed them, made little comments about her puff pastry spinach cups and bruschetta with avocado and balsamic reduction and zucchini bites, breaded, baked and drizzled with garlic aioli.

"Shall we do the cake?" she announced when she couldn't think of anything else to say. "Who knows where the birthday boy is?"

Gus appeared, as if summoned, Ruby at his side. After everyone sang, he said, "Make a wish, Rabbit," and lifted Ruby onto his hip, like she was still small, and not nearly nine years old. Ruby squeezed her eyes shut for a moment, then blew. Fiona cut the cake and slid the goopy pieces onto paper plates. The icing was slick, starting to separate. She'd overmixed it. And it was too sweet, too.

While everyone was eating cake, a delivery guy arrived with a teetering stack of damp, hot pizza boxes, even though there was still plenty of food laid out on the counter.

"Gus?" Fiona said as he pulled out a fistful of cash he should not have.

"It's all good, Fi." He thrust it at the driver while everybody protested and threw money at him, which Gus left where it landed. As the children scrambled for it, Ruby stood against the wall with a finger hooked in her mouth.

"Go get some," Fiona said. "That Shane kid, his mothers need to teach him manners. Look! He's going to hog it all. And Liam. He just got a twenty." She wanted to go get some for herself, for her and Ruby and Gus, because she was pretty sure that he'd taken the cash from the coffee can. That was money she was saving for a trip home to England. Or part of it.

Fiona pushed Ruby forward. "Go." Ruby took the push, but then backed up against Fiona and shook her head.

"Never mind, I get it, love." Fiona held her closer, her hands crossed over Ruby's chest.

Ruby didn't eat any of the pizza. She ate the spinach cups. She ate the bruschetta. She ate the zucchini. Even though pizza was her favourite.

Fiona cornered Gus in the basement, where he was looking for the Magic Carpets. "Did we leave them at the hill last week?" he said.

"I wasn't there."

"But do you remember me and Ruby bringing them home?" Gus pulled aside the toboggan with the broken rail. "We had four of them."

"Was that pizza money from the can?"

The tattoos that coloured his arms from wrist to shoulder looked like black paint in the dim light, but she could see his new knuckle tattoos clearly. *Ruby. Love.* A birthday present to himself. He traded two pairs of last year's rental snowshoes for them.

"Shit," Gus said as a box of dead Christmas lights toppled to the floor.

"Did you take the money from the coffee can?"

"I did." He jammed the box of lights back onto the shelf. "I'll replace it long before we'll have enough to go anywhere."

"It was the idea of it, though." Fiona touched his hand. *Love.* "You know? Just having it there, adding to it. It means more than the sum of the coins and the bills."

"I get it." He took both her wrists in his hands. *Love. Ruby.* "I'll put it back. I promise."

When he couldn't find the Magic Carpets, Gus grabbed the broken toboggan and a snow disc he found beneath the rubble of outdoor stuff under the stairs. His good gear was well-organized in bins on shelves, but the rest of it landed here, in a musty pile just outside the light cast by the two bare bulbs, one at either end of the damp basement.

There was Ruby, sitting at the top of the basement stairs, the door to the living room closed behind her.

"How long have you been there, love?" Fiona put a hand on Ruby's shoulder and kissed her head.

Ruby shrugged.

"Too loud?" Gus held out a hand. Ruby nodded, taking it. "Want to come outside with me?"

"Oh, it's so cold," Fiona said. "And late."

"We know cold," Gus said. "Right, Rabbit?"

Ruby took his hand. *Ruby.* Gus pushed open the door and the music suddenly blasted down the stairs, and the light too.

Gus held up the broken toboggan like a trophy. *Love.*

"To the great outdoors!"

There was a swell of cheers, and then scuffling and thumping as people shrugged into coats. Ruby looked back as she stepped into her fur-lined boots. She smiled. Fiona waved and smiled, and then she watched the procession from her place halfway up the dark stairs: jeans and leggings and boots and jackets. The dirty linoleum and the puddle of melted snow from the boots.

It was Willy's fault Fiona ever set foot in British Columbia in the first place. She flew six bridesmaids and Fiona—unmarried maid of honour—to Whistler for her bachelorette celebrations, even though it was April, there was little snow, and she had no connection to the place other than the fact that a DJ she loved was performing there on the second night.

A red-eye to Vancouver, a limo the rest of the way, past impressive mountains and ocean and forests. They even spotted a scrawny mama bear and a little cub grazing under some power lines.

Fiona hadn't slept, and she'd had a lot to drink on the plane.

She felt weary and iridescent, a vibration prickling her from under her skin. This buzzing ache demanded motion. Action. But mania was unpredictable. She took a pill that would knock her out. She would start from scratch when she woke. She would not ruin Willy's celebrations.

She lay naked on the bed and did not sleep. She listened to the partying on the pub patios and the amplified hip hop from the stage—some mountain biking festival was in full swing—and when the phone rang, she didn't answer it. When Willy and the girls knocked on the door to collect her for dinner, she opened it a crack and said that it was something she ate and Willy moaned and the girls offered to bring her ginger ale and soda crackers and Fiona said no need, no need, she'd feel better in the morning, but thank you.

Night two of no sleep.

Whistler buzzed with a frenetic energy so intense that Fiona was sure that if she stepped out—even just into the hallway— she would be flattened by the sexual, youthful yearning and the sweat and the inebriation and the lack of inhibition and the filth falling off the muddy bike armour and the stench of those alien helmets and the terrible stomping. Everyone stomped.

Willy came alone the next morning. Fiona ignored her knocking. It was believable—she could be in the shower, or out for a walk or at the pool—but Willy kept knocking. She knew better. Fiona went to the door and opened it that same little crack.

"It might not be food poisoning," she said. "It might be catching. Planes are such cesspools."

"Bullshit." Willy pushed her way into the room. She wore yoga pants and a tank top and clutched a water bottle, and if she was hungover, she didn't look it. She'd been to the gym on the second floor. "You're doing your crazy thing. And I'm here to tell you that you simply cannot. It's *my* bachelorette holiday and you have a job to do, Fi."

"I know," Fiona said. "But I'm sick."

"You're not sick. You're having an episode. You have medication for that. You can do this if you want to. You're hiding, that's what. Indulging yourself."

"I'm not," Fiona said.

"Right, because you're fine. Do not pull your crazy out now. Come to brunch with us."

Fiona put a hand to her stomach. She actually did feel nauseous. "I don't think I should."

"But you *will*." Willy pulled Fiona's hand away and held it tight. "You're slipping, and while it's normally my job to shore you up, you will come down to brunch, and if you spend the entire time vomiting into the bread basket, so be it."

In the lineup at the restaurant, three men behind them talked loudly about a fourth.

"Warranted, he was dancing like an asshole."

"The bouncer overreacted."

"He didn't. He had every right to kick him out. That place has a bad enough reputation as it is. Norm was doing his best to clean it up."

They lowered their voices. Fiona was desperate to know what the absent friend had been kicked out for. She tried to let it go. She sipped her mimosa and nibbled at her poached eggs on Dungeness crab cakes and listened to the others talk about vows and dresses, but she could not take her eyes off the group of men. There was an empty chair at their table. Was that for the friend? She couldn't hear them at all now. Fiona needed to know what happened. She wanted to know who the fourth man was, what he looked like, how he spoke, what he had done the night before—at a bar, she could guess that much—and where was he now? In jail? Maybe he'd come up for a party weekend and got arrested. For what? What did he do? She had to know. She *had* to know. She put a hand to her gut. She felt the churning panic that came with this kind of obsessive thinking. It only got worse once they were seated.

"Fi, will you?"

"What?"

"Ride the ATVs with us."

"No, thank you."

"They give you helmets. You can go as slowly as you'd like. We might see another bear!"

"No." Fiona stood up. "Excuse me."

"Sit, Fi."

"I'll be right back."

"Fiona!" Willy called after her.

She approached the table with the three men. Nearly vibrating with that terrible need to know about the fourth man, she pulled out the empty chair and sat.

"What did he do? The fourth man."

"Excuse me?" The man beside her leaned back. He parked one elbow on the back of his chair and looked her up and down. "Who are you?"

"Did he get into a fight?" Fiona leaned forward, lowering her voice. "Did he do something to a girl?"

"What are you talking about?"

"Your friend. I just want to know what happened. You were talking about him and then you just stopped." Fiona sped up. "You said something about a bouncer having every right to kick him out, and then you stopped talking and I really, really need to know." Her words were coming in such a rush that she could hardly get them out in order. "If-if-if he did something, if he was jailed—I mean arrested—for something. If he's okay. I just need to know."

"Who the fuck *are* you?" the man across the table said. "It's none of your business." He waved for the waiter.

Fiona put her hand on the arm of the man beside her. "You have to understand, I just want to know. That's all. I don't care what he did. I'm not mad at him. I'm not going to judge, I just—"

The waiter arrived, and the maître d' too.

"Can I help?" the maître d' said.

"Yes," said the man across the table. "We have no idea who this woman is, or what the hell she wants—"

"But you *do* know what I want! I said so. I was very clear."

"Miss, let me escort you back to your table." The maître d' put a hand on her shoulder.

"Get off me! I just want to know what happened to your friend! I'm Fiona, so now you do know me! And you know what I want. You *do*. Please. Please?"

Willy was at her other side now. She pulled Fiona out of her seat, using all her strength. "I am so, so sorry. She's not feeling well this morning. It was a long flight yesterday and then the car ride to get here. She is simply exhausted, aren't you, pet?"

"I'm not. Let me go, Willy."

The first man stood. "I'll walk you out," he said. This relieved Fiona, because he might still tell her what happened to the fourth man. And this one—the one called Gus, who was coming with them right now—was a beautiful, beautiful man.

Willy, holding tight to Fiona's arm, steered her through the lobby and into the elevator and up to her room on the sixth floor. The beautiful man escorted them, not saying a word.

"He could come in," Fiona said.

"He can't." Willy grabbed her shoulders and steered her inside. She held the door open just long enough to add, "*Do not leave this room.*"

On the other side of the door, Fiona could hear Willy insisting on paying for the men's meal. As their voices faded towards the elevator, Fiona considered going after them. After *him.* She held her hands out in front of her. They shook. Always an indication that a few benzos and a glass of wine was in order, followed by a nap.

She'd find him after her nap.

Even after the pills and wine, she couldn't sleep. She didn't normally like tattoos on a man—on anyone, really—but she liked them on him, even though she hadn't really seen what they were. They covered both arms, from his wrists and all the way up and under his short-sleeved T-shirt. She wouldn't normally like a man who wore a T-shirt to brunch at a fancy hotel either, let alone one with a polar bear in a hammock between two palm trees smoking a marijuana cigarette, but the fact remained that when she crawled into bed and tried to sleep, she could think only of him. Only him. *Gus, Gus, Gus,* as she made herself come. She fell asleep, at last.

When she woke, it was nearly midnight. She ignored the texts and voice mails from Willy and got dressed to go out. Fiona found Gus at the third bar she tried. He didn't seem surprised to see her. He looked at her as if he knew her through and through already. As if they'd already fucked. He put his hand around her waist and introduced her to a towering, husky, hairy man. This was Mike—the missing fourth man—and his wife, Sarah. Tall, long dirty-blond hair, muscular arms, a short silver spaghetti-strap dress that shimmered like fish scales over just a hint of a baby bump.

"I wouldn't even know that you're pregnant," Fiona said.

"My toilet knows every single morning when I'm kneeling in front of it," Sarah yelled over the thumping bass. "I would be at home sleeping, but I'm here instead, to make sure Mike doesn't get into trouble tonight. My older kid is at a sleepover. I think this is what I used to do for fun?"

"But now you're not so sure," Fiona said.

"Now I am not so sure," Sarah said with a laugh. "I spend most of my shifts on the ambulance plugging my nose because all the smells make me want to barf. All the smells!"

Mike grabbed Sarah to dance, so Fiona was left with Gus and the two other friends whose names she never bothered to remember, then or since. She pulled Gus onto the dance floor and ground her ass against his crotch. She hung her arms around his neck and rubbed her tits against his chest. She slid up and down the length of him and felt like a dark, scrawny slut among the beautiful, strong, pink-cheeked snow bunnies. She wanted to fuck Gus right there in front of everyone, like an amateur porn movie. But she didn't feel like an amateur. She felt like she should be getting paid for this. There were cameras all around, and everyone was watching. Everyone was watching. That's right, *everyone.*

"Come with me," she whispered in his ear. She led him out of the bar and away from the thumping music and along the village stroll to the hotel and in through the back entrance past the trash compactor and a trio of kitchen staff smoking by the door—because that was dirtier and she was aiming for absolutely filthy—and up the service stairwell because there was filth in that too, even at the Fairmont the concrete landings were stained in the corners, and the smell of the underground parking garage leaked up. Exhaust fumes and spent fryer grease. The cold metal banisters and blue-white lights in little metal cages. She was taking him to her room, but they'd only climbed three flights before she backed him against the wall and shimmied down until she was crouched in front of him. She undid his belt and pulled out his erection. He hadn't said a word since leaving the bar, and she worried about that, but not enough. She put her mouth on him and he put his hands in her hair, her chandelier earrings swinging across her cheeks.

DECEMBER 21

Gus and Ruby were gone by the time Fiona awoke the next day. Gus had taken Luke's keys away, so he was asleep on the couch—where was Aubrey?—his enormous nearly grown feet clad in socks with robots on them, one hairy arm dangling to the floor. Even though he was not Mike's son by birth, there was something about him that stirred a kind of recognition in Fiona. She didn't like it, or the thoughts that came with it—if she let herself go there, everyone would be horrified, except perhaps Luke—the mingling of disgust and attraction. She tried not to be alone with him, because when she was, she offered him innuendoes and sultry looks, even as she admonished herself for doing so. She'd looked up MILFs on porn sites and made herself come watching clips of supposedly teenaged boys fucking middle-aged women. That was one thing. But she would not actually be that stupid. She would not actually make that mistake.

There was a note propped against Fiona's jar of loose tea.

School ends early today.
Pick Ruby up at noon.
I won't be back in time.
Love,
G.

Love.

She'd just turned the kettle on when she heard Luke plodding upstairs to the bathroom. When he came down and into the kitchen, he already had one arm in his quilted plaid jacket—was that Mike's?—a toque pulled over his messy blond hair. Those robot socks. Fiona felt a surge of innocent affection for him then. Luke was a good kid. She was the wicked one. She'd known him since he was younger than Ruby. She was definitely the wicked one.

"Sorry about the mess," he said.

"It's not your fault."

"Some of it is." Luke fished his boots out of the jumble at the back door. He didn't bother with the laces.

"Would you like something to eat?"

"No, thanks."

"A cup of coffee? I don't suppose you drink tea."

"I'm good." Luke glanced at the loaf of bread and jars of peanut butter and jam Ruby had left out.

"I could make you some toast. A sandwich?"

"I can do it, thanks." He slathered two pieces of bread, slapped them together and took an enormous bite. Still chewing, he looked around at the array of tipped-over cups and soiled paper plates, a chair on its side, a pool of red wine on the tiles. "I can totally help you clean up."

"No, thank you." For so many reasons, but especially because sometimes—too often—she *was* far too stupid for her own good.

She saw him to the door and stood behind him while he finished putting on his jacket—she was sure it was Mike's. She noticed the wear on his leather belt, and the shape of his wallet in his back left pocket. The rim of his underwear stretched across his smooth, golden back. He dug in one hip pocket, then the other.

"Gus took them," she said.

Fiona found his keys in the bowl by the front door, amidst the jumble of their own keys. This seemed inordinately intimate, even as she plucked them out and dangled them above his beefy hand. "You drink too much, Luke."

"That's what my mom says. And Mike. And Gus. And Aubrey."

"So?"

"It's not a problem."

"Yet," Fiona said.

"Sure, yet."

"Did Aubrey stay the night?"

He shook his head. "She's babysitting today."

Why was he looking at her like that? What wasn't he saying? Fiona took a deep breath. *Sort yourself out, Fi.*

His keys. She glanced down.

He had a bottle opener on his key ring, and a picture of him and Aubrey at the rodeo photo booth, slipped into a little Perspex frame. She said, "Back in the seventies, couples would throw their keys into a bowl and the women would pick out another man's keys at the end of the night and go home with him."

Luke took the keys. Did a minute pass? Was he saying something without saying it? See? This is why he should go.

"You should leave, Luke."

"Yeah, I have to get to the store."

"You do." She didn't have a clue if he did or not.

"Want me to take anything for Gus?"

"What?"

"A sandwich or something. Maybe some coffee?"

"Oh. No. No, thank you," Fiona said. "I'll make him a lunch and take it to him later. Do you want me to bring you one too?"

"Nope, thanks." Luke spun his keys on his finger. "Aubrey's coming by with the kid she's looking after and we're walking up to the gas station for hot dogs."

After he left, she cleaned up the house, and with that done, she phoned Gus to see what he'd like on his sandwich, as if she'd planned to make him one all along. It seemed like such a sweet thing, to bring him lunch.

"Or maybe you want to walk up to the gas station and get hot dogs?"

"Luke and Aubrey already brought me back a couple," he said. "Isn't that funny that you had the same idea."

Fiona left the house with plenty of time to get to Ruby's school. It wasn't snowing, and the sky was a bright-blue wash from one side of the valley to the other. She pulled on all her layers and laced up her boots and slipped her sunglasses on. She passed the public school first, sprawling and squat, all the classrooms brightly lit, artwork hanging on the walls and the desks grouped in fours, and the teachers all looking so capable. Fiona would rather Ruby went to Mount Casper Elementary, because the Cayoosh Learning Co-operative was just too small. Maybe Ruby simply hadn't found her best friend yet because that particular girl went to Mount Casper. Maybe Ruby's best friend was in one of those warm classrooms with their walls plastered with twenty-five versions of Van Gogh's sunflowers. One best friend, that's all. Every little girl needed just one best friend. At least to start with. Triads and murders could come later.

"That's not how you do it," Gus said one day when they were waiting for Ruby after school, watching all the little pairs come out.

"And what do you know about little girls and best friends?"

"You don't shop for them like you're buying a car," Gus said. "I know that much."

"It's always a good thing if you have more cars to choose from."

"She's not going to miss having the friend she's never met."

"I would argue that she already does miss that friend."

"I know about friends," Gus said. "You find them where you are. Cayoosh is exactly the right place for her. Why would you want her to be a cog in the public system when she can go to a democratic school?"

Where was Ruby?

"If she were in public school, they would have speech pathologists, and counsellors, occupational therapy. The teacher would force interactions, like working in assigned pairs. Or splitting off into groups."

There she was, with Shane and Liam not far behind her.

Fiona straightened. "Those little shits." She waved and Ruby waved back.

"I bet you it will be Anna," Gus said. "Or Skye. Just give it time."

"No, you don't understand," Fiona said. "Anna is Skye's best friend. Skye is Anna's best friend."

There's no room for Ruby. You need to know about girls. You need to know how those kinds of friendships start, and last, to the exclusion of others. They start out as two little girls, holding hands, and for that to happen, there has to be Ruby—all alone—and another little girl all alone too. Like her and Willy, on the first day at Harrogate.

—

Fiona walked along the trail rather than the road that went through town. She gave herself plenty of time, but when she got there, all the children were gone, including Ruby. Fiona checked her watch: 12:15 p.m. She reluctantly opened the door and stepped into the warmth of the foyer. The skylights and stained glass brought in so much light that the small space felt much bigger, and bright with the children's art bunting its way around the room and the rainbow mural everyone had worked on last spring. There was a square of couches in the sunken centre of the space; when the building had been the youth drop-in centre, that was the favourite spot, and those were the same ratty couches with slouching cushions spotted with old gum.

Mike came striding down the hallway with a stack of papers in hand.

"Hey, Fiona."

"I'm here for Ruby." It was only when she was alone with him that her body betrayed her and did things like sweat, and erupt in goosebumps, or turn on palpitations like a switch had been thrown. When it was the two families together, or even just the couples, Fiona could keep it together.

"Gus picked her up."

What was that look? Was he just looking at a parent of one of his students? Or the wife of his best friend? Or was he really looking at *her*, someone whose body he had possessed, if only once, and furtively?

Fiona wanted to say, Will we ever talk about it? Will we ever do it again? Was it so terrible? Is it so bad? Sweat dampened her skin, beneath her winter layers. That night on their family trip to Mexico, almost a year ago, had been so humid. When she'd touched him, her hands slid across his chest and came away damp. Sweat dripped off his brow, down the cleavage of her bikini top, pooled in his navel, slicked their skin where she sat on his lap. This sweat now, with its accompanying light-headedness, was not the same. This was the all-over flush of nausea. Fiona swallowed.

"I was supposed to pick her up."

"His client was a no-show. He didn't call?"

"He may have." Fiona put her hands in her pockets. No phone. She turned to go. "They're probably at home already."

"He said he was taking her to the shop." Mike glanced down at the papers. Maybe a lesson plan for growing beans in the spring, in little pots that the children would craft out of old newspapers, a list of spelling words to go along with it: *grow, plant, green, shoot, dirt, tend, light. Wait.* He smiled at her. A warm smile, but not personal. The smile he would give any parent of a student.

"Okay, then. Thanks."

Fiona made her way to the front doors, waiting—or not waiting—for his footsteps to follow her.

Fiona had been looking forward to walking home with Ruby. Ruby often let her hold her hand, which felt special given all the times when Ruby didn't let her touch her. She'd reach for a hug, and Ruby would set off in the other direction. Or she'd try to help her out of the bath, which used to be the other way Fiona could hold her, after wrapping her in a big thick towel. She'd pull her onto her lap and comb out her hair. But Ruby wouldn't even let Gus help with her bath now. If she'd been able to walk home with her daughter hand in hand, she might've been able to steer the two of them onto the couch, to sit close and watch the Food Network, legs touching. Sometimes Ruby would lean her head on Fiona's shoulder, which made Fiona sit so very still, breathing shallowly.

She mostly chose Gus over her, which rarely bothered Fiona, as it usually suited her just fine too. But sometimes she wanted to be the one Ruby reached for. Maybe, if she promised they would watch one of the videos Gus made when he was still competing, Ruby would settle beside her. Ruby loved those, even more than shows about cake decorating or the best places in the world for street eats. *Epic Snow Day, Slice Master, Heli Drop Hell.* Hours and hours of footage of Gus and other champion snowboarders performing ridiculous stunts, soundtracks of thrasher metal or teeth-grinding hip hop and edits so frenetic that Fiona got the same kind of headache that she used to get from strobe lights in nightclubs back home in London. Then, she'd take ecstasy, or Willy would cut a delicate little line of coke for her, and the headache would disappear. If she was sitting with Ruby on the couch, she could just close her eyes. The headache would still be there, but no way would she get up to get a paracetamol, because then Ruby would move too. She'd slide to the floor and sit cross-legged, arms on the coffee table, and no coaxing could get her back onto the couch.

Mount Casper Outfitters came into view. Fiona let a truck go by, and then another and another. Two more, loaded with snowmobiles. An empty school bus. The ambulance, with Sarah driving—she didn't see Fiona, or she was pretending not to—and her partner in the passenger seat, no one that Fiona recognized.

Fiona watched the warmly lit storefront like it was a movie screen. The climbing wall stretched along one side, behind the racks of jackets and pants and thermal underwear and technical socks. Ruby was monkeying along the top, her toes gripping the moulded holds. Gus sat on the stool behind the register, writing something in the trip binder. Two steaming mugs sat on the counter in front of him. He looked up suddenly. Did Ruby call for him?

Ruby glanced over her shoulder. Was she talking now?

Fiona squinted. What did she say? What would she say to Gus that she would never, ever say to Fiona?

Look at me?

Look at this?

Watch, Daddy?

What did she *say*?

Maybe nothing at all. Gus was better with Ruby's silence than Fiona was, which meant he caught her unspoken requests and comments better than she did. But Ruby sometimes spoke to him, and maybe this was one of those times. Ruby had talked and babbled to everyone and anyone when she was a baby. It wasn't until she was a preschooler that she started to choose her words carefully. And she never repeated herself. After a time, she didn't say much at all. For nearly two years, she'd been mostly mute. *Selectively mute,* the child psychologist in Vancouver said. Very selective, it seemed. She *selected* Gus to speak to sometimes. She had not selected Fiona for months.

Ruby looked right at Fiona then, but didn't see her for the lights reflecting on the inside of the windows. Just midday and the sun was already sliding behind the mountain. Ruby turned away again, and reached for the next hold. She'd felt with her foot and moved along, closer to the last hold, which would put her above the stack of bouldering mats. Once she got there, she leapt away from the wall and landed on the mats, grinning. Gus laughed. He lifted the mug, reminding her. Ruby ran to the counter and took it from him, the big mug looking enormous in her tiny hands.

Fiona could not enter that movie. There was no part written for her in that scene. If she opened the door and walked in, Gus would hand her his mug of hot chocolate, and for some reason that seemed like a particularly terrible offence.

She headed home instead. She waited at the four-way stop that the town council proposed to replace with a traffic light. It was soundly voted down, as if there was some kind of prestige that came with living in a town with no traffic light. She went into the kitschy Emporium with its old-timey storefront and bought a box of candy canes and a package of silver garland. Gus and Ruby would get the tree. It was distinctly possible that they already had, and it was leaning against the house by the woodpile. She was only meant to notice it once it was inside. The inside was hers as much as the outside was theirs. Once Gus brought the tree in, she'd clear the corner by the couch for it. She'd get it screwed into the red metal base and tweak its posture. She would clean up the trail of pine needles without complaint, and make some joke about getting new carpet with built-in pine scent. The tree was never quite right, but that was a tradition in and of itself. She would say it was too small. Too big. Too scraggly. And then she would pointedly rearrange a few of the decorations the two had hung—usually the two robots, one pink and one blue, that Gus bought her when Ruby was a toddler. Meant to be the two of them. She'd have the blue one chase the pink one all around the tree over the course of a few days, like a very slow stop-motion movie. That didn't seem right this year. Even when she was standing right beside Gus, even when he was about to make her come, she wanted her pink robot to be far away from his blue robot. Ruby would never let that happen, though. She liked the robots together, hanging near the top, face to face, cold, flat faces kissing.

After Fiona told Willy about Gus emptying the coffee can to buy pizza, Willy insisted on buying them all tickets to London.

"Christmas in London," Willy said. "Which is exactly as enchanting as it sounds."

"I didn't tell you so you could feel sorry for me," Fiona said.

"I don't feel sorry for you," Will said. After a mutual pause, she added, "Well, I feel sorry for you all the time, but this isn't about that."

"There was barely two hundred dollars in there, Will. It was his birthday. I'm a bitch for making a big deal of it."

"True or false: Two hundred dollars for you is twenty thousand dollars for me?" When Fiona didn't answer, Willy laughed. "Oh, come, Fi. It will be brilliant," she said. "We're going to roast a swan. Can you believe it? An actual *swan*. And you can go up to your dad's for a night or two. You can endure him and your deplorable aunt for that long, and then I'll send you all home with suitcases full of fabulous presents. Ruby looks so good in red, and I don't just say that because of her name. I have a dress for her. Collette picked it out when we were shopping for her own holiday dress. Taffeta and a velvet sash and a Peter Pan collar. I know Ruby doesn't like dresses, but she will love, love, love this one. I promise. Come, Fi. *Please* come."

"I'm just not sure what's happening." Fiona lit a cigarette. "Sometimes I think we're okay, and it's only me, and all I need is time. But then I just wish that he'd stay at the store longer or get booked for a long backcountry trip. I don't want him to come home. I don't know what's wrong with me."

"Sure you do," Willy said. "That episode in Mexico. Your boring old lunacy. Terrible combination. Look, just get him here. We'll show him a good time. Kumar adores him. He loves all that rugged wilderness stuff, not that he'd actually do any of it. Gus loves to tell a good story. Gus loves a good beer. They have a lot to offer each other. They could be great friends."

"Gus is 'great friends' with everyone."

"So, he'll be fine," Willy said. "Come."

"I think a trip is a bad idea right now."

"Maybe it would actually be good for the three of you to get away."

"We got away last year to Mexico, and that didn't work out so well."

"Just the three of you." Willy lowered her voice, even though Kumar was visiting the H&M factories in Jakarta and Collette was away at school. "It would do you good, as a family. After last year you need to rewrite the holiday. Maybe it's not too late. Maybe you'll change your mind."

"My mind isn't made up."

"Fair enough," Willy said. "Considering your mind is never made up. Not ever. Not really."

Last year.

Mexico.

Gus, Fiona and Ruby rented the upstairs apartment just above the main street of a dusty little surfer town.

Mike, Sarah, Liam, Aubrey and Luke rented the suite below.

There were far too many people on holiday together in Sayulita, which was not far from Puerto Vallarta. The apartment was nice enough, with whitewashed walls and little geckos scuttling along the rafters. Everyone but Fiona went to the beach at least once a day, if not more. Fiona liked the tiled deck around the pool and the large, faded patio umbrellas that easily adjusted to keep the shade. She was content to be alone, and though she was always happy to hand out snacks and sun hats and slather sunscreen on Ruby, no matter how hard Ruby tried to pull her out of the gated yard, she didn't go. She stayed behind and read her books, with the clattering din of the town's business as good a white noise as the hushing of the surf.

"Come on," Sarah said, maybe three days in. "You have to dip just a toe before we go home."

"We'll carry you down there and throw you in," Mike said.

"No, we won't." Gus kissed the top of her head.

"You have to," Sarah said. "You might never be in Mexico again."

"I do not care for the beach," she said.

"*She does not care for the beach,*" Sarah said in her bad impression of Fiona's British accent.

Gus knew why she stayed put. He also knew that she could barely consent to allow Ruby to play in the ocean. In fact, she hadn't consented, not properly. The ocean was tremendously filthy—tests had been done—seven times the acceptable E. coli count. And it teemed with sharks and jellyfish and other horrible things with wet, gawping mouths or stingers lying in wait just under the sand. On the beach, sand stuck to everything and was so hot that going barefoot was not an option.

And Christmas hadn't felt like Christmas at all, though the little kids—Ruby and Liam—didn't seem to mind. Sarah invited their condo neighbours for brunch, an elderly playwright from

Vermont and the two couples from Wisconsin. Mimosas and pancakes and bacon. Sarah had brought maple syrup and party crackers and paper hats and Gus wore a Santa costume for about two minutes before he jumped into the pool with it still on. No presents, everyone had decided. It was expensive enough to get there. So, nothing to open. Nothing to admire. No disappointments. Less is more, Gus said. Experience trumps trinkets.

"Cheers," Fiona said, and they all took a drink. She looked around at what Sarah had pulled together, these thousands of miles from home, and wished that she'd thought of it. And also wished that she could bring herself to go down to the beach and offer that one toe to the warm Pacific Ocean, just to say that she'd done it. Just to show Ruby about pushing past a fear. But, once stuck, it was nearly impossible for Fiona to unstick herself. That was an old story that she constantly wished she could rewrite but that only added to itself, chapter after chapter. It was a very long book by now.

Ruby went to the beach after brunch, along with the others. She went every single day. Of course she did, because when they booked the trip, Gus had made it clear.

"Ruby is going to the beach," he said. "She's going to eat fish on a stick from the lady at Los Muertos, and she is going to buy something from the guy who pushes the wheelbarrow full of candy up and down the beach, and she is going to eat tacos at El Ivan. And she is going to have surf lessons."

"I could just stay home," Fiona said. "That would be so much better than all of you suffering my constant anxiety and disapproval. And I'm not being passive-aggressive. Not in the least. Truly. Everyone would be better for it."

"We are a family, Fiona," Gus said. "It wouldn't be Christmas without you. Ruby wants you there more than anything."

"Did she tell you that?"

"You know what I mean."

"Let's go somewhere else. Let's go to London. Please, let's go to London."

"The trip is booked. You agreed to it."

"That was in August." Fiona leaned against him, and he didn't stiffen.

He put an arm around her, his temple against hers. "Were things better in August?"

"I think so."

Gus pulled away. A cool wash of silence swept between them.

"Look, never mind about me. You can make it worse for Ruby," he said. "Or you can make it better."

Ruby got sick. She'd spent Boxing Day morning at Los Muertos playing with two local girls at the far end of the beach, delighting in being with kids who didn't expect her to talk. The two girls carried on a story between them, Ruby could tell from the little stick families they made, and the pebble houses. They gave her a family of sticks too. Two long ones, two short. The girls built their pebble neighbourhood, adding dirt walls and little fenced-in paddocks, until the girls' mother ran across the sand and yanked her daughters away.

"*Sucio!* No!" She pointed into the forest, to a narrow, murky stream, strewn with garbage, chicken carcasses spilling out of a bag under a footbridge. She yanked Ruby out too, looking up and down the beach.

"*Donde esta tu mamá?*"

Ruby pointed to her father, who was running across the hot sand, calling her name. He thanked the woman and then carried Ruby to the water.

"Let's rinse you off, Rabbit."

They swam past the break to where the water was calmer. Ruby looked back at the people on the beach. The waves lifted her up and down, which made it look like the people were going up and down, not her. The water was clear, so much so that she could see the clean sandy bottom as she treaded water, and the chipped polish on her toes. Her mom did it before they left home. Matching pedicures.

"We won't tell your mother, right?"

Ruby absolutely did not want him to tell her mom. If they did, she wouldn't be allowed to come to the beach again. That was for sure.

But then she got sick just a couple of hours later. She spent the afternoon on the toilet, groaning and crying. Gus sat on the floor beside her, holding her hand while she simultaneously vomited into a plastic bowl and shat into the toilet.

"Sorry, Daddy," she whispered.

"No, Rabbit." Gus stroked her hair, damp with sweat. "I'm sorry. I should've known better."

He cleaned her up and wrapped her in a big towel and carried her out of the bathroom at last.

"I heard her say something," Fiona said.

"Not now," Gus said.

"She's getting dehydrated." Sarah put her wrist to Ruby's forehead. "She's really warm. I saw some Pedialyte at the Oxxo. I'll go get some."

"I'll go," Mike said. "Our resident medical expert should stay with Ruby."

—

When the worst was over, Fiona put Ruby to bed for a nap. She stripped her clothes off and put on a fresh pair of underwear—happy, dancing, bespectacled fruit—for her to sleep in. It was too hot to wear anything, but naked was not okay. She pulled the sheet over her and sat on the edge of the bed and stroked Ruby's forehead until she fell asleep, and then she crawled onto the bed beside her and stared at her sleeping daughter and marvelled at each sour breath and how amazing it was to love this small person while a raging storm of doubt about everything else roared on, engulfing her entirely. No, not quite, because there was Ruby, the easy one to love.

How could it have been such a long day? When Fiona woke, it was dinnertime. And it was still Boxing Day. Not long after Ruby woke, the others went next door to El Corazón—they had a reservation—and Fiona made toast and poured a ginger ale for Ruby and a beer for herself. They watched Mexican cartoons on mute, and Fiona made Ruby laugh with voiceovers. *That's my bottom! Why are you looking at my bottom? Look away, scoundrel. Look away!*

Ruby fell asleep on her lap, while the cartoons flashed silently in the dark. Mike came back alone, a beer sweating in each hand.

"Some rich, stereotypical Texan is buying everybody beer. I brought you one." Mike switched to a Southern drawl. "Merry Christmas, Miss Fiona." He ditched the accent. "And I came up to give you the message that everyone is going to the club. I'll stay with Ruby. I'm exhausted."

"No, thanks. This has been the longest day ever. I am knackered, even after having a nap."

He looked at Ruby. "Want me to put her to bed?"

"Sure." Fiona stretched, the cool sweat from the beer bottle trailing down her arm. "Thank you."

"She's a kitten compared to Liam."

When he picked Ruby up, she nearly poured out of his arms, like so much sand, her sleep was so deep. Fiona followed him into the bedroom. He laid Ruby on the bed and she hardly stirred except to park her finger in her mouth. The fan turned lazily overhead. He brushed Ruby's hair away from her face.

"She's so tired," Fiona said as they closed the door and returned to the couch and the beer.

"She had a rough day."

"I don't even want to get into how avoidable that was. This place is a cesspool." Another swig of beer. "That sewage on the street after it rained the other day? It was burbling through the manhole covers."

"That's why the sidewalks are raised."

Fiona shrugged.

"I know you don't want to be here."

"Of course, Gus told you how ungrateful I am to be in paradise with my family and friends."

This time Mike shrugged.

"What else did he tell you?"

"It doesn't matter. Come outside for a minute," Mike said. "I have strict instructions from everyone—even the Texan—to show you the moon."

"It's a moon."

"But this is a *moon*."

Fiona followed him onto the balcony. The moon was impressive. More than half full, the grey whorls on the surface were a clear contrast to the silvery white. The sky around it was dappled with stars against darkening indigo, a ripple of silver surf underlining the horizon.

They leaned on the railing, side by side. Down below, the playwright sat in the dark by the pool, staring at the moon too.

"Do you think he can see us?" Fiona said.

"Do you want him to?"

With those five words, the distance between the moon and the ocean in front of them suddenly expanded, making the air between her and Mike thinner. She couldn't make her breath move past her throat. It just sat there, doing nothing at all. She gripped the railing with both hands and bent her head, focusing on the concrete deck surrounding the pool, with its cracks filled with dirt, the worn-out paint where bare feet and flip-flops had worn it away.

It was a dirty apartment, both up and down. Every surface was sticky with cooking residue and salty ocean damp. The rail was rusty, and dangerously loose.

Think of these things. Not the hot, thin air between her and Mike.

"Do you want another beer?"

Fiona nodded, still with her head bowed.

When he came back, she took the beer and put it to her forehead, like she was in a commercial for Dos Equis. She felt an easing, as if the moon was back in its proper alignment, and she could take such deep breaths. This wasn't a big deal. It *was* that simple.

"Do you like to be alone?" Fiona said.

"Not particularly, no."

"I do."

"Is that your way of asking me to go?"

"Sometimes I want to be alone, and at the same time have someone with me."

"I'm not sure I get what you mean."

"Being utterly alone," Fiona said. "With people around."

Mike reached for her hand. He'd never held her hand before. She didn't want to know why he was now, but she had to admit that it made sense somehow. She knew that, next, his hand would slide up her arm. Maybe up to her neck in the same motion, landing on her cheek and cupping it, and then the mutual leaning in.

"I'm going to bed." She turned to go inside, but Mike had a gentle hold on her wrist. There was the bedroom door. Ruby was in there. It was cooler and dark in there, with the steady *hush, hush, hush* of the fan. She should pull away and go into that dark room and lie on the bed beside her child and think that it was enough. His fingers along her pulse. The waxing gibbous moon.

He let go of her hand and slid both of his up under her sundress, along her thighs, two fingers catching on the narrow band of her panties where they curved over her hip. He pulled down, as casually as if he'd done it so many times before, in this place, at this time, with her, on this night.

Her panties pooled at her ankles, and for a moment everything seemed suddenly and incredibly juvenile. She was fourteen, in Hussein's bedroom right off the front door while his parents were out getting groceries. They did it on the floor because his sister was upstairs and his bed creaked. He gave her a pillow for her head, which had seemed like the sweetest thing. And a towel for after. He'd just come inside her when the key turned in the lock. He asked if he could keep her underwear, and she let him. He was six years older than her, almost twenty. She thought that must be something people having sex did. But she didn't want *his* underwear. What she remembered now was knowing that they'd get caught, and doing it anyway, and then, when they weren't caught, she was disappointed, which made no sense at all.

The playwright glanced up just then, even though they hadn't made a sound. He waved. Fiona's pulse raced. Did he think Mike was Gus? Did he?

Fiona stepped out of her panties and pressed her knee against Mike's leg. He slid a finger into her, his thumb on her clit.

"Not out here," she said.

Inside, Mike sat on the tired couch and pulled her to him.

He unbuttoned his jeans and slid them down under his hips just enough. She straddled him. There were a lot of things they should be talking about. He loved Sarah, and only Sarah. He was absolutely devoted to her. Even now, while he was doing this. He didn't even like Fiona. She'd heard him tell Gus that he preferred more weight on a woman, hips and a wide, flat stomach, breasts enough to lose your face in. Fiona was a bird. Nothing supple about her. Why was he letting her get away with this? Why was she letting him get away with this? Why was she letting herself get away with this, when she had to know by now that she rarely had her own best interests in mind? It seemed so simple to do it, and just slightly more difficult to stop it.

Fiona had said no to tickets to London, but Willy kept calling. Either to keep pushing the idea of a visit or to try to get her to talk about what happened last year in Sayulita.

Since they were girls, Willy had made sure to commemorate the dates of "Fiona's Messy Things," in order to nail the complicated feelings in place before they could topple Fiona into a mania or a depression. Fiona's mother's death, for example, or getting caught trying to steal a pair of lovebirds from Kew Gardens, the tragedy of Princess Diana, the time Aunt Noreen found Fiona inside the running car in the tiny garage at the bottom of the garden and slapped her face over and over, which did nothing but make her look beat up when she did come to in the hyperbaric chamber. Gus didn't know about any of these anniversaries. He knew that Fiona's mother died when she was young, but he didn't know the details. Pressed, he wouldn't even be able to tell you how old Fiona was when it happened.

Fiona finally picked up one of Willy's calls, just two days before Christmas.

"Willy, hi!" And before she could reply, Fiona swept right by her and took off. "Why don't you come here at Christmas. It's magical! Maybe not now, because you've missed all the big stuff, but for sure next year."

Fiona described the celebration the town threw when they turned on the lights strung on the enormous pine tree behind the cenotaph, with hot chocolate and gingerbread cookies. And then the solstice party, with a big bonfire. "Everyone goes," she said. "There's always music. Fiddle and guitar at least, and those stupid hippie drums they hold between their legs. Where is a bodhran when you need it, am I right? Oh, and there's an old man that brings his saxophone some years. And we go carolling, too. Even in the cold. It's so cold, Willy. But we dress for it. That's how you enjoy it. You dress in layers. Lots of layers."

"That sounds amazing," Willy said.

"Because it is amazing."

Fiona could picture Willy, sitting at her telephone table in her vast Kensington flat, because she didn't like to wander around her home and talk on the phone. That little oak table with its attached chair had belonged to the flat when Willy's grandmother was born there in 1927 and must've been fairly new then.

Fiona said, "You know, sometimes I think you fancy yourself to be a hipster, the way you won't use your phone anywhere else except that seat. Like insisting on playing vinyl records."

"I don't own a single vinyl record," Willy said. "And as for my phone, you know that I use it everywhere, for everything except actual conversations, which I like to focus on. Like this one now. Look at me, delightfully focused when I sit here on my telephone chair at my attached telephone table, *circa* who gives a shit, with *bum bum* scrawled across the surface in indelible marker by someone who cannot stand it when I talk on the phone. Thank you, preschool Collette."

"Have you tried surgical spirit?"

"Fiona, please. I know what you're doing."

"That makes one of us."

"You've just talked for"—she paused, clearly to check—"almost twelve minutes and told me exactly nothing about you and Gus and Ruby. I know you, Fi."

"You think you do," Fiona said. "And I'm not."

"Not what?"

"Shitting bats."

"Shitting bats right now or not," Willy said, "you need to come home for a break, before you lose it."

"I can't leave quite yet. I have to figure things out with Gus."

"Not necessarily," Willy said. "Sort it out when you get back."

All of those things were true—the bonfire, the lights, the carolling. Just not true for Fiona, who rarely went. After Ruby and Gus left, all bundled in layers, she would curl up on the couch and be still, letting the solitude settle into her bones. No layers necessary. No chilled breath clouding her vision. No candles and flashlights and lanterns bobbing in the dark. No children screeching and chasing each other with sparklers and pine boughs. But maybe, if Willy came next year, she would go.

"It's always a wonderful time, Willy. It's exactly what you'd imagine a small mountain town Canadian winter to be like."

Their Christmas was quiet. The tree was beautiful. Ruby emptied her stocking one item at a time. A bouncy ball. Comic book. And all the rabbit things: an eraser, a chapter book, shoelaces, a small tin, a magnet for the fridge, a little stuffed bunny that could fit in her pocket. A mandarin orange. A sack of chocolate coins at the very bottom. Hot apple cider and French toast for breakfast. Fiona gave Ruby a boxed set of Roald Dahl books—her favourite—and Gus gave her a Swiss Army knife, a folding shovel and new snowshoes. Ruby hugged them both. If she wondered why each card was signed by just one parent, she didn't ask.

DECEMBER 31

Between Christmas and New Year's Eve, Fiona slept a couple of hours each night. She woke in the morning with her skin vibrating. She leapt up without worrying about waking Gus because he was sleeping in their bed upstairs while she was spending her nights fully dressed on the sofa. She showered regularly, so the clothes stayed clean, right? Except she wasn't sure when she'd last showered.

Fiona packed food into a box for their traditional New Year's Eve at the T'Sek Hot Springs up the In-SHUCK-ch Forest Service Road. They'd all missed it last year, because of Mexico. This year, she'd told Gus she was not camping at the hot springs, and so they'd need just enough food and drink to last them until midnight. She'd wakened early—or had she not gone to sleep at all?—to make apple and squash soup, and rosemary and sea salt crackers. She made too many of those—ten dozen of the little buggers—so she made a spinach artichoke dip to go with them. She made a tourtière, because she'd been meaning to make one ever since she'd been in Canada. It wasn't out of the oven yet. She was working on cinnamon sugar pinwheel cookies—festive, right?—when Gus came down, barefoot and in just his pyjama bottoms, his abs screaming for attention. Fiona was always amazed that she could be equal parts pissed at him and attracted to him.

"What's all this?" he said. "We're having hot dogs on the fire. Same as always."

"We don't *have* to have hot dogs on the fire, same as always."

"Did you bring up the sleeping bags?"

"No need." Fiona shook her head. "We're not staying over this year. Remember?"

"You didn't mean that, did you? This is a lot of food for just an evening." Gus came up behind her and kissed her neck. "We could have the tourtière in the morning. Great for hangovers."

"I've got to get these cookies into the oven."

"It's just one night." Gus poured himself a cup of coffee and leaned against the counter, way too close for Fiona's comfort. She needed that space to set out the baking trays, but she resisted saying that out loud.

"You'll be warm enough," Gus said. "That's what these sleeping bags are made for. Winter camping. This is my *job*, Fiona, making sure that people stay warm out there. We have an entire store of things that can keep you warm."

"I don't want to stay overnight."

"You *will* want to," Gus said. "So, let's be prepared."

"Maybe next year." Oh, and here were all the other things. Water crackers and a round of brie, a jar of olives stuffed with feta, mandarin oranges. Hot dogs, buns, marshmallows, graham crackers, two bars of chocolate. A bottle of champagne. Two bottles of wine. Beer. Packets of cocoa.

"This is enough food for a week."

Fiona laughed, and fed him a cracker. Then moved in closer and fed him another. "How do those taste?"

He swallowed. Nodded. "Not as good as you."

Fiona blushed. She glanced at the pinwheel dough, the oven, the timer for the tourtière. The clock. Ruby, who was never up before ten unless school forced her out of bed. 0918. Fiona pulled Gus towards the living room and her pile of fusty blankets and pillows. He'd built up the fire in the stove on his way to the kitchen, so the room was cozy enough for Fiona to take off the clothes she'd worn since Christmas.

After, they lay with their legs entwined, his head at one end of the couch, hers at the other.

"That was nice," he said.

"I hate it when you say that."

"If we separate, you won't have to hear me say it." Gus smiled. "But then, you won't be getting any of this either." He bucked the air.

"What rule says that? Never mind, I don't want to talk about it." Fiona's throat constricted with each word, so much so that the last one barely made it out.

"You want in the shower first?"

She shook her head.

"Want me to grab you some clean clothes?"

"No. These are fine. I'll change after I have a shower."

"When will that be?"

They both looked up as Ruby made her way down the stairs, her hair endearingly matted at the back of her head.

Gus stopped at the top of the highway and put chains on the aging winter tires before they started the two-hour drive up the road along the lake before splitting off to the north. The logging road was gravel and sand, slick with compact snow and ice, and hugged the shoreline of the long grey lake, frozen all the way around, but not quite at the middle, where a thin line of shadowy slush was the backbone of the skinny, slithering serpent.

Separate. Fiona gripped the door handle and barely spoke during the ride. *Separate.* Her seat overlooked the very edge of the road, which was also the drop-off to the lake below. *Separate.* He'd said it so casually, when he had never been the one to bring it up before. A joke. He was playing her somehow. And it had to do with the fact that she hadn't showered. He was pointing at her. *I'll get Ruby because you smell, and no one should be making homemade crackers at three o'clock in the morning.* He loved her best when she was clean and smelled good and could barely put together a box of mac and cheese with a side of carrot sticks. That's the Fiona he loves. Not this one. This one he wants to *separate* from. And why is he saying that? Fiona says *divorce.* Because they are adults, aren't they? Can't they talk about it like adults?

Every time Gus took a turn, her stomach lurched around the corner too, sloshing and cramping.

"If you need me to stop, let me know."

"Maybe you should let me know what separation looks like."

Gus shot her a very definitive look. *Shut up, Fi.*

Ruby, tucked between them on the bench seat, held an empty laundry detergent bucket for Fiona. She bounced it on her knee. The hard plastic handle bounced against the bucket, *tap, tap, tap, tap, tap, tap, tap.*

Fiona put a hand on the bucket to make it stop. "Why don't you put on some music, Ruby?"

Ruby handed over the bucket and fished in the box of cassette tapes and found their favourite, Simon and Garfunkel's *Bridge*

Over Troubled Water, the album that always put her to sleep as a restless baby, combined with the bumpiest dirt roads they could find. She was saying something with that choice, and now that it was playing, so was Gus. He glanced at her as the piano swelled. Where was their bridge to get them over these shitty waters?

Fiona *was* weary. She did feel small. And she desperately wished for earplugs. She wished for silence. She wished for a truck that wasn't almost as old as she was so they wouldn't be stuck playing the same old tapes. Especially this one that was their favourite. Or used to be their favourite, but now was littered with lyrics that were so many tiny cuts.

Fiona wished for a broken bridge. A flat tire. She wished for a big tree across the road. Engine trouble. Something that would turn them around.

Mike's truck and camper were parked in the campsite between the hot springs and the river. He and Sarah were hanging the last of the Christmas lights when Gus pulled in. There were at least five long strands that met in the middle, which made the place look like a Christmas tree lot. There were lights all around the camper too, as if that's where you'd go to pay for your tree. A fire roared in the big pit, and beside it was a huge pile of wood that Mike brought up in a little trailer behind the truck and camper and had already stacked.

"Looks amazing!" Gus said as he hopped out. "Boys already in the tubs?"

"And Aubrey too. They're in the big one," Sarah said. "There are three other people here, I think. That's it. A couple who are camping in a tent, and one old man who may or may not be sleeping in his car."

"I don't know how he made it up the road," Mike said. So far, he'd managed not to look at Fiona, still sitting in the truck. It was a bit of a game for her, to see how long it would be before he spoke directly to her. Outside of school, that is.

It did not feel like a game tonight. She rolled down her window.

"Mike," she said. Either he pretended not to hear her or he actually didn't. "Mike!"

"Yeah?" He answered without looking at her.

"That middle string fell," she said.

"Thanks, Fiona." He looked at her then, but more to assess which Fiona had arrived at this party.

Which Fiona, indeed.

Gus grabbed a couple of towels and took Ruby's hand. "Let's go have a dip."

Ruby shook her head.

"You want your suit? Everyone else is skinny-dipping."

She shook her head again.

"Is Liam in a suit?" Gus asked Sarah.

"Nakey."

"So you want a suit?" When Ruby nodded, he fished it out of a shopping bag stuffed behind the seat and handed it to her. "Hop into the camper and get changed." Ruby hesitated, her swimsuit in her fists. "Go ahead, it's okay. No one's in there." Gus lifted her up to the door of the camper and helped her inside.

Fiona sat in the truck and smoked a cigarette while the warmth waned. Once she stubbed it out, she pulled on layers one by one, then stepped out. It wasn't windy, thank god, but it was shatteringly cold, and because she did not want to be there in the least, she felt the cold even deeper in her bones. She could not unclench her jaw.

"Have a drink, Fiona." Sarah handed her a thermal mug with coffee and rum.

"Thank you." She sipped it slowly and stood still, hoping to preserve what warmth she could, but then she noticed Sarah shifting from one foot to the other, swaying as if she was rocking a baby, and did the same. Tick tock, tick tock, I'm a little cuckoo clock.

She wanted to go into the camper and stay there, but Gus would get angry and Mike would tease her and Sarah would be so nice, offering her another hot drink or the use of the toilet in the tiny closet by the door. So Fiona stayed outside. She would go in when the others did. And then she would want to go out. The camper was a big one, but not big enough for four adults, one enormous teenager, another teenager, two little kids, and Mike's repulsive, slobbering old dog, which probably weighed as much as Liam and Ruby put together. They would be in, and she would want to be out. They would be out, and she would want to be in. The equation would not work, so she stood still by the fire, not even able to rock. She took an inventory. Two pairs of wool socks, good winter boots. Silk long johns and undershirt, fleece leggings, ski pants, long-sleeved fleece shirt, down vest, parka, fleece neck warmer, knit hat with flaps, deep hood with furry trim, gloves. She remembered one more thing: ski mitts to slip overtop of her gloves. She went back to the truck to look, but she couldn't find them. She took her gloves off altogether and lit another cigarette.

She heard Gus whooping, and then he and Ruby ran past, heading for the trail to the tubs. He was naked except for his boots, a six-pack of beer in hand. Ruby, in her swimsuit and snow boots, held on to his other hand, clomping along, trying to keep up. Fiona had bought that two-piece suit in the summer. Yellow-and-white-striped boy short bottoms and a cropped top. Not a bikini top, but not a tank top either, she was noticing now. Or Ruby had grown. The swimsuit looked all wrong on her now. It bunched between her bum cheeks. The curves at her waist looked almost womanly. She was only nine years old. *Almost* nine. Not nine yet.

"Ruby!" But what was she going to say? Come back here and take that suit off! And then what? She'd go in naked? Fiona would never let her. So she wouldn't be able to go at all. What about her underwear? No. Not her underwear. Fuck, Fiona. She could hear Gus now. Give it a fucking break.

Ruby stopped in her tracks and spun.

"Come with us!" Gus hollered. Ruby jumped up and down, waving at her.

Fiona shook her head, and he and Ruby were off running again. They disappeared into the forest at the trailhead, and in a moment Fiona heard Gus whooping again, and a big splash, and then Luke's low voice and Liam's laughter and nothing but silence after silence after silence from Ruby.

When Sarah finally left to join the others, Fiona carried the food into the camper. She stepped over the old dog they called Ophelia, which was a terrible thing to do to a beautiful name, and sat at the dinette, shivering in the warmth and unpacking everything they wouldn't be eating. She pulled a bottle of red wine out and dug in the miniature kitchen drawers until she found the corkscrew. She got a plastic tumbler from the cupboard and filled it half-full. She moved the boxes of food to the other bench, which made more room. There was a deck of cards, and a stack of board games. A few supermarket mysteries and a copy of *The Mosquito Coast*. Fiona opened it to the first page, but didn't even bother pretending to read. Was she a bad parent for letting her child hang around such a display of genitalia? What if Luke got an erection, sitting in the hot water beside Aubrey, with her breasts all buoyant and her pubic hair a waving shadow between her legs?

A child should not be subjected to that.

Ruby felt very small in the big tub. She was a fairy. The others were giants, with long, fat shadows cast by the line of candles flickering along the edge of the tub. The light lit the steam and the surface of the water. She'd wanted her and her dad to take a smaller tub, just the two of them. But Gus said no. *We came up here to hang out with these guys, Rabbit. We want to be together.*

"Like in Europe," he said.

"They do this in Europe?" Luke said. He and Aubrey—she was wearing a suit, so Ruby *wasn't* the only one—sat at the far end. He had an arm stretched along the cedar deck, the other around Aubrey. Mike and Sarah floated along one of the long sides. Gus and Ruby had the other. Liam had the opposite end all to himself.

Ruby kept her back to the others. She listened to them talking and laughing, but she didn't want to look at their shadowy faces or their naked bodies. Liam and Luke both had waterproof flashlights that they kept dunking under the water. When Ruby had first got into the tub, she saw Luke's penis bobbing in a halo of red pubic hair. And Liam's too, small and trembling between his legs. Pervert, Liam said. Then we all are, Mike said, laughing.

Gus handed out the beer.

"Can I have one?" Liam said, and everyone laughed.

"You can have a taste," Mike said.

Liam swam across the tub to his father, making a wave that lapped at Ruby's chin.

"Rabbit?" Gus said. "Do you want a taste of mine?"

She shook her head.

"Have you tried it before, Ruby?" Luke said.

"Sure she has," Gus said. "Lots of times."

"What did you think?" Luke said. "What did it taste like?" He was trying to get her to talk. Like everybody else. Ask the right question and maybe she'll say something. Dummies.

"Luke." That was Aubrey. "Leave her alone."

The man from the station wagon got out of the smallest tub, his old man balls swinging low, lit by the lantern he had hung from a nail. He said hello and good night as he passed, a towel wrapped at his waist, his lantern a glowing circle disappearing down the trail.

Luke helped Aubrey out of the tub. "We'll go grab that one." He took their beer and followed her, both of them mincing quickly along the icy boardwalk, barefoot, steam lifting in tendrils off their bodies. Luke slid into the water as Aubrey stripped off her suit. Once, Ruby heard Shane tell Liam that Aubrey was fat. But she wasn't. Ruby could only see the outline of her, and then her profile when she turned. She looked like a mom-shape. The shape most mothers were, but not her own. Her mother was bony, and small all over. Aubrey was shaped like a fairy-tale mother. Like she should be wearing an apron and a bonnet. A little waist and a bigger bum and big wobbly boobs. Aubrey stepped into the pool, sending whorls of steam up around her. No one else was watching. Ruby was the only one. Aubrey put her arms around Luke's neck, and he drew her closer. *Penis and vagina,* Ruby thought.

Fiona saw their flashlights bouncing in the dark as they all ran back. They climbed into the camper, one after another, shivering and laughing and soaking wet. Fiona slid along the dinette bench and wedged herself against the window to make room for all the bodies and the dripping and the talking. Ruby sat beside her, wrapped in a towel. Fiona lifted her onto her lap and smelled the minerals like an egg rinse on her wet, dirty hair. Sarah offered her a quilt, and she wrapped it around both of them.

"Did you have fun?"

Ruby nodded.

Everyone else got changed around them, bumping elbows and sorting through the heap of underwear and long johns and so much fleece.

Aubrey and the boys finished first, and headed outside with the sparklers Fiona brought. Bring all the fun things. Someone will notice. All the fun things.

"Keep them for midnight!" Sarah called as she clambered out after them, even as they were lighting them up.

Fiona and Ruby watched out the window as the slivery sparks lit the dark just beyond the fire. Liam waved his sparkler in circles. Luke was spelling something.

f-u

f u c k

Aubrey laughed. Sarah stalked over to him, and then she slapped his hand and Luke was laughing. He wrote something else.

s o r r y

Sarah lit a sparkler off Luke's. In the dark she looked like his little sister. Her sparkler shimmered, shooting out tiny pricks of light as she wrote in cursive against the dark.

I l o v e y o u.

Liam lit another one too, and so did Luke.

poopdick

And another one from Sarah.

R U D E.

Mike took the hot dogs and buns and headed out into the cold. "I'm going to get the fire built up again."

When he was gone, Fiona made a *tsk* sound with her teeth. "There won't be any sparklers left for midnight."

Gus pulled his ski pants up and reached for his jacket.

"It will be midnight," Fiona said again, "and there won't be any sparklers left."

"Might be."

"Well, they're for midnight."

"Does it matter?"

"No. Not really, I suppose." Or it shouldn't. And so that was why she said that, when in fact she wanted to run outside and grab them all—lit or not—and stuff them back into the package and scream at them. These are for *midnight!*

Ruby shrugged off the blanket and climbed up to the bed over the cab. She pulled off her swimsuit and rooted around for her clothes. Her naked little bum was at Fiona's eye level, pale, smooth, with a tiny little star nestled between her cheeks when she bent over. Her daughter's asshole. A child's asshole.

It was horrifying, and for a moment Fiona had no idea what to do.

"I don't want to see your butt," Gus said.

"Get yourself decent," Fiona said.

Ruby wanted to go out with her father, not after him. If he left first, she might not go out at all. There were too many people and too much dark, and she wasn't sure how the door worked, and then there were those teetery accordion stairs with no railings and she would probably fall and then Liam would laugh and Luke too, and maybe even her dad, but that would be a love laugh and he would come pick her up and carry her to the fire, and maybe even lift her onto his shoulders. But she didn't know how the door worked and she didn't want to be standing there pulling at it and pushing and trying that tiny lever up and down and side to side. That's not what she wanted. She swung her legs over the edge and leaned forward into his arms.

"Let's go look at the stars," her father said. "The sky is clear."

When the clock on the microwave said 11:49, Fiona started pulling on her layers. She drank the last of the bottle of red before she zipped up her jacket. She glanced outside. Gus stood at the far side of the fire, Ruby on his shoulders. A giant in the shadows of the flames. They and the others formed a circle around the fire, their faces lit, words and laughter puffing out into the cold. Mike had Sarah folded into his parka. Luke was looking at his phone, a small rectangle of white in the dark. He glanced up and said something and then everyone was counting.

Ten! Nine! Eight!

The time on the microwave must be wrong. Fiona could still get out there. She could hustle and be there beside the fire by the time they got down to one. But the wine sloshed in her belly, and would it be so bad if it was the microwave's fault? It wasn't her microwave. So, it wasn't her fault.

Seven! Six! Five!

They didn't want her out there anyway. No one so much as looked at the camper while they counted down. No one shouted for her. *Fiona! Come out! Join us!* That might've been a different thing. If they called for her to come out. If there was an invitation.

Three! Two! One!

Happy New Year!

Gus lifted Ruby off his shoulders and kissed her. He said something. Fiona squinted. Did Ruby say something back? She hugged him tight. She wasn't saying anything now. The others whooped and hollered and hugged and kissed. Sarah kissed Mike, long and sweet. Fiona could not look away, even though she wanted to. She could go out there and kiss him too, if she wanted to. Because now everyone was kissing. Sarah kissed her boys, and Gus. Gus kissed Liam and Luke, and Aubrey. Mike grabbed Gus and kissed him on the forehead. Gus shoved him away at first, but then he pulled him roughly to him and gave him a kiss on the lips. Luke and Aubrey roared with laughter, and Sarah too. Liam glanced over at Ruby, the two of them standing alone and apart.

Fiona could see it coming, but she couldn't get out there in time to stop it. Liam shuffled closer to Ruby, until he was right beside her. Ruby pulled away, but not before Liam pecked her on the cheek and took off into the darkness. Ruby put her hand on her cheek and began to cry.

She slid the window open and called to her. Ruby looked up. "Come in, love."

Fiona helped Ruby out of her jacket and ski pants. She lifted Ruby up to the bed over the cab and zipped her into a sleeping bag. Ruby's eyes were red, her lids heavy. The furnace was a hot, dry *hum* coming from the vents at the end of the kitchen cabinet.

"Go ahead and fall asleep," Fiona said. "Daddy will carry you to the truck when we're ready to go home."

Ruby tucked her hands under her cheeks and closed her eyes.

Gus stumbled up into the camper about half an hour later.

"We all need something hot to drink. Can you put on the kettle? Sarah says not the front right burner. It doesn't work."

"We should get going."

"Sure." He fished in his pocket until he found his keys. He tossed them at her, but she didn't catch them.

"Gus," Fiona said.

"I sure as hell can't drive."

"You *said* you would."

"No, you said *you* would."

"Gus." Panic rose in her throat. "Gus, you said you would just have two drinks. Just two."

"Sure, I said that."

"Right. So?"

"I also said that we should sleep here, because it's really, really dumb to drive all the way back to town in the middle of the night on an icy dirt road."

"You did this on purpose?" Fiona's voice rose. It wasn't even a question. *You* did this on purpose. You did this on purpose! Because she knew he would. Even if she stupidly hoped the evening would go as *planned*.

"It got away from me," he said. "Or I let it."

"What got away from you? Your word?" All of a sudden Fiona could smell her own body odour, and it was rank.

Ruby's eyes popped open. For a moment, she thought she was at home. Woodsmoke, loud voices, a warm bed. But this wasn't her bed. And the fire was outside, with more voices, and tall, flickering flames. Cold air threaded in at the seams of the old camper, despite the furnace. She chewed on her finger.

"So now what?" her mother said.

"Now we sleep over."

"Where? *Where?*"

"You and me and Ruby up there."

"All three of us?"

"It's only one night," her father said. "Actually, only a few hours."

"And where the fuck is everybody else going to sleep?"

"Mike and Sarah on the dinette bed. Liam said he'd sleep on the floor. Luke and Aubrey have a tent."

"I want to go home. Now."

"I'm drunk, Fiona. If you want to go home so badly, you drive."

"I'm drunk too! I've had that whole bottle of wine." Fiona poured a shot of rum and downed it. Gus snatched the bottle and the glass and did the same.

"Cheers," Gus said as he poured a second shot. A third. "And so we'll stay. It'll be fun."

"I want to go home."

"Then go."

"I would walk. If it weren't so far."

Ruby waited for her dad to say something next. He didn't, though. He just stood there with the empty little glass like the kind he put her maple syrup in when he made pancakes. Shot glass. Like from a gun. Maybe because you could shoot them from a special gun.

"I'm not sleeping here," her mother said. "I won't."

"So you're going to keep everyone awake all night by reading *The Mosquito Coast* by flashlight in the bathroom?" He picked up the book and threw it down in front of Fiona.

Ruby didn't want to hear any more. She didn't like wondering what was going to happen next. She didn't want to imagine her mom driving onto the lake, the ice creaking around the truck and then giving way, making a gawping black hole and swallowing her up. She didn't want the three of them squished together up here. She didn't want her father to drive them home, either, though. Sleep would be good. She could sleep all the way until morning and wake up wherever she was supposed to be, either here in the camper or at home. Ruby loved being carried inside and up to bed in the dark, pretending to be asleep but really being awake, enjoying the smell of her father's clothes: laundry soap and woodsmoke and sweat and tools.

"You think this is hilarious," her mother said.

"I don't recall laughing once in your presence this evening."

"Then wipe that fucking smile off your face."

"Done."

Silence again.

Someone put on a coat or took one off. Above Ruby, the ceiling was covered in digger and dinosaur stickers, and one small, glittering unicorn in the corner. She could touch it if she reached out, but she kept her hands under the blanket and kept still. She didn't want them to think about her just like she didn't want to think about what would happen next. Were they going home now? It would be a cold, bumpy ride. She'd curl up on the bench between them, her head on her mother's lap, and she might sleep, but she might not, and so she'd look out at the black, starry night while her parents did not talk and her father drove very,

very carefully because people are not supposed to drive when they're drunk. He's a good driver, though, so it would be okay. It's always okay. Ruby squeezed her eyes shut.

Someone picked the keys up off the floor. The door opened. Suddenly the voices outside were louder, the fire crackling was louder, and the rushing river beyond was loudest of all. The door closed, and it was quiet again for a moment.

"Hey!" Mike hollered from the firepit. "Where are you going?"

The truck door slammed, and the engine caught and stalled, then caught again.

"Fiona! Don't go!" Sarah shouted. "You shouldn't drive!"

Ruby's mother replied with tires crunching into the hardpacked snow, the cold engine's splutter fading away towards Casper as fast as she could go.

Ruby opened her eyes. There was the ceiling, still in its right place. The dinosaurs and diggers and the unicorn, equally unlikely, really.

There was her father at the sink, filling the kettle. He lit the burner and set the kettle onto it. He glanced up at her, but not before she shut her eyes tight. She remembered to relax them, like a real sleeping person's eyes would be, but not fast enough.

JANUARY 1

Fiona did not end up in the lake, perhaps because she drove so slowly that it took her twice as long to get back to the highway. When she got home, and even before she took her boots off, she grabbed a piece of paper and a pen and sat on the edge of the couch with one of Ruby's picture books propped on her lap.

She held the pen above the paper. If it touched it and she began to write, she would not stop. She needed to be sure before she began.

First, though, the house was too cold.

Still clutching the paper and pen, she checked the thermostat. Twenty. She checked the one in the kitchen. Also set to twenty. But she could see her breath, so it wasn't twenty. She looked at the indoor/outdoor thermometer, which reported that it was six degrees Celsius inside the house, and minus ten on the back porch.

They'd only been gone since noon. There were probably still embers in the stove. All she needed to do was put a log in there. Open the door and put one of the small logs in. She put a hand to the wood stove. It was still warm. But she would not. The stove was not her domain. Gus needed to be accountable for *something*. She turned the thermostats up to twenty-five, all four of them.

They should've gone to the UK.

By which she meant that she and Ruby should've gone.

She should've gone. She should've gone and taken some time to think about things. To think and think and think and try to figure out what should happen next. What would make the most sense? She should be thinking. But she could only spin on the same few thoughts. Go, don't go. Go, don't go. Polarized thinking did not take care of the details. The what and when and where and with whom.

One little log.

The baseboards were cold. She would just sit there in the dark, shivering. It would not be the worst thing.

Dear Gus.

My love.

Gus.

You know exactly what this is about.

When you

Fuck. Fuck. Fuck. Fuckfuckfuckfuck.

Fiona left the book and the paper and the pen behind on the couch and went upstairs and got undressed and stepped into the hottest shower, her head ringing with everything that she would write in the note. Not a note. A note was a small thing. It hardly weighed anything at all. She would write a letter. Pages and pages that—when folded—would barely fit into the envelope, but she would stuff them in anyway and prop it up against the mantel with Gus's name written on the front in thick black marker. Make no mistake. GUS. Not too soon, though. The letter had to come last. Just before she and Ruby walked out the door with their suitcases.

—

Ruby was four and a half the August that Gus and Mike had matching broken arms after they rolled the ATV down a muddy hill into the creek. They had VIP tickets to the music festival at the base of the ski run because the sponsor was also one of Gus's sponsors. The amphitheatre was new since the Winter Olympics, a pair of steepled hands made from cedar, with the mountain looming up behind it. It was a full day of bands performing for at least a thousand people, all there for the mountain bike competition that Gus would not be racing in. He was still a VIP, though, so they got to lay out their blankets in the fenced-off section of grass with the best views and sound. There was a sea of blankets and coolers and so many beautiful people that Fiona didn't know where to look. She wanted to look everywhere all at once. Ruby sat between her legs, bouncing to the music.

The sun set behind that bare summer fortress of a ski hill, and dusk fell over everything, the light dusted with the dirt from the bikes ripping down the hill. When Mumford & Sons came onstage as the final act, everyone leapt up from their blankets to dance, after all day politely dancing in the designated section by the beer garden. At first, Fiona was pissed. They should sit. So everyone could see, all the families with tiny babies, the old couples with their picnic baskets and low cushioned chairs, the group of young people tripping on something, all of them flat on their backs, marvelling at the sky. But they were all getting up too. Everyone was dancing as they started their cover of "The Boxer."

"Fiona!" Gus pulled her up, then Ruby. "It's our song!"

Promises. Lies. She'd never really paid attention to the lyrics before. Resistance. Lie, lie, lie, lie, lie, lie.

"Let's dance!" He lifted Ruby onto his shoulder so she could see. She balanced there, while he took Fiona's hands and pulled her close, singing along. He danced with her at first, tugging and swinging, until the music found her and she really was dancing. Ruby beamed, her hands on either side of Gus's head. When the song was over, Fiona kissed Ruby's dirty knees on either side of his cheeks, and then Gus. They were still kissing when Ruby patted their heads and pointed up. The first star.

"Everyone make a wish," Gus said for her. Gus and Ruby squeezed their eyes shut, wishing. Fiona never made wishes. They were dangerous, like the Sirens. Luring, and then smashing against rocks. But she loved this, watching her husband and little girl make wishes. So hopeful. So sweet.

After the shower, when she was dry and warm and the room was fogged with steam and she was just about to open the door to the dark, cold hallway—why wasn't the furnace working?—she thought about writing all kinds of things on the mirror. She also thought about Ruby, fresh out of the bath, smelling like her orange-scented bubbles, standing in front of the sink, reading the messages. *Fuck you, Gus. You asshole.* She lifted a finger and put it to the glass.

I love you, Ruby, she wrote instead.

And a little heart with a happy face underneath.

Ruby woke up beside her father. There was snoring, but it wasn't him. She surveyed the camper in the grey light of dawn. Ophelia heard her and looked up from her bed, thumping her tail on the floor. It was Mike snoring. He and Sarah were a red and an orange double sleeping bag with a head. Liam was a green cater-pillar in his sleeping bag on the floor.

Did her mother make it home okay? Did anyone have phone service up here in the big wild middle of nowhere? Was she sup-posed to worry? Her father slept soundly, which meant that he wasn't worried. Ruby decided not to be worried until he was.

Besides Mike's snoring, Ruby heard the thrum of the furnace and the rush of the river. She was thirsty and she had to pee, but instead, she lay back down and stared at the ceiling. She picked at the unicorn sticker until it peeled off nearly perfectly. She stuck it to the back of her hand, but then realized that someone would notice it there. She lifted up her T-shirt and stuck it between her nipples, pushing hard to make it stay.

Ruby could not bring herself to take a turn in the tiny bathroom, even after everyone was awake. She cringed when she heard her father's long stream of pee hit the water, then Liam's. *Tinkle.* Pause. *Tinkle.* She could not pee in there with everyone listen-ing. She couldn't wipe herself knowing that Sarah was standing right outside the door flipping pancakes and boiling water for coffee and hot chocolate. Sarah glanced up at Ruby, sitting up on the bunk with her legs dangling down.

"Did you sleep?"

Ruby nodded.

Mike was in the bathroom now. He peed and peed. It lasted forever. Absolutely forever, and then he farted. "Sorry."

"Light a match, for fuck's sakes." Gus counted out cards for Uno. How could he joke about it? It was just so horrible.

"I would"—Mike's voice boomed through the door—"but it might make the whole camper blow up."

Ruby desperately had to go pee, but she would not. She'd wait until they were on their way home and ask her dad to pull over. Then she remembered that her mom took the truck. Never mind. She could make it until she was home. She squeezed her muscles against the cramp in her gut. She refused a glass of orange juice and nibbled at her pancake, staring out the window at the glare on the new snow and the bright-red jujube of Luke's tent, wobbling as Luke and Aubrey moved around inside. Luke emerged first. He stretched and yawned, then hopped through the snow to the river's edge, where he stood with his legs apart and fished in his pants.

Ruby looked away. If she watched him, she might just pee her pants right there at the table, and that would be the worst thing of all. When she thought it was safe, she looked up again to see him hopping back to the tent, his pee still steaming in the snow behind him. Ruby slid her hand under the table and up between her legs. She pressed hard. Harder and harder, hoping the pain would make her bladder forget.

They were talking about the hot springs, how the place needed new pipes. The taps were so rusted it was hard to get any of the creek water in. That's why it was so hot in that one tub. Let's go in again after breakfast. One last dip before we hit the road.

She could pee in the tub. She would swish her legs and let it out slowly, slowly. No one would notice, but they would all be bathing in her pee, which was funny and gross and completely embarrassing all at the same time.

—

It took a long time to get all the strings of lights down, but once they were all packed up, it was time to go. Her dad would ride in the front with Sarah and Mike, while the kids rode in the camper.

"It'll be fun," Aubrey said as they gathered to climb the stairs. "Like sitting at the kids' table."

Which was never fun.

"Don't worry." Luke's cheeks were burnished red from the cold, his nose dripping. "We'll make sure Liam is nice to you."

Ruby hopped inside. Ophelia greeted her, wagging her tail. That helped, even with Liam there, staring at her. He held a juice box in each hand.

"Which one do you want?" he said. "And no pointing."

"Don't be a jerk," Aubrey said.

"Apple or grape?" Liam kept on. "Say which one."

Luke grabbed both and gave them to Ruby.

"I've seen her say stuff to Gus," Liam said. "You can talk to us too, you know." He didn't say it like a party invitation, though. He said it like he blamed her.

"Like she'd want to talk to you, Mr. Shane." Luke slid onto the bench.

"Stop saying he's my boyfriend!" Liam punched Luke in the arm.

"Did I say he was your boyfriend?"

"Enough!" Aubrey said. "The ride back is bumpy enough without your bullshit. Both of you."

The truck rumbled down the road. Ruby had never felt carsick before, but she thought she might be now. Probably. Maybe. Maybe not.

The four of them sat at the table, Luke and Aubrey on one side, Liam and Ruby on the other. Luke dealt four hands of Uno.

"How is she supposed to play?" Liam said.

"She can point to a colour for wild cards," Aubrey said.

"What is she going to do when she gets to the last card?"

"She can hold up one finger instead of saying Uno," Luke said.

"You're supposed to *say* Uno."

"Like I said, shitwad, she can hold up a finger." Luke stuck up his middle finger. "This one, if she wants."

Ruby tried not to smile, but then Luke winked at her and she couldn't help but grin. She picked up her cards and arranged them by colour. She also had a Wild Plus Four card. That one was for Liam. She'd play it on his turn, even if she still had colours to play. No one would know. No one ever challenged her hand.

It was dusk when Fiona heard Mike's truck outside. She pulled aside the curtain just enough to look out without being seen. There was Gus, saying goodbye and then going around to let Ruby out of the camper. She hopped down into his arms, and when he set her down, she smiled and waved at the others, as if they were friends and not just the children of Gus's best friend, the ones who had pretty much ignored her from birth. When the truck pulled away, they all waved like they were leaving on the longest road trip ever. Gus shouted thanks and see you soon and then he took Ruby's hand and they walked up the path together. All of it made it seem like the night before had been just so much fun. Because Fiona wasn't there to fuck everything up.

Fiona hadn't gone to bed at all. She'd sat on the couch in the dark and freezing house until her fingers were numb, and then she got into the shower again and scalded herself from head to toe, which had to have been a little after five in the morning. About an hour after that, there was a knock on the door. A dumpy woman in one of those walking sleeping bags of a down coat waved at her through the window. At first Fiona couldn't place her, but then she remembered that she was the secretary at Cayoosh.

"Happy New Year, Fiona!" she said. "I'm here to put some wood in your stove. I hear your furnace is on the blink. You're not supposed to be home."

Fiona cracked the door. "I wasn't feeling well."

"Oh, well. There you go." Sunny was her name. Third-generation hippie. "I'll just go, then. Unless you need anything?"

"No, thank you," Fiona said. "I'm feeling better, thank you."

Fiona got dressed and shovelled snow in the still pitch-black dark.

New year, clean path. It was symbolic, which she would not point out to Gus. She cleared it, swept it, and then scattered ice melt from an ice cream bucket in neat swinging arcs while she backed up to the porch. She ignored the ugly view of the hydro substation across the street. She did not write the letter, right? It wasn't on the mantel, was it?

It wasn't. Of course it wasn't. The letter that she had not written was not on the mantel. Was she disappointed? Or relieved? She could write a note right now. Before he walked through the door. Short. Scrawled. *It's over.* Folded. She could stuff it in the palm of his hand and fold his fingers over it. Done.

A cold gust swept in with Gus and Ruby.

"Jesus," Gus said. "It's freezing in here!"

"The furnace isn't working for some reason."

"I know. But the wood stove works perfectly fine," he said. "Sunny was going to come load it up for us," he said.

"Which goes to show you planned the overnight," Fiona said.

"And I'm guessing you sent Sunny away and just wallowed in the cold? When is the furnace guy coming?"

"I didn't even know it wasn't working," Fiona said.

"I asked you to call about the furnace two weeks ago," Gus said.

Fiona pulled Ruby into a hug. She smelled of campfire and maple syrup, which stained her shirt in an oblong blotch.

"If you had told me . . ." Fiona tried hard to keep her tone even, but she knew that she sounded like a bitch. She tried again. Softly. Softly. "If you had told me, I would've called. I'm sure I would've."

"I did tell you," Gus said. "But I wasn't in a rush about it because we have the wood stove. And when you're not going to be home for a while, you can get a friend to load it up for you."

"I was home."

"You couldn't let her help you?"

"I'll call. I will deal with it." Fiona kissed the top of Ruby's head. "Happy New Year, love."

Ruby stood on her tiptoes and kissed her on the cheek.

"Would you go make a fire in the stove?" Fiona said. "You, my perfect thing, are the best fire maker."

Ruby nodded and scampered off.

"How was your drive home?" Gus said.

"The truck and I are in one piece." Fiona pushed her tongue against her cheek. "I wore a seat belt. Did you? Did Ruby? Are there seat belts in campers?"

"You were too drunk to drive."

"You let Ruby ride the whole way home in the back of a camper?"

"Right."

"Campers are not meant for that, Gus. It's unsafe."

Ruby was back at their sides. How long had she been there? For a slice of a moment, Fiona wanted to berate Ruby. Don't sneak up! This is an adult conversation. You're not stupid. You know that we're having a private conversation! Go away!

Instead, she put a hand lightly on Ruby's head and glared at Gus.

"Everybody is fine," he said. "They played Uno. There were juice boxes. Maybe even chips. Were there chips?"

Ruby nodded.

"Come on, Rabbit," Gus said. "I'll run you a bath."

Fiona sighed. Ruby pressed against her. Her hair smelled of woodsmoke.

"Don't let Ruby ride in a camper or trailer or motor home while it's driving ever again. In the event of an abrupt stop, she'd become a projectile. A crash would be catastrophic."

Gus reached for Ruby's hand. "Come have a bubble bath, Rabbit."

Ruby hugged Fiona again.

"Thank you for getting the fire going." Fiona kissed her on the top of her head. "No more camper rides, okay?"

Gus stood at the bottom of the stairs, arms folded. Ruby looked from one parent to the other, until Fiona gave her a playful shove. "Off you go, love."

Ruby climbed the stairs behind her father. As he ran the bath, she stripped off her clothes and got into the tub. Gus turned off the taps, then sat on the toilet beside her and read to her from *Hatchet*. She was mostly listening, but even more mostly she was thinking of the bumpy ride home. After two rounds of Uno, Luke boosted Aubrey up to the bed. He got up there too. They zipped themselves into one sleeping bag. We better not roll right over, Luke said. So they inched to the other side and spoke in low voices. Liam leaned over the pile of Uno cards and whispered, "Do you know what? They're humping. His penis is in her vagina *right now*."

Her dad stopped reading. "Ruby? Are you listening?"

"Yes." Humping, bumping. Bumping, humping.

He started reading again. Beyond the words, Ruby heard the back door open and close.

Before Fiona finished the cigarette, her fingers were numb from the cold. The sun had just slipped behind Mount Casper, leaving the mountain tinged with pinks and purples. The town was already in dark shadow. The sky above was a deep turquoise, with silvery wisps of cloud catching on the mountain's peaks. The valley plunged into night so early now. The days were punishingly short, and when the sun set, the nights were the blackest dark—long and heavy and very, very cold.

All that beautiful food that Gus had not brought home. Where was it? At Mike and Sarah's? Some snowbank? Fact was, none of that food was here and so they needed groceries. Now. Right now. Fiona stubbed the cigarette out under her boot. She'd go get groceries. That was a good enough reason to go somewhere. She'd wear Gus's ski gloves. Those would warm up her hands.

—

The fluorescent lights in the grocery store buzzed overhead as Fiona aimed her cart through the automatic door. One of the cashiers waved at her. Her daughter was at Cayoosh too. Was she a bit older? She must've been on scholarship too. Fiona pretended not to see her, or the two women in the first aisle that she knew from yoga, back when they had the money for her to go. As she collected groceries into her cart—fumbling and dropping things because of the gloves, which were so warm that she just couldn't bring herself to take them off—she focused on each item so that she didn't have to look at anyone. She did not want to talk, and she did not want to do small talk most of all. Apples, oranges—Ruby was eating three or four a day right now—broccoli, carrots. In the meat section she selected two packages of ground beef and a whole chicken. When she turned up the bread aisle, there was Mike at the other end with a loaf in each hand.

Fiona backed up, but not before he saw her.

"That was a dramatic exit last night."

"Gus and I . . . there was a misunderstanding."

"How does that work? You thought you were going home, and he thought you were staying?"

"Something like that."

"That's a pretty big mix-up."

There was a point on the drive back from the hot springs where the road veered sharply to the right. A driver could plunge straight into Lil'wat Lake if they didn't take the turn properly. As she approached it, she thought about not turning. She could sail off the short, rocky cliff and belly-flop the truck onto the ice. The truck would rest there for a minute, maybe long enough for her to get out and scramble back to shore, and then the ice would crack, the truck would tip and slide and sink.

Maybe she could get out. But she wouldn't.

Tip. Slide. Sink. Into the ice water. She would succumb to the cold before she had a chance to drown, unless she could will herself to sink, eyes wide open in the black waters as her sodden clothes dragged her down.

She slowed at the turn, and then slowed to a stop in the middle of the road. She looked across the moonlit ice to the open water far beyond, and the trees at the other side like black, jagged teeth.

"You were drunk," Mike said.

"We all were."

"The rest of us didn't drive anywhere. We were worried about you. I worried about you. All night."

"I got home okay," Fiona said. "Just like you and Gus do when you drive drunk. Except for that time you drove your truck into the ditch by Nairn Falls."

"Leaving last night was really dumb," he said. "One of your dumber moves. You need to know that, if Gus wasn't clear."

"Driving home from Whistler when you're drunk is also a dumb move," Fiona said. "Especially when done repeatedly over the years."

"At least it isn't on an isolated logging road," Mike said. "When you might not be in your right mind."

"My right mind."

"You know what I mean."

Fiona steered around him. "Look, I'm here to get groceries, not to discuss my mental health with you. Then I'm going home to make supper for the man who lied to me to trick me into going up to the hot springs under false pretenses, and the child who will not tell me what it was like to ride home in the back of your camper."

"I'm sorry." Mike put his hand on the handle of the cart. "There's always more to it, isn't there."

That moment in Mexico was an impossibility. That night and this one simply could not coexist.

"Are you okay?" Mike said. "Will you be?"

"I'm fine. I'll see you on Sunday."

"You're still coming?"

"I am still coming." Fiona gave the cart a hard push, forcing him to let go. "Every fucking Sunday."

Fiona grabbed a loaf of bread—any bread. She needed milk and yogurt too, but she got in line to pay instead. She had to get out of there. She couldn't stand the thought of Mike in the store behind her, picking up a bag of oranges or a jar of mayonnaise or talking to a parent from Cayoosh, leaning on his cart and smiling. He was massive. He took up all the room. All the oxygen.

She picked the line with a cashier she didn't know, but then the woman collected her water bottle and handed over the keys she'd had on a plastic coil around her wrist to the woman who was the mother of a Cayoosh student. She put her own water bottle down and smiled at the next person in line. There were two people ahead of her, with not much in their carts. The cashier glanced past them and beamed at Fiona. Fiona turned to the old woman behind her in line.

"I forgot my wallet in the truck," Fiona said. "If you'll excuse me."

Out in the parking lot, people rolled carts to their cars and trucks, the wheels clattering on the salted pavement. Country music leaked out of the Legion next door, and the rhythmic stomping of the annual New Year's Line-Dancing Marathon. A diesel truck rumbled by pulling a trailer of snowmobiles. Fiona climbed into the truck and sat there with her hands in her lap, and no groceries.

She sat there until Mike brought out his groceries, two bags in each hand. He'd parked along the street and didn't see her watching him as he waited for a car to pass. Someone shouted his name and he looked up with a smile as the manager from the ice rink ran over. The kids from Cayoosh skated there once a week. Mike leaned against the truck, legs shoulder-width apart, arms folded. He was the possessor. He possessed the bread aisle. He possessed that truck. He possessed that body. He possessed his life all the way to the dark corners and all the way to the basement too. He was the one who owned what happened in Mexico. It was more his, somehow, than hers. He grinned and laughed, and at one point shuffled all his bags into one arm so he could playfully punch the man on the shoulder. Why not own him too? And the conversation. He was a big, strong, happy man. He took up the space and used it for himself and allotted it to others only as he saw fit. He owned more than his fair share and he was the man who knew how good he had it.

Unless Fiona took it all away. Because she could, if she wanted to.

When they were first home from Mexico, she was afraid she might blurt it out at a Sunday supper. She kept her mouth shut for weeks, afraid that if she opened it to say so much as please could I have a bit more wine, the admission would fall out of her mouth. But then, after all, she'd managed not to say anything.

How was it fair that he was so big and she felt simply reduced? Instead of ejaculating inside her and adding something, it was as if he'd taken something away instead. She was smaller. Unsure. So uncertain that she wasn't even sure of that. Or had she always been so small? Maybe that was it. She was a very small thing, and had been mistaken all these years. She was no bigger than a pebble, one that anyone could keep in a pocket, or a little box. She was skulking, when she should not be. Mike was never going to tell. But what if she did? Would it fill her out again, at the edges?

Fiona pulled out of the parking spot too fast and almost hit the old lady from the lineup. When she slammed on the brakes, Mike looked up and lifted his hand like she was just another person he knew. He was not afraid. He had never been her lover. She kept both hands on the wheel and caught up to the truck towing the snowmobiles. She followed it along Meadows Road for a while before pulling off to the shoulder.

This road did not lead anywhere. Not anywhere that she could go right now, anyway. It turned into gravel and then there was a fork. To the left was the road to Meager Creek. To the right were the narrow dirt switchbacks that climbed up to another road that wound along a plateau before climbing up some more and ending at an old mining town with abandoned cabins and a giant hole in the earth. Bralorne. Gus took her there once. It was summer, and Ruby was newly walking. They brought sandwiches and cookies and a cooler full of ice and beer. They sat on the porch of one of those cabins and watched Ruby toddle in the tall grass. It was a very good day, when she thought back on it.

There were only so many ways to get out of this dark valley. This road—inaccessible in winter unless you had a snowmobile—the precarious logging road along the ridge above Paradise Valley, the Lil'wat Lake Road with its contemplative sharp turn up through six reserves, after which the road was just a broken-up four-by-four puzzle that arrived at the north end of Harrison Lake, and then the most-used route: Highway 99, through the Sea to Sky Corridor, past Whistler and Squamish to Vancouver, about three hours away with winter conditions and proper tires.

Vancouver felt like an impossible destination to Fiona. It was unreal to Fiona that she could drive there right now. She knew that for some people Casper was just a stop at the gas station for shitty coffee. It should be for her too. She was a person on her way to the city, where she could buy a pretty dress and then wear it to a French restaurant and sit with a bottle of wine and a tureen of *lapin à la cocotte* and a fat, smart novel. But the surrounding mountains held her in place. There was no leaving the valley.

Ruby trailed behind the six other kids as they pushed out the doors of Cayoosh's main building. They scampered up onto the snowbank, but she didn't. She was alone in the middle of the short breezeway that led to the Namaste Room—a converted shipping container that was dented and rusty on the outside but warm and cozy inside. They were not supposed to walk along the breezeway because of the roof, which was angled and troughed, built for a herb garden they'd plant in the spring. Built, too, to hold a lot of snow. Mike shovelled after every snow. Still, *I don't trust it*, he'd said to her father. *Should be steeper.* They'd passed a joint between them by the firepit in the backyard while Ruby whittled a stick into an arrow. *There's a gap along one seam. And a sag at one end. I've called the contractor, but they're busy in Whistler for another couple of weeks.*

Mike was up there now, clearing off the snow. *Crunch, scrape, wump.* Until he saw her there and stopped.

"Ruby! Use the path, kiddo."

The other kids peered at her from the stamped-down trail along the top of the snowbank on one side.

"Stupid," Shane said.

Ruby didn't climb up the snowbank. Before Mike could warn her again, she ran straight for the doors.

The walls of the Namaste Room were lined with photographs taken by Shane's mom. Her name was Moe Walz, and she was a very famous photographer. Everest. Kilimanjaro. The Yangtze River. A golden temple in Nepal. An elephant in a cloud of dust somewhere in Africa. A child washing a tin cup at a tap in Bangladesh. A crest of slate-grey mountain in Patagonia, and Shane's mom, and his other mom—he called her mama—too, both with their arms raised, his mama obviously pregnant, triumphant, the blue sky behind them, a glare on their sunglasses. There used to be some of Shane too, but one of them was of him as a fat baby, sitting naked in the middle of a dirty tarp with cocoa beans drying all around him. No one even said anything, but one day in grade one he took them down and put them in the garbage.

Liam, Shane, Anna, Skye, Nino, Tag and Ruby.

The Namaste Room had wide cushioned benches with jumbles of pillows along the walls, and a floor made from cork and brought to a polish, and a shelf stacked with yoga mats, with a Tibetan singing bowl on top, and a small Buddha with his eyes closed and his hands on his knees, palms upturned, and an incense holder, which had only collected dust ever since a few parents brought up the issue of fragrance pollution. Prayer flags hung from the ceiling, in all the colours of the pillows—red, yellow, orange, green, purple. The children sprawled out on these, waiting for Gus.

Liam, Shane, Anna, Skye, Nino, Tag and Ruby.

"Where is he, Ruby?" Shane said. "Where's your daaaaaaad?"

"I bet he's hungover," Liam said.

"What's hungover?" Anna said.

"If you don't know, then I'm not going to tell you." Liam squeezed an imaginary headache.

"You don't even know either," Nino said.

"Luke is hungover all the time," Liam said. "All. The. Time."

"I know what it means," Tag said. "Ruby's dad drank too much beer, and now he has a headache and he can't get out of bed except to barf."

But that was *Tag's* dad. Not hers. Tag's dad was the one who drank too much. He was the one who went away to a place that helps people stop drinking.

"She knows." Shane clutched his stomach and feigned an epic barf. "Is your dad at home barfing-kissing the toilet?"

She'd never seen her father barf. Definitely not from too many beers. He didn't drink any more beer than any other dad. He drank less than her mom. Even if she drank wine mostly and it was hard to compare because one was in a fancy glass that you could just keep pouring into.

"Huh, *Wabbit*?"

Rabbit was her father's name for her. Only his. He was the only one allowed to call her that. Ruby balled her fists up. She glared at Shane so hard that he looked away, when he was never the one to look away first.

"Is that why your parents can't pay for you to go here? He spends all the money on beer? If he's so famous, why do you wear pyjamas to school all the time?"

Leggings and a T-shirt. Not pyjamas. Not pyjamas!

"That's not nice," Anna said.

"He's so famous, but he can't pay for school because he buys beer. All of it. Like, all the beer in the world. A million cans of beer. Beer in the morning," Shane chanted. "Beer at lunch, beer at supper, beer a whole bunch!"

That rhyme didn't make any sense.

"I'm going to tell." But Anna pushed up her glasses and did not actually get up to go get help.

"Don't, Anna." Skye took her hand. "Don't tell!"

"Did he have too many beers?" Shane was beside Ruby all of a sudden. "Did he sit on the couch in his underwear and drink beer and watch TV?"

"She doesn't have a TV," Liam said.

But she did. Was he trying to help? Or was he trying to make it worse?

"*Wabbit* doesn't have a TV?" Shane laughed. "That doesn't surprise me."

Ruby clenched her fists. Don't call me Rabbit. Do not call me Rabbit! You don't get to call me Rabbit! Only my dad!

"I have a TV in my room," Shane said. "And it's big. Bigger than this one." He tossed a pillow at the modest-sized one mounted on the wall. He hit it so hard that it wobbled.

The children gasped.

He was the only one with a TV of his very own.

Liam had a TV in the living room, he reported. "I can watch whatever I want."

Not true. Not true! *Luke* decided what they were going to watch. Except when Ruby was over, and Sarah put on the Food Network because she knew that Ruby liked to watch the chefs race around trying to beat each other with the best dish.

The twins—Anna and Tag—lived in a yurt in the woods, way back in the new reserve built up on the mountainside after the flood, and they didn't even have a bedroom of their own. They had bunks on one side of the wood stove, and their parents had a double bed on the other side, and if they wanted to watch something, it was on the computer and it was about molecules or the Roman Empire or the origin of flight. Their mother's family was Lil'wat *infinity*, Tag liked to say. Since the dawn of time. She came once a week to do Ucwalmícwts lessons for all the classes. Their father was from Musqueam Nation, and came up here because he was a freshwater biologist. If Ruby had to have best friends, maybe it would be Desirée Pierre—all those *e*'s in her name—and Dan Grant, who never asked her questions, not ever, just smiled at her and offered her the bowl of chips at a picnic or an extra scoop of ice cream at movie night, even while he talked a mile a minute himself, and his wife knew every pun there ever was and used them all.

Nino didn't have a TV either, but he could watch whatever he wanted on the computer, so he mostly watched clips of people falling on their faces or dogs that told fart jokes, or magicians teaching magic tricks step by step, because he'd gotten a box of magic tricks from his grandma in the mail and he was going to do a magic show for Talent Night in two weeks. Skye's mother had a TV in her bedroom, but she was the only one who watched it. She didn't think children should watch television. The ads poisoned their impressionable minds, which is one of the reasons why she signed Skye up for the Cayoosh, because there were no logos permitted. Not on clothing, not on backpacks, not on shoes or hats or watches or water bottles. Lunch boxes weren't an issue because lunch was provided—made by the students—and the parents took turns bringing a nutrient-rich snack. There were fifty families involved with the school, and eighty-four students, so that meant snack time one or two times in the school year, depending on how many children you had, and if they were in separate rooms. The classes—*pods*, actually—were mixed ages, so a six-year-old and a nine-year-old brother and sister could very well be in the same group. Children benefit from learning and growing within a multi-age environment. So the brochure said.

But sometimes the children were grouped by age. For this field trip to the Tiffen Creek cabin, for example. Everyone was nine years old. Except for Ruby, who was going to be nine very soon.

The TV was in the living room at Ruby's house. Sometimes she watched it. Sometimes she didn't. Her mother was the one who watched it the most. Sometimes, when Ruby came home from school, she'd find her mother watching cooking shows. Sitting upright, as if she'd just sat down, or was just about to get up. Or as if she'd heard Ruby on the front steps and had rearranged herself as Ruby was opening the door. Sometimes Ruby hurried to sit with her right when she walked in the door, still wearing her jacket and boots, and sometimes even her backpack, because if she waited, her mom might get up and turn it off and then wander around the house picking up one thing and putting it down for a while before sitting down to read a book. Which was not something Ruby could sit with her for. Which was different from them both looking at someone discussing why you should use heirloom tomatoes in a pasta sauce.

"Hey, Rabbit." Shane wiggled his nose at her. "Where's your dad? Where is he?"

Ruby looked at her feet.

"What? I can't hear you."

"Maybe he's up a mountain," Anna said. "With customers."

Footsteps outside—breezeway, not snowbank. It was him! Thank goodness.

A gush of cold air swept in tendrils of snow when he flung open the door.

"Dudes! Let's get this thing planned." He grabbed Ruby and gave her a rough kiss on her head. "My favourite human."

Ruby broke into a grin. He dumped a big backpack by the

door and sat, pulling Ruby onto his lap. Shane would tease her about it later—*baby, baby, baby*—but who cared.

"Shane, Liam, Anna, Skye, Nino, Tag. And Ruby too. Who's got a checklist for me?" Ruby held out hers as the others scrambled forward with theirs. "I don't need to see yours, Rabbit. I know you're good." Gus took Shane's. "You still need to get the dried apples. We're going to want those in our oatmeal in the morning, trust me."

"My mom is getting them tonight."

"Good, because I do not want to miss out on dried apples in my oatmeal, my friend."

Not friend.

"Don't worry." Shane grinned. "Hey, what do your knuckles say?"

Don't show him, Daddy. Don't. But Shane grabbed Gus's hands and read them both. "Ruby love." He glanced at Liam. "That's really nice."

"That's for Ruby," Gus said.

"Duh," Shane said.

Ruby's cheeks burned. They would spontaneously combust if he didn't stop talking.

"And this one too." Gus pointed to a rabbit on the underside of one arm. "I had to put it there because I already had so many tattoos by the time she was born." He noticed Ruby then, her red cheeks and damp eyes. "Okay, kids. Enough about my ink. Let's talk fruit leather."

"I got the fruit leather," Tag said.

"He did not," Anna said. "Me and Skye went to the store and got the trail mix *and* his fruit leather."

"All good," Gus said.

"I got the powdered milk," Liam said.

"Right on, Liam. Nino? Hot chocolate?"

"Lots and lots."

"Which is a very good thing," Gus said. "Because it is cold out there. Cold, cold, friggin' cold." The kids laughed. "So, layers, right? You've got all your layers? Thermal underwear—wool is best, and I know most of you have a good first layer—and then a fleece or wool mid-layer, then wind- and waterproof layers. No cotton, you all know that. And good technical socks. And a spare pair, and another pair to sleep in. Nothing worse than cold, wet socks. Wet socks mean cold, wet feet, which equals bad news. And where we're going? Very bad news." He pulled a leather cord out of his shirt, with a small, soft deerskin bag cinched at the bottom. He worked it open and emptied several tiny white bones into the palm of his hand.

"What is that?" Shane leaned right in, about to pick one up.

"No touching." Gus pulled away.

"I know what they are," Liam said. "Toe bones."

"Gross!" Skye said.

"Cool!"

"So cool." Shane and Nino looked closer.

"I lost two toes to frostbite."

Once the kids had a good look at the bones, Gus took off his right boot and showed them the smooth, scarred space where his two smallest toes used to be.

"This is serious stuff. We need to be prepared. Don't be like me. I got stuck out overnight with a broken-down snowmobile and I wasn't prepared. I didn't have the Ten Essentials." He upturned his backpack onto the floor. "I'll dump out my stuff and you guys can match the gear to the list."

Navigation. That was actually Ruby's compass he lifted up in one hand. In his other hand was a dog-eared map and a GPS.

"Navigation," Shane said in a bored voice. "Light," he added in the same drone, as Gus picked up his headlamp.

Next, a small tube of sunscreen.

"Duh," Shane said. "It's winter."

"Snow sunburn is real," Gus said. "Call this category Protection. Sun, bugs, chafing."

Shane and Liam snorted.

"You've never had crotch chafe?" Gus said. The kids giggled. "When a pair of shorts or your ginch rubs the wrong way?"

Stop talking, Daddy. Ruby reached for the next item to get him talking about anything else. The red first aid kit. Inside were several bandages with little bunnies on them. She held the kit tight when her dad tried to take it from her to show the kids. She would not let go. There were the bunny bandages, and also a menstrual pad. He kept one in there in case anyone needed it on his tours, but also because it made a really good bandage for a bad bleed.

"Luke and I take a much bigger first aid kit guiding," Gus said. "We'll go through that another time. Just know we've got you covered. Now, a knife." He pulled his grandfather's knife out of the worn leather sheath on his belt. He'd died long before Ruby was born, but she'd seen pictures of him beside deer he'd shot. "You don't need a heavy one like this. Any little Swiss Army knife will do."

"Unless you have to kill something," Nino said.

"It's never come to that," Gus said. "You could learn how to use a snare and tuck one of those in your kit, though."

"To kill *wabbits*," Shane said under his breath.

Even if she had not eaten in a million days, Ruby would never *ever* kill and eat a rabbit. She would kill and eat Shane first.

Willy called at six o'clock in the morning.

"I know it's hate-me o'clock there, but I've decided that I'm buying you and that exquisitely gorgeous little girl of yours tickets to come visit me and my exquisitely gorgeous little girl. You need to come home. I can hear it in your voice. I can read it in your texts and emails. You're just about to fall apart, Fiona."

As Willy talked, Gus let out a fart. He threw the covers back and got out of bed, leaving the stench behind. He padded out of the room and down the hall towards the bathroom.

"I'm already in pieces, Will. But I'm good at it. I have the thoughts. I don't do the thing. Everyone else is none the wiser. Being in pieces is not uncharted territory for me."

"It's different right now," Willy said. "I can sense it. I know it's about Gus. So put the pieces into a suitcase and arrange to have them and Ruby delivered to the airport and put onto the plane. I will reconstruct you once you are here, from however many pieces. I do like a puzzle. So does Collette."

"A puzzle isn't the same."

"I can put you together," Willy said. "I've done it before. Let me."

The shower started in the bathroom.

"It's been awful," Fiona said.

"But he hasn't found out about Mike?"

"No."

"Good. Everyone has one hall pass, right?"

"It's not even about Mexico. It was so long ago. That was just one thing and there are so many. I hate this place. I hate him. At least, I'm nearly certain that I hate him. In relation to me, that is."

"I can clear my schedule for two weeks from now, so come then. That gives you time to get Gus warmed up to the idea. It's just a visit. That's all. No need to make any big decisions right now. You have all the time in the world to do things right. Come see me. You will survive until then. And then you will come, and I will be grossly demonstrative when I see you at the airport. There will be a giant sign, and flowers, and balloons. Maybe even a teddy bear."

"Oh, Will." Fiona groaned. "Not a teddy bear, please."

"For Ruby, you nitwit."

Fiona sat up and reached for her cigarettes. "She's not that kind of kid."

"What kind of kid is she, then?"

"She's serious. And sweet." Fiona slid into her housecoat and slippers, stuck the pack in her pocket and headed downstairs. "She doesn't like gifts you'd give a regular kid. But she's gracious."

"What does she like?" Willy said. "I'll get her all of it."

"She has a pocket knife, which she loves. She loves those paracord bracelets."

"No clue."

"Rope, woven into a bracelet. She's always wearing the same filthy purple one." At the back door she shrugged into Gus's parka and switched her slippers for his big boots. She stepped out onto the porch and lit a cigarette. As Willy looked up flights and read out departure times and layovers, Fiona gazed up at

Mount Casper. It was a giant silvery wedge at the edge of town, turning a breathless blue as the sun began to rise.

The flight details came in an email that afternoon. Fiona showed Gus the printed tickets after she'd tucked Ruby into bed. Gus was doing the dishes. She placed them on the counter where he could see them without drying his hands. They looked very formal, with names and dates and times. It was quite pleasing to look at.

"It's so nice of her to buy them." She tried to keep her voice even. "We'll only be there three weeks."

"Which is too long," Gus said. "I've never been away from Ruby for that long. And that's a lot of school to miss."

"Come on, you don't care how much school she misses. You take her away all the time. Mike wouldn't mind. He'd call it life learning and send her off with a camera and a journal and a package of brand new coloured pencils."

"I could come too."

"During your busiest season?" Fiona felt a flutter of panic in her gut.

A pause. The air thickened.

"You don't want me to come."

Another pause.

"I'll take Ruby up to see my dad and my aunt."

"You hate your dad and your aunt." Gus dried his hands.

"I don't hate them," Fiona said. "Not at all. Ruby should know them better. She has a lovely relationship with your father. And she had that with your mother too. Before she got sick."

"You need a letter from me." Gus slid the tickets across the counter to her. "To cross any border with her. I have to sign it. And I won't."

How did he know that? Had he been checking in case she left without telling him, and took Ruby with her? Because he wasn't checking for himself. If he left with Ruby, it would be just across town to Mike and Sarah's. He had nowhere else to go, really. No one would be waiting for him with a stupid teddy.

"You will, though." Fiona reached for a glass that still had a bit of water in it from the night before. She swallowed it, hoping to quell the burn at the back of her throat. "Please? It would be a lovely trip for Ruby. You can hate me for my part, but let her go see her auntie and grandad. And Willy and her foul little child."

"Collette is not foul," Gus said. "She's a snob. Entirely different."

"Please, Gus."

"No." He shook his head. "I will not, because I don't trust you to come back."

"We'd come back. This is Ruby's home."

"But is it yours?"

"Of course."

"I know what you're doing, Fiona. I know how this works." He was barely whispering now. "You have it in your head to go, and in your head there is no other way this is going to play out. So, you go, and maybe you come back—"

"We *would* come back."

"So, you go, take all your medication at all the right times, catch all your trains on time, feed yourselves three meals a day, stick to a smart itinerary, and when the time comes, you get on the plane, you get off the plane, I pick you two up and you both sleep on the ride through the mountains."

"Exactly."

"The only problem with that version is that at every turn you might not take your meds—or hell, even if you do take them—and then I hear that you're staying and Ruby is going to try out for a prestigious ballet school, or that you've talked Willy into buying you a little cottage so you can try your hand at being a market farmer because you told her I slap you every day at a quarter past four."

"She wouldn't believe me," Fiona whispered. "Not if I said it was every day."

"Everyone believes you eventually," Gus said. "After you've worn us all down."

Worn us all down. Just say nothing. Let him be the one to say something.

"It's not happening." Gus plunged his hands back into the dishwater. "I won't let Ruby go. When we end this at last, she stays with me. She never crosses a border with you."

"When we end this *at last*?" Fiona's throat squeezed out the words. "I haven't made any decisions. Have you?"

He shook his head.

"So, that's okay." She put a hand on his arm. "Let Ruby and me go on this trip. Maybe it will help things. Maybe we'll come back and things will be better. There is no need for *when* or *at last*. Come on, Gus." She leaned forward to kiss him. "Please."

"I know what you're doing." Gus scrubbed and rinsed Ruby's favourite plate—melamine, with dancing rabbits. A first birthday gift from his parents. "You think you can talk me into something I have zero intention of going along with. But not this time." Was that a hint of a smile on his face? "It took a while, I'll admit, but I know how to do it now. Make the decision and stick to it, no matter what you say." He scrubbed at a pot. "I know you, Fiona. I *know* you. I know that the best thing is to stop you and make you wait for yourself to catch up. If only I'd known that before. But I do now. Because I know you."

"Last year I rented a storage locker." Fiona picked up a wine-glass dappled with greasy fingerprints. "With a roll-up door, like a little garage. You were in Whistler with Ruby. Remember? Commentary for the kids' dirt bike competition? I drove the truck right in and shut the door and left it running. The manager heard the engine and opened the door."

"Fiona—"

"I had sex with my cousin when I was twelve. That was my first time. Not fourteen, with Hussein, who was nearly twenty, and not my age, like I told you when we met."

"Girl or boy?"

"What?"

"The cousin."

"Boy."

"Who was it?"

"Doesn't matter."

"How old was he?"

"Seventeen."

"That's rape."

"I wanted to do it. It hurt and I liked it. He came in my mouth. I liked that too. Even though it made me gag."

Gus's face was pale. "Ruby with a seventeen-year-old boy. Would that be okay?"

"I didn't say it was okay. I told you something that you don't know about me." Fiona straightened her shoulders. She set the glass down and took the dishtowel from his shoulder. She picked a bowl from the rack. She wiped it dry, and then wiped it again. And again. The bowl gleamed. She kept wiping. "Want another truth? Or maybe a lie?"

"Neither." Gus took the bowl from her and put it away in the cupboard.

"I did heroin." She picked up the dirty wineglass again. "For about six months, when I was eighteen. Until Aunt Noreen threw me into prison."

"Probably a very nice rehab," Gus said. "You can stop talking any time. And you know you should. Listen to yourself. You're talking in fast forward. Classic batshit-crazy Fiona. Look, there is a bottle of lorazepam beside your bed. There's one in the medicine cabinet. There is one in the junk drawer. There is at least one in each of your purses, as well as your makeup bag. There is one in the glove compartment. Go find one."

Fiona pulled open the nearest drawer and took out the orange pill bottle. She uncapped it and tipped the pills into the sink full of soapy water and dishes.

"Fiona!" Gus wrenched her wrist away with one hand and drained the water with the other. "Now we have to wash these all over again! Or do you want Ruby passing out after she has a drink of orange juice from one of these cups?"

"Highly unlikely." Another bottle from atop the fridge. She uncapped this one too, then tossed the pills into the garbage. "Once, I faked a vaguely eastern European accent and offered a blow job to an old man I met on the train. He was in his seventies at least. He took me to dinner, and then he took me to his apartment and told me to put my hair in pigtails and we looked up porn about old men and little girls and he banged up against me for ages until I got him off with my feet. He gave me five hundred dollars. I'd just turned sixteen. I met him once a week for that whole summer, until his wife came back from Australia."

She dug another bottle out of her purse. This she threw across the room and hit the garbage can.

"Slam dunk," she said. "That's what you call it?"

"I call it mania."

"Oh, come on." Fiona lifted the wineglass, about to throw it expertly into the bin too, but then stopped and headed for the fridge, where she contemplated the choice between boxed red or white wine. Upon investigation, she found the white was almost empty. She tried to dunk that into the garbage, but it clattered to the floor. No matter, it was recyclable anyway. She filled the dirty glass with red, noting a little bit of muddy ash at the bottom.

"When I was twenty-one, I stole a very expensive ring from an antiques shop, just because I liked it. Another time, the cops picked me up because I was running around Hyde Park with no clothes on."

"You were on medication by then."

"I was off them at that particular time."

"Were you high?"

"On drugs? Or manic? Sure. Either one. Ask Willy. She'll tell you. She knows better than me. She's the one that brought me clothes to go home in because all they gave me was a paper gown, like at the doctor's." Fiona took a sip. It did taste ashy, which was not that bad at all. "You know me, right?" She pointed the glass at him. "You *know* me."

Up next? The three things that would hurt him the most. She held two of them tight in one fist, two marbles covered in diamond shards. She opened her hand, expecting blood. The third thing was not available. Not like this. Not yet. Perhaps never.

"At some point in your life," Gus said, "you will need help."

"I've had help. I *have* help," she said. "A psychiatrist prescribes all of my medication. You see her name on every single bottle, even if you never ask about my appointments with her. Her phone number is on the bottles too. Feeling inspired to call so she can make you feel good about trying to force some quetiapine down my throat?"

"I'd be happy to start with the lorazepam."

Fiona laughed. "If you knew anything about my medication, you'd know what each one is for."

"Is the quet—" He grasped for the word. "The other pill. Is it upstairs?"

It was, but Fiona shook her head. She didn't want to turn into a zombie right now. She needed her faculties. She did not want him to help her up to bed and give her a glass of water with a straw so she could sip it because she kept missing her mouth if she tried to drink it without a straw. She hated straws.

He filled the sink again, to wash the dishes in clean water. "Should I expect the phone call where they tell me you're at the store rearranging all the canned goods by colour again?"

"See? That doesn't help. You're making fun of me. In the meanest way. Like a horrible boy at school." The glass orbs cut into her fists. If she unclenched her fists, there would be blood.

"That's not fair."

"You have a part in this."

"I do."

Her fingers unfurled and the two worst things slipped out of her hands and fell, shattering on the tile floor.

"I had two abortions." *Leave it at that. Leave it, Fiona.*

"You never mentioned that to the doctor when we were trying to have another baby."

He dried his hands and folded his arms across his chest, biceps pushing against his T-shirt. She could see his pulse throb at his neck.

"Because they were yours," she said. "I didn't want you to know."

Gus stared at her. The throb intensified.

"I did get pregnant. Twice. And two times I went to Vancouver and had an abortion. I did not want another baby. I did not want another baby with you. I did not want a baby at all."

Gus fell forward, catching himself with his hands on his knees. He exhaled with such force that she thought he might pass out. He breathed in heavily, then out, over and over again. And then she saw drips on the floor. Tears. He was crying!

She should've kept those two tiny not-babies in her fists forever, because they didn't matter to her. Their expulsion was an immediate relief for her, but she knew it was the opposite for Gus.

Willy would be so disappointed. Why did you tell him *now*? How cruel, Fiona. You know better. This is you, unravelling. Come to me. We can fix this.

This was unfixable.

There was no way to pick up the glass. Everything would always be worse now.

She was sorry. I'm sorry, Gus. Please forgive me! But she wouldn't say it out loud, because they were embryos. Collections of tissue. Not infants at all. Not babies.

"What about Ruby?" Gus looked up, his face the very definition of beseeching.

"What about her?"

"Did you want her?"

"I love her, but no. I didn't want her. Of course not. I'd just met you. I was in a foreign country. Entirely alone." Fiona put the wineglass to her head, half wanting to smash it there. "But then I *did* want her. I love her."

"What about those other babies?" More tears. Snot running down. "Those are your babies too! Just as much as Ruby is."

"No. No, that's not true. Tissue and blood. Zygotes. That's all. It's my body!" She screamed it. No. No, Fiona. Be quiet. She should say she is sorry, because of course she is.

"I didn't mean to hurt you," she whispered. "But I couldn't have those babies."

She remembered sitting in the waiting room in the building on one side of the busiest intersection in the city and listening to the traffic congest the four corners and the SkyTrain going to and fro overhead, and the crying of the teenaged girl who sat all alone across the room. She remembered thinking that she should go sit with her. She remembered thinking that Gus would cry like that. She was right. Here he was now, crying exactly like that.

She still needed his signature, and if he'd been reluctant before, there was no way he'd ever allow her to take Ruby to England now.

Fiona had blown this up.

"Those were my babies," Gus said to the floor. He looked up at her. "And you knew that I wanted them. You said that *you* wanted them."

"I thought I did. But then I didn't. And I couldn't talk to you about it, because you would not stop talking about kids, Gus." *Shut up, Fiona.* "Because that's all you would talk about. Our kids. A carload. Siblings for Ruby. A brother, a sister, maybe one of each. Or more. We can get rid of the truck and get a minivan. I can't wait to hold another baby in the middle of the night. Their heads are so soft. They smell so good. Their tiny fingers and little toes. All those tiny clothes with snaps and zippers. And stacks and stacks of cloth diapers, which are just so foul and depressing." *Shut up, Fiona.* "You're like a fucking little girl, Gus. A little girl with her dollies."

"Because I wanted a family?"

"You got a family." Fiona heard how feeble it sounded. She slid backwards, until she bumped into the Fiona behind her, and the two of them collapsed on the kitchen floor. *Shut up, Fiona. Stop talking.* She crawled to the garbage can and fished in it until she found the pill bottle. She undid the cap and tipped the contents into her mouth. She swished the pills around in a big mouthful of wine. When she tasted them dissolving, she swallowed the slurry, followed by the rest of the wine. Gus didn't budge at first, but then he lunged for her and nearly shoved his whole fist down her throat to make her vomit, when one or two fingers would've had the same result.

They waited too late on the night Ruby was born. Gus said that they could make it to Squamish in an hour, maybe a little more.

Even in the snow? Fiona swayed, paced, braced herself against the wall in the nursery, which was the warmest and cleanest room in the house. The contractions were far enough apart to stay put for now. When it passed, she draped the green blanket over the crib instead of the rocker. The rocker was her prized possession. A gift from Willy, it glided back and forth instead of rocking, so it took up very little room, and looked like a very expensive—if understated—piece of furniture. She opened each drawer of the little bureau Gus had found in the alley and repainted, creamy yellow with egg yolk pinstripes. Clothes in every colour for the baby they did not yet know was a girl.

You're doing great, the nurse said on the phone. It's too soon to leave. There was no point. Not yet.

Gus rolled tennis balls on her lower back. He made her raspberry leaf tea that was supposed to thin her cervix, but not too quickly.

Fiona began to make ugly faces with each contraction. Willy had warned her that this meant the baby was coming soon.

Gus massaged her shoulders, but now she didn't want him touching her at all. The nurse phoned again, and after she checked in with Fiona, she wanted to talk to Gus. Fiona could tell by the way he left the room and spoke in a low voice, and then did not come back right away after he hung up, that something was wrong with the plan.

Fiona said, "It's the highway, isn't it?"

"There was an accident," Gus admitted. "The highway is still closed in both directions, and it's been hours now. Hobs will call as soon as he gets the go-ahead."

Hobs who drove a snowplough for Highways. "We could follow him," Fiona said.

Gus nodded. "Yes. Absolutely. As soon as he calls."

Fiona gripped the crib and hung her head into the pile of blankets. Everyone had sent one or made one or given her one of their baby's old ones. It was a pile, like the mattresses in "The Princess and the Pea." A big contraction folded her over the side of the crib.

The phone rang again.

"Sarah," Gus said. "Am I ever glad to hear your voice."

Fiona listened until another contraction flattened Gus's voice into a thin, hot line of pain. When the contraction eased, Gus was still on the phone. She heard *alternating lanes*, and brightened immediately.

"The highway is clear for one lane," Gus said. "Sarah is taking us in the ambulance."

"No ambulance!" Fiona shook her head. "I don't want Sarah to see me like this. Please, let's just drive behind Hobs."

"He couldn't wait for us," Gus said. "He's already headed south."

"No ambulance."

"You could lie down," Gus said. "And the nurse said we had to."

Fiona had to go to the bathroom. She needed to poo. When she sat on the toilet, she realized that her vulva felt boggy and swollen. She reached between her legs and felt the baby's head, a slick, imminent evacuation. She wiped herself and slid to the floor. If only it were as simple as squeezing her legs together.

The hospital bag sat downstairs by the door. Made from leather, moss green and supple. Willy had sent it, already packed with treasures. Bassetts Sherbet Lemons. A small jar of hand cream Fiona had never heard of. A bamboo headband. The softest slippers for Fiona and a creamy-white romper for the baby, made from even softer angora.

"Gus!" Fiona yelled, and then louder. "Gus!"

He came running, and when he saw her on the floor, his face blanched.

"Sarah's coming!"

"Sarah is not delivering my baby!"

"She's delivered babies," Gus said. "I haven't."

Fiona bellowed through another contraction. She rolled onto all fours, taking only a moment to pull herself up to vomit into the toilet, which was already a stew of blood and shit. She flung shaking fingers up to the handle to try to flush away the smell and the mess. Someone flushed it for her, and it was not Gus. It was Sarah, in her dark-blue uniform pants and T-shirt.

She closed the lid and sat on it.

"Let's meet this baby!" She unfurled a sterile roll marked OBS onto the little counter and pulled a portable doppler from her kit. Her partner stood at the door with Gus, writing things down.

Fiona rocked back and forth, her back an arch of hot pain. She felt a terrible crawling, stretching sensation all over her body.

"I need a shower," Fiona said. "A really, really hot shower."

"You don't have time for one," Sarah said. "After." She picked up a pair of sterile scissors and came at her.

Another contraction gripped her. Her water hadn't broken yet. If this baby could be born in the caul, then all good things would come to her. She'd be blessed, from birth. Just as soon as she'd had the thought, Fiona felt a gush, and then the floor under her was slick with blood-tinged fluid.

"No meconium," Sarah said. "That's good, Fiona. Come on, hon. Let's meet your baby!"

Gus started crying when Fiona delivered the head, which seemed to Fiona to be the strangest sensation, that one person's head could be sticking out of another person. Another grinding bellow and push, one shoulder, two, then the baby slid out so fast that Fiona didn't have a moment to register that Sarah was putting her—*her!*—on her chest and covering the two of them up with all the blankets from the stack in the crib.

"We get a little stork pin when we deliver a baby," Sarah said. "This will be my third." She fitted a cap on the baby's head. One that Willy sent, also angora, with stripes of greys and browns, and two little bunny ears.

While Fiona delivered the placenta, Gus put the baby in his shirt, against his skin.

"Little rabbit," he said. While the baby was being born, there had been another accident on the highway, fatal this time. It was totally closed again. There was a long conversation with the ambulance dispatch, the medical director, the nurse manager of Casper's clinic, the midwife they'd been seeing in Squamish, and the nurse they'd been on the phone with. The local health nurse would be there in half an hour for a well-baby check. Everyone agreed that it would be best to keep baby and mom home.

Mum. Mother. Mummy.

The women in the valley liked to be called *mama* if they were at all into attachment parenting. The *mommies* were the ones who sleep-trained and hired nannies and got organic produce boxes delivered to their houses from the local CSA.

Fiona was supposed to be a *mama*, but all she could hear was her little-girl self running up the garden behind her own mother, reaching for her housecoat and screaming *Mummy! Mummy! MUMMY!* Why was she in the garden in her housecoat? It was raining, Fiona remembers—

"Let her find your nipple." Sarah put the now-diapered infant onto her chest. "We'll get her going. Watch, she'll find you on her own."

Fiona put a hand on the baby's little bum, made oddly big by the terry cloth diaper from the service Willy had arranged. She put her other hand on her tiny, warm, bare back, covered in down, the ridges of her spine like vestigial dragon nubs. Wisps of shiny yellow hair stuck out from underneath the bunny hat.

The baby squirmed around until she bobbed her wobbling head near Fiona's nipple. She let Sarah help the baby latch, and when she did, the pain pierced right through Fiona, and she hated it immediately, even as the weight and warmth of the baby on her skin was absolutely delicious.

Ruby listened to her parents yell at each other about tickets to London to see Aunt Willy and her snobby daughter. She would love to see Willy, and her grandad, and even Great-aunt Noreen. A trip on a plane is a fun thing, with pretzels in little packets, and an entire can of ginger ale to herself. With a plastic cup of ice on the side. But the idea of this trip was not fun. It might not happen, unless her father signed a piece of paper.

Ruby did not know what heroin was, or blow jobs, or why it was a big deal if her mother parked her car in a storage locker. But she did know other things, like about stealing, and having sex with an old man for money when you're just a kid, and being picked up by the cops. She knew *batshit crazy*, because her dad said that all the time, like it was a nice thing to say, even though Ruby knew it wasn't. He only said it to her mom when they were fighting, but that was a lot of the time, so it was said a lot of the time. Batshit crazy, which just sounded dark and like it'd stink like guano, like those caves her dad took her to.

She did not want to think about sex. And not an old man.

She pulled her blanket over her head as she heard her dad come up the stairs. He paused to look in on her before going into the bathroom and doing the things that meant he was going to bed. Pee. Teeth. Splash his face.

Twelve-year-olds are not supposed to have sex, either. And seventeen-year-olds are not supposed to make them have sex. Luke was seventeen. He had sex with Aubrey all the time. They were the right age. If someone tries to make you touch them and they're way too many years older, you tell someone. That is abuse and you go tell a safe adult. Even if they're not too many years older. What if it was Shane? And he tried to make her touch him? What about when Skye said she put her finger in Anna's vagina? And Anna said that was okay with her, except it wasn't actually her vagina. Only her vulva. Like putting a hot dog in a bun, not poking your finger through a doughnut.

Ruby didn't want to fall asleep thinking about gross things, but that's what happened.

When she woke, it was still dark. Her clock said it was just past 5 a.m., but she couldn't fall back to sleep. It was too cold. Her dad had definitely not loaded the wood stove before bed. And the furnace still wasn't working. The house was cold enough that Ruby could see her breath as she got dressed in all the layers she'd wear to go snowshoeing, plus her fuzzy housecoat on top. After she went to pee—careful not to actually sit on the icy toilet—she checked on her parents. Only her dad was in the bed.

Ruby tiptoed down the stairs, avoiding the creaks. Her mother was not on the couch. Neither were the blankets and pillows. She crept into the dark kitchen, lit only by the bulb above the stove. Her mother was curled up on the floor by the table, her head on a pillow, covered in the two blankets. One wrist rested in a mess of crimson vomit beside her. Wine barf.

Ruby found a new roll of paper towel. She gently lifted her mother's hand and moved it out of the way, and then used the entire roll to clean it up. She stuffed the dirty paper towels into a plastic bag, and tied it in a knot, like Sarah did when Ophelia barfed up in the house. Ruby kissed her mom, almost gagging at her barf-up wine breath, and then she traded her housecoat for her parka and her slippers for her snow boots. Before she put on her really good ski gloves, she wrote a note.

Snow cave.

Before she set it on the table where they put all their notes, she added three tiny drawings, no bigger than dimes. A bunny, a heart and a snowflake.

The moon made more light than the stove had. It gave the field of snow a blue glow. Her well-trodden trail was a dark-blue rivu-let connecting the house and the forest. Ruby ran all the way to the cave, to hang on to the warmth she already had. She did not stop to look at the stars. She did not stop to look for lit windows in the middle of the night, where people were up, arguing like at her house, maybe. But probably not. More like a new baby up crying or a grandma who couldn't sleep.

Once she was in the cave, she sat cross-legged in front of the rabbit warren, still dressed in all her layers. The rabbits were still snuggled up together on their down bed. The peg family was too, on a twig-and-twine bed she and her dad made together, with a mattress made from an old baby sock stuffed with more of that woodsmoke-smelly down, and a scrap from one of his old flannel shirts for a blanket. Everyone was tucked in just right for the night. Ruby unfurled the sleeping bag she kept there in a waterproof stuff sack, and arranged it on the foam mat. She took off her boots and crawled in. Once she pulled the hood over her toque and cinched it tight, she looked like a caterpillar.

A warm one. Or a worm one! She laughed at that, even though it wasn't actually very funny.

Not funny.

No laughing.

Nothing's funny.

Worms and caterpillars and middle-of-the-night yellow lights in hard houses. Not funny.

Ruby fell asleep, hot enough in her four-season bag that she dreamed of swimming in Mosquito Lake. Her dad threw her in over and over, past the swampy edge, which is why they always had that lake to themselves. No one wanted to swim past the murk to get to the clear water. No one wanted to sunbathe on the thin, muddy edge of shore before the forest rose up thick behind them, the trees like giant, looming soldiers. But the water past the weeds was so clear that you could dive under and open your eyes and see fry, even though the bigger supper-sized trout liked the darker, colder waters of the deeper down. Ruby woke up with trout on her mind. There was a stack of rainbow in the freezer in the basement.

In her dream, she talked with her dad, back and forth. No big deal. She wanted to talk with him now. She'd tell him about the dream, the memory of swimming, about knowing what "batshit crazy" meant. And wanting rainbow trout for breakfast. She wanted to ask him why any ten-year-old would have sex with a seventeen-year-old. She wanted to say how much she liked getting thrown into the lake, and that sometimes she worried about when she'd get too big.

"Rabbit?"

The bough door shook, and then her dad squeezed through, on all fours.

"Did you sleep here?"

Ruby nodded.

"Thanks for the note." He sat beside her and handed her one of the oily banana muffins from the gas station, wrapped up tight in plastic, and a little carton of chocolate milk. He pulled her into a hug and kissed her forehead. "Thanks for cleaning that mess up this morning. That wasn't your job."

"It's okay," she whispered.

"It's not okay," Gus said.

Ruby broke the muffin in half, and put one piece into her father's hand.

He handed it back to her. "I ate mine on the way here. I've got to get to the store." He looked very silly crawling towards the door. "I need to get ready for Helena."

Helena, his client, the old lady who was famous for hiking ten thousand miles in one year before she turned twenty-five, way back when hardly any girls did really long hikes at all.

"Come give me a hand," he said. "You can see Helena, and then we'll drop you at school before we head up the mountain."

Ruby unzipped the sleeping bag, letting out all the warm as she hurried into her boots and parka.

Out in the heron-grey dawn, halfway along the path under the power lines, Gus stopped ahead of her and turned around.

"If your mom and I didn't live together anymore," he said, "who would you want to live with?"

Without hesitation, Ruby pointed at him. Before she could even lower her arm, she felt like she was going to barf up the muffin and chocolate milk. She burst into tears.

"Oh, Rabbit! I'm sorry." Gus pulled her into a tight hug. "That wasn't fair. Can you pretend I didn't ask you that? Can you imagine we were just walking along and I wasn't a total asshole?"

Ruby nodded into his coat.

He pushed her away and shook his head. "What a shitty thing to say to a kid. I'm sorry, Rabbit. Forget I said it. Look." He bent and scooped a handful of snow. "I'll eat my words." He shoved the snow into his mouth and chewed and swallowed while Ruby looked up at him, a small smile on her face. What if a dog peed on that?

Her father nodded in the way that said he'd heard her loud and clear. He winked. "I checked first. Pee's not the worst thing I might've picked up."

Ruby held his hand for the rest of the way along the trampled path. She wondered when the other question would come. Or maybe it wouldn't, being that he already felt bad about asking her and that she cleaned up the barf too. She wanted him to ask, though, because it was an easy answer. *Do you want to go to England with your mother?* The answer to that would be yes. It made her squirm to hold one answer in one pocket and the other answer in the other pocket, when they didn't match at all. Like a plastic hedgehog and a big pomegranate-flavoured marshmallow, which she'd had once, as big as a deck of cards. It tasted like pink eraser.

Helena and her two friends arrived just minutes after Gus unlocked the door. She flung open the door and opened her arms, bedecked in a shimmering mauve fleece track suit.

"Darling! I'm back!"

"Helena! So great to see you. Charlotte, Lakshmi, you too." He hugged them all. "You remember Ruby?"

"I do," Helena said. "Are we still engaged in one-way transmissions?"

Ruby nodded.

"Can I hug you?" Helena didn't wait for an answer to that. She hugged Ruby, and then held her away to look at her. "I do believe you are growing. And I do believe that I have a little something for you." She fished in her ancient external frame pack and pulled out a big bag of the buffalo jerky Ruby loved, from the company she owned and ran in New Mexico.

After her father found her something better to eat than the terrible muffin—instant oatmeal and astronaut ice cream from the store—he walked her across the street and left her at the door of the school with Liam, who was only still outside because he was waiting for Shane. Liam glanced at her, and then promptly looked away. The other kids were playing in the field. Bright-blue skies today, so they'd probably get to stay out. There was Shane, slouching up the sidewalk, a long stick in hand. He poked the snow like it was an avalanche probe. Poke, step, poke, step.

"Get out of here." Liam gave her a little push, and then a harder one.

That was fine by her. Stupid Liam doing everything stupid Shane told him, like he didn't know how to say no, even though he said no to Ruby all the time.

Ruby jumped down the steps and waited until Shane looked up, at which point she gave him a big mean ol' stare, knowing he wouldn't do anything about it because her dad was right across the street, out on the sidewalk, putting down salt. Ruby wanted to grab Shane's stick and run into the forest with it and hide it so he'd never find it. But her dad might see that too, so Shane could have his stupid stick. And Liam could have Shane.

JANUARY 14

Fiona sat on the couch with Ruby in her lap, watching the Food Network. When they heard Gus's truck turn onto the street, Fiona shifted Ruby onto her feet and got up. She wanted to meet him at the door, to apologize immediately. Fiona put her hands on Ruby's shoulders, not sure if she should tell her to go upstairs or stay. In the end, she said nothing at all, and crossed the cold floor in her sock feet to stand at the curtain and watch as he parked. Snow drifted in delicate whorls under the street lamp at the corner. The roof of his pickup was capped by the pompadour of snow that had gathered while he was up the mountain with Helena.

When Fiona had woken up from the quetiapine stupor, a few hours before Ruby came home from school, she'd topped it up with just one milligram of lorazepam to keep her down enough that she could stay out of her own way. She'd managed that, and was now drugged to the point where she regretted everything she'd told him. Most of all, those two secret babies, in shards on the ground.

She'd written out her apology in antipsychotic shaky script.

I'm so sorry that I hurt you.

But she couldn't bring herself to apologize for the abortions.

I'm sorry that I didn't tell you how I felt. I didn't know how, and I couldn't make the words come. But please know that I am sorry.

She'd also called the village office and purchased a plot in the graveyard, and a headstone. He could pick two names. Maybe that would help.

Gus stared at her, hands on the wheel, until Ruby joined her in the window. He lifted a hand. Ruby lifted one too.

That got him out of the truck.

"Hey, Rabbit," he said as he came in the door. He picked her up and swung her around. Even though Fiona could tell that Ruby didn't like it, she didn't say so.

"I want to apologize—"

"You know," Gus whispered after he set her down and Ruby headed back to the couch, "I was thinking that Ruby was three when you—"

"I am so sorry."

"You're sorry you told me." Gus threw his coat onto the pile on the bench beside the door. "If you were actually sorry about what you did, you would've told me sooner."

"There are things you don't tell me," Fiona said. "That's only human."

Ruby turned up the volume on the TV.

"Are you going to take your boots off?" A chill washed down Fiona's arms as she heard the drugged slur, and the wine behind it. She licked her lips and tried again, trying very hard to put edges on all her words. "Can I get you a beer?"

"No."

"Want to take your boots off? Want to come into the kitchen? I can make you something to eat."

"No, thanks." Gus walked over to Ruby and kissed the top of her head. "I just came to say good night to Ruby." Without looking at Fiona, he added, "I'm going to stay over at Mike and Sarah's."

That cold chill again.

Ruby's eyes welled with tears, but she didn't look away from the TV.

"I'll be here when you wake up, Rabbit." He kissed her head again. "Go upstairs for a few minutes. I'll come say a bonus goodbye when your mom and I are done talking."

Ruby turned the volume up even more, and then scampered up the stairs without looking at Gus or Fiona.

"Door shut," Gus called after her.

Snow melted off Gus's boots and pooled on the wood floor. Fiona reached for a towel and squatted to wipe it up.

"Stop." Gus yanked the other end of the towel. "Leave it."

She kept wiping, so he yanked hard, and Fiona fell back. Her mouth formed a thin, hard line. Her cheeks burned pink.

"Oh, so strong." She made a grab for the towel, but Gus held it out of reach. "Such a big man. Gus, the heavy."

Gus balled up the towel and threw it at her. "Just listen."

The two of them suddenly noticed Ruby standing at the bottom of the stairs.

"Upstairs," Gus said.

Ruby shook her head.

"Go to your room," Fiona said.

Ruby sat on the bottom step.

"I told you to go to your room!"

Ruby shook her head.

"Fine. I'll take you up, then." In one motion Fiona grabbed Ruby's wrist and twisted so hard that Ruby slipped off the step and landed on the floor. Fiona dragged her onto her feet.

Fiona looked at Gus, even as she knew—she *knew*—that she should be attending to Ruby. She felt compelled to give this moment, this *mess*, to Gus, and this was how she was doing it. She stared at him for seconds upon seconds, and then she narrowed her eyes, pinning the next few seconds on him too, with such sureness that it was like she was pinning an actual badge on him, through the skin, reaching further in to secure the backing against the sharp post. Then, with those bloody fingers, she pushed Ruby hard enough that she fell again.

This was a fulcrum. Fiona could see the shape of it even as Ruby stumbled backwards. Gus knocked Fiona aside and swept Ruby up in his arms, settling her on his hip as if she were a toddler. Fiona landed on her hands and knees at his feet.

"I wish I was surprised," Gus said. "But I'm not. Ruby is coming with me to Mike and Sarah's."

Ruby put her finger into her mouth and bit down. A hot red bracelet circled her wrist. She curled her head under his chin, laying her cheek on his chest as it rose and fell with each breath. She squeezed her eyes shut tight.

Fiona sat back on her haunches and shook her head. "No, no. Gus, please. I wanted to apologize. I bought a plot at the cemetery—"

"Not now, Fiona."

"You don't understand!" She shook her head even harder. "Not for me! For the babies."

"Not now!" Gus shouted. And then, more softly, "Not now. Okay?"

Gus moved one hand up and pressed Ruby's head against his chest.

Ruby felt little in her father's arms, like that first time he took her snowshoeing. She was three, maybe. She remembered the pyjamas she was wearing, fleece top and bottom with bunnies with an *x* for a mouth. He drove the truck way far up out of town

and behind the mountain. He helped her on with her new snowshoes, and then they hiked through the trees to a little waterfall
frozen into the shape of a chair. A fairy chair, her dad said.

On the way back, Ruby was too tired to snowshoe. He'd held
her like this then. She rested her head, eyes drooping. She fell
asleep, but woke when she heard a crack. They were about halfway across a small clearing. Wake up, Rabbit! Her father set her
in the snow, looking down at her with panic eyes. Another crack.
They both looked up to see an icy cornice slide down, sending
pebbles of snow ahead of it. Her father tossed off his pack and
picked Ruby up again and started running as the pebbles grew
into boulders behind them.

The avalanche widened, boulders of snow rumbling down
the slope, and then a fat, wide blanket, crumpling towards them.
He kept running.

Ruby thought they should go back for her new snowshoes.
No, baby, no! Her father held on to her too tight. She started to
squirm. But he clutched her to his chest, held her head with one
hand and ran, his snowshoes kicking up a spray of snow with
each step. The avalanche bowed out behind them, and by the
time they were in the shadow of the forest, it was all over.

Her father set Ruby onto her feet. He bent forward, hands
on his knees, and gulped for breath. He shook his head. "That
wasn't supposed to happen, Rabbit."

Ruby chewed on her finger through her mittens.

Her dad looked up at her. She had not been afraid, but something shifted when she saw him look at her, his face full of relief.
All of a sudden she completely understood, even if she didn't,
really. Her lips trembled, and she began to cry.

After they left, Fiona took more quetiapine, but not too much. She picked up her phone to call her psychiatrist, but she put it down. She picked it up again to call Willy, but she put it down again. She went to bed instead, propping herself on her side with pillows in case she vomited. She closed her eyes, letting her body sink into the thick, quiet blank that came with those pills. If it could shut her up long enough to get a grip, that would be a good thing.

She woke up late in the afternoon the next day. The sun had already slipped behind the mountains—she'd missed it entirely. The remaining light was thin and grey, and so was the house. Not a single light was on, but she could smell the wood stove, and she couldn't see her breath. She sat up, taking several long moments to let her mind arrange for her body to stand up and walk downstairs, gripping the railing on both sides. It was either Saturday or Sunday, she guessed. Or else Ruby would've been at school, not sitting on the floor watching the Food Network. She could've been watching TV at Mike and Sarah's, but here she was.

"You came home."

Ruby nodded. She let Fiona pull her up onto the couch beside her. Fiona put her cold hands on Ruby's warm head.

"Hi, Ruby love."

Ruby took one of her hands and kissed the back of it. Fiona noticed that her fringe—excuse me, her *bangs*—had been trimmed.

"Did Aubrey do that?"

Ruby nodded.

"It looks nice."

Ruby turned her attention back to the TV and the bowl of cereal in her lap. She was watching a Food Network program called *The Tudor Table*. It made Fiona hopeful for their trip to England, if they got to go, because her father loved watching television with Ruby.

The narrator sounded like he was just about to fall asleep.

"Someone get that man a cup of strong coffee," Fiona said. "Right?"

Most of the meals consisted of meat, he droned on. *And not only the typical meats found on our tables today, but many others too, such as pigeons, sparrows, heron, pheasant, woodcock, partridge, blackbirds and peacocks.*

"Peacocks!" Fiona exclaimed.

Someone in Tudor dress slapped a dead peacock onto a chopping block, and then reached for a mug. *People did not drink water. It was often contaminated with sewage, so they drank ale. Rich people drank dark red wine.*

"Imagine that," Fiona marvelled. "No water? You'd be drinking wine. Even at your age. Isn't that incredible? Isn't it? Isn't it incredible?"

Answer me. Answer me! Look at me when I speak to you. Talk to me. Talk to me. Say something! Isn't it incredible?

Fiona felt a full-body shiver. Suddenly she needed all the lights on, so she took a moment to flick them on, one by one. Kitchen, basement, hall, stairs, bedrooms, bathroom. The living room was last. Two standing lamps and it still was dim. Dreary. There was a hanging work light on the porch. She retrieved that and hung it from the ceiling fan and light that hadn't worked since before they moved in. She plugged it in and beheld the icy-blue cone of light it produced. It was awful. She yanked it down. This brought two arms of the fan down with it, and a cloud of dust.

Ruby didn't even look up. She stirred her cereal. She liked it when it was nearly mush, which she'd eaten longer than any other child Fiona knew. The spoon scraped on the side of the bowl. The noise struck a terrible, rageful note deep inside Fiona. It took no effort at all to see it—grabbing the bowl and throwing it against the wall and screaming in Ruby's face, "What is the opposite of shut the fuck up?" But it did take every effort not to do it. Fiona backed away. Isn't it incredible? That you can *not* want to do something and do it anyway?

Instead, she collected the laundry from the two bedrooms. Ruby didn't look up when she walked by with that either. The elegant peacock was being plucked now. *Preserve the head to adorn the pie later, and the feathers and feet too, so it appears to be alive when you set it upon the table.*

Fiona stuffed the laundry into the machine and turned it on. She thought about staying down there. Giving herself a kind of time out so she wouldn't say something terrible to Ruby. But instead, she went back up to the kitchen, where she made coffee, then poured herself a cup and looked at the calendar. Thirteen days before she and Ruby could be on a plane away from here. Maybe by the time they came back, winter wouldn't be holding on so tight. The days would be longer. The snow would start to melt. Somewhere under all that dirty white would be the sidewalks and trails and the first green shoots of spring. Along with a sea of soggy dog shit and mud.

JANUARY 16

They were late leaving for Mike and Sarah's. Ruby's parents were arguing about walking or driving, and because of this, Ruby was sitting on the floor, her snow pants half on and her warmest toque in her lap. They'd be too hot in the truck.

"It's a five-minute walk." That was her dad. "It's so nice out tonight. Clear enough to see a million stars."

"I happen to have seen at least ten million stars. You two can walk," her mother said. "I don't even want to go."

There was a pause in the conversation that made Ruby squeeze all her muscles in fear of what one of them would say next.

Her dad spoke. He did not sound very nice. "You'd rather hang out here like a happy family instead? Or maybe you want to talk?"

In the next long pause, Ruby blew out slowly, her lips pursed in a tiny *o*, like Mike had taught the Cayoosh kids to do one day when they were all arguing with each other so much he actually yelled at them to sit down and quiet up. She wriggled into her snow pants, pulled on her warmest toque—and gloves—and reached for the door. On second thought, she pulled off one glove so that she could write a note on the pad hanging on the wall by the door.

Blow out your lips like a tite o. Im going now. See you ther.

Once Aubrey helped her off with her jacket and snow pants, Ruby went straight to the dog's bed. Big old Ophelia always shuffled over to make room for her. The dog breathed heavily as she slept, her side landscaped with old dog bumps, rising and falling steadily. Sarah assured her they were just fatty deposits, nothing serious. Even still, Ruby didn't like to touch them. The firm wobble made her queasy. So she'd mapped a way to put her arm over Ophelia's greasy fur to keep from touching them.

"Liam's upstairs," Sarah said, squatting down. "Want me to tell him that you're here?"

Ruby shook her head. She patted Ophelia for emphasis.

The last time their mothers made them play together upstairs, Ruby spent the whole time sitting in a corner looking at a book on rocks and minerals while Liam worked on some kind of elaborate marble run. She'd picked up a piece and offered it when she thought it made sense, but he shook his head and told her maybe she should *tell* him where she thought it should go.

Maybe she could get Aubrey to cut her hair again. She liked that. She'd have to be careful when she looked for her, because one time she knocked on Luke's door and he made a noise that she thought was a kind of yes, but when she opened the door, she saw Aubrey in just a bra, sitting on top of him, riding him like a rodeo horse.

Ruby knew a couple could get pregnant like that, unless he had a condom on his penis. It wouldn't be so terrible for there to be a baby. Ruby could help take care of it.

—

Before she and Gus set off on the walk, Fiona had tucked Ruby's note into her glove. She was going to bring it up with Mike. What was he doing to help her? What about the new language arts teacher they hired? What was the point of a learning plan when a kid was still writing like that?

Actually, no. She would not bring it up, not tonight. She would make an appointment. Did that hippie school even make appointments?

When they arrived, she took her gloves off and transferred the note discreetly to her bra. Gloves and toque in jacket pockets, jacket on a hook already populated with at least eight other items. Boots off and set to one side of an impossible jumble. Fiona unwound her scarf and draped it and her bag over the newel post, which was the best way to ensure she'd find them later. Complimentary slippers on. All knitted by Aubrey, polyester, in the same style as the ones Aunt Noreen had knitted for two entire decades before the turn of the century. They were retro now, of course.

Gus had gone on ahead of her, into the kitchen with the beer and wine. He'd only had his quilted lumberjack coat to shed, which he'd tossed into a pile of outerwear on the floor that smelled musty with boy and man and dirt.

There was a fire in the fireplace, and the wood stove was ablaze too. The house was suffocatingly hot. Fiona stepped outside for a moment. The porch was cluttered with every piece of sports equipment, even a plywood skate ramp in pieces that would be put back behind the garden in the spring. There was an old bench from an ambulance, with a motel lobby ashtray on a pedestal beside it. It was there for party smokers, although Fiona was the only one there who smoked on this particular night.

As soon as she sat and lit her cigarette, the cold took hold of her. No matter—she would rather be out there in just yoga pants and a T-shirt than inside. An ambulance turned the corner; no doubt who that was. The lights flashed a brief red-and-white greeting, followed by a single bleat of the siren.

Sarah hopped down and collected her lunch bag and jacket and stethoscope and said good night to her partner.

"Fiona!" she called up the driveway. "Aren't you cold?"

"I am." Fiona nodded.

"Let's go inside, woman." Sarah waited for Fiona to get up. "You can take the lasagna out while I go have a quick shower. This day has been a *day.*"

Fiona did not ask what kind of *day* required verbal italics. She would go in, though, because her fingers were going numb. She stubbed out her cigarette and held the door open for Sarah and her armload of work detritus, and then she made her way to the kitchen to take out the crappy grocery store lasagna that she very much hoped was on a tray at least.

Gus leaned on one counter, Mike leaned on the other, each with a beer in hand.

"I'd love one," she said as she looked around for oven mitts. "Kind of you to offer."

"Oh, sorry, Fi." Mike cracked one open and held it out to her. She took a long swallow. She set it down to don the oven mitts, so filthy and pocked with burn holes it was hard to tell that there was a laughing moose on each one. The insides felt crusty and sticky. She threw them off and used a dishtowel instead, but it was a little damp, so as soon as she got a grip—no tray under it—she felt the heat and dropped it back onto the rack, unsteady in its cheap foil pan. The cheese dripped over the sides and onto the bottom of the oven, where it sizzled. The oil boiled at the edges. She put on the oven mitts again and yanked the heavy thing out and set it down hard on the bare counter. She let the mitts drop to the floor. That disgusting old dog wandered over and took one back to its bed, where it gnawed on it, one paw trapping it between the other.

"You good?" Gus said.

"Perfect, thank you." She kicked the other oven mitt towards the dog. "Where's Ruby?"

Ruby was in the living room, playing chess against herself.

"Can I be white?" Fiona sat on the floor beside her. "White is way ahead."

Ruby gave her a sly smile before she shook her head and cleared the board, pushing the white pieces into Fiona's lap and keeping the black ones for herself.

"Do you want to go first?" Fiona said.

Ruby shook her head.

"White doesn't *always* have to go first," Fiona said.

Ruby nodded.

"Fine." Fiona moved a pawn two steps forward from a knight.

Ruby moved a pawn two squares too. Fiona knew that Ruby liked to free her bishops early, so she could zigzag all over the board, so Fiona moved a pawn in place as a decoy. Ruby didn't go for it.

The whole while, Ruby's ill-written note was in her pocket. It felt much more important than this one game, which clearly demonstrated that Ruby's intellect was not in question. She saw Mike go outside.

"I'll be back, love. You can play both sides if you want." She followed him.

Mike stared into the old freezer at the far end of the porch.

"Mike," Fiona said. "I want to talk to you about something."

"Sarah told me to get a bag of blackberries for the cheese-cake." He sorted through a shelf stuffed with fruit picked and frozen in the summer. "She's going to cook them down while we eat."

"Can I show you something?"

Mike turned, the bag of berries in hand. He held her gaze for just a tiny moment longer than the question called for.

"It has nothing to do with that," Fiona said.

The relief on his face was instant. It made Fiona ill to watch it redden his cheeks.

"It's this note that Ruby wrote." She reached into the neck of her sweater and pulled out Ruby's note. "Her writing is not improving. For a kid who doesn't talk, writing is very important. You know this. So why isn't her writing getting any better?"

"It is improving," Mike said. "I see it. Her teacher sees it."

"I don't see it."

"Do you look for it?" he asked. "Do you encourage it, like we talked about in the fall? Do you get her to write lists? Notes to her grandparents? Type on the computer? These are things we've talked about, Fiona. Lots of shit we do not talk about, and do not need to talk about, ever, but this is absolutely something that we have talked about and can keep on talking about. When I am at work. Right now, you are my best friend's wife, and Ruby is my niece."

Fiona wouldn't say out loud that she was not, technically, his niece, but she was pretty sure that he understood the message from the look she was giving him.

"You should go inside," he said.

"*You* should." Fiona lit a cigarette.

Without another word, he did just that.

Fiona sat on the freezing ambulance bench in a cloud of smoke and icy breath. She tapped her ash into the tray. Another ashtray came to mind. The one her father sent her that arrived the day of the first bonfire at the lake, when the ice was finally thick enough to skate on.

Fiona didn't go. Because the ashtray told her not to.

A heavy green glass pentagon, with a notch on each side. Fiona had bought this ashtray for her father on the pier at Blackpool the summer just after her mother died. The wind blew off the ocean, and the waves slapped the beach over and over. No one was even on the beach save for an old man and a dog. And there was Fiona's Aunt Noreen, screeching gleefully as she body-surfed the waves, her fluorescent-orange swimsuit and matching bathing cap like an unmoored buoy in the stormy waters.

"Stupid woman." Fiona's father sat beside her on the bench, a cigarette dangling at the side of his mouth, stuck to his lip with saliva, while Fiona ate an ice cream cone. She was wearing a striped halter top, red and white. Purple sateen shorts with white piping. She was cold, covered in goose pimples. She'd stepped on a piece of glass that morning and got a small cut under her big toe. She hadn't told her father or Noreen. She crept into the bathroom and quietly looked through her father's shave kit—Old Spice and Mitchum and Aquafresh—for the little white stick he used when he cut himself with the razor. She pressed it against the blood and it stung. It was the holiday right after the terrible thing. The one her father didn't cancel.

Her father had mailed the ashtray, along with a pack of Embassy cigarettes and a note: "For old times' sake." It must have cost him a fortune to send it, and she was unclear as to why he had done so now.

She had got as far as the parking lot at the lake, but she couldn't get out of the truck. She sat there in the dark, the ashtray in her lap illuminated by the flames of the bonfire. She smoked one Embassy after another, even though they were stale.

Out there was murderous ice and a dark, endless forest beyond, both waiting to swallow everyone up. Cracks and fissures and the teeth-grating slice of ice skates etching the surface with drunken whorls. All the dead life beneath, rocks and the weeds, slimy and swaying in the murk. And sleeping beasts in dens dug under towering trees, swaying and snow-capped, as if nothing was amiss.

The ashtray was warm in her hands, even though the truck was cold.

"The ice is safe," she said out loud to herself. "The ice is safe."

Gus and Ruby were on opposite teams for hockey, slinging hockey sticks back and forth. Parents against kids, because it wasn't just dads. One of the mothers had been on the national women's team for five years.

The ice was safe. The local search and rescue crew was in charge of it. They'd been checking it for weeks, and they hadn't removed the orange cones and the caution tape until they were more than absolutely sure. *It's safe. It is safe. Of course it's safe.*

—

Fiona stared at the rusted rim of the motel lobby ashtray perched on its flaking golden tripod, one leg bent just enough that it leaned but did not tip. Fiona ground out her butt but let her hand hover above the stand for a moment. She wanted to push it over. Very much. She clenched her hand closed. *No.*

Yes, actually. She kicked it over. It made one thunk, tipping out the little ash of her cigarettes. No more than that, because either Mike or Sarah cleaned it out after every party. When she stood up, she kicked it again before righting it, bracing the base with her foot and tugging the bend back into shape, so when she stood it back in its place, it didn't lean anymore.

After dinner, Fiona stared at the ravaged lasagna pan, nothing left but a slick of orange grease and a crust of lasagna gristle. A cutting board covered in crumbs, one dried-up heel of the store-bought garlic bread. A bowl of baby carrots. Those ones that aren't, really, just carved to thumb-size from bigger carrots, with their smooth ends and no skin and taste of bleach. She knew better than to get up and clear the table. She'd tried it often enough that she didn't bother anymore. So she sat there, repulsed. Half listening to Sarah's work story.

"The helicopter let them off at the glacier and they set up their tents. And when it got dark, they lit up a bunch of glow sticks and played tag. She was having a great time. Her friend said that she'd never heard her laugh so much."

"Past tense is never good," Gus said.

"Just wait," Sarah said. "She and her best friend stayed up to watch the sunrise, sitting in their sleeping bags at the edge of the icefield. The friend said the sunrise was a magic trick. She swears it came over the horizon twice. Like it skipped itself."

"Maybe it was magic," Aubrey said.

The rest of them waited for the ending. Gus and Mike, Luke drawing Aubrey so close she was almost sharing his chair, and Liam, elbows on the table. Ruby was listening from Ophelia's bed.

"She lifted her knees and her sleeping bag shifted. She started sliding. Her friend screamed and reached out, but she was out of reach, speeding down the icefield and then over the edge, and she was gone."

"Holy shit," Gus said.

"How far did she fall?" Mike said.

"At least three hundred feet."

"Oh my god," Aubrey said. "That is so sad."

"But what a way to go," Gus said. "And on your birthday."

"I agree," Sarah said. "The friend said that as they were sitting there watching the sun rise twice, the girl said it had been her favourite day of her entire life."

Fiona stood. She collected the lasagna pan and salad bowl.

"No, no," Sarah protested. "Please don't, Fiona. Sit, sit."

"Imagine that was your last day," Aubrey said. "And it was your favourite. That's amazing. What would your favourite day be, Luke?"

He blushed. "Somebody else go first."

Fiona hated these kinds of questions. These dinner party chats about things that don't matter. It wasn't small talk, because good friends don't do small talk. This was big talk. As if they were all so much closer than two couples who would chat about the alpine forecast, or their children's soccer teams, or how Cayoosh should do a fundraiser for the earthquake in Nepal. Fiona tried to think of something to say. She didn't want to not say anything at all, because they would prod. Prod and push. Come on, Fiona. A life like yours? Can you pick one? Normally she could handle the ribbing, but not this night. She was not fortified. Her favourite day. Pick one, Fiona.

Gus was already talking. "That day that Ruby and I went up to the fairy chair. I never told you, Fiona, but there was an avalanche. Just a little one. It didn't touch us, but it scared us, right, Rabbit? It made me think about losing Ruby. But I didn't. That's what made it so miraculous. So perfect. I would do that day over and over again, just to have that same feeling again. I still had her. My heart was the opposite of completely shattered."

Fiona swallowed the last of her wine. She could ignore a small avalanche. Couldn't she? She could. It was like *almost* getting hit by a car. Or *almost* getting pregnant. Gus had never been at risk of losing Ruby because the avalanche had just *almost* hit them. She could ignore him not telling her. It was no surprise. He'd said it often enough. I tell you something and you give me that look or you lecture me, or you don't talk to me at all. So he probably *almost* told her all kinds of things. And of course, Gus's favourite day wouldn't be a day with her. She was not kidding herself. Certainly not. She reached for the bottle, but it was empty.

"How about you, Mike?" Sarah glared at Gus. Trust another woman to be the only one who noticed that Gus had just leaned over the table and slapped Fiona across the face. The mark still burned on her cheek. Fiona put her hand to her cheek and felt the heat there.

"Last year," Mike said. "On that boat to the Marietas Islands in Mexico."

Another day that did not include Fiona but was adjacent to her.

It was only two days after they slept together. Would she call it sleeping together when it's twenty minutes on a shitty couch?

Two days after they fucked. She did not want to be stuck on a boat with everyone. So the others went without her.

"The breaching whales," Mike said. "The stingrays leaping out of the water. The grouper the captain caught. The ceviche!" Everyone murmured in agreement. The best ever. Unbelievable. "Those hammocks at the front of the boat. And swimming off the back. And the tunnel into the island. You swim through the tunnel and come out onto that amazing secret beach."

Like thousands of other tourists. All flocking to the tiny island with the doughnut-shaped inlet at one end. It's pretty much a cave with a huge hole in the roof. That's what Gus said when he told customers about it. Ruby swam the whole way from the boat by herself. With a life jacket, he added. She's such a strong swimmer.

"There were a lot of blue-footed boobies," Liam said. And then everyone was giggling.

"And the sunset on the way back," Mike said. "Just lying there on the pillows, tired and happy and sunburned, with all my favourite people around me, my wife leaning against my shoulder. Easily my favourite day."

Fiona knew this was when she should just sit absolutely still. She should not say anything, and she should not get up, and she should not reach for anything, unless it was to get a pill from her purse. A shut-me-up pill. A help-me-into-the-truck pill. But she sat back in her chair and laughed. Seriously. How could Sarah still have no idea?

"What?" Sarah smiled. "What's funny?"

Mike levelled her with as much of a look as he dared, without the others wondering about it. Did they wonder? Fiona looked at each person at the table. One after another. No one?

"Does anyone have any questions for me?" Fiona put her cold hands against her burning cheeks.

"Sure," Sarah said. "What's your favourite day?"

All of Mike's favourite people were on the boat. But not Fiona. How about that. He'd seemed pretty fond of her just a couple of days before that spectacular boat ride. They'd had their own spectacular boat ride, just her and Mike. Fiona laughed again. But it was true that one did not have to feel any affection at all for a person they might fuck. Did fuck. Fucked once. Spectacularly.

"I'm going to fill the pitcher." Mike put his hands on the edge of the table and scraped his chair back.

"Fill the pitcher," Fiona said, with a guffaw on either end. "Do you want me to come too?"

"I'll help," Sarah said.

"Take this." Fiona pushed the lasagna pan across the table. "It's so dirty."

This set off more giggles that she could only stop when Ruby appeared at her side. She draped her arms around Fiona's neck. Fiona took a steadying breath. She closed her eyes and mapped the slight weight of Ruby's cool, slender arms on her hot skin.

"We should get going." Gus put a hand on Ruby's shoulder.

Oh no. Not yet. Fiona was still thinking of her favourite day. Okay, okay, here it was. An alpine meadow and a carpet of wildflowers and tiny strawberries underfoot. You couldn't help but step on them, sending the ripe, sweet fragrance into the air. Gus and Ruby ran around her while she lay on her back and watched the clouds amble by. They brought her strawberries and popped them into her mouth one at a time, like candy. Tell them about that day.

Say: *Strawberries. Wildflowers. Clouds.*

Tell them it was so sweet, in so many ways.

"I bet that woman shit herself on the way down," Fiona said instead. She dug her fingernails into her palms, waiting for pain to shut her up.

"Okay, so what are we talking about now?" Sarah said.

"That woman who died today," Fiona said. "I bet she shit herself."

"I wouldn't know, actually." Sarah suddenly sounded like Aunt Noreen when a tourist asked her for directions to the *sexy pub*. The one with the peelers.

"My mother did," Fiona said. "When she died."

"There are children at the table," Gus said.

"You sound like Aunt Noreen too." She wagged a finger between Sarah and Gus. "You in on something?"

"And that's us." Gus stood. "Time to hit the road."

"What's the big deal?" Fiona said. "Kids know about shit. Especially eight-year-olds. And nine-year-olds!" She wagged her finger again, this time between Liam and Ruby. "Am I right? Poop, feces, diarrhea, dump, crap, shit, turd?"

"I'm nine and a half," Liam said.

"Kids love a good shit story," Luke said with a nervous laugh. "It's true."

"Fiona. This is our dinner table," Mike said. "We don't talk about bodily functions at the dinner table."

Another nervous laugh from Luke. Aubrey stared at her hands in her lap.

"My mother lost her bowels," Fiona said. "That happens to people when they die. I was eight, like you, Ruby. Barely eight, actually. I could smell it from down the hall."

"That's very sad," Sarah said. "And entirely inappropriate table conversation, Fiona. Time for you to go home."

"It was sad. Terribly sad. I cried for three months. Every night. Every day at school I'd shut myself in the bathroom and cry until my blouse was soaked. The headmistress must've let me, I realize now. It was exhausting."

One does not speak of deceased persons at the table, Aunt Noreen said. It is simply not acceptable. Go to your room at once.

But I'm not finished my tea! The plate brimmed with tinned beans and stewed tomatoes and soggy toast, and a sausage. Just one. Always just one sausage.

Up to your room! Aunt Noreen bellowed. No tea for you and your filthy mouth!

Up the stairs and there was the room on the way to her own. Her parents' room. How could Aunt Noreen sleep in it? She would see it from the bed, the broken plaster around the hook in the ceiling beam. Why didn't her father fix it? Why hadn't he taken down the hook? Her mother hanging there like an outfit in a closet. Shit trickled down her legs and dripped onto the floor. She wore her light-blue velour housecoat, gaping open to show her nightgown with the tiny periwinkles all over. Just one slipper. One peach slipper—Mummy's slipper is *coral*, darling—the other one had fallen to the floor and was speckled with shit. She'd managed to put her hair in her big soft curlers, but hadn't tied the scarf over them yet. The scarf was on the floor. She'd surrendered to this wretched, relentless conviction sometime between rolling her hair in curlers and tying on the scarf.

"But did the woman crap herself, Mom?" Liam said.

"Liam." Mike put a hand on his shoulder. "Time for bed."

"You would know," Fiona said to Sarah. "You'd smell it. Don't you cut off their clothes, if it's a traumatic death?"

"She was clearly and obviously dead, Fiona." Sarah stood up. She put the salad bowl into the lasagna pan. She put the pan on the cutting board. She lifted all three and headed for the kitchen. After two steps she turned back. "We don't work on someone who is that dead."

When they got home from Sarah and Mike's, Ruby stood waiting for the argument to start. She did not take off her coat or boots, because she figured she and her dad would end up going back. But there was no argument. Her mother collapsed on the couch. Gus put a blanket over her, right up to her shoulders, but he didn't take off her coat or boots. Ruby bent to help her off with her boots, but Gus pulled her away. He just shook his head and steered her to the stairs. He sat her on the bottom step and helped her out of her layers.

"Mom," Ruby whispered.

Gus shook his head some more. Ruby pointed, trying to tell him that it was never good when her mother just sat and stared at the wall above the TV, at that spot where there was absolutely nothing at all.

Gus took Ruby by the hand and led her up to the bathroom.

"That wasn't much fun, was it?" He sat on the edge of the dirty tub.

Ruby shook her head as she brushed her teeth.

Gus rubbed at the grime. "When we get back from the field trip, let's put on those silly aprons Grandma sent and do some serious cleaning."

Grandma Far Away, Ruby called her, not only because it took two days to drive to her and Grandpa's house, but now she didn't even live there. She lived in a care home, and didn't know who Ruby or Fiona or Gus or even Grandpa was anymore.

But she could still sew.

These aprons were a mishmash of fabrics with UFOs and happy green Martians and Christmas trees with kittens peeking out.

Ruby nodded. She loved it when her mother got into her cleaning mood and cleaned for a week straight. She never ate, she hardly slept and never even left the house. Robot Clean Mode, her dad called it. Beep, boop.

"We'll give the whole place a clean."

Ruby rinsed her toothbrush, and her hand where the spit had dripped. She knocked the water off the edge of the equally grimy sink and replaced the toothbrush in the plastic cup, also dirty. She showed her dad the cloudy, viscous fluid pooled at the bottom.

"Gross," he said.

"Gross," she said.

Once, Ruby had seen a show where a house blew up. It was a show about trajectory, or maybe velocity, and how far debris can fly when things explode. It was an old house, and they were exploding it on purpose. It blew up in a mushroom of fire and smoke, and then they played it in slow motion, showing what happened in each room.

The walls sucked in, then out, then crumbled away, the couch, the beds swept out and into pieces carried away on the wind. Everything in ruins. Ruby imagined an explosion that blew her mother high into the cold, cold clouds, as if an invisible giant had yanked her away. She and her dad would hold on. They were stronger that way. Their feet might come off the floor, but they would hold on to the last post standing, just to be sure to be there after to marvel at the absolute nothing that was left.

Ruby tried to picture this slow-motion demolition, but all she could think about was her mother at the dinner table, talking about her own mother's poo trickling down her leg.

Gus pulled her to him. "She's not feeling well, but she'll be okay. Let's think about nice stuff. The trip up the mountain, okay? Can you help me decide what treat to bring?"

He got a little notebook out of his lumberjack coat, and a pen from the floor of the bathroom.

It would be chocolate. He always ended up bringing chocolate.

"I always bring chocolate, but Skye is allergic to dairy, and the twins aren't allowed any refined sugar at all." He held his pen over the list. "Honeycomb? Too sticky?"

Ruby took the notebook and flipped to the page with the list of the kids' names. She pointed to Anna, then Tag.

"What's with them?" He offered her the pen.

She wrote *veegin* in her neatest letters.

"Gotcha," he said. "That means Jiffy marshmallows are out, but the ones from the health food store are a maybe. They don't have gelatin or refined sugar. Made with sweet and gelatinous wing drippings of woodland fairies. Is that acceptable?"

Ruby laughed. *Ded farrys!!!* she wrote. Then, *Just do not tel.* And a happy face.

He crossed out *chocolate*. He crossed out *honeycomb*.

Glow sticks?

Ruby nodded.

Stupidly expensive hand warmers?

Ruby took the pen and put nine checkmarks beside that.

Shane didn't deserve hand warmers or glow sticks. But it would be mean not to give him any. Her dad was nice to everyone, even if they were just a stupid bully who was going to grow up and be a giant, walking turd. Imagine a walking turd with hand warmers and a glow stick!

Ruby heard her mother coming up the stairs. She stopped in the doorway of the bathroom.

"What are you doing?" she said.

"Cleaning up your mess." Her father said it like he would tell off someone who tailgated him all the way to Whistler. Not like he'd said the words *marshmallow, honeycomb, chocolate.*

Ruby used her cold bare foot to gently close the door. Not all the way, because her mother was leaning on the door jamb. But enough.

"I love feeling supported and appreciated," her mother said in her most British accent, which she used for exactly times like this. "What treasures, both of you." She took hold of the knob and opened the door wide before slamming it shut so hard that the towel rack fell off the wall. Then, through the closed door, "I love you, Ruby. Good night."

Ruby trembled. This was the Upsy Daisy mom, the one who might spin into the room and announce that they would be spending the day making eight-strand friendship bracelets to send to refugee children new to Canada. Or she might be the mom who crawled from her bed to the toilet and back and only spoke in a whisper to tell her how much she loved her and that she would try so, so, so hard to stay.

Stay.

"Hey, Rabbit." Gus shook her wrists. "Come back."

Her mother had a tattoo on her wrist. The phases of the moon and the word *stay.* What did that mean?

"Are you nervous about the mountain trip?"

She shook her head.

"Everyone has a buddy," her dad said. "Except you."

She liked the trips with just her and her dad, or when he let her come along on guiding trips with customers who loved a kid who could handle themselves like she could. They had kids with them sometimes, and were always saying, Look, she doesn't need a break. She doesn't have blisters. She's not complaining of cold hands. She doesn't need a snack.

She should feel sorry for those city kids. She was used to it. They weren't. But she liked it.

"Liam is a good friend, you know."

Ruby shrugged.

"He could be."

Ruby shrugged again.

"Except for that little shit Shane." Her dad grinned. "Am I right?"

Ruby nodded. It was okay that she didn't have any friends her age. She didn't need any. She had Luke and Aubrey. Mike and Sarah. Her dad.

"When I was your age, everyone was my friend." Gus brushed her hair. "Even the dumb kid who always had dried spittle in the corners of his mouth and walked on the balls of his feet. Even the jerk who always picked on that kid. But you're different, Rabbit. Your friend is coming. It's like your mom said. A girl just needs one good friend."

When Ruby went down to get a glass of water, she saw her mother, stripped down to her panties and bra, asleep on the couch, curled up like it was comfortable, even though they got that couch from the alley behind the hockey centre and it was droopy at both ends and covered in rough mustard-coloured fabric that left stripes if you sat on it with bare skin. It still smelled of the hot dog machine, because that was right beside it in the rink for a million years.

Ruby filled her favourite glass at the kitchen sink, and then stopped to look at her mother's face illuminated by the front porch light no one had turned off, through the open curtains no one had closed. Her mother had a long neck, not like Ruby's. Small ears, not like Ruby's. Her hands looked exactly like Ruby's, though, stubby fingers where you'd expect to find long, slender ones. Somehow, she still looked pretty when she held a cigarette. Her breasts were squished between her arms, angled to tuck her hands under her chin. The curve of her waist to her hips would be perfect for a fairy slalom. Her underwear was hardly there. Just a string of creamy lace high across her hip and disappearing into her butt crack one way and into the crease between her legs the other way. Normally her mother only had an eraser-sized patch of hair, but there was more now, growing in as a carpet of stubble. Ruby pulled the blanket over her mom, even though it was warm in the house, with the wood stove glowing orange in the dark.

She stuffed two more logs in before latching the door and going back up to bed. When she was all snuggled under her duvet, she remembered she'd left her glass of water on the coffee table, but she was too drowsy to go all the way downstairs to get it.

Ruby was already awake when her father turned the hall light on. As he loomed in the doorway, she closed her eyes, because she liked him to wake her up.

"Rise and shine, Rabbit." Gus knelt and swept her hair out of her face. He left his hand on her head as she stirred. "Time to go."

He got her base layers ready while she padded to the bathroom, stopping in the doorway of her parents' room, surprised to see her mother lying naked on her side of the bed, her hair messed up, legs akimbo, dark bushy hair at the V. There on her side table of books and pill bottles and balled-up tissue was the glass Ruby had filled with water in the middle of the night. The one from Head-Smashed-In Buffalo Jump, with its tidy line of buffaloes lining up to topple over the cliff. There was no water left in it. Ruby wanted it back. No one else used that glass except her. She picked it out in the gift shop when they stopped there on a trip to visit her grandparents in Pincher Creek. She paid for it with her own money.

She grabbed the glass and was halfway out of the room when her mother called her name.

"Hey, baby." She reached an arm out, beckoning her back. Her mother's voice sounded dark and filmy, like the room. Her parents' room always smelled of a musk that was the combination of all her mother's perfumes and creams and powders, but there was another smell this morning: people musk, tangled-together musk, sweating-under-the-same-blanket musk. "Thank you for the glass of water."

Ruby knew better than to shake her head, but she didn't nod either.

"I woke up on the couch and saw it there and thought, hey, that kid loves me." She pulled Ruby closer and kissed her twice, once on each cheek. "That glass is so special to you, which made your gesture even more special to me. It gave me the energy to come up to bed." Ruby tried to give her no look at all. Her mother laughed. "It did! Come here."

She pulled Ruby onto the bed with her and cuddled her like she was some kind of baby.

"Let me give you some warmth before you head into the snow." She covered Ruby's forehead in kisses. "One for each kilometre. Six, round trip, right?" And one more. "Let me give you one more, for good luck. And another, just because."

Ruby kissed her once on both cheeks. She wished the kisses had left a mark, little kissy pucker marks, like hearts her mom could wear while she was gone. She'd get her mom's red lipstick from the dresser and put it on and kiss her again, to leave those cheek hearts, but as she rolled across the bed to get out on her dad's side, she put her hand in a wet spot. She yanked her hand away, wiping it on her pyjamas. It was probably just water. Or sweat. Though it felt slimier than either, and made her forget about the lipstick.

Her father helped her get dressed in her first two layers. Wool socks up to her knees over silk long johns, silk long-sleeved undershirt, merino over that. He held her hand as they went downstairs. He'd already made coffee and set out toast with peanut butter and jam. A banana. A glass of milk. The radio was on to Mountain FM, so low that Ruby couldn't make out the songs from the table by the windows with the black morning outside. Gus stood at the counter, packing a stuff sack with the last of the food. Zip-lock bags of dried soup. A package of pepperoni sticks.

"I'm going to warm up the truck," he said. "You all set?"

Ruby nodded. Then he was gone and it was dark and quiet, except for the radio. Ruby sat in the small circle of light from the fixture that hung above the little kitchen table. The light swung ever so slightly, giving depth to the shadows; the toaster, the pile of coats by the back door, the fridge. Ruby heard the truck engine revving, then the steady *shick, shick* of her father scraping the ice off the windows. She heard her mother's footsteps overhead, which made the light swing wider, stretching out the shadows. Footsteps on the stairs? The hall light came on. Ruby sat straighter. She set down the triangle of toast.

"I couldn't go back to sleep," Fiona said from the doorway, the light behind her casting her into a dark outline of mother. "I'm excited for you." She padded across the kitchen and sat in the chair across from Ruby. She took Ruby's hand and squeezed it. "I'm going to miss my little fire starter."

The fire was already started. There was even a stack of wood by the stove. All she had to do was open the door and put it in. She never did, though. It was like there was a spell on her mom, or the stove. Or the wood. Or all of it.

"Good breakfast?"

Ruby nodded. She could call Mike or Sarah or Luke or Aubrey and they'd come put more wood in. But not Luke,

Ruby remembered—he was coming on the trip. But that still left almost everybody else. Anyone in the whole town would help her mom, if she just asked.

"Stay warm." Ruby squeezed her eyes shut, waiting for her mom to hug her too tight and gush too much and thank her over and over for saying something.

A kiss on the head.

"You too," her mom said. "You be safe. Listen to Daddy." Another kiss on her forehead. "I love you, my favourite thing."

Ruby hugged her tight. She smelled of sweat and wine and that bedroom smell.

As her mother disappeared into the dark to go back upstairs, Ruby picked up her toast. But then Gus came in the front door and Fiona stopped in the pool of light on the stairs. Ruby could see the two of them. Her mother above, her dad below, like a scene in a movie.

"Good morning." Fiona pulled her housecoat around her and sat on the step. "Are you all ready to go?"

"What happened last night?"

Ruby knew to turn her attention to her empty plate if she wanted them to keep talking like she wasn't listening.

"You enjoyed yourself."

"I didn't even know you were there, let alone what you were doing, until I—" Her dad's voice slid into a whisper. Not her mother's, though.

"You enjoyed yourself," she repeated.

"Can't say the same for anyone at dinner."

"Seemed to me that everyone was having a grand old time," her mother said. "At my expense."

"I'm not getting into this," her father said. "Ruby! Truck's warm. Let's go!"

Ruby took her plate and glass to the sink. She couldn't quite reach the taps without the stool, so she set the dishes to one side and pushed the stool in place and climbed up. She turned on the taps and squirted some soap onto the plate.

She couldn't hear what they were saying until she turned off the tap.

Something something lawyer something something you're not taking her to London.

"I bloody well am!" her mother bellowed.

"We'll see about that, Fiona." Ruby heard Gus slap the banister. "Rabbit! We're going to be late!"

Last summer it got so hot that they all slept on the trampoline one night, with thin sheets and good pillows. Her parents fell asleep fast, one on either side of her, but Ruby stayed awake, watching for shooting stars and looking at her parents, their faces calm and slack with sleep. Ruby listened to the warm wind tickle the cottonwood trees, their tall, quiet sway, back and forth. When the chill of dawn came, they all snuggled up under the one sleeping bag Fiona had dragged out. Ruby fell asleep then. She slept so hard that her mother had to wake her up to put on sunscreen. That was a perfect night. The most perfect night in a book about perfect nights.

"You always tell me not to yell at her," Fiona said just under a yell.

"Because you do it a lot," Gus said. "She doesn't need it from both parents. Rabbit, let's go."

Ruby rinsed the plate and the glass. She set them in the drying rack beside the sink. She wiped her hands on the dishtowel and ignored the knot in her gut that was telling her that she had to use the washroom. She didn't want to go up the stairs past her mother. She would wait until they were at the school and everyone was getting ready. Everyone would have to go before getting into the van.

Ruby sat in the Great Hall with her backpack at her feet, listening to the other kids talking about their talismans. Anna had brought a piece of amethyst. Tag brought his lucky pocket knife. It had two blades and scissors and even tweezers, and his name engraved on it. Nino brought a square from a prayer flag.

"You picked that?" Shane asked. "I thought you were bringing the golf ball."

"My dad said to bring this," Nino said. "But I snuck the golf ball too."

Shane brought a big silver coin. "From Las Vegas," he said. "The luckiest."

Liam brought his treasured arrowhead.

"You didn't even find that," Shane said.

"Luke did. He gave it to me."

"Let me see."

Liam took off his glove and fished it out of an inside pocket. Shane snatched it from him before Liam had even opened his hand all the way.

"Give it back!"

"No." He gave Liam his coin. "You can have this."

"I don't want your dumb coin. Give me back my arrowhead!"

"Maybe later." Shane pocketed it. "Don't be a baby. I'm just borrowing it. That's what friends do, dink." He grinned at Ruby. "How about you, Hop Hop?"

"Leave her alone," Liam said.

"Probably just her lucky daddy," Shane said.

And then Nino showed them his bright-orange golf ball and told them how he could always hit his target with it. Tree, wall, rock. When he used his slingshot, he never missed.

Ruby had a collection of key chains distributed amongst the zippers on her coat and backpack. Gus brought them back from snowboard competitions. He didn't compete anymore, but he judged and was a commentator and celebrity guest. Ruby had key chains from Whistler—of course—Apex, Telluride, Chamonix, Park City, Catina, Aspen, Mont-Tremblant, and a few that she couldn't remember where they were from because they didn't have the name of the town or the mountain on it. She had a moose (Jackson Hole maybe?) and a hot-air balloon (Vail?) and a snowflake and a snowboarding Santa with a naked bum.

Her favourite was a plastic rabbit she'd attached to her jacket pull. It was tiny, but looked real. Her father had one too. His was brown, with a black nose. Hers was grey, with a black nose. Gus made it to replace the rabbit's foot that her grandpa once gave her. Ruby loved him enormously, but she did not want a rabbit foot. Her grandpa had been a park ranger in the Rocky Mountains his whole life. He'd wrestled a cougar and didn't even have a scar to show for it. He was old now, and his bones cracked and popped when he stood up. When he sat down, his grizzled white beard touched his big belly. He had the best stories in the world, but he thought it was okay to offer to teach her how to skin a rabbit, and how to roast it over a campfire, when it wasn't.

He'd dangled the rabbit foot in front of Ruby. "I made this when I was a boy," he said. "I know how much you love rabbits."

Ruby took it. Smooth and soft, with a dented gold cap and a rusty chain with a ring. She slipped it into her pocket and held her dad's hand. When they got into the truck, she gave it to her father. Gus rolled down the window as he drove and tossed it out into the bush.

"That's where it belongs," he said. "Am I right, Rabbit?"

She nodded. He was absolutely right.

The next day there was the key chain beside her bowl at breakfast. It was a small grey rabbit that fit in the palm of her hand. She looked up at Gus, wondering.

It was one of her own toy rabbits. He'd screwed a tiny eyelet into its back and attached a chain and ring. There was a bit of glue at the base of the eyelet. Ruby picked it off.

"This way you can still have a lucky rabbit's foot," he said. "Four of them."

Ruby kissed him, and then she ran upstairs and found another little rabbit just like it, only brown. She folded it into his palm.

"We can both have lucky rabbit's feet?" Gus said.

Ruby nodded. After breakfast, he took her down to the basement and let her drill the tiny hole and screw in the eyelet and then he pinched on the chain and threaded on the ring.

Mike was there to see them off. He rounded the children up now, steering them out the door. But Ruby hadn't used the bathroom yet.

"Let's go, gang," Gus said.

She took his hand to tell him. She'd been waiting, and then she forgot.

"Need something, Rabbit?"

Skye and Anna came out of the bathroom, heads together, laughing. They had been in there so long, and now it was time to go.

She should've gone down the hall to the bigger bathroom. But that hall was pitch-black except for the Exit sign at the far end. No one else had gone that way. Ruby opened her mouth to ask her father to wait. To tell him that she needed to use the bathroom. It was no big deal. Just make the words come out. But Shane was staring at her, and Liam too. Shane mouthed something at her.

Baby. Baby. Baby, baby, baby.

She dropped her father's hand. He went ahead, shouting at Luke to put the sled on top, last.

What was Shane saying now? She couldn't make it out. He sneered at her and picked up his bulging backpack and walked away. She wanted to know what he'd said. She'd made out the words *dad* and *fuck*, which was bad enough. She stood in the middle of the hallway with her pack at her feet and her eyes closed, trying to piece it together. *Your dad is a fuck.* Or *Your dad is a fake. Go fuck your dad.* She ran after Shane and grabbed his arm. He spun and then was so surprised it was her that he almost stumbled.

"What do you want?"

But Ruby couldn't say it. She opened her mouth and tried to make the words come out, but she just couldn't.

"What do you want, retard?"

Gus and Mike were outside in the dark, loading up the van with Luke. Gus looked up. For a moment Ruby thought that he saw her and Shane standing there. He'd know what that meant. He'd know that she needed him. But he said something to Mike and then he was grinning. He took Anna's pack from her and stacked it on top of the others. He leaned down and looked right at Anna and said something nice to her. Ruby could tell by his face. He was being nice to her. He wasn't a fuck and he wasn't a fake.

"Let go!" Shane twisted away, but Ruby held on tight.

"Leave him alone." Liam pushed her and she tipped over, landing on her backpack like an upturned turtle. "Weirdo."

The boys opened both doors, letting in double the amount of frigid cold air. Now it was just Ruby, alone in the Great Hall, the room dense with silence except for the hum of the vending machine at the far end, full of granola bars and dried seaweed and fruit leather and trail mix.

Ruby pulled her arms out of her pack and stood up. Another rush of cold air.

"Rabbit?"

Don't call me that anymore. Don't call me Rabbit.

Gus picked up the backpack and held out his hand. "Ready to go?"

Don't call me Rabbit anymore.

"Van's waiting, kiddo."

Ruby walked ahead of him. She sat in the last seat available, front row, beside Nino. He twisted around to talk to anyone but her.

Ruby listened to Gus and Luke go over the plan for the day. They'd park by the power line and cut in along the trail from below, along the creek bed. They'd stay south of the treeline and get to the cabin long before dark. The next day they would build snow caves in the morning, and head home after lunch. Ruby could take the lead with that, her father said. She built a great one in the woods in town. You should see it.

"A winter wabbit hole," Shane said with a smirk. He made an O with a thumb and index finger of one hand, and poked his other index finger in and out and in and out.

Don't tell where. Don't tell where.

Don't, Daddy.

Ruby's stomach ached. She had to pee and she had to poo, and one was so much worse than the other that when she felt the hot wetness pool in her lap, she was just relieved that she hadn't pooed herself.

The smell of urine filled the van.

"She peed her pants!" Nino yelled. "It's going to get on me!" He undid his seat belt and scrambled over to the bench behind.

"Hey!" Anna said.

"Hold up back there," Gus said. "What's going on?"

Why weren't they laughing? Why weren't they pointing at her? Quiet was worse. It made the smell worse. It made her damp, clinging layers worse. It made the heat worse. It made everything worse. She wished they *would* laugh. Gus pulled to the shoulder. He put on his four-ways, undid his seat belt and crouched in the space between the two front seats.

"Rabbit? Did you have an accident?"

Ruby nodded, and then she began to cry.

Gus lifted her out of the van and led her around to the back. It was still dark out. The rear lights of the van lit their breath. The van rumbled. Exhaust billowed out. Ruby's stomach churned.

"Oh, Rabbit."

"Don't call me that anymore!"

She felt him jerk at her words. He didn't say anything, just helped her strip off the wet bottoms—because she'd been sitting, her socks and boots were still dry—and put on her spare pair. "Don't worry. The other kids have spares too. We won't need all of them."

Ruby shivered. She still smelled pee. "I have to poo," she whispered.

"Right now?"

"Yes."

"Okay." Gus rooted in the back of the van and found the roll of toilet paper. "I'll give you a little privacy," he said as he ducked around the side of the van.

Ruby crouched. The cold of the ploughed road spread along her damp, naked thighs. Salt crunched under her boots. The van jostled a bit. Were they watching her? No. Her father wouldn't let them. Luke wouldn't let them. They were singing "The Grand Old Duke of York."

And when they were only halfway up, they were neither up nor down.

She strained, but nothing came. She held her breath and tried again, and then suddenly a stream of diarrhea splattered down, splashing her boots and the snow all around.

"Daddy!" she cried.

"Oh, Ruby. Rabbit, are you going to be okay?" Gus helped clean her up, and then he tossed the paper towels over the snowbank. "Do you want to go home?"

Until he marched them out of sight.

She shook her head. She did want to go home, but she was not going to tell him that. Never.

"You sure?"

No way was she going to ruin the trip for all the other kids. If she dared to, everything that was already awful would get worse, worse, worse.

When she got back into the van—Luke had sopped up the urine as best he could with paper towel—the other children didn't say a word. Gus pulled the van back onto the highway, the tires crunching on the fresh salt. They drove along as the sky turned from black to the deepest blue, and then lighter and lighter until the stars faded. The children didn't say anything until they turned off the highway and onto the ice-slicked Tiffen Lake Road. Gus and Luke got out to put the chains on. Ruby plugged her ears and squeezed her eyes shut so she wouldn't have to listen to Shane go on and on and on. Back on the road, she couldn't do that, because her dad would see in the rear-view mirror. It wasn't as bad, though. The chains crunched and the heater fan blew and the radio blared in the front, so Gus and Luke couldn't hear the children whispering. Ruby could, though. They held their noses and talked about diapers and babies and ugly, stupid, dumb bunnies.

Fiona slept until mid-morning. When she woke, she felt as refreshed as if she'd slept for three days straight. She might do that, she thought. She might have a shower and eat a piece of toast and drink a glass of orange juice and a cup of coffee, and then she would go back to bed. She would ignore the fusty smell of unwashed sheets and questionably consensual sex—he woke up with a start to find her straddling him, and told her to stop, but after she pinned him down with all her weight for a few moments while he glared at her, he absolutely enjoyed himself—and the pile of dirty laundry spilling out of the basket in the corner. Gus's underwear, his stiff socks, his dingy T-shirts, all of it touching her slips of underthings, her soft shirts with capped sleeves and gracefully scooped necks, a pair of his jeans suffocating a pair of her bamboo leggings, speaking of non-consensual.

They must be kept apart.

No touching! God. *Unacceptable.*

She leapt out of bed and toppled the basket onto the floor. The clothes were a pile of hibernating snakes, legs and sleeves and underwear tangled and warm and filthy, undulating. She knelt on the floor and went to work. Gus's things to the left, hers to the right. His pile grew exponentially faster—his jeans were bigger; his shirts were bigger. He was bigger. In all the ways, he was bigger. And she was small. So small. Tiny satin panties with delicately hopeful lace trim, leggings that hardly kept a shape at all. A short, empire-waisted dress with three-quarter sleeves made from organic jersey cotton. She picked it up and held it in two fists. This was part of the problem. She was not the sort of person to wear this dress. It wasn't even a dress. It was a tunic. Rhymes with *eunuch.* Exactly. She wore it over leggings, with what Gus called "funny mommy" knee-high socks. He didn't say funny *mummy.* He said *mommy. Maw-me,* so it didn't even rhyme, when it absolutely could. The socks were decorated with things like unicorns, flowers, goldfish or the Union Jack. Almost all of them were from Ruby. Her favourites were the simple striped ones. Her new favourites were the ones Ruby gave her at Christmas. Soft bamboo, green and blue and black stripes. When she left the house, she put on gumboots. Wellies, for God's sake. As if she was Lady Whatsit driving around the estate in an old Land Rover. As if she was the kind of person who liked living in shapeless cotton layers and boots with pink flowers on them, as if that made them any less ridiculous.

She sat between the two piles of clothes now, such an overly simplified metaphor that she had to laugh. She placed her laundry at the bottom of the basket and then Gus's on top—more cheap metaphor. She put on a sweater. Gus hadn't packed the

the stove before they left, but it didn't matter. It was just the one night. Neither of them had called the furnace guy yet. It was cheaper to use up the cordwood.

She took the basket down the hall to Ruby's room. Her laundry was neatly contained in a little basket by her closet. She usually wore the same clothes for as many days in a row as possible, so she never made much laundry. Fiona had stopped asking her to put on something new. Or nice. For a while, she'd insisted on underwear at least, but she'd stopped that too. Whenever she noticed the absence of an underwear line, she had to work to not say anything, because the things she wanted to say were the things her aunt would say to her, and those were not things that anyone should say to an eight-year-old.

You'll get piss dribbles on your skirt when you sit at your desk, and then you'll stink, and the kids would have something to say about that, eh? What if the wind gets the best of you? Everyone will see your backside and what a laugh. And what a surprise your fingers will get to go in for a scratch and find your fanny saying hello and how do you do.

Ruby didn't like seams of any kind. She didn't like clothes that were too tight. She wore a size or two larger than she measured; she was so small she still fit into a size five. She didn't like socks. Too "bunchy" at the toe, or too tight at the top. She didn't like anything with buttons or snaps or fitted collars. She didn't like anything made of "crunchy" material, which meant anything other than soft jersey. What she wore to school looked no different from—and sometimes actually were—pyjamas. Meanwhile her closet was stuffed with gifts Willy had sent, new dresses on wooden hangers with the store's name burned in, protected in muslin bags, and boxes of top-quality hand-me-downs from the undyingly snobbish Collette, whose wardrobe could not deny an unhealthy obsession with ponies.

Fiona carried the heaping basket downstairs, cranking every thermostat she passed, with the small hope that doing so would knock the furnace back into action in the basement. Living room, kitchen, bathroom.

The stairs to the basement were cold underfoot—her slippers were upstairs beside the bed still. She knew that all she had to do to be warm was to put the laundry down, turn around, go up the stairs into the living room and put a log in the wood stove. But it was not her domain and, furthermore, she was terrified of it. It was a raging hot beast that could burn the house down. She didn't understand the flue, or how much wood to put on, or how to make it burn slowly. She kept forgetting that the glass was searingly hot and that the ash needed to be shovelled out.

When Ruby was a baby and Gus was away at a competition in Vail, she managed to smoke them both out of the house. The fire truck came, but it was hours before they could go back inside. She'd had to go to Sarah and Mike's. She hadn't touched the stove since.

The concrete floor was so icy that she dropped the basket and skipped over to the door that led up to the yard and stuffed her feet into a pair of Gus's running shoes. The insides felt clammy and foreign, shaped to his foot, not hers. They were big on her, and so she had to slide-walk back to the basket, which had tipped over.

There was a time when she had carefully separated their laundry into darks, colours and whites. She used to have a laundry station in the bathroom, three canvas sacks that hung on an aluminium frame with the designation printed on them in flowery cursive, as if that made the whole affair more palatable, when in fact it was always about dirt and sweat and stains and bodies leaking. Darks, colours, whites. With the American spelling of *colors*, which irritated her beyond explanation. She'd bought it and brought it home unassembled in the box. When she saw the spelling, she wanted to return it right away, but it was a three-hour drive back to the city.

Ruby was a baby then, and she hated being in the truck, if a baby could really hate anything. She'd squall and writhe and turn her head, staring wide-eyed out the window as the trees and the sky slid by at an admittedly dizzying speed, until she'd fall asleep, exhausted.

"You could sit back there with her," Gus had said.

"I could."

"Then you could just lean over and give her the boob."

Fiona stared at him, not wide-eyed at all.

"It's something to try. Sarah hangs over and she hardly has to shift in her seat."

"Does she."

"Hers are bigger. And Liam was bigger when he was that age. You'd have to twist a bit, but I bet it would work if you angled it up a bit with one hand." He reached over and grabbed her breast through her shirt, lifting and squeezing. "Ruby could latch on." When he let go, there was a milk stain on the green linen. Another moment later, there was a matching one on the other side.

Gus pulled onto a logging road, stopping in a pullout above the Cheakamus River.

"Isn't this nicer?" Fiona said as Ruby latched on, murmuring happily around her nipple, reaching up and stroking her cheek.

—

Fiona opened the door of the washing machine and scooped up armfuls of the laundry and stuffed it all in together. She hadn't separated by colour since the laundry system had fallen apart. Or, more pointedly, had broken apart because Gus leaned on it once too often while keeping Ruby company when she consented to have a bath, which was a rare occasion in and of itself. Fiona had been downstairs, putting away clean dishes, and heard a crash that had stopped her short. She'd frozen with a mug in one hand and one of Ruby's plastic plates in the other—and then she heard laughing and she'd carried on, stacking plates and bowls, sliding cutlery into their sections in the plastic organizer that fitted into the drawer. Teaspoons, soup spoons—they'd had soup that night, carrot ginger—small and large forks mixed together (which she did not like), butter knives. They were still laughing. Gus's low chortle and Ruby's high-pitched cackle. Chortle and cackle. Like two witches in a children's picture book. She'd made a note of it. Where was that notebook now? Fiona dumped a scoop of laundry soap into the machine and closed the lid. Was it one of the spiral ones? Or one of the hardcover ones? She went to the bottom of the stairs and stepped out of Gus's running shoes, leaving them neatly side by side, pointing to the first step, as if they were about to climb the stairs all by themselves.

At the top, Fiona remembered two things. One, she should wash her good coat. Or would she have to take that to the cleaners? Was it open? No, of course not. The owner went to the Philippines for a month over Christmas, so he wasn't home yet. She'd dig it out and look at the label. She could probably wash it on gentle, but she shouldn't put it in the dryer, which ran too hot no matter what the setting. The other thing she remembered was that she'd written the note on the witches at the back of the notebook Ruby had given her for her birthday two years before. Its lines were much too dark, but because it was from Ruby, she'd tried to use it. In the end, she just could not. It was spiral-bound, with a hard front and back, and a picture of a rabbit—no surprise—on either side. The rabbit wore a bonnet, and was carrying a basket of Easter eggs. Fiona's birthday was in April.

"Did you get it out of the Easter display?" She was asking Gus, who would've had to help Ruby pick it out and pay for it. It had an Emporium sticker on the back. $2.99.

"Ruby picked it out," Gus said.

"But you paid for it at the counter? Or did Ruby?"

"Ruby did."

"Did she say anything?"

Ruby would've just put it on the counter with the right amount of money and the cashier would smile down at her. Aren't you a cutie? A cute little notebook for a cute little girl. You're Ruby Tenner, right? And Gus would smile. Do you like to snowboard too? Ruby would nod. That's two ninety-nine, dear. I'll put it in a bag for you. Here's your change. See you later, sweetheart. Ruby would smile her thank you, and that'd be it. After all, the whole town knew that Ruby couldn't speak. But that wasn't true. That wasn't true at all. She could. She just chose not to.

Fiona could even understand that, if she let herself be kind. If she let herself be honest.

DURING

Ruby pretended to be asleep for the rest of the ride. She did feel a lot better, but she kept her eyes closed because the kids were still talking about her as if she wasn't there, which was better than them talking *to* her. She wished she could close her ears too.

"What a freak."

"Who pees themselves when they're nine years old?"

"She's only eight." That was Liam.

"So why is she even on this field trip?" Shane. "It's for nine-year-olds *only*. We should undo her seat belt and open the door and push her out."

"Then you'd have to touch her stinky butt." Nino.

"I'm not touching her," Tag said. And they all chimed in. *Not me! Me either. No way. So gross. You'd get it on you!*

Gus parked the van at the Tiffen Creek trailhead and the children spilled out into the snow without any of the jackets or coats they'd peeled off in the hot van.

"First things first." Gus handed out avalanche transceivers and the children all hung them around their necks. Then he went around, setting each one. "We'll practise with these tomorrow, but you should get used to wearing them whenever you go into the backcountry in the winter."

While Gus was adjusting Skye's transceiver, Shane whispered in Ruby's ear. "Smells way better out here. Right, Liam?"

"Get your layers on," Gus shouted. He disappeared around the back of the van to help Luke unload the snowshoes.

"What a baby," Shane said. "I can't even breathe. She stinks so bad!"

"It's not that bad out here." Liam didn't look at Ruby when he said it.

"I can even see the shit splashes on her boots." Shane sneered at her. A mean little braggart, her mom called him. A horrid little boy.

Ruby followed her father. She would stay with him at all times. She wouldn't let herself end up alone with the others, not even for a minute, not even with just one of them. Even when her dad had to go pee, she would follow him and wait nearby. She watched him pee all the time at home, but she wouldn't let the other kids know that. It was weird, wasn't it? It was weird to watch your father pee, even if he was walking her home from school through the woods, talking about cloud formations, and he said hang on a sec, Rabbit, and he pulled it out and aimed at a tree and kept talking about cloud formations. Nimbus, cumulus, cirrus, and then he'd put it away and zip up his pants and they'd be on their way.

But then it was weird to be in the hot tub with naked adults, right? And Aubrey and Luke too—were they adults? Penises bobbing between legs, pubic hair that looked like anemones, and boobs and beer and candlelight and the cold, cold night. And Liam too.

All of a sudden Ruby's pockets were weighed down with priceless gold coins. She could embarrass him. She bet no one else knew that he sat around naked with a bunch of old people.

He wouldn't want the other kids to know that. She would say it, if she needed to. She would talk. She could talk. Or maybe she couldn't. But if she could, that's what she'd tell them. Liam sat in a big bathtub with his brother with no clothes on and his mom and dad too and even Gus. Ruby and Aubrey were the only ones wearing suits. What do you think about that?

But that sounded weird too, that she and Liam were together with his floaty dink hanging out.

Shane would say they were making babies. That's what he always said when a boy and a girl were just standing next to each other working on a project at school. You're having *sex*. You're humping each other and making babies. Fingers in an O, another finger poking in and out.

But I had my suit on!

Doesn't matter. He can stick it in the side. Fingering the O.

The children moved slowly. The air was thin and crisp and so cold that when Ruby inhaled, her chest felt hot. The back-country cabin was a two-hour hike for grown-ups, so her dad and Luke figured it would take the kids three. Ruby knew she could do it in less than two hours even, but no one else had backcountry experience like she did, especially in the winter. They were going to do an hour and a half to the big downed cedar, and then have lunch there. Then snowshoe for another hour, then a snack, then the last half-hour would be the hardest, straight uphill to the cabin, protected from the wind by the steep rock face that rose behind it. But it would take all day if they stayed at this pace. The group had been trudging along for almost two hours and had only managed to make a quarter of the distance.

The sky was a bright, hopeful blue above them, and the snow glistened on the wide trail, dug deep by cross-country skiers on one side and flattened by snowshoes on the other. It was a popular trail, and they'd already met a couple making their way out. They'd said that there was no one else at the cabin, and they hadn't seen anyone else on the trail.

"Because it's a weekday," Gus said.

"That's probably it," the man said.

"Hey," the woman said. "You're Gus Tenner, aren't you?"

"He is!" Liam said. "He was in the Olympics."

"I remember," she said. "How cool to have an Olympic medallist take you out here."

"He only won the silver," Shane said.

"You try doing that," the man said.

The woman gave each of the children a caramel, nearly rock-hard from the cold. "Don't eat it yet," she said. "Keep it in your pocket for that moment when you think you can't take another step. Then pop it into your mouth and it will taste like heaven."

Ruby slipped her candy into her pocket, and when she did, she noticed that her lucky rabbit was gone from her zipper. She looked at her feet. She looked on either side of the trail. When had she lost it? She had to go back! She could follow the trail until she found it and then she could catch up. Her dad could come with her, and Luke could go ahead. Or she could even go with Luke. Or she could go by herself. Her dad would let her, right? Or did Shane have it? Did he steal it in the van, when the jackets were all in a jumble? That was exactly something Shane would do. It was absolutely a Shane thing.

She needed the rabbit. To lose a good luck thing was to turn it right into a bad luck thing. And now it was out there in the

snow being bad luck. She started to cry. And then she lunged for
Shane, knocking him to the ground. They wrestled as she tried
to shove her hands into his pockets.

"Get off me, freak!"

"Whoa! Ruby!" Gus pulled her away. "What's going on?"

"Bet you won't make her say she's sorry. Because she can't!"

"Shane."

"She attacked me!"

"That's enough!" Gus knelt at her side as she wept. "What's
the matter? What is it?"

Ruby cried and cried.

He picked her up, snowshoes and all. "Why are you crying?"

Someone laughed. Well, not someone. Shane. Shane laughed
and laughed.

"Hey," the candy lady said. "That's not nice either."

Ruby lifted the naked zipper pull.

"The rabbit."

Ruby nodded, sobbing.

"It's okay, I'll give you mine." Gus set her down and worked
his rabbit off his zipper. "You're my good luck charm. I don't
need this one." He worked it onto her zipper, and right away
Ruby began to feel better. "Better?"

Ruby nodded. "Thanks, Daddy," she whispered in his ear.

The children started grumbling shortly after they said goodbye
to the couple.

"We've got to move faster, gang," Gus said.

"Come on, superheroes," Luke said. "There's a princess at the
cabin and she needs to be rescued!"

Superheroes do not go with princesses. Ruby trudged along beside her father as the others chased Luke, their backpacks bouncing, snowshoes kicking up snow.

Luke spun the story long enough to get the children to the first pit stop a full hour later than planned, which wasn't that bad, all things considered.

Then, when they were all settled, Anna said, "I don't feel so good," leaned forward and vomited into her lap.

"Gross!" Shane howled with laughter, while the other children just stared, their red cheeks like alarms against wan faces.

"Okay, honey." Gus leapt up and lifted Anna away from the others as she threw up some more. "It's okay."

As Gus was getting her cleaned up and calming her down, Tag vomited too, then sprinted awkwardly away from the group. He wrestled his pants down just in time to shit a stream of diarrhea onto the snow, the hot mess melting a trough under his bum. He didn't make it far enough that the others couldn't see him. Shane pointed and laughed and laughed, crowing, "You just crapped your pants!"

Tag was stuck there, his backside dripping with excrement and nothing to wipe it with. Ruby stood to one side and didn't look, her father's rabbit attached to her zipper and folded in her hand. She was not going to lose this one. It was good luck for both of them now. Her father rooted through the sled for the toilet bucket, a five-gallon bucket with a lid and a roll of toilet paper inside. They'd use the outhouse behind the cabin—which might or might not have a damp-swollen supply—but he'd brought the bucket to put in a corner of the porch for the middle of the night, when the kids wouldn't want to dash to the outhouse in the snow. It was cold, and far, and even Ruby thought it looked like a towering four-legged monster in the shadow of the moon.

"Here," Gus said. "Take this to Tag."

She had to plug her nose as she got closer. When she handed it to him, he yelled, "Go away! Don't look!" When she got back to the sled, her father and Luke were trying to decide what to do.

"You could take Anna and Tag home. Or we could get all the kids to the cabin."

"Or we could *all* go home."

"But we're closer to the cabin than the trailhead. We only have a couple of hours of good light left."

"Help!" Tag wailed. There was a pile of dirty toilet paper beside him, but he was still grunting and splashing diarrhea onto the snow.

"Fuck, Gus. I don't know. This sucks."

"Gus!"

Ruby spun. Who was that? Not Tag.

Skye was bending over with her hands on her knees, vomiting.

"You're okay, Skye." Gus ran to her and tucked her long ponytail up under her toque. He rubbed her back. "You'll be okay, honey."

Luke and Ruby stood by the sled, staring at Skye and the mess spewing out of her.

"Luke!"

"Yeah."

"There's a roll of paper towel in there somewhere. Get it out, would you? Set up the stove so we can melt some of this snow and wipe their faces with a nice hot cloth. Tag? I'll be over there in a minute, buddy."

Tag whimpered.

Anna sat in the snow, her face almost the same blue-white. Her glasses drooped at the end of her nose.

Skye sat on her backpack. "I want to go home!" she wailed.

Shane, Liam and Nino stood so far away from the rest of the group that Ruby could hardly see them in the slanting afternoon light

"Liam! Give me a hand." Luke rifled through the stuff sacks. "I can't find the paper towels or the stoves."

Liam headed for the sled.

Shane and Nino backed up even farther as Skye threw up again.

The vomit and diarrhea stood out like paint bombs on the white snow. The smell was everywhere. Ruby pulled her neck warmer up over her mouth and nose. They should go home. They should turn around and go back to the van and maybe along the way she'd find the rabbit and then she and her dad would both have good luck charms because maybe Gus lost all his good luck when he took his off. That's when all the mess started.

Luke finally found the stoves, and was setting them up while Liam scooped snow into two tin pots.

"Everyone is going to be just fine." Gus came back to the sled. "Let's carry on to the cabin. Everyone will feel better in the morning. All we need is a good night's rest."

The children were little twists of impossibly bright colours against the backdrop of snow.

Anna and Tag held hands and cried. "We want to go home," Anna said between sobs.

Skye was still crying. "Me too!"

"*We* don't want to go home," Shane said. "Why should a couple of people wreck it for everybody else?"

"Three people," Liam said.

"I kind of want to go home," Nino said. "What if we all get it? I kind of don't feel very good either."

"It's Ruby's fault," Shane said.

Ruby shook her head. She wasn't sick. She just had to go to the bathroom and waited too long. *I just waited too long! I feel fine!*

"She started it."

"Shut up, Shane." Gus pointed a finger at him. "Shut the fuck up."

"Gus," Luke said. "Dude."

"Sorry." Gus shook his head. "I'm sorry, Shane."

"I'm telling my moms, and they'll tell Mike. You'll never get to take us on any more stupid trips."

"What if we phone for SAR?" Luke said. "Get them to come get the kids. They could get the snowmobiles going. Get the kids a ride out of here."

Gus shook his head. "We can't do that on account of a few kids with an upset tummy. What if someone who is really in trouble needs SAR and they're busy rescuing us from a stomach bug?"

"They'd be fine with it. SAR isn't only for idiots who go out of bounds."

"But what about the guy who wanders out of bounds and dies of hypothermia while we're totally capable of handling this?"

"Not his lucky day." Luke shrugged. "Should've stayed in bounds."

"We're both in Search and Rescue, Luke. We can take care of these kids. We'll take them to the cabin and get a fire started in the stove, and we'll hunker down for the night. We won't do the snow caves tomorrow. We'll go home. First thing in the morning. How does that sound?"

"No snow caves?" Shane whined. "My moms are going to be so mad! This sucks! You guys suck!"

Gus suddenly reached for him, and Ruby was sure that he was going to slap him across the face, but Luke grabbed his wrist and forced his arm back down to his side.

"We'll manage," Gus said. "We'll all take care of each other whether we like it or not. I'll call Mike if we have to. But not yet. We've got this, kids. We can do it!"

Gus took Ruby aside as the three boys who were still feeling okay collected their packs. Luke was putting away the stove and piling the other children's packs onto the sled.

"I want you to go ahead and get a fire started in the wood stove, okay?"

She wanted to go back down the trail and find the rabbit so she could give it to her dad. He should have a good luck charm too. But there was no way he'd let her go now. She'd have to look tomorrow and hope it didn't snow.

She'd been to this cabin so many times that it felt like they owned it, and just had to share it with other people sometimes. She knew the trail all the way from where Gus had parked the van. As he talked, Gus rooted in her pack. "You've got everything in here you need, just in case?"

Ruby nodded.

"All right, you run ahead and get it nice and cozy for us, okay? I'm going to send Luke along with the others one at a time. I'll come last. You're feeling okay? No more tummy ache?"

Ruby nodded again.

"You okay to do this? It'd be a big help. A really big help. You'll get to be the hero." Gus gave her a hug. "How cool is that?"

Ruby shrugged.

"You're good?"

She nodded.

"All right, then, Rabbit." Gus hugged her so tight she was pretty sure he didn't hear her when she told him not to call her that. She wasn't going to say it again. She hadn't meant it. Not really.

He planted a kiss on her forehead. His lips were cool, and his nose was red and wet. It dripped onto her cheek. "Gross, sorry." He wiped it off and kissed her again. "You wait, Rabbit. This is the kind of thing they're going to remember. It's going to be good. When you get to school on Monday, everyone is going to know that you're the one who went ahead all by herself and got the fire going. You're going to be the cool one. I promise."

Ruby didn't think so. On Monday, everyone would be talking about how she peed herself in the van and splattered poo on her boots. It won't matter that the other kids got sick. No one would talk about how nice it was to arrive at a warm and cozy cabin. Because they wouldn't even notice that it was warm. They'd only notice if it was cold. Then they'd complain.

"Off you go."

"I love you, Daddy."

"I love you too, Rabbit."

—

Ruby could hear someone vomiting as she took off down the trail to the cabin. Was that Nino now too? The sky was turning indigo above the small clearing, glowing turquoise where it butted up against the snow. It was darker in the forest, with long, dull shadows lacing across the dirty trails. When the cabin came into sight, it was a dark, boxy shadow against the black. It looked scary without her father beside her. Thankfully, it had four walls, thick windows, a door, and even a little wood stove, unlike some of the other open-sided, dirt-floor cabins she and her father had hiked or skied or snowshoed to.

Ruby glanced behind her. She couldn't hear anyone coming up the trail. She stopped and found her headlamp and put it on. She hadn't realized how dark it had become until she turned it on. The light was so bright that the forest around her seemed that much darker. Before, she'd felt like she was at the front of a lineup. Like the others would be along shortly. But now she felt small and cold and alone. She hurried to the cabin and sat at the bottom of the stairs to take off her snowshoes. She was going to start the fire first, and then go to the raised outhouse, but her stomach squeezed with cramps. She barely had time to grab her stash of toilet paper and make it to the outhouse and get her pants down before letting loose a stream of diarrhea that splattered onto the pile far below.

Maybe it was her fault. Maybe she had made everyone sick.

She sat there for a long time, a quiet howl of icy wind at her bum, just to make sure that she was finished. And then she got herself dressed and made her way back to the cabin. She stood just inside the door, happy to see a giant stack of firewood along the wall. She thought of the woman who gave them candy. She tried to remember the man, but she couldn't, other than that he'd had a beard. She thought of the two of them hauling the wood in from the pile. She pulled her fire starter kit from her pack, but then didn't need it because there was a box of matches on the shelf above the plywood table, and a plastic bucket of kindling. There were a couple of empty boxes from mac and cheese, and a newspaper too, so Ruby balled up a few pages and opened the door to the stove and set them in the middle and built a teepee of kindling above it. She took a match from the box and before she struck it, she looked all around her to make sure there was nothing flammable nearby. She lit the match and let it catch and then she held it to the paper and it licked the flame and started burning and she dropped the match and shut the door just a bit, like her dad had showed her, to get the air going in. There was no window in this door, which made it hard to know what was going on. When smoke billowed out, Ruby remembered the flue. She pulled it open and the flames lit up. She sat on the floor and waited until she thought her father would add more kindling. She did that, and once that caught nicely and was burning, she put on the smallest log she could find. She left the door of the stove open a crack, just like Gus did, and then she stood up and had a look around, wondering which bunks she should take for her and her dad.

She chose the ones closest to the wood stove, and why not? She was the one making it cozy, and so she and Gus should be the warmest. She put her backpack on the bottom bunk and threw her jacket onto the top bunk, to claim it. And then she sat on the edge of the bottom bunk and heard a rumble. A low rumble. Her dad? With the sled?

She cocked her head to the sound. It was definitely coming from down the trail.

Cougar?

Wolf?

Not a river.

Not a plane.

Or maybe a plane?

A helicopter?

Ruby overturned an empty wood box and stood on it to look out the window. It was almost completely dark. The window shook. Someone had made a mobile from beer bottle caps, and it jingled against the glass. Then the whole cabin began to shake. The door to the stove swung open and Ruby could see the blazing fire within, the orange flames so bright against the dark. The emergency was the wood stove. She needed to get the door closed and latched. The cabin was made of wood, except the tin roof. It would burn down like a house in a cartoon. Columns of hungry fire and then a charred frame and then ha, ha, ha and *poof*! A pile of ashes on the ground and the roof suspended mid-air for just a second before crashing down. Just like in the cartoons.

Ruby's hands shook as she latched the wood stove door closed. Blood pounded in her head. Her throat felt dry. It was quiet again, but something really terrible had just happened. The rumble was a horrible thing, and even as she knew exactly what it was and only a little about what it meant, she didn't know anything at all, except for this stove, getting hotter, the sooty pipe creaking as it heated up. When the crackling of the fire settled into a quiet blaze, and it was the blackest night outside, and all she could hear was a mouse scurrying along a rafter, she sat on the bunk and turned off her headlamp to save the batteries and waited in the smoky dark.

———

Mike waited outside the school for Sarah to pick him up. The sky was a thin blue wash of twilight along the spine of Mount Casper, and it was so cold that when he got into the truck, the opposing heat was cloying.

"Had to shovel the breezeway roof again," he said by way of hello. "Now the contractor says he won't make it for another month."

"So much for getting what you paid for," Sarah said.

Mike turned the heat down, then the radio on. The radio news was just starting, the familiar jingle for the top of the hour. It was four o'clock. There was a shooting in Surrey. A fire in an empty factory in Vancouver's harbour. Port access would be limited for the next few hours. The opposition praised the elderly women who'd been arrested protesting the pipeline. Then the weather. Cold, cold, cold. Rain and sleet at the coast. Snow at higher elevations. Sarah turned it down low when the sports report began.

It was quiet except for the heater, and the susurrus of tires on the slushy road. Mike put his hand on her knee. She pulled up at the grocery store and ran in for a moment, but then got talking to a fellow paramedic. Mike watched them through the store's big windows, pooled in the cool glow of the fluorescent light. Sarah held a loaf of bread in one hand. A bag of carrots in the other. Mike turned up the radio. The Beatles' *Blackbird*. Luke was learning to play that on the guitar. Mike sang along now. People often told him he had a good singing voice. A parent of one of his students was the conductor of the community choir and had invited him to join as a tenor, which he was considering, except practice was Thursday evenings, and he liked to stay put once he was home from work. The street lights blinked on, and all of a sudden he could see the houses that lined the street, and the gas station beyond, and then there was Sarah coming out, smiling.

The woman only had two candies left when she and her boyfriend reached their truck. The Cayoosh van was parked at the other end of the ploughed clearing. "I like the emblem," she said. A hand with a tree growing out of it, a river circling around. "If we had kids, they'd go to a place like that, wouldn't they?" There was a Cayoosh River too. She'd noticed it a few times on their way from Lil'wat, the crossing marked by a weathered little sign at the end of each narrow bridge. When she looked it up, she learned that a white settler named it that after his horses drowned in that creek, whether that was true or not. His horses were cayuse, some of the ones caught from the wild, tamed and then traded by the Xeni Gwet'in people farther north in the Chilcotin.

As she put the candies in a cupholder on the dash, she heard a tremendous *whump*, and then a deafening rumble. The trees shook off the snow, and suddenly the pines were deep green and standing at attention, as if it were spring. She knew in an instant.

The children. The snow. The dusk.

How many candies did she hand out? Six? Seven?

Too many.

The street lights came on when Fiona parked the truck in front of the house, lighting the low cloud and the high banks of snow. Warm yellow blocks of light shone from all the homes along the street, except for hers. Fiona hadn't thought to leave any lights on, so the house was dark as she carried the groceries up the path.

She could see her own breath once she was inside, which was her own fault. She would not build a fire.

Instead, she put on her warmest sweater, Willy's scarf and one of Gus's ski hats and turned her attention to her shopping. A loaf of crusty bread, a wedge of Stilton, a jar of olives, a package of Genoa salami. A bottle of wine. A pack of cigarettes. A miniature cheesecake, glazed with garishly gelatinous red raspberry coulis.

Willy would have a meal waiting for when Fiona and Ruby arrived in London. It would be the middle of the night, and so it wouldn't be a proper sit-down meal. It might be like this, but better. All of it would be better. The bread, the olives, the salami, the wine. Even the cigarettes and the lighting. There would be no cheesecake, though. Maybe éclairs instead. Willy and Fiona had a history with éclairs, so it would be an inside joke. Éclair o'clock! They would laugh, and Ruby would yawn, and then Collette would show Ruby to the room beside hers— Ruby wouldn't *say* good night to anyone, but she'd wave, and give Fiona a hug—and then she and Willy would talk quietly even though the children were at the far end of the hall and the flat was sprawling and there was no reason to keep their voices down.

The problem was that it was too cold to *not* start a fire. Gus and Ruby wouldn't be back until tomorrow late afternoon. She would not call Mike. Maybe she had Aubrey's number somewhere?

Fiona went as far as to open the door of the wood stove. It was still warm, with a small pile of powdery embers flickering excitedly at the gust of fresh air. Kindling first. A bucket full of kindling was within arm's reach, even. Some kindling, and a small log or two. Later, a bigger log. It wasn't hard. It was stupidly easy, and yet she could not. Instead, she shut the door, put all the groceries back into the bag, and carried it upstairs and got under the covers with the bag on the bed beside her, and none of the lights on, and the cold, cold house all around her.

She needed to take her pills. But then she didn't, did she? Gus was the one who made her take them. He made her go to the psychiatrist, all the way down to the city, once a month. He drove, to make sure she actually went. He was the one who made sure that each little section of the pillbox was filled and emptied on schedule, daily. It's a deal breaker, Fiona. If you don't take them, we're done. I can't do this anymore.

We're done.

If that was in fact the case, then her obligation had surely shifted in this regard.

Fiona had such dark thoughts. And then the bright glare as everything was illuminated.

A switch. Dark. Light.

Dark.

Light.

Sometimes so bright that everything, everyone, every idea was encircled by a hot, shimmering aurora borealis of potential—she missed that so much.

She could have it back. She actually could. She and Ruby would pack for London, and Fiona would just leave out the pills. A simple omission, is all.

Fiona lit a cigarette and stayed awake just long enough to stub it out, and then she fell asleep.

—

The cabin was warm.

The forest was quiet.

Ruby turned on her headlamp and unpacked everything onto the bunk.

Her thermos of mint tea, getting cold now.

Cherry berry fruit leather.

Avalanche transceiver.

A bag of cashews.

A small notebook and a mechanical pencil.

An emergency blanket, still folded in its package.

A beeswax candle and a lighter.

A box of stormproof matches.

A bright-orange whistle.

The lanyard with her house key on it.

A bar of chocolate.

A bar of chocolate? A surprise from her dad. When did he put it in there? She would have just one bite now, and then she would wait for him and share the rest with him. She broke off a piece. As it slowly melted in her mouth, she heard someone running up the steps. They're here. It had taken them forever, but maybe it had only been a few minutes. The door opened and Liam stumbled inside, landing on all fours. He was panting and didn't get up. He stayed there heaving and retching. Was he going to barf too?

Fiona woke up to the sounds of a parade of pickup trucks racing for town. They all pulled into the seniors' centre parking lot. She could hear the doors slamming even from here. The house was colder now, infused with a creeping blue-grey dark. She was hungry, but the groceries in the plastic bag beside her didn't appeal

to her now. She folded back the covers and sat on the edge of the
bed, shivering. She wanted to be in better spirits. She wanted all
the lights on and the wood stove so hot that she could boil the
kettle on it and make herself a cup of tea. She wanted to sit on
the couch and read in the delicious silence, and then she wanted
to take a bath with a cigarette and go to bed early or late, either
one would do. Instead, she padded through the dark rooms in
her bare feet until she could hardly feel her toes for the cold. She
didn't need to pack much for their trip. She and Ruby would
need so little when they left. Just a coat, really. And boots.

Liam had not moved from all fours. He didn't get up, and he
didn't lie down. He stayed put, bawling, his head bent, snot
stringing down and pooling on the dirty floor. Ruby put another
square of chocolate in her mouth and then she knelt beside him
and offered him the bar. He sat up and batted her hand away,
sending the chocolate bar skidding under the bunk. Was he
going to barf?

He looked around. "There's nobody else here?"

Ruby shook her head.

He sprang to his feet. "Then we have to go save them!"

Ruby retrieved the chocolate bar and broke off another piece.
If her father was here, he would say you go for it, Rabbit, so you
go ahead and eat the whole bar at once if you want. Mommy isn't
here to tell us not to. Maybe just save me one bunny nibble.

"Come on!" Liam leapt to his feet. "Let's go!" He grabbed her
jacket and threw her snow pants at her. "We have to go back!"

Go back? Weren't they all on their way? Ruby got dressed as
quickly as she could and followed him outside. She hesitated on
the steps.

"There was an avalanche." Liam started to cry again. "Don't you understand, stupid? They all disappeared!"

Before, the children stood in the clearing with their backpacks at their feet, each of them with a wedge of orange in one hand and a candy in their pocket. Then a layer of hardened snow cracked ten feet below the surface and slid forward, waking up the snow that weighted it down. Both layers cleaved off the mountainside high above them. They broke up as they rumbled and tumbled down. The children watched the growing bank of snowy cloud roll over itself for several stunned seconds. Then Gus screamed *run, run, run!* The children scrambled for the trees, their snowshoes slowing them, legs akimbo with aluminum and plastic.

The backpacks sat still, obedient little colourful boulders.

When the snow settled, all of it was covered. There were no children. No backpacks. No Gus, or Luke. It was as simple as that. They were there, and then they were not. Five children, with cold feet and churning stomachs. The air had smelled of citrus and vomit, and now, moments later, it smelled of loam and pine and broken rock.

Ruby knew she needed to take her transceiver and the shovels from the cabin. The school ones, with CAYOOSH etched on the blade, were with her dad. But here were two, bright orange and folded and packed in a dairy crate that also contained a first aid kit and three foil emergency blankets. She lifted out the shovels, but then she changed her mind and grabbed the whole crate, as heavy as it was. She put it down again and handed Liam the two shovels. Her dad would need them if he couldn't find the sled and the school shovels. If anyone was buried, he and Luke would be sliding their probes down, up, down, up, down as near to the rescue signal as they could. Maybe no one was buried. Maybe Liam just got separated from the group. Maybe he had no idea what he was talking about. So there would be no one to rescue from under the snow. She and Liam would need to be rescued, or not rescued really. They'd need to be collected. This was how it would go: Luke would stay with the other kids, and Gus would come across the avalanche field to get her and Liam. But what if there was another avalanche? Maybe he'd get a helicopter.

Ruby ran ahead of Liam down the path, the crate bouncing against her thighs, the hard plastic cutting into the palms of her hands. She forgot her gloves. That was a bad thing. Someone would have a spare pair. Or she could put her dad's on, to warm up her hands.

Liam followed her, still crying, stumbling down the moonlit trail with a shovel under each arm, his boots sinking in the snow when he stepped off the worn path. He had no flashlight, no headlamp, no backpack, no snowshoes, but the low cloud had lifted, so at least it was clear. Dark and clear was better than dark and cloudy, or dark and snowing.

Ruby didn't like to think about all the equipment that Liam didn't have. His things must be on the other side of the clearing, with the sled and all the food and the other kids with their stomach cramps and diarrhea and her father and Luke figuring out how to get Ruby and Liam back.

Just before the trail opened into the clearing, an owl glided out of the trees, up and along in a long arc. Ruby stopped to watch it, silent and majestic as it lifted up towards the moon, heading for the stars. She watched it until she couldn't see it anymore, and then she turned her attention to the clearing. Liam was whimpering behind her. Where had they taken a wrong turn? This wasn't the narrow path of the creek. This wasn't where the footbridge rested under ten feet of snow, waiting for spring to let it out again. This wasn't where she and her dad had dipped their tin cups into the cold, cold water and looked up to see a mama bear and two cubs on the other side. *Hey, bear,* her father said softly. Back up, Rabbit. Easy does it. Give the whole place to the mama bear. This is her home first. Then ours.

They'd gone the wrong way. This was Liam's fault, because she knew this trail and he didn't and so it was his fault that they ended up at the wrong place, and now they were in serious danger because her father always told her to stay put. If you get lost in the woods, you stay where you are, Rabbit. You're a tree. You don't move. I'll come to you.

But Liam was pushing past her, a shovel in each hand, ready to dig. He clambered atop a fallen tree, and then jumped from it to another one. A fence of broken trees before a steep, rugged mountain of snow. This was all wrong. But then it wasn't, either, because there was a broken trail post, the orange marker a flash of colour in the moonlight.

Ruby was suddenly electric with fear.

"Daddy!" she yelled. "DADDY!"

Liam froze. He turned and looked at her, his expression tightening into another sob. He squeezed his eyes shut and shook his head hard and fast before opening them again and glaring at her.

"Come on!" He wedged both shovels under one arm and reached out a hand so that she could pass him up the crate. He set it on a branch of a fallen tree, but it slid off and crashed down into deep blackness, and then it was just the two of them standing at the top of what used to be a smooth white meadow but was now snow upon snow upon snow, dirty white boulders of it piled atop each other, and a black slash of broken forest on each side.

Ruby turned on her transceiver. A staccato of beeps cut the cold silence. She scrambled up onto the white scree and headed for the closest signal, the beeps speeding up as she crawled on all fours, her hands shrinking and stiffening in the cold. She was on top of a signal now. The constant beeping ran together in her ears, one long scream swinging from her neck as she dug, her fingers numb. The snow was hard, and her shoulders ached. When she stopped to catch her breath, she looked around for Liam. She didn't see him, and she didn't see him, but then she did. He was standing still, a tiny, dark statue staring up at the field of snowy rubble and the mountain beyond it. The shovel lay at his feet. His face was lit enough that Ruby could see he was glaring at the mountain just as he'd glared at her.

She started digging again, but she couldn't feel her fingers. The beeping was ceaseless. She could feel it in her teeth. She fumbled the shovel, and when she tried to pick it up again, she simply couldn't. It lay on the snow, bright orange and cheerful against the white. She pulled her arms up into her coat to warm up her hands. She thought about the tiny bones in the pouch around her father's neck. That wasn't the only time he got frostbite. It's not the worst thing, he said. The worst thing would be dying. What's a little frostbite compared to that?

Ruby appraised the hole that she'd managed to dig. It was big enough to curl up in, maybe. Somewhere under there, straight down, was a warm rabbit warren like the one she and her father had carved in her snow cave. One of the children could be down there. Rabbits plucked their own softest fur, tucking it all around with the leaves and grass. They might have a fireplace, and a kettle hanging on a hook, like the one in her cave. Two armchairs carved from snow and a tiny cherry pie. Who was down there? Who was sitting by the fire with a blanket over his lap? Shane or Nino or Luke or Tag? Or was it Anna, or Skye? Or maybe all of them, sitting around the little table with mugs of hot cocoa and a plate of cookies. The rabbits would fuss over them. We never have guests! Let me find another chair. Let me pour you some more cocoa. Would you love some of these tiny marshmallows? Would you like another cookie? Can we get you anything at all? We might be down here together for a frightfully long time.

There was the owl again, swooping overhead. And the moon, hanging low and fat. And two children standing still. And the beeping, beeping, beeping, beeping, and the creaking and scraping as the snow shifted and packed down harder and harder as the night stretched out ahead of them, the indigo sky dappled with stars.

Fiona woke again when her phone rang. There were three missed calls from a number she didn't recognize, and this one from Mike. She did not pick up. He hadn't called her in over a year, and now he was calling her when Gus was away, and Ruby too.

She silenced the call and drifted back to sleep. The phone rang again, and she ignored it. It rang again, and again. Mike, Mike, Mike. And then it rang a fourth time.

Sarah.

Had he told her? Had she found their emails? There'd only been a few. Fiona had deleted them on her end, and had assumed that he'd deleted hers. They'd only texted a handful of times. Erase them, Mike told her, unkindly. So, he must have too, right?

Or he wanted to come over. He'd made some excuse to get out of the house and he was going to come over. Let him. She wouldn't answer the door. Or she would answer the door.

She turned her phone off and fell back to sleep almost immediately.

She woke up moments later, or hours later, to a pounding on the front door. Blue-and-red lights wound around and around the bedroom walls. The bag of groceries had overturned on the quilt and the olives had leaked. The room smelled of brine, and the salami, sweaty and folded in its waxed paper.

"Mrs. Tenner!"

She went to the window, pulling the curtains apart just enough to see a constable down below, looking up at the dark house. If she didn't turn on the light, he would think she wasn't home. If she slid back into bed and waited for him to leave, he would leave. And then she would shut her eyes and the blue-and-red lights would still be flashing and she would hear his pounding until she knew what he was there for. But she didn't want to know, and so why should she go down and open the door and find out? It would not be good. It would be bad, and why would she want to hear a bad thing? Why now? Why not later, in the flat grey light of dawn or the bright blue-sky blaze bouncing off the snowbanks? Why not wait for the light to shore her up? Why would she want to know now, when whatever the awful thing was could be illuminated by light instead of told to her in the black of night? Knowing in the light would spread the bad thing away from her. It would thin it out. Knowing now would hold it close around her, pinning her limbs against her body, pressing against her throat. Suffocating her.

If she opened the door and he spoke the words now, she would suffocate. The house was cold. Her bed was warm. The night was long enough as it was. There was no reason to turn on the lamp beside the bed, or the light in the hall, or the porch light outside. It would all stay dark, and he would drive away, and in this manner the issue was decided.

Only it wasn't, because the front door was unlocked, and the cop came right in, stomping up the stairs with snow staying frozen on his boots, because it was that cold in the house.

"There's an avalanche," he said. "Up where Gus and the kids are. You need to come with me. I'll take you to the other parents."

They were fine, of course. A mother doesn't lose a child this way. A husband and wife don't separate like this. This is not what anyone meant.

"I need a moment," she said. Ruby was so good outdoors, she probably rode the snow like she was surfing a beautiful wave, like Gus taught them. *Swim in it. Keep your head up.* Of course she was okay. She was absolutely fine.

The officer went downstairs so she could change her clothes. She'd slept in all those layers and was damp and cold with sweat and smelled of olives and salami and sharp cheese. She pulled down her pants and kicked them away from her. She stood there, not sure what to put on. What was the dress code for a tragedy like this? A tragedy that will pull the whole town, the valley, the mountain itself, into a dark, bottomless hole with sharp teeth angled inward, barring any escape. She took off the shirt, and then her bra and panties, and for a brief moment she was standing there naked and covered in goosebumps before she opened the drawer and pulled out a pair of emerald green satin panties edged with lace, and a bra to match.

Fiona went to the closet and fingered the hangers: a tunic, a tunic, a long grey sweater, a button-down shirt in periwinkle, a pair of jeans, another tunic, leggings, leggings, leggings. She wanted a fitted dress, something with a zipper up the back, in a brilliant colour. Fuchsia so vibrant it would attract humming-birds, a buttery yellow, apple green. Something you'd wear in spring. Clothes a person would never wear if something terri-ble was happening. The dress she put on was Ruby's favourite. Robin's egg blue with a pattern of leaves so tiny they looked like polka dots. Sweater, jacket, toque, snow boots from where she'd kicked them off earlier.

Ruby needed to go back to the cabin. The beeping-beeping-beep-ing that used to be a sound outside her head was now inside her head, and it made her want to throw up. She was getting sleepy and starting to feel warm. She took off her coat, then felt a sud-den surge of panic. She remembered a story her father told her about a skier who got lost out of bounds. When they found him, he was slumped—naked and dead—against a tree trunk not far from a sign that would've led him back to the groomed trail.

Naked, her dad explained, because when you become hypo-thermic, your body gets confused and you start to think that you're warm even though you're just about to freeze to death. That skier had taken off every last bit of clothing except for his socks and his boots. He'd hung each piece neatly on the branches of the tree above him, like so many colourful flags. That's how they spotted him from the helicopter. They saw his neon-green ski jacket, and then his bright-blue pants. Lastly, his legs sticking out from under the lowest branches, blanched and still.

Where was Liam?

She couldn't see him.

He needed to come with her.

She scrambled over a mound of snow and spotted him digging.

When she reached him, she took his hand and pulled him away from the hole. He'd dug down to his knees, chipping at the hard snow.

"Let go!" He twisted his arm out of her grip. "We have to get them out."

No they didn't. Her dad would take care of that.

And there was no rush, either. The ones under the snow were in a warren, being kept warm by a tangle of soft brown rabbits. They had a fire. And hot chocolate. The rabbits were looking after them.

She turned off her transceiver, but she could still hear the beeping, incessant and piercing. Her ears rang with it, and with the cold.

Liam let her switch off his transceiver too, and pull him behind her, over the rubble and over the tangle of fallen trees and back to the cabin, which was still warm. Ruby opened the door of the wood stove and slid in two more logs. She left the cast-iron door open, to light the room by the flames. Liam was cast in shadow, shivering and holding his hands out. His nails were painted black, which surprised her. Ruby broke the rest of the chocolate bar in two. Liam stuffed his half into his mouth, his teeth chattering as he tried to chew. Ruby offered him her thermos of cold tea. He drank it all in three big swallows, and then handed it back to her, chocolate still stuck in his teeth.

"Sorry."

Ruby wasn't thirsty anyway. She pulled two overturned crates up to the fire. She sat and waited for Liam to sit too. When he did, she pulled out the candy from the woman on the trail. Liam fished his out of his pocket too. They unwrapped them and popped them into their mouths. The caramel was a hard, smooth, sweet, small thing. As she was sucking it, she heard Liam crunch his, and then she heard the familiar dull *whop whop whop* of a helicopter overheard. Liam leapt to his feet. He ran outside and was hollering and screaming. I'm here! We're here! Help!

Ruby just sat by the fire. A smooth, hard, sweet thing. Smooth. Hard. Sweet.

Stay put, her father said. Stay put and I'll find you.

AFTER

Ruby heard the helicopter land. After the rotors fell silent, she heard shouting. Her father would be in charge of the rescue. He'd come for her when everyone else was safe. This is what he did, so he would be the leader. He was the one who knew the most about everything in the wilderness. He knew more than anyone, and he was teaching her, which is why he let her go ahead to start the fire. He trusted her. And she had made a good fire and so he was right to send her ahead. The cabin was warm and ready, and when the other children came, they would need to take off their clothes, which would be funny. But you always take off wet clothes if you don't want to get hypothermia. Get right down to the nakey-nakey, he said. And then put dry clothes on and get warm. If they found the packs, their spare clothes would be okay. Because imagining them all naked, standing around the stove, was really funny, and nothing should be funny. Not right then. Not about this. This was not funny. She had to stifle a giggle. Luke and Anna and Skye and Nino and Liam and Tag and Shane, all naked. Shane! Naked. And, well, she'd seen Liam naked already.

It didn't matter, she realized.

There would be blankets in the helicopter. And foil emergency blankets too. She should go get those and bring them back here. This could be SAR base. It was warm and dry. Anna was allergic to wool. Were the SAR blankets wool? She would give Shane his last. That's what happens when you're mean. You get the emergency blanket last. And the last square of chocolate. But then she remembered that she and Liam already finished the chocolate. Her father had more. He always had a bar in his pack. Chocolate is everything, he said. It fuels your body, and it tastes good, and it makes you feel better. It raises morale, he said. He noted her quizzical expression. Lifts your spirits, he said. Makes people cheerful. If you're lost, or cold, or you have a blister. Chocolate, Rabbit. Chocolate makes everything better, even for just a moment or two. Same with a candle. A little tiny light, a little tiny bite. Does wonders when everything else is going down the drain.

The door flung open and a man Ruby had never seen in her life came striding across the cabin towards her.

"You're a sight for sore eyes!" he bellowed. Cold air swirled around him, and suddenly Ruby's ears were ringing, the transceiver noise a constant high, thin sound, like when her mother sometimes drew her finger around and around the edge of her wineglass.

"Are you okay?"

He was enormous and entirely clad in snow gear, right down to a balaclava. He took it off and squatted in front of her, with an expression like he was in pain, even if he seemed fine. He ripped off his gloves and grabbed her shoulders and looked into her face with bright-blue eyes and snot dripping at the end of his nose. His cheeks were damp with sweat and he was talking; his breath smelled of garlic and beer. He ran his hands down her arms, checking her to see if she was hurt. Ruby wanted him to put his gloves back on and his balaclava and go back out into the night and leave her alone. Her father would come get her when it was time to go home. Not this man. Not this stranger who was running his hands all over her now as the ringing in her ears grew louder. Lifting her hands and squeezing her arms and legs and circling her waist with his hands.

He sat back on his haunches for a moment. He was explaining something. What was he saying? She could only make out a few words behind the ringing.

"Let's get you to the helicopter." He picked up her coat and shoved her arms into it. He zipped it up, but she wrested herself away and unzipped it and threw it to the floor. The man looked around and spotted her pack. "This it? You want to take this?" He stuffed everything into it, hooked it on his arm and then reached for her hand. "Good to go."

Ruby shook her head. Not without her father.

He said, "Fuck, kid," and lifted her up and carried her. No one but her father carried her like that. Ruby twisted and kicked. She punched his arm and then his side as he hauled her out of the cabin. He set her down on the porch to try to get the coat on her again, but she dashed past him and back inside. She ran to the bunk and wrapped her arms around the post.

The man wasn't saying anything now. He glared at her as he easily pulled her away from the bed. She fought him while he put on her coat, but he won. He zipped it up and pulled the hood over her head and then he picked her up and flung her over his shoulder and carried her and her backpack out of the cabin and into the night. Ruby kicked him, and pummelled his back. Through the ringing in her ears Ruby could hear another helicopter. The first one, leaving? Another one, coming?

Then she went limp, as if she'd been unplugged. But the ringing got louder.

"Kid?" He set her down. "You okay?"

Ruby stood in the snow. The ringing. And shouting. The staccato of shovels stabbing the snow. The beeping again.

The man held out his hand. "Ready?"

Ruby nodded.

"You're not going to bolt?"

She took his hand and they walked down the trail. He helped her over the tangle of fallen trees and up the steep cliff of rough snow. At the top, a dozen people were digging around four probes. A dozen more walked in a row, sliding their probes in and out of the snow. A generator rumbled, and lights glared down on the snow from telescopic poles.

Someone was running over. Someone was picking her up. Someone was carrying her to the helicopter. Someone was putting a blanket around her. It smelled of wool and dirt. Liam was beside her, bent over with the blanket right up over his head, like a cloak. He looked like a wizard or a beggar. He was sobbing, with snot and tears running down his face and dripping off his chin. The engine roared. The rotors shuddered and then spun lazily at first, and then faster and faster. Liam wiped his face with the blanket and looked at her. "I couldn't find anyone. I couldn't find them. I was digging and digging and I only found a glove." He shuffled under the blanket and stuck out his hand. He was wearing it. The glove was pink, with a silver snowflake on the back.

"Was this Anna's?" Liam put his hand right up into her face. "Was this Anna's or Skye's? Do you remember who was wearing this?"

The RCMP officer could not—or would not—tell Fiona anything other than the school group had been in an avalanche.

"What about Ruby Tenner?" she said from the passenger seat. This is all she'd said since getting dressed. *Ruby Tenner. Gus Tenner. Ruby. Gus. Ruby. Ruby.*

He drove her to the seniors' centre and walked her in. She let him, because she wasn't sure what else to do. She glanced down at her right hand, fully expecting to see Ruby, holding on to it. She glanced to her left, at the officer, and saw Gus, eyeing her critically, silently instructing her to hold it together.

Mike and Sarah stood in the middle of the room, awash in cold yellow fluorescent light, made worse by the even colder and mismatched yellow paint on the walls.

Fiona's ears rang. The ringing got louder as Mike approached her.

"Ruby?" Fiona said. When he didn't say anything, she said it again, louder. "Ruby!"

"We don't know." Mike pulled her into a hug. Sarah joined him, sandwiching her. "Search and rescue is up there now."

"We haven't heard about any of them. A skier called it in."

Sarah was still hugging her, even though Mike had pulled away. She pressed her cheek to Fiona's. Her breath smelled of hummus. "They should've been at the cabin hours ago. The cabin would've been safe. I'm sure everyone is okay."

"The timing doesn't make any sense," Mike whispered.

Fiona noticed Shane's parents next. He called the taller one Mom. Moe was quite beefy and masculine-presenting, in the way that Fiona was often attracted to. She was the photographer. Elise—Shane called her Mama—was the gestator, so to speak. She was tiny, fine-boned, and hardly looked up to the task, but she'd just given birth to Shane's sister a few months earlier. The baby was secured and asleep in a colourful wrap arranged so deftly around Elise's small figure that it reminded Fiona of how she never got the hang of those wraps. She'd given up and used a strapped carrier for Ruby. This marvel of dexterity did seem befitting of a yoga instructor who got invited all over the world to teach.

Moe stood at the folding table with a coffee urn, another urn with hot water, a box of sugar cubes and a plastic bowl filled with coffee creamer. A stack of paper cups. She had scaled Everest twice. And Manaslu and Annapurna and Mount McKinley. This woman had trekked through Nepal and Albania and was the parent of one mean little bully and, the most hopeful thing of all, a brand new baby. She took two paper cups and let the rust-coloured coffee fill each one. She looked around for a spoon for the creamer, but when she didn't find one, she abandoned the cups and returned to her wife, who sat on one of the two chairs nearest the window, the baby at her breast now. They looked out, up at Mount Casper, even though it was just a darker shape against the prevailing night.

Sarah steered Fiona to a couch. She sat beside her, thigh to thigh, a hand on her knee, as if she was not directly involved in this tragedy. As if her boys weren't up there too.

"Liam?" Fiona said. "Luke?"

"They're with the others," Sarah said, as if that would make any difference.

"What if they almost find Ruby," Fiona said, "and they're calling her name and she won't call back?"

"They'll find her."

"They will. Of course they will. Excuse me."

The lights buzzed louder as Fiona stood. She was going to go to the coffee table, where a volunteer had added hot chocolate sachets, a tea sampler and a mug of spoons, but she veered towards the hallway and she locked herself in the bathroom at its far end.

She sat on the toilet and peed, resting her head against the wood panelling. She heard a helicopter overhead. The main door opened and closed, opened and closed. All the heavy winter boots clomping across the floor, and the accompanying male voices of the search managers, trying to keep it down.

Eventually there was a knock at the door.

"Are you okay in there?" It sounded like Sarah, but with a thicker voice, stopped up with fear and uncertainty.

"Is there any news?"

"Open the door?" When Fiona didn't, Sarah kept talking. "They're bringing Liam and Ruby down."

"Is she okay? How is Liam?"

"They're safe," Sarah said. "They're taking them to the clinic. Everyone is going over there, even though it's just Ruby and Liam so far, and the helicopter hasn't landed yet."

"Did you hear me?" Sarah said. "She's okay, Fiona! Come out. We'll go together."

Fiona covered her face with her hands and wept. Her shoulders shook. The tears soaked her cheeks and palms and ran down her chin and neck and soaked the front of her dress too. More tears slid down her wrists, wetting the loose cotton cuffs.

On the other side of the door, Sarah sighed. "Well, come or don't come. You know where we'll be."

Fiona did want to come, but she could not move from the toilet, where her dress was gathered up around her waist and her panties strangled her knees. She wiped her face with toilet paper, tried to arrange her limbs, new to her in this role of mother of child who has survived an avalanche that killed other parents' children. She wasn't sure how to stand up, even. If one leg should still follow the other, or if there was a way of walking she had yet to learn.

She would go to Ruby, but first she had to get out of this room, out of this building, and find one of the SAR people to drive her across the village. Correction, she did not want a ride. She would run. She would run there.

The paramedic told Ruby that the helicopter was landing behind her school, but it landed in the field behind the public school, not Cayoosh. There was a field at Cayoosh, but it was small and wild, and lined with tall pines. There was no playground. The forest is our playground, Mike said. The backcountry is our recess. The playground at the public school was brand new.

A paramedic lifted Liam out first, then Ruby. There was a stretcher waiting for each of them, which was good, because she'd worried about sharing with Liam. Mount Casper Elementary had a merry-go-round and a jungle gym with two red slides side by side, like a giant forked tongue. Monkey bars. A climbing wall. They had a climbing wall at Cayoosh too. The one at Cayoosh was way better.

The inside of the ambulance was brightly lit. Was this Sarah's ambulance? Where was Sarah? Ruby didn't recognize the woman murmuring to her as the driver shut the doors and they pulled away. She was different from the one in the helicopter. How are you feeling, honey? Are you in any pain? Frostbite, I bet? Were you buried? Can you talk to me?

Buried?

Ruby shook her head.

The tea party with the rabbits. Tiny nut cakes with sugar roses on top. Little crustless sandwiches and a fire in the pot-belly stove. The kettle would still be hot.

It was a short ride to the clinic. Someone had tacked posters on the ceiling on the way in. Something to look at while you lay there. Cats, unicorns, a poster of Mount Casper at sunset. Ruby kept her eyes on those. Anna's mother reached out and took her wrist.

"Did you see her?"

Shane's big mom leaned over her, her face so blotchy with tears that one dripped right on her cheek.

"Excuse us." The paramedics steered the stretcher through the emergency room doors.

"Did you see Shane?" Moe called after her.

The doors wheezed shut. The paramedics lifted her onto a bed and then the man left right away, taking the stretcher with him. The woman lingered for a moment, one hand muffling her radio. With the other, she pushed Ruby's bangs out of the way, and then she kissed her on the forehead and smiled and patted her arm and told her she'd check in on her when she came back with the other children.

Ruby watched her go. The ringing in her ears stopped. She caught a glimpse of Liam in the next bed, then a nurse pulled the curtain. Liam had looked at her, like he might say something, but then Ruby was staring at the blue-checked curtain and her nurse was peeling off Ruby's clothes and helping her into a gown and saying things like, Do you have any allergies to medication? Do you have any medical conditions? Asthma, maybe? How are you feeling, Ruby? Any numbness or tingling anywhere? I'll get you a warm blanket. Did you know that we have a blanket warmer? That's it right over there in the corner. Wouldn't it be nice to have one of those in your house?

A big metal box with two doors, like a fridge.

We keep blankets up top, and saline down below. Do you know what saline is?

Ruby shook her head. The nurse popped a thermometer in her mouth.

Close your lips around that, hon.

When it beeped, the nurse looked at the number. You're perfect, she said. Absolutely perfect. No warm saline for you. I'll get you a warmed blanket, sweetheart. I'll be right back.

The other nurse rolled a machine towards Liam's bed. She pulled the curtain back. Liam was staring at the ceiling. When the nurse drew away the blanket, Ruby caught a glimpse of him naked. He glanced over at her. There was his small penis resting between his skinny, pale legs, and he didn't care that she was looking at it. It didn't matter. Ruby lifted her hand to wave, but she just kept it in the air for a few seconds. He did too, the one with the glove. Then the doctor and nurse unrolled a puffy white sheet over him. It was connected to the machine by a hose, like a dryer hose. As it inflated, the doctor turned a knob on the machine. Ruby's nurse went to the warmer and collected a bag of saline while the other nurse held Liam's arm tight and stuck him with a needle.

He didn't even wince.

He kept his eyes locked on Ruby's as the nurse set up the IV and started the drip.

Then the nurses were gone, and the doctor too. Someone was screaming in the foyer. Someone was crying. And someone else was yelling. Screaming and crying and yelling.

Ruby hopped off the bed and, with the blanket wrapped around her, shuffled over to Liam. She pulled a chair up to the bedrail and kneeled on it so she was eye level with him. The machine hummed.

"It's warm under here," Liam slurred.

Ruby slid a hand out from under her blanket and under the puffy sheet. It was warm. She reached in farther. There was Liam's side. His hip. His stomach. Smooth and soft. Ruby left her hand there, palm flat on his skin.

More commotion in the foyer. This time, angry yelling. A scuffle of some kind, and then one of the nurses speaking firmly, and then softly, and then Mike's voice.

"My parents," Liam whispered.

Ruby pulled her hand away.

The door wheezed open and Mike and Sarah ran across the room. Ruby could see them coming through the gap in the curtain. Mike flung the curtain aside and for a moment he and Sarah stood there, not sure who would go first, but it was just a second. Just one second, and then they were both reaching for Liam. They touched him all over, just like the man had touched Ruby in the cabin. Shoulders before elbows, elbows down to wrists. Sarah touched each fingertip on one hand, but Liam wouldn't let her take the pink glove off his other hand.

Sarah wept, her nose swollen and dripping. Mike put a hand to Liam's cheek and leaned over the bed.

"What a terrible thing, Liam."

Liam's eyes were heavy. "I tried to dig him out."

"I know you did. I bet you were digging so hard."

And then Sarah noticed Ruby there, a heap of blanket with her small blond head sticking out.

"Ruby, honey," she said. "Oh, Ruby."

Mike picked her up, blanket and all, and cradled her in his arms like she was a baby. He sat on the edge of the bed with her and started to cry. His shoulders heaved as he curled over her, his tears splashing onto her face. He wiped them away, but it would've been okay if he hadn't. It would've been okay.

Fiona walked in on this, Mike crying with her daughter in his arms. Comfort he was not entitled to.

"Ruby," she said.

Ruby reached for her. She was too big for Fiona to cradle in her arms, but she did it anyway, using a strength she knew was limited. Mike set a chair beside her, but she did not sit. In fact, she could get home with this strength. Ruby cried into her neck, making her collar even more wet. Silent tears, eyes squeezed shut. This child needed to go home. This strange emergency strength was actually growing. She was certain that she could make it all the way home carrying her like this, at a run.

"Thank you, everyone." She headed for the door.

"You can't just go!" Sarah said.

"Fiona, sit." Mike chased her with the chair, but she ran faster. The strength God gave three mothers to lift an eighty-foot fallen tree off a Brownie pack on a backcountry hike, a toppled vending machine off a small child in an airport, or, more locally, to swim against the current in the Lil'wat River to snatch a toddler who'd fallen in while picking blackberries along the shore. Hysterical strength, it was called. She could feel it boiling her blood.

"Nurse!" Sarah yelled. "She's leaving with her daughter!"

Mike blocked the door.

The nurse studied Fiona for a moment, staring her right in the eyes, long enough for Fiona to put together a firm and fierce gaze back. She said, "Tell me why I shouldn't take her home."

The nurse put her hand up when Sarah made protesting noises.

"You'll bring her back in the morning?"

"I'll stay up with her all night."

"If you take her, it will be against medical advice," the nurse said. "You'll have to sign on that."

"She wasn't even *in* the fucking avalanche!" Fiona adjusted Ruby in her arms and marched past the other parents, all silently watching. Through the automatic doors, still shouting. "I'm not signing any fucking papers. Nothing happened to her!"

The beeping sped up as they approached the far corner of the debris field. Three rescuers slid their probes down, down, gently down until one resisted. They dug carefully and swiftly and found Nino's left hand first. Fingernails too long, the cuff of his down jacket pushed up to his elbow. A bloody scrape on his wrist. They kept digging gently, along his arm and the bunched-up jacket, and away from it too, looking for the rest of him. He'd been reaching up. Or had he? Was this just the way the avalanche had left him? His arm above him, fingertips pointing skyward. But he was looking down. Black hair in his face. Cheeks as white as skim milk, and cold. Someone said leave him. Leave him, there's nothing we can do except dig for the others. Someone turned off the transceiver around Nino's neck and put a yellow tarp over him and the hole he was reaching up out of.

Then came joyful hollering, a little way away in the shadows cast by the lights.

"He's alive!"

"Over here!"

The paramedics rushed over with their kit and oxygen tank, volunteers sliding behind them with the stretcher baskets piled high with blankets.

Luke blinked slowly, his eyelashes crusted with ice. He was pale as Nino, but tiny breaths clouded in front of him. Just small puffs, cool and insufficient. A paramedic slid an oxygen mask over his head, adjusting it above his ears. The plastic fogged up. Luke was trying to say something.

The rescuers worked to untangle him from a puzzle of branches and snow and dirt.

"Anna?"

"Do you know where she is?"

"I have her," Luke slurred.

"Luke," someone said. "You don't have her. You're all alone here, buddy."

Another voice: "We'll get you out. Hang tight. It's going to be okay. Give us five minutes and you'll be on the helicopter. We'll get you out of here. Think warm thoughts."

Which was just so stupid.

"I have Anna with me." Luke groaned. "I'm holding her hand."

And the thing was, he was holding her hand. As they pulled away cedar branches and knots of dirt and snow, there she was, her hand in his, her torso between two skinny lengths of pine. One pink glove with a silver snowflake on the back. The other hand mid-grasp and naked. A green bandage on her thumb, dotted with smiling monsters. No glasses. A plastic rainbow bracelet on her wrist. *Best Friends.*

They pulled him out and they pulled her out too.

"Is she okay?"

Swiftly, they cut off his cold, wet clothes and laid a sheet of warm packs over him, and a foil emergency blanket, and one of the search and rescue grey wool blankets, and a dry, slouchy hat on his head. He was being lifted up, men on four corners, a paramedic running beside him carrying the oxygen tank. She was saying, "Bring the girl. Keep working on her! Bring the girl!"

Luke looked up at the paramedic. He knew her. She looked frantic and terrified, like she was the one running from the avalanche.

"Don't leave Anna," he whispered, but she didn't hear.

Bring her. Because he'd been holding her hand, Luke thought. Because they found her with him. Because even as the snow had hit him from behind and knocked him down and he'd let go of her for just a moment, in the very next moment he was upon her, smashing down on her, and he'd said sorry, in that tiny second that he had, when he knew what was happening, and everything that he needed to do, and so he reached out and grabbed her wrist, and when the crashing stopped and his ears were ringing with how loud it all was, she slid her hand into his and held on like that.

Bumping along. Voices loud. Beeping, beeping, beeping. It was a wonderful sound and it was a terrible sound. How many hadn't they found yet?

"Dig!" he tried to yell. "Keep digging!"

But it was muffled under the mask and the generator and the deep-black night overhead and the depth of stars above that. He knew what he was looking at. He knew those stars, but he couldn't think at the moment. Right now, he had no idea.

The paramedic didn't know that Anna's back was broken. When they didn't rush her to the helicopter, she looked up from squatting beside Luke, an IV catheter in hand, and saw them lay out her body beside another one. They'd gone back to dig out the boy? Or was this a third victim? Two yellow tarps on the brightly lit snow.

The rotor started a lazy circle, then went faster and faster. Someone yelled, "The tarps!" But it was too late. The rotor wash blew the tarps into the trees as the helicopter lifted up. It wasn't the boy who'd been reaching up; it was another girl, wearing only a T-shirt and panties and no boots, as if she was just getting ready for bed. As if she were about to change into her pyjamas.

The paramedic knew Luke, and she knew that child too. Skye Bellamy. The daughter of a friend. The last time she'd seen Skye, she'd been sitting in the front seat of her mother's van at the gas station. She had a book in her lap, a stuffed animal in the crook of her arm. A purple plastic bracelet on her wrist. *Best Friends*.

She wanted to jump out of the helicopter and lift Skye into her arms and breathe for her for as long as it took to get her colour back. She could breathe for her forever. She could carry on like that for years and years, if at the end it would mean Skye would breathe for herself again. If it would mean that her cheeks would pink up and she would blink open her eyes and laugh.

The helicopter lifted away.

"Let's get you to your parents," she said.

"The kids?" Luke said, more clearly now. "Gus?"

"Let's get you off this mountain."

Luke closed his eyes. For a moment, the paramedic thought he was sleeping. But then he opened them, and they were puddled with tears. He reached up and pulled the mask off his face.

"I don't want this."

He kicked off the blankets and the warming sheet.

He wanted to be breathless and cold. He wanted everything to be emptied out of him, permanently.

By the time the sun rose, there were four small bodies resting side by side under yellow tarps on the snow. Nino, Anna, Tag, Skye. A new contingent of rescuers from North Vancouver had relieved the locals and were now doing a grid search of the field in a line, two feet from each other, sliding probes down into the snow and feeling no resistance, save for a tree or rock. There was no more beeping. About an hour before, they'd dug out a fifth transceiver, but just the transceiver. No body. No person.

They were looking for Shane, and they were looking for Gus. Slowly and methodically, because the rush was over. Everyone knew that the rush was over. It was a new day, crisply bright. Everyone wore sunglasses to cut the glare of the sun on the snow. The generator still hummed, the lights were off, and SAR command was still in the parking lot and here too, with a folding table, binders and clipboards, a laminated topographical map, and a bank of radios, charging. There was a carafe of coffee and a stack of paper cups. Packets of cream and sugar. Skinny wooden stir sticks. A tray of doughnuts from the bakery at the grocery store. A box of mandarin oranges. Someone was eating a cruller. The avalanche risk was low. It was a terrible, beautiful day in the narrow, snow-swollen valley.

—

Fiona had carried Ruby straight up the stairs and set her in her and Gus's bed. She pushed aside the groceries and stripped off the duvet with the brine stain. Ruby stayed curled up, as she'd been in Fiona's arms. Her eyes were closed, but Fiona knew that she wasn't sleeping. She was taking herself away, like she used to do when she was a toddler and became overwhelmed at loud birthday parties or stores with too many things crowding racks and shelves under humming fluorescent lights.

"I bet you're cold." Fiona pulled all the blankets out of the wardrobe and layered them over Ruby. "I am. Silly Mummy wearing a dress and no tights. I'll be right back." She went to Ruby's room and got her blankets, and downstairs to collect the ones from the couch, and lastly to the basement to find as many sleeping bags as she could, which was a lot. Six altogether, plus a camp quilt and three packages of foil emergency blankets from the survival pack that was supposed to be in Gus's truck.

She hauled all this upstairs and layered it on top of Ruby, who still hadn't moved or opened her eyes. Blanket after quilt after tacky crocheted throw from Gus's mother after blanket and sleeping bag and foil layers in between.

"Cozy?"

Ruby didn't move.

Fiona went downstairs and found every candle she could, and a box of matches. She set the candles on a plate and lit them all. Not too close to the bed, but enough to make a barrier of warmth in between the window and where Ruby's head rested on Gus's pillow. The frost on the inside of the window began to thin, so she knew it was making a difference.

This business about the furnace was madness. She pulled out her phone and called the sat phone to tell Gus exactly that.

No answer.

No matter. Gus would be back and the first thing they would argue about would be the furnace. And then they could go downhill from there and undo whatever was left, because most of it was already undone before he took the children up the mountain.

And now this.

She dialed him again. Just the very remote-sounding tone of no connection.

She sat beside Ruby and put the phone in her lap. She put her hand on Ruby's forehead. She was warm. Just right.

This was Gus's side of the bed. Two milk crates secured by zap straps was his table, a coffee table book leveling the surface so his lamp wouldn't tip over. *Dutch Windmills*, a gift from his mother after a painting holiday there two summers ago, just when she was getting to be more forgetful than her friends, and didn't paint one windmill herself, confused about how to put a painting together.

Fiona glanced at Ruby. Her face had relaxed. She was sleeping now.

Fiona knelt on the floor and began emptying the two crates. Mountain sport magazines, several unread books, a box of condoms with just two left. Nail clippers, a notebook and pen, drawings by Ruby, a few of her books. His *Star Wars* lunchbox from when he was a kid that he used for special things. She knew what was inside it.

Everything Ruby. Still, she opened it, sorting through her funny drawings and her first attempt at printing her name, and his. And a few letters from his mother, which she hadn't known were in there. Probably sweet recollections about Ruby before the Alzheimer's took hold. She unfolded one. Dated two years ago. They'd come for Easter, and also to see Ruby and Fiona off on what was supposed to be a two-week visit to England that had turned into six weeks. This was written shortly after their return.

Dear sweet boy,
Thank goodness they are both home safe and sound. You know I worry about you and Ruby, and now this trip is another reason to worry. What if she simply hadn't come back? What if next time she doesn't? I cannot imagine what an international custody battle would look like. Imagine, little Ruby over there, with only Fiona. And not speaking.
She needs help, Gus. Supports. Resources. A proper school, perhaps. It's good to hear you talk about leaving Fiona, and while I know that it upsets your father, I do think it's best—

Fiona leaned back against the bed. The floor was so cold that her legs felt apart from her. Or maybe they actually were. Maybe this letter, written in sharp, slicing retired-schoolteacher cursive, had actually cut her off at the waist. Maybe she was bleeding out right now, all over the floor, and Ruby would wake to find a dead mother, just as Fiona herself had when she was eight.

The SAR manager had said that the avalanche happened between the creek bed and the bridge, like she'd know exactly where that was.

The creek bed and the bridge? *Did* she know it?

No, but she could imagine a creek bed. She could imagine a bridge.

Downstairs, someone let themselves in.

If it was Gus, he could come up and find them. But as soon as she heard the heavy steps, she knew it was Mike.

He said, "You know Shane?" His voice was thick.

Fiona nodded.

Anna and Skye and Nino and Tag and Shane.

"I just had his moms in last week." Mike rubbed his face with a hand. "I got frustrated and called him a bully. I actually used that word. I was at my wits' end with him, but I shouldn't have used that word. And now I can't take it back." He sucked back a big breath and began to weep.

"They still haven't found him?"

"Shane? No."

"Gus?"

He shook his head and cried harder. Fiona got up, unsure about her legs, and then pleased that she could walk to him, take his hand and lead him to Ruby's room. She sat on the bed while he tried to find somewhere to stand. The ceiling sloped to the window, and the floor was a mess of Lego and books and art supplies. He was too big for the room. Too tall and broad, too hefty, too hairy, with his lumberjack beard.

Fiona remembered running her hands down his carpeted back in Sayulita and coming away with her palms wet with sweat. He hadn't seemed too big in that room, with its vaulted ceilings and whitewashed walls. Here, he was the entirety of the outside coming in—mountains and trees and rivers and sky. He sat on the bed beside her and it creaked in protest. He was so much bigger than Gus. He smelled of body odour, and an oily, earthy scent. Luke smelled like that too. Would Liam? Did little boys become bigger boys and then men who carry the musk of their father?

But Mike wasn't Luke's father. Not really.

"Will they find Gus?"

"Not alive," he said. "No."

"But they might?"

"Not alive," he said again. His voice caught. "Him or Shane."

"What if they were just swept away?" Fiona said. "What if they're alive?"

"No." Mike picked up the stuffed rabbit that Gus gave Ruby. "He's gone. Shane is gone. They're all gone."

Fiona wished she could touch his lips and tuck back in all the things he was saying. This wasn't like Mike, to be completely void of hope.

"They'll find him," she said. "They'll find him and they will find Shane."

"You don't even sound like you believe that." Now there was an edge to his voice. "*Search* and *rescue* are suggestions. Not guarantees."

"They'll find them." Fiona said the things she wanted to hear from Mike. "They know what they're doing. They know where they *are*. The general area, at least. They won't stop looking until they find them."

"I can't believe any of this." Mike hugged the rabbit. "I cannot believe that Ruby has lost him. That we've all lost him, but Ruby especially. That could ruin her."

"I remember being so sad when my mother died," Fiona said. "And I did feel different from the other kids. Immediately."

"I doubt you were ever like the other kids," Mike said.

"Everything changed when she died."

"But it's different when you expect it," Mike said. "Your mom had cancer."

"She hung herself, actually." Fiona inhaled, catching her breath and holding it long enough to feel faint. "I was the one who found her."

"That's terrible," Mike said. "Truly, Fiona. Gus never said."

"I never told him." Fiona shook her head. "He would've just blamed my mental illness on her. I didn't want that. My mum was a beautiful, generous and very funny woman. And so kind. Polite too, very proper, even though we ate baked beans on toast three times a week."

"And now you've made this about you," Mike said. "Again."

"She always wrote thank-you notes on perfumed paper, like we were rich." Fiona reached for a small framed picture of her mother in big glasses and a perm. Ruby had taken this from her own bedside, years before. "This is her."

"This isn't the conversation we started." Mike stood up. "I'm sorry that your mother killed herself, but this is not about you right now. It's about Ruby, and Gus, and Luke and Liam, and the other children who I cannot name right now because if I do, I will collapse and not be able to get up, walk down the stairs and drive away from you. This is not about you. Not eight-year-old Fiona. Not your dead mother. Someday, when this is easier to talk about, you and I can sit together and I'll tell you how worried Gus was for you, and how it broke his heart over and over whenever you fell apart."

"She didn't kill herself."

"She did? Or she did not?"

"She couldn't stay anymore," Fiona said. "That's all."

Mike stepped into the hall but turned away from the stairs and went into her and Gus's room instead.

Fiona called after him, "What are you doing?"

"Ruby is spending the night at our house." He said this so plainly that Fiona almost nodded. But then she got up and rushed past him. She bent over Ruby, whose eyes were still closed.

"Call the clinic," he said. "Your choice. We watch her for the night or she goes back to the clinic with the social worker."

"I didn't see Emháka there." Fiona straightened.

"She was in the family room," Mike said. "With the other parents. Which is where she should be focusing her time."

"I agree!" Fiona flung her arms out. "The nurse said it was fine."

"She didn't say it was fine. She said it was against medical advice. And she regretted giving you even sort of permission as soon as you took Ruby out of there." He pulled back bunches of blankets and foil at a time, peeling and peeling away until Ruby was revealed to be a very small, sweaty ball, curled up with her finger in her mouth. "She was going to send the police. And Emháka."

"You can't take her." Fiona grabbed his arm with both her hands and squeezed tight. He twisted away easily. "I'll tell. I'll tell Sarah everything."

Mike ignored her. "Hey, Rubes," he said as he lifted her into his arms. "You awake?"

"She's not."

Ruby opened her eyes.

"Hey, hey, hey," Fiona said. "Let's put you to bed in your room? Or do you want to sleep here with Mummy?"

"I call the police or I take her to our place," Mike said.

Fiona considered this for less than a minute. She ran down the hall for the rabbit and tucked it in the curled-up sadness that was Ruby. "Take your rabbit with you, okay?"

Ruby nodded.

"This is just for the rest of tonight," Fiona said, crowding Mike as he carried Ruby down the stairs.

Mike set her down and helped her on with her coat and boots. She put on her backpack.

"You don't need that, baby. You're only going for a few hours," Fiona said. Ruby twisted away. "Okay, take it. It's just a few hours. It'll go by fast because you'll be asleep, and then I will be there. I love you."

"Try to get some rest." Mike picked Ruby up again. "The helicopter will go up again at first light, if it's clear."

"I'll come get you—" Fiona's voice caught. She stood on tippytoe to kiss her daughter on the cheek. "I'll come get you first thing in the morning. I'll be there before you even wake up."

Mike set up a camping mattress beside Liam's bed. Liam was already asleep. He looked sweaty, like he'd just run around the field three times.

"Sarah and I and the doctor decided it was best to bring him home and keep an eye on him here," Mike said. "Your mother wasn't wrong. She just went about it the wrong way, that's all."

Mike reached for Liam's dresser and tugged out mismatching pyjamas from the bottom drawer.

"Bathroom first?"

Ruby shook her head. She put her arms up, like a baby. He helped her get changed.

Then he said good night, and that if she needed something, it was just him, because Sarah was at the hospital with Luke.

"You know where my room is," he said. "I don't think I'll sleep a wink, but you come wake me up if you need me. We'll get your mom sorted out in the morning."

Mike said it like *mawm*. Not like the flower, which is how her family said it. *Mum*. Even if her mother was the only one who spelled it with a *u*.

Liam's room was dark except for the spinning night light, a little box with stars cut out of blue Cellophane. The box spun slowly around the light bulb, dappling the snowboard posters and Lego figures and the basketball hoop on the back of the door and boxes of cars on top of the low shelves with stars.

Her mother was not there when she woke up. Sarah came home from the hospital while Ruby was in the bathroom. She and Mike made a stack of sandwiches, and then he headed off to the hospital. Sarah called Ruby's mother a few times. She didn't answer.

"I'll try her again later." Sarah slipped her phone into her pocket. "She probably finally fell asleep. Let's let her rest for a bit? Okay?"

Ruby nodded.

"Do you want some breakfast?"

Ruby shook her head, and then she nodded. She meant *no*, she couldn't imagine eating anything ever again so long as she lived, even to one hundred and ten years old. She also meant *yes*, please, give me everything to eat, right now, because I am starving and could eat a dozen hamburgers stacked up like the caps in the children's book with the mischievous monkeys. Sarah brought an armload of cereal boxes to the table. Ruby ate three Luke-sized bowlfuls, a full two and a half bowls more than she ever had eaten before.

Ruby was just finishing her third bowl of forbidden-at-home sugary cereal when her mother banged on the front door. Ruby hadn't been able to think about anything other than whatever she was looking at, so she was thinking about the fridge, and the pictures and artwork and grocery receipts and bills and a dried rose tied with a piece of ribbon and flea medicine for Ophelia held up by a magnet clip with a grinning dog's face and a bow tie instead of a collar. On top of the fridge was a stack of dusty baskets and a row of grimy vases and one of those little balsam airplanes you build from flat pieces, a slingshot and a set of walkie-talkies. The last few things were up there because when Sarah or Mike took stuff away from Liam for time outs, that's where they put it. Not for very long. Just long enough to make him feel sorry if he didn't already and then they'd give it back. Ruby's father never took anything away from her. He only gave her things—

"Ruby!" The outline of her mother's head appeared in the little frosted kitchen window.

"I'll let her in," Sarah said. "Okay?"

When Ruby didn't reply, Liam hollered from the living room, where he was playing video games.

"Want me to let her in, Mom?"

"I will." Sarah squatted in front of Ruby. "Do you want me to?"

Ruby nodded.

"Sarah, oh my goodness." Her mother pulled Sarah into a hug. "I'm so glad that your boys are okay."

She touched Ruby's face, and then rubbed her arms, up and down, before gripping her shoulders so tightly that Ruby flinched.

"Sorry, sorry." Her mother relaxed her grip. "You've got Liam's clothes on, of course. Look at you, comfy as comfy gets, right? Grey sweatpants." Fiona named each piece. "White T-shirt with a snowboarder silhouette. Socks?"

Ruby showed her the too-big wool socks.

"He's got such big feet now," Sarah said. "I looked around for a pair of Aubrey's, but I couldn't find any."

"Do you want a sweater?" Fiona said. "I brought you the one with the fuzzy rabbit on the front."

Ruby shook her head.

"But look." Fiona dug in her big purse. "It'd be so warm."

Sarah leaned against the counter. "I offered her a sweatshirt, but she didn't want it."

The grey sweatshirt hung from the chair. Ruby took it now and put it on, leaving the hood up.

"There," Sarah said. "You'll be warmer now."

Her mother held up the sweater. It was raspberry red, with rolled cuffs, and the rabbit was white angora, with a pink bow at its throat. Willy had sent it for Christmas. "What about this one? Wouldn't you like to wear it instead? You look like an escaped convict."

Ruby lifted the spoon out of the bowl, soggy flakes dripping off it. She let it drop back in, under the island of mush, down to the tepid milk.

Sarah took the bowl away and stood there with it for a moment, looking at Ruby's mother like she was waiting for something. She kept staring at her until Fiona lifted Ruby from the chair and sat herself on it with Ruby sideways on her lap, her feet dangling in Liam's wool socks, grey with white-and-red stripes at the top, the same kind her dad was wearing, up there on the mountain. Wool was good for the cold, and for the wet. His feet would be toasty warm, while he found his way home.

She hopped off her mother's lap, shrugged on her backpack and shoved her feet into her boots—tight because of Liam's big socks—and beckoned for her mom to join her. Ruby had to go home and get a few things, and then she would go find search and rescue and get them to take her up there with them. If she went up there, her father would know she was there and would come to her.

He had been alone for less than twenty-four hours. Ruby was absolutely certain he was waiting exactly wherever the avalanche had carried him. He might've surfed it. Or at least kept enough of himself above it, swimming in it, like he taught her to do. He might be injured, but that's okay. If he couldn't start a fire, he'd be keeping himself warm under cedar boughs until he heard the searchers' whistles. He had a really good emergency blanket. Not just foil, but bright orange on one side. Anyone would see that from the sky. It was big enough for him and Shane. He'd have Shane safe and sound under the bright orange, under the boughs, like a papa goose. Unless they got separated in the avalanche and then maybe Shane was alive somewhere else. Or he might be dead, because even if he went camping in the snow with his moms sometimes, being out in the wilderness alone is very different. Not like it looks as a picture hanging on the wall, when everyone is happy and the sky is blue and there is so much hot chocolate in the thermos that it seems like it will never run out.

Their breath puffed out in front of them. Fiona tried to hurry Ruby along the shovelled sidewalks, but Ruby moved like a robot, each booted footstep loud and clunky.

"I didn't bring the truck because I thought you could use some fresh air. Also, I didn't have time to clear the snow off. It's a nice day, though. I didn't think to bring sunglasses. So much winter sun on all this snow. It'll be a good day for the searchers. I've got a good feeling about today. Do you?"

Ruby nodded.

"Good. Positive thinking leads to positive outcomes," Fiona said, not believing one word of it. "Let's get you home. I'll run you a bath. Would you like bubbles? Or some Epsom salts? You like those." Willy had sent Ruby the rose bath salts for Christmas, in the same package as the sweater. Everything in that box smelled like roses, even the book she'd sent Gus about the Franklin expedition—*Frostbite! Starvation! Cannibalism! Dreadfully exciting. xo, Willy.*

Gus didn't read books. The ones he stacked beside his bed? Never cracked, even though each one of them was about something he'd be fascinated with. Everest. Missing hikers on the Pacific Crest Trail. Grizzly attacks in Kamchatka. He hadn't read a single book in all the years Fiona had been with him. She couldn't imagine life without at least two books on the go at the same time and a tower of them waiting to be read. Not a single book. This should've been a clue.

The first gift she'd given him was a book. After Willy and the others reluctantly left Fiona behind and returned to England, Fiona stayed with Gus in the two-bedroom basement suite of Mike and Sarah's place. Gus had five roommates to split the exorbitant resort-town rent: two Australian brothers, and three best friends from Quebec who came to work and ski for the season. The low-ceilinged suite was always too hot because the forced air was controlled by Sarah and Mike upstairs, who kept it very warm once Liam was born. When you added the constant heap of damp, sweaty gear, it was almost muggy, and always chaotic, and messy. After the brothers got into a fist fight that resulted in two broken noses and a busted coffee table, Fiona made a joke about *The Lord of the Flies,* and when she found out that none of them had read it, she bought a copy for Gus. In the end, it was the other five who read it. She wondered if Gus had a learning disability, but over time she realized that he just really hated reading. When she and Gus moved to Casper—followed shortly by Mike and Sarah when she transferred to the Casper station—he left the book behind, which hurt her feelings more than she cared to admit.

Suddenly, Fiona realized that if Gus was dead, the year-count would end here, measured from just before *The Lord of the Flies* to now.

Right here.

Nine years and nine months.

Nine years last April. No matter how many years slid by from now on, that number would never change. It was a different kind of finality than she might've felt if he'd actually left her. Leaving her would've been an insult, not an ending. A thing committed upon her. Imagine they find him up there today, which was entirely possible: he would come down and be in hospital and maybe even profess a renewed love for her. More than likely not, though. He would be sweet to Fiona, and want Ruby by his side, but this would never be a cute human-interest story about the marriage that was dead until the husband almost died in a terrible tragedy that claimed the lives of five beautiful children but restored the love he had for his wife.

Marriage over, duration nine years three-quarters, if you count from when they met. It was never official. No shotgun wedding, no courthouse, no rings or vows. But a marriage, nonetheless. One that could not be retroactively salvaged by an unexpected tragedy.

She wanted to say something to Ruby about Gus. Are you scared? Are you sad? I'm so sorry. This is a terrible thing. What had her father said to her when her mother died? *Don't look! Come away from there, Fiona! For Christ sakes, Noreen, ring for the ambulance! Ah, you stupid woman, Cathleen!* He held her legs up, hugging her shit-stained feet and crying, until the police came and led him out of the room.

Take the girl away! the constable bellowed at Aunt Noreen. Why haven't you? He pushed Fiona into the hall and slammed the door.

She and her aunt stood in the dim hall, listening to Fiona's father wailing. A cylinder of pallid sun from the ox-eye window in the stairwell lit the far end, the dust motes churning lazily. What a shock, Noreen said. We've all had a terrible shock, haven't we? I'll run you a bath, love. Scrub it off and get yourself dressed. We'll have lots of company and I don't want you smelling like the privy. Fiona realized her hands were brown with shit.

"What a shock," she said. Fiona knelt down and put her hands on Ruby's cheeks. "We've all had a terrible shock, haven't we?"

Ruby nodded. Then she hugged Fiona so tight, and for so long, that when she finally let go, Fiona fell back on her bum. She pulled Ruby onto her lap, no matter the icy sidewalk.

"This is the worst thing," Fiona said. "Nothing will ever be as terrible as this." This was meant to be a comfort. This was the thing Fiona had wanted her father to say to her that day, when the funeral home porters, dressed all in white with starched creases on their pants, wheeled her mother's body into the street, zipped in a bag made from stiff burgundy vinyl, belted onto an aluminium gurney that collapsed so they could slide it right into the back of the van.

It was not the worst day. They would find her father. Also, it was too cold to be sitting on the sidewalk, and people were standing at the windows of the houses Ruby could see, watching them. One of them was on the phone, staring right at Ruby. When Ruby tried to get up, her mother held her tighter, until a van rumbled by slowly, tires crackling on the salted road. The van had all kinds of poles and boxes and antennas on the roof, and bright lettering on the side. CTV NEWS. Her mother leapt up, sending Ruby tumbling.

"Shit." Fiona took her hand and pulled her up. "Let's go." She hurried, too fast for Ruby. She kept tripping on her boots stuffed with Liam's socks, quickly bunching up at her toes.

That van had something to do with the avalanche. Ruby was even more certain when her mother pulled her onto their block and Ruby could see straight down Portage Road, all the way past the tracks to the seniors' centre and the fire hall at the base of the hill. There was the new fluorescent-green SAR truck, and the fire trucks too. The CTV van parked in front of another van with the same kind of robot stuff on top. CBC NEWS. The second van had a pole that went up, up, up with a satellite dish at the top, and a small, spinning something, glinting in the sun. Fiona knew the CBC. It was the only radio station her mother listened to in the kitchen. She liked the classical music, but also the news at the top and "bottom of the hour," a phrase that made her and her father laugh.

Ruby wrestled her hand free and started running, her pack bouncing against her hips.

"Ruby!"

They would know something. The news people. The SAR people. That's where she should go. Maybe the helicopter hadn't left yet. She got half a block before her mother caught up with her, only because of those stupid socks.

—

Fiona settled Ruby on the couch and went upstairs to run her a bath. Ruby sat there for a moment, staring at the milky window, frosted on the inside, the house was so cold. But as soon as she heard the pipes creaking, she ran downstairs to the laundry and pulled out her warmest dirty clothes and layered up as best as she could and grabbed her pack—it still had everything she needed, including her father's good luck charm—and slipped out the back door and ran.

She would wait at her snow cave. If she couldn't get up there, she would just have to wait for SAR to find him. Maybe she should've left a note, but he would know where she was, even without. He told her once that if her mother was sick, or needed help, to run to Sarah and Mike's, because he knew she wouldn't speak to a 911 operator. Still, he told her, if you dial it and don't say anything, they'll come. But if you need ... He closed his eyes tight, looking for the right word. But if you need *help* with something about Mommy, go to Sarah and Mike's. And if you can't go there, meet me at the snow cave. Even if it's the middle of summer. This is our spot. We can build a fort. We can hang a hammock in the spring.

As the steam from the bath rolled out into the cold hall, Fiona called and called and called for Ruby, but the house rang empty. She hadn't expected an answer, but maybe she'd hear her footsteps. When she didn't, she thought that Ruby might've fallen asleep on the couch. Fiona would lay a blanket over her and sit with Ruby's head in her lap while the bathwater turned cold. She would sit beside the child who had not died and watch her breathe in and out and she would be thankful. She wouldn't think of Gus. She would only think of Ruby, and how they would get away from here on that plane in nine days. They would go, and never come back to this awful town and that murderous mountain.

To begin with, comfort a grieving child.

The couch was empty, though, the afghan pooled in one corner, a throw pillow on the floor, a book splayed open on one arm.

No Ruby.

There was no point in looking for her. She was at her cave, and Fiona had no idea where it was.

The steam smelled of roses. The bathwater seared her frozen feet as she stepped into it. There was a vase stuffed with them, sitting on the corner of the tub. She reached to take one into the bath with her, to pluck each petal and set it afloat like a tiny red raft, but now there were no roses. No vase. It was a hallucination, but seeing as there was no one there to witness the discord between her perception and truth, it wasn't really anything but a disappointment to find that she couldn't touch the roses and wonder who had sent them.

The helicopter squatted in the middle of the field at the elementary school like a frozen black monster. Ruby wanted to watch it, wait for it to *do* something, but it was too cold, and it had started to snow, tiny flakes like an icy mist.

In the cave, Ruby lit one of the thick, short survival candles that burned for three hours. She opened an energy bar and ate it.

It's important to never get hungry when you're out in the bush, Rabbit. Always have something in your pocket. Don't wait too long. If you feel hungry, you've waited too long. Had the three gigantic bowls of cereal really happened? She was so hungry. She had waited too long.

It was getting dark out now. The snow thickened into fat flakes. When she left, it would be deep and soft on the ground. It would be up to her ankles atop the old snow. It would be powdery and sweet, and everything would look fresh and new and lit by the moon. It was a wicked trick that nature played, making her think that everything was quiet and beautiful.

The entrance to the cave was a raft of cedar boughs bound together with twine. More like a lid. She pulled it away and held the candle up. Snow fell over itself to get in. The flame flickered, and then extinguished. She would have to go home. She would have to go, because everyone would be worrying about her, and that would be awful, when they were already worried that Shane and her father were still up on the mountain. That's who they should be worrying about. Not her. Not even the dead ones. When you're dead, no one needs to worry about where you are anymore.

She left the candle in the snow cave and took the garbage from the energy bar with her. She put on her headlamp to see in the deep-blue dusk and the forest dark and started for home. At one point she looked back and had to search to find the entrance to the cave. The new snow had topped everything, but there it was, darker against the white. Ruby turned and went on her way. She would always know where it was. And so would her father. He could meet her there, if he didn't want to go home. If he thought her mother would be mad at him for—

For what?

That morning a million days ago when it was time to leave, Ruby came down the stairs and they were already arguing. It wasn't even daytime. It wasn't even nighttime either. It was just a dark in-between.

The papers are on the table.

I'm not signing them.

Why not, Gus? It's a holiday. Just a holiday. I'm not taking her away.

Her mother was at the back door. She'd just come in? Or just gone out? No cigarette. Pink cheeks.

Sign them. Let Ruby have a bit of fun. Get her away from this little town stuck in the mountains. Let me show her some of the world.

It's not like she's never left this place. She's a well-travelled kid. She's been to England three times!

They never ask to see these papers anyway. It's a formality. Besides, you'll let her go, Gus. Right? You won't punish Ruby by not letting her go.

Maybe. He'd nodded, but to himself. He kept nodding as he leaned over the table with the pen in his hand. He signed the papers.

He said something as he set the pen down.

What? Her mother stepped closer.

Sometimes I think I hate you.

Gus—

He sucked back a big sob and hugged her. Really hugged her. I'm sorry, Fiona. I'm so sorry.

She kissed him, long enough that Ruby felt a kind of sour tingle in her belly.

Sometimes I think I might hate you too, Fiona said.

—

Sometimes he didn't come home. Before. Sometimes he stayed at Mike and Sarah's. Sometimes he stayed at the store on a blow-up mattress in the backroom. He took Ruby with him a couple of times. The first was when her mother pulled everything out of every closet and screamed at them both to make up their minds about the crap they wanted to keep because the house was too small for all this shit.

Gus held Ruby to him, his hands firm on her shoulders. Stop, Fiona. Just stop for a minute.

But she'd kept flinging things at them. Jackets and tennis rackets, a deflated soccer ball, a plastic grocery bag full of mittens and gloves.

These don't even have pairs!

Was that when he told her to go get a clean pair of underwear and pyjamas? They stayed at the store that night, the two of them on the air bed. They watched funny videos on his phone. Cats falling off things. People falling off things. And a video of animals being rescued: A dog beaten up and abandoned in a ditch, another dog hauled up by climbers after it fell off a cliff. A cat cut out of a drainpipe. A shivering, exhausted dog lifted from an ice floe, hauled onto a boat by a man wearing a thick red suit. He looked like Santa. And the last one, a truck backing up to a dumpster at the edge of the woods, with a woman holding a ladder.

Watch this, her dad said. Ruby looked up at him then and saw that he was crying. Watch this one, he said. It's really good.

The woman slid the ladder into the dumpster and then the truck peeled away so fast that she almost toppled over. A mama bear bounded out of the woods, and then one by one, three tiny bear cubs climbed up the ladder. The mama waited for them to run into the trees ahead of her, and then she swung her head over her shoulder and looked at whoever was filming before she galloped after her cubs.

Maybe she's saying thank you, her father said.

Ruby thought that maybe he was right, but maybe he was wrong. She had another feeling too, some kind of anger towards the mother bear. She didn't understand why she was so angry at that stupid bear. That stupid bear who couldn't get her own babies out of a stupid garbage can. She took Gus's phone and found another video. Cats in boxes. She laughed and laughed, because when she laughed, Gus did too, and she liked to hear him laugh.

Fiona should phone Mike and ask him to go into the forest. Or maybe Luke knew, if Gus had told him, or even shown him. He was so proud of it. But then what? Mike would go get her and drag her home and as soon as her back was turned—or not even—Ruby would bolt out the door again, so it made more sense to leave her be. Leave her alone. She was not a child who wanted to be held in any way right now.

Not Ruby.

She always wanted space. Distance. Enough room to get away in an instant. Out of reach. At the edge. Never coming closer. Come give Mummy a kiss. Her arms open, her toddler wandering off. Come back, Ruby! When she was not even in school. And then when she was. Don't go away. Stay inside for a few minutes. Sit with me.

Don't push her, Fiona.

I never push her.

You do. *Say something, Ruby. Tell me one thing about your day. Come here and sit with me. Why won't you sit with me? Why won't you talk to me?*

Gus did such a good impression of her, right down to the accent. Fiona hated it.

He wouldn't be making any mean impressions of her now, would he?

That is a horrible thing to think, Fiona. Just horrible.

Think of what you should be doing, if you are not going to look for your small, devastated child in the cold, dark night. What will you say to the social worker if she comes calling? Oh, don't be ridiculous, she has all those dead children and their families to manage. Two from her own community, so that will most certainly keep her off my back.

Fiona should take something to the families, gathered at the seniors' centre again today, to support each other and especially Shane's family. Were they waiting for Gus too? That thought had not occurred to her, but it helped. It meant she would be welcome there. She was one of them. And if she ran into Emháka Joseph, the social worker, there, she'll tell her that Ruby is with Sarah or Mike or Aubrey or whoever isn't at the centre, or asleep in the truck, utterly beat from the excitement, poor thing. What could she take to show her sympathy without seeming to be boasting about her child not being dead?

She could make cookies. Or muffins. Why not both?

She hurried down the stairs and flung open the cupboard doors. Flour, baking soda, baking powder, oatmeal, chocolate chips, and the butter in the owl-shaped ceramic keeper Aunt Noreen sent her for her birthday one year. *It looks so odd in the cupboard,* she wrote in the thank-you card, *so delicate and pretty beside all the ugly things.* She set it down, lined up all the ingredients. Oatmeal chocolate chip cookies and blueberry muffins. She ran downstairs to the chest freezer. She pulled everything out until she found the blueberries and she didn't put anything back, leaving it in a sweating, cold pile on the concrete floor. There simply wasn't time. A plastic bag of blueberries that Gus and Ruby had picked in the summer. Wild ones, tiny and sweet. Gus and Ruby had eaten them in handfuls, until Fiona took them away to freeze. We'll want them in the winter, she said. When everything at the grocery store is dull and has no taste and costs a fortune. Here we are now. Fiona held up the bag of frosted jewels. Ta-da! Colour, in the deepest slate grey of winter.

She took the bag upstairs and dumped the berries into a bowl. She didn't need a recipe. She made cookies and muffins often enough. One or the other in Ruby's lunch every day. Her phone buzzed across the counter. Willy. Fiona declined the call. She did not have time to talk to Willy right now.

While the cookies cooled and the muffins baked, Fiona wrote down the names of the children and their parents. She flipped through the Cayoosh directory. Shane, she could remember him because he was the bully. Liam, of course—but he was fine, so that didn't matter—and who else, Skye and Anna who were not Ruby's best friends. And never would be now. Fiona stifled a laugh. So much for that. Anna's brother who? She found Anna's name, and below her, Tag. Right, the one Shane sometimes referred to as Label. And Nino, that little boy with the single dad. The handsome, sad farmer whose wife died all of a sudden when Nino was a baby. He was in the crib, asleep, while she mixed bleach and ammonia to clean the bathtub and died right there on the bathroom floor. Now his son was dead too. What would he do? How could he do anything? Maybe he would sit in his barn or on his porch or in his truck and just watch the sun rise and set over Mount Casper until he was frozen solid. Or maybe he would plant strawberries and not let anyone pick them just so he could smell something sweet on the warm wind that swept down the valley on summer nights. Something to push away the stench of death. A dead wife. A dead son. And in such unlikely ways. If it was her, she would think she was cursed. Fiona bristled. She *was* cursed. They were all cursed. What difference did one dead wife make?

She wrote the names onto an index card and slipped it into her purse.

Shane. Skye, Anna. Tag. Nino.

The timer on the oven chimed.

The muffins were sunken in the middle, and rock-hard at the edges. No clue what that was about, but they were ruined. There were plenty of berries. No matter, scrape them into a pan and leave them, maybe she could toast the mess and turn it into granola. "Muffin Bite Granola." She could market that. She might. When she had a minute, she'd look online and see about copyrighting the name. Actually, she had a minute now, didn't she? Where was her computer? She ran into the living room, then back, because of course the recipe was on the computer, which was on the counter. Well, that minute was gone now.

She mixed another batch, concentrating hard on following the recipe this time.

While she waited for the muffins to bake, she took off her sweater. This project was making the house a tiny bit warm. Why hadn't she thought of that before? Keep the oven on, the door cracked. It wasn't gas, so no one could accuse her of trying to kill herself or Ruby.

When the timer sounded, she pulled the muffins out and overturned the pan onto the cooling racks. What a mess. Fiona set them upright and in order. She'd have to wait for them to cool. She stared at them, poking them every once in a while to see if they were ready. She recited the names of the children in her head. It would not do to forget one.

Shane, Skye, Anna, Tag, Nino.

Shane, Skye, Anna, Tag, Nino.

When the muffins were cool enough, she put them into a basket lined with a linen dishcloth. She put the cookies into her best tin—from Rifle Paper, of all things, rich pink roses on a black background, and she didn't even mind if she didn't get it back. Such things simply do not matter at a time like this. Where was Gus? Had they found him yet? It was awful, just awful.

She braced herself against the counter. What if they found him alive and all this time she's been thinking that he's dead? She'd have to rearrange everything in her head to make space for him to come back. She'd have to take care of him, and of course, she would. She would nurse him back to health and wait however long was necessary so that she could leave and no one would call her a bitch for it. If he left, even right away, no one would blame him. He was everyone's favourite. *Is* everyone's favourite? If he makes it down the mountain, his darling status will skyrocket, even higher than when he brought the medal home from the Olympics.

She never fit in here.

She saw Willy leaning on the counter by the stove. You never tried to fit in here, did you?

"I did so," Fiona said. "Look at all of this beautiful baking."

Willy didn't know what she was talking about.

Fiona went upstairs to put on just a little makeup. Tasteful. Respectful. The kind a wife bothers with when her husband is lost on the mountain. She'd leave her hair as it was, in the casual ponytail she'd done that morning. She couldn't look too put together. Of course she couldn't. She couldn't look proud and she couldn't act boastful. She couldn't be the relieved mother and the grieving wife at the same time. She'd have to be somewhere in the subdued and silent space in between.

When she arrived at the seniors' centre, all the news cameras turned on her. But she'd come from behind the building, knowing full well they were there.

"Have to be quicker than that!" she said.

No one was at the door, and so the cameras kept filming while she tried to balance the cookie tin on her knee and pull the handle. The tin fell and the lid popped off, so she had to set everything down to scoop the cookies back into the tin, snow and grit and all.

"Good grief!" she said when she managed to get the door closed behind her. "Hello. Hello, everyone."

She smiled, and hoped it was sympathetic and empathetic at the same time. Mike came forward and ushered her farther into the room. Someone took her coat and hung it up on one of those mobile racks, like the ones they had in the church basement when she was a little girl.

"I've brought muffins," she whispered. And then she said again, louder, "I've brought blueberry muffins and oatmeal chocolate chip cookies!"

She went around the room. There was Nino's father, and Skye's parents, and Shane's mothers, with the baby asleep with her head on Moe's shoulder. Fiona hesitated in front of them, holding out the basket and tin. "Have one, please. In a hard time, it's very important to eat. To maintain your energy." Both women glared at her, refusing the cookies and muffins, Moe wrapping the arm not holding the baby protectively around her wife's shoulders. They didn't like each other, Mike told her once. Isn't that what he said? Shane's family is going through a hard time. Moe has a temper, and everyone is tired with the new baby, and so we have to be understanding about where Shane gets this behaviour. "I see you're supporting each other," Fiona said. "This is good. In hard times, we need each other. No matter our usual feelings. Failings. I guess I mean both, really."

Why weren't they saying anything to her? They had this in common, this terrible thing. Gus was lost. Gus was dead. Was he dead? She spun to look at Mike.

"Do we know? Do we know that Gus is dead now?"

"Come sit down, Fiona." Mike reached out, but of course he didn't mean for her to take his hand. "Come sit down over here." He gestured to a seat away from the other parents. Why would he do that?

"In a minute." She still had to offer Anna and Tag's parents cookies and muffins. "I am so sorry for your loss," she said. And then she remembered that there were two children and so she should say *losses*. "For your losses, plural." She held out the basket with the muffins, the tin sitting along her arm. "Please, take one. It's so important to eat."

The mother—Fiona had no idea what her name was and couldn't very well look at the index card now—silently took a muffin. The father shook his head, his eyes moist, cheeks burnished red.

"I should've brought napkins too. I'm so sorry." The twins' mother stared at her. Was that about the napkins?

"Come, sit." Mike was at her side, his hand on her arm.

Desirée! That was it. Desirée and Dan. "Desirée, Dan, please accept my condolences." Mike gripped her arm.

"I am so sorry about Anna and Label."

Desirée looked up, confused.

"Tag!" Fiona shouted, but Dan had heard. He glared at her as he stood up.

"What did you say?"

"Tag," Fiona whispered. "I'm so sorry."

"You called him Label."

"Danny, please." His wife took his wrist. "Please don't."

"Everyone is upset," Mike said. "She needs to sit. Fiona, you need to sit."

"Not anywhere near us," Dan growled. He did not sit down.

"I don't need to sit."

"You *do*," Mike said.

He led her across the room with a firm hand at her back, and an elbow too when she tried to twist away, to a chair in the hall beside the bathroom.

"Apologize!" Dan roared behind her. "Come back here and say his name correctly."

She tried to stand, but Mike's hands on her shoulders were heavy.

"Let me go," she said. Then, "You're hurting me!"

Mike sighed. "Stop, Fiona."

"Oh, don't sound like such a defeated king. I am a free member of the realm." She returned to the sad lineup of parents, slumped and folded and spent, all save for Dan, standing tall and furious and red in the face. She stopped in front of him and said, carefully and clearly, "I am so very sorry for the loss of your two beautiful children, Anna and Tag. I misspoke. I'm upset. We all are."

Dan received the words, and did sit down, so Fiona took that as a kind of forgiveness.

She put the lid on the tin. She would place them on the table with the plates of sandwiches and the tray from Valley Foods with its sad, sweating cheese and rolled-up deli meats, stacked like logs. They could help themselves.

"What is that?" Moe said.

"What?" Fiona hadn't said anything. "Are you speaking to me?"

"What the fuck does that say?"

"I'm sorry, what are referring to?"

"The lid on the fucking cookie tin." Moe threw a paper cup, hitting the tin square on.

"There's no need to swear." Fiona glanced down at the tin. What was wrong with it? Mike took the tin from her, turning it away from the parents. "What's the matter? I don't understand."

"Read what it says on the fucking tin," Moe said. "Out loud."

Such pretty, curling letters, surrounded by roses. "Stop and smell the roses?"

"Stop and smell the roses." Moe handed the baby to Elise and stood up, glaring down at her. Fiona shrank. Her skin loosened, her teeth started to shift in her mouth. "You bring a cookie tin that says *stop and smell the roses* to a room full of parents whose children have just died? Our children are *dead*. You cannot understand what's happening to us. You can't!"

Elise was up now too, and Dan and Desirée. All arms and pats and gripping shoulders and moving in closer to each other like it was a stage direction. Did they know each other? Fiona was confused. Had she organized the parents correctly? Yes, Elise was Shane's mother. And Moe. That little shit's mothers. A dead little shit is still a little shit.

A smash, and she was reeling backwards. The basket of muffins emptied onto the scuffed linoleum floor. The cookie tin landed with a metallic thud. That was Moe. Now Elise gave the baby to Moe and slapped Fiona, hard across the cheek. The rest of them towered over her, yelling, but she'd shrunk so much by now that she was level with Mike's boot and their voices were tiny, indecipherable shrieks.

"Get up," Mike said.

"What did she hit me for?"

"*A dead little shit*? You fucking bitch!" The baby wailed as Elise shouted. Moe held her back with one arm, the baby safe in the other. "You fucking cunt!"

"Little baby has big ears," Fiona said. "Everything you say matters."

"Get her out of here, Mike." The look on Moe's face was clear: if he didn't get her gone, she would.

Mike pulled Fiona up and pushed her into the coat racks. She stumbled and landed under the musty, woodsmoke-smelling apparel. She reached a hand out.

"Get up yourself."

She turned on her knees, her ass to him. She had to bite her lip not to say something about him coming in her ass. She would not say it. She wouldn't. She felt herself growing back into her skin, her teeth settling, her hands big enough to push through the door.

"Go home," he said. "Don't come back."

"This place is for me too." As she stood, Fiona managed to let just those words out. The compulsion to bark out the inventory of their night together was painful to hold back. "While my daughter was asleep in the other room and his wife was at the pub." She said it quietly.

"Here?" Mike's eyes widened. *"Now?"*

Fiona put her fingers to her lips and squeezed them shut.

"This is *Gus's* fault!" Elise screamed from the other side of the room. "You're not welcome here! You're not one of us! It's his fault."

"Don't come back." Mike led her to the door and waited for her to go through. When she had, he leaned out of the building, gripping the door jamb. "And don't pull your bullshit with me. I know more about you than you think I do. Remember that."

He tried to slam the door shut, but the hydraulic arm slowed it down.

"I don't understand what's happening."

"None of us do, Fiona. But some of us are trying to keep our shit together."

"Have you ever been the wife of a man who is still under the snow? The wife of the man who took those children into the woods? Am I a widow?"

"Probably." He hung his head then and lifted it a long moment later. "But you are also the mother of a little girl who just lost her father."

"I know that."

The door was almost closed, but now he swung it open again.

There it was, a sudden realization on his face. She wasn't the only one having those over the last couple of days.

"Where is she?" he said.

"At home."

"By herself?"

"Of course not." The cold, dark house. Had she come back yet? "Of course I didn't leave her alone."

"Who did you leave her with?" Ruby, who'd never been looked after by anyone other than Mike's family, including Aubrey.

"It's none of your business."

"She's at home alone, isn't she?"

"I just told you that she's not alone." Fiona pulled out her phone and found Emháka Joseph's number. "You think she's at risk? Go on. Call the social worker."

"Fine, Fiona." Mike wiped his face with both hands. "But she should be with her mother at a time like this. Who is watching her?"

"None of your business," Fiona said.

"You have a sitter?"

"None of your business."

"Now isn't the time for her to be with a sitter for the first time. We can have her at our house any time. Or Luke and Aubrey can go to your place."

"No, thank you." Fiona put her phone away. Emháka and Mike were having an affair. Who knew what he'd say to get Ruby taken away. "I know about you and her."

"Give it up, Fiona. Emháka is a grandma of eight with a husband in a wheelchair!" Mike rolled his eyes and yanked so hard on the door that it gave in and slammed shut.

Fiona had never seen so much action up in this tiny corner of town. It was usually just seniors coming and going to bingo and exercise classes, and the fire trucks in and out, to crashes on the highway or medical calls. But now there was a phalanx of cars and pickup trucks parked along the street. The two bay doors to the fire hall were rolled up, the fire engines pulled out to make room for folding tables and chairs, the interior ablaze with lights, the trucks polished and gleaming against the falling snow. People were milling around. A man held a dog on a leash. A trio of teenaged girls whispered to each other, pointing at her.

A pickup idled at the corner; someone inside looked back, over his shoulder.

Someone else was looking right at her too, an older woman with a plush teddy bear in her arms, and also holding a Mylar balloon with a crying unicorn on it. She was aiming for the stairs, where people were building a makeshift memorial, like the ones on the news. Surely not here. Surely this little town was better than that. That was for other people. Not this little town, and these small children. But it was. Stuffed animals and wilting, freezing flowers from the grocery store, bundled in plastic and ribbon, candles alight in jars, quivering and sizzling as the snow fell.

"Don't," Fiona said. "Please."

But the woman went ahead and set the bear down amongst the detritus of grief.

"Take it away."

The woman acted as if she didn't hear her.

"Please?" she said. "Please take it away?"

"It's for the children." The woman mumbled a prayer and crossed herself. "Not you."

"Is that what you think?" Fiona was dumbfounded. "What use do dead children have for soggy stuffed animals from the dollar store and overpriced, out-of-season floral arrangements from Peru?"

The woman bristled but didn't say anything more. She walked away with her hands in her pocket and joined a clutch of elderly women in the fire station bay. She told them everything. Fiona watched her do it. They all looked over at her and frowned, arms crossed. They were talking about her now. That Fiona Tenner, thinking she's in charge. If she knows so much, why is her husband still up there and her daughter *who knows where.*

Fiona leapt into the middle of the stupid memorial. She snatched up the bear and hurled it across the lot. "This accomplishes nothing," she yelled. "It just makes you all look stupid!"

The women stood there, staring.

"Fiona Tenner?" A man rushed forward, well-dressed, his face matte with powder. One of the reporters. Well, of course there would be reporters. And why not? It was a huge story. Dead children. Dead celebrity athlete. Huge.

"Yes."

"Could we ask you a few questions? Maybe at Gus's store?"

"I suppose you could." She tossed a scowl at the old ladies.

"Great! Let us give you a ride." He helped her into the passenger seat of the news van, then he climbed into the back and another man drove. They were at the store in two minutes. She let them in, turned on the lights, noticed that Luke must've been keeping the stove warm, because it was toasty in there. It smelled of Gus, which made her feel even warmer.

"I love bringing him his lunch here," she said. "We have all those little tin lunch boxes and beeswax wraps. He sells them." She pointed to the shelf with all the water bottles and silicone snack bags. She stripped off her coat, right down to the pretty blue dress with the spaghetti straps. She took off her boots and her knee-high socks. She shimmied out of her underwear and helped herself to a very expensive pair of technical silk knickers she'd always wanted, turquoise with a tiny black-bear print. She pulled them on and tossed the box back onto the display. That done, she arranged herself on the armchair beside the wood stove. She brushed her long black hair out of her eyes and started to talk. She didn't stop for a very long time.

—

The house was dark, and no smoke came from the chimney. Her mother's favourite Elastica song was on a loop, top volume. Ruby stood on the porch and looked in the kitchen window. If she was a robber, this house would be easy. The back door was never locked. None of the windows locked. A robber could get in any way he wanted. The front door too, although sometimes her mother locked that. A robber could come in and take whatever he wanted. What would he take? Her mother's jewellery that she never wore. The laptop and the stereo. Her dad's camera, if he could find it. What would he take of hers? She imagined her room and the small wooden box filled with rocks. Yellow-and-orange agate from their camping trip to Devil's Elbow. Blue agates from Ellensburg. Thunder eggs from Madras. Jade from when her dad took her to Banff with him for a film festival one of his movies was shown at. Quartz crystal and amethyst. The fossils they took from the Grand Canyon when the ranger wasn't looking. That's what a robber would take.

Once she was inside and had taken off her boots and jacket and turned off her headlamp and flicked on the kitchen light, she noticed the mess. Flour on the counter. A heap of bowls in the sink. The oven still on and the light glowing. Cooling racks and muffin tins and cookie sheets and a smashed egg on the floor, congealing. A pan of sunken muffins that looked more like her mother's Yorkshire pudding, tipped over on the counter beside a big empty bowl. The lid for the butter dish broken in half, sitting in the dustpan, the broom propped beside it.

There was no note, only this mess. There was no one. Her mother's purse was gone from the closet. Her snow boots too. She was out somewhere. Looking for her? She didn't know where the snow cave was, so where would she look?

Upstairs, Ruby found the bathtub still full, the water cold and the surface slick with flattened bubbles that smelled of roses. She'd put in both bubbles and bath salts. Both bottles were empty. Ruby took off her clothes and slid into the cold water. It was like the lake on the hottest day of summer, shocking at first, and then not, and she liked that. It made her think of sunshine and digging in the sand and Gus lifting her onto his shoulders and throwing her into the water. She slid under the water and closed her eyes. She held her breath for as long as she could.

She turned her head in the milky, fragrant water, and even though it stung her eyes, she saw her father beside her. Minnows circling, the muffled noise of her laughing, and taking pictures. He took her hand and counted, bubbles releasing with each number. He got all the way up to thirty-nine seconds before he pushed her up out of the water. Ruby gasped. She plunged her head again, but he wasn't there, and neither was her mother.

When Fiona came home, a fire blazed in the stove and there were long puddles of melted frost along the bottom of each window. Ruby was in her bed, lying very still.

"Ruby?" Fiona perched on the edge, the springs complaining. "We have to talk."

Ruby's eyes were closed. Too tight. She clutched her stuffed rabbit in the crook of one arm, both hands in tight fists.

"I can tell that you're awake." Fiona put a hand on her shoulder. "Look at me, love."

For a moment Ruby remained still, and then she rolled onto her back and opened her eyes. Icy blue, long blonde lashes blinking.

"You used to talk to Daddy," Fiona said. "Sometimes. It's okay to talk to me now."

Ruby stared at her.

Fiona's eyes were dry and clear. Had she cried yet? She realized she hadn't, and she felt suddenly adrift, like she'd put things in the wrong order, and now found herself on a part of the path that she shouldn't be at yet. "Have you been crying?"

Ruby shook her head.

"You've been in here since we got home?"

Ruby nodded, even though they both knew that wasn't true.

"You took that bath and didn't go anywhere, right?"

Ruby nodded.

"Come here, love." Ruby scooched over and sat on Fiona's lap. "You're so warm. It's so cold out. Thank you for the fire."

Ruby rested her head on Fiona's shoulder.

"I love you," Fiona said. "And Daddy loves you, no matter where he is."

Ruby tightened her hug. So tight that Fiona had to work to get her next breath, but she would not ask her to let go. "They'll find him."

"Yes," Ruby said.

Now tears slipped down Fiona's cheeks. That one word was a beautiful golden butterfly and she would *not* scare it away.

"Have you eaten anything?"

Ruby didn't nod her head, or shake it, and for a small moment Fiona waited for her to speak.

No. Yes. I did. I didn't. I'm hungry. I don't want to eat.

I miss Daddy.

I want Daddy.

But she didn't speak again, and she didn't say those things, but even as she didn't say them, she did, because all of that was clear to Fiona, and for once she could understand why Ruby didn't bother saying much. It never came to any good. Everyone in the world should just shut up. Perhaps Ruby had it right all along.

The darkness of dusk pushed further into the blank indigo of night. Ruby fell asleep in her arms. Fiona laid her down, and lay beside her, the two of them under the quilts Ruby had retrieved from the pile on Gus's side of the bed. Cold air slipped through the house now that the seals on the windows were not frozen shut. Fiona eased out of Ruby's bed and went downstairs to assess the mess she'd left in the kitchen. Ruby had cleaned it all up.

JANUARY 19

When Fiona woke in the morning, her head was clearer. The first thing she thought of was that she should not have spoken to the reporter. What had she said? She couldn't remember.

She turned on the TV and found a morning news program. It was a segment on baking frittatas. She could see past the woman to the picture window that overlooked Georgia Street. It was just barely snowing in the city. Just a few fat, drifting flakes.

Frittatas, then deep cleaning behind appliances, and the debut album from a local singer-songwriter who perched on the edge of the sofa looking bewildered and meek while she was interviewed and who came to life only incrementally when the commercial break was over and the show returned to her sitting on a stool, strumming a pink guitar and warbling about some heartbreak.

Then, at the top of the hour, there it was.

A town plunged into grief.

"Five children dead and their Olympic-medallist guide, killed in an avalanche. We go live to Casper, where our reporter has been learning about this terrible tragedy."

"Yes, good morning, Leona." The journalist stared at Fiona as he spoke. "There are more questions than answers today, as this close-knit community grieves for their lost children and the man who was charged with their safekeeping."

He was the one who had taken her to the store, with the cameraman who couldn't stop looking at her dirty underwear on the floor. Now he was standing in front of the school field with the SAR helicopter in the background.

"As you can see, Leona, the helicopter is grounded this morning. The snow is falling and the skies are socked in, and so the recovery efforts—downgraded late last night from a rescue mission—are temporarily on hold. There are two bodies still to be recovered from the avalanche site."

He consulted his notes.

"Shane Chapman, aged nine, and the body of Gus Tenner, the adult guide responsible for organizing the trip into the back-country. He was not an employee of the private school that all five children attended, but many viewers will recognize his name from his years as a competitive snowboarder and Olympic silver medallist. Tenner owned a guiding and outfitter business here in Casper, and was well respected as a capable, careful, knowledge-able guide."

Cut to clips of various people commending Gus with sol-emn faces. There was the cashier from the grocery store, crying. He was very kind, she said. And such a good father. That poor little girl.

A shot of the storefront. More teddy bears and flowers. A balloon wavering as traffic passed along the slushy street. Had all that been there last night?

"I had a chance to speak with Gus Tenner's wife yesterday. Here's what she had to say about the tragedy."

Fiona sat up. There she was in the shop, by the fire. The basket of muffins and the stupid cookie tin behind her on the counter.

And her underwear on the floor. No one could tell what that was, surely.

"The parents are grieving. And angry. Of course they are. They're confused and sad and struggling too right now. I want them to know that I feel their pain. Gus is gone, and our daughter and I will have to come to terms with that. It must be said, though, this was not Gus's fault. It was a terrible tragedy. He would not have taken those children on that trip if it was not safe, so everyone can just go ahead and stop thinking that. It's a knee-jerk reaction, and an ignorant one at that."

Back to the reporter in front of the helicopter. Fiona leaned forward, waiting for more from what she said to the man at the store. They'd talked for nearly an hour, hadn't they? This was what he chose? But no. That's not the message. That's not what she was saying. She didn't mean to bring up guilt or blame at all. And then she remembered Shane's mother slapping her. She put a hand to her cheek. It was still tender.

The reporter was still speaking to the host, the screen split in half. It was snowing a little here, but not much. Not enough to stick to the helicopter, or the reporter's coat. Behind the colourful couch in the studio, the fat flakes had turned to rain.

"Tell us what the Avalanche Centre has to say about this tragedy, Dean."

"Yes." Dean nodded. "The avalanche risk was considered moderate in the immediate area of the incident that morning."

"And what does that mean?"

"The Avalanche Centre advises caution with that rating, Leona."

"Caution."

Gus was cautious with his customers. He was more than cautious with the kids from Cayoosh. The rating was wrong. Or the reported rating was wrong when he checked it. Or it changed all of a sudden.

"Yes, caution."

There was a pause.

"Should those children have been on that trail, Dean?"

"Well, the Avalanche Centre has issued a statement saying that the conditions were not ideal at that particular time. And that their thoughts and prayers go out to the victims' families, and the entire town of Casper."

"A lot to think about. Our thoughts and prayers are with the families too on this most difficult day. What a tragedy. For all of the town of Casper. Thank you, Dean."

A nod, and then it was all studio. The host leaned back in her chair and turned to a man beside her. The weatherman? Fiona never watched this show. They were going to talk about it. Candidly. Unscripted.

Fiona switched off the TV.

She knew exactly what to do. She needed to get the binder Gus kept up on the shelf behind the cash. A file for each trip included a pre-trip checklist that had a line for names, next of kin, destination and route, alternative route, time expected back, and avalanche rating as of that day. She needed to see what he wrote down for the avalanche report. That would explain everything.

She walked the alleys, impassable to vehicles by this time of the year but packed down enough by skiers, sledders and snowmobiles, even though they weren't supposed to go down the alleys. Even still, she stumbled with every few steps, sinking to her bare knees and catching snow in her boot as she pulled her foot out. She came out behind the shop.

She hadn't brought her keys. The little window above the door was lit, she could tell even in the rising sunshine. That was the office. She made her way between the store and the fireplace shop, over snow freshly fallen from the eaves. The front of the store was dark. Locked. She put her hand to the glass and peered in. The lights were off, shrouding the racks of technical jackets and backpacks in shadow, the coils of rope hanging off the wall like sleeping snakes. The door to the backroom was open a crack, a sliver of light pushing out.

Fiona banged on the door.

"Luke!" Of course, it was him. Who else would it be? He was the only other one with a key. Besides Ruby. Where was Ruby?

Asleep in her bed. Yes. She looked in on her before she left. This shop was Gus's other baby.

She owned this store now. This was her shop. Her baby.

"Let me in!"

The door at the back opened wider. Luke poked his head out.

She banged and banged the door. "Open the door!" She kept banging while Luke made his way to the front. And then she saw Aubrey behind him. He'd been back there with her. When he opened the door, Fiona pushed past him. "What were you doing back there?"

"Hiding," Luke said. "From everything."

"The store was supposed to be open fifteen minutes ago."

"You want me to open the store?"

"I do."

"Seriously?"

"Yes."

"Kids are *dead*. Gus is *dead*. Me and Liam and Ruby almost *died*."

"But you didn't die, so you can open Gus's store for him and help out that way, right?"

"Mrs. Tenner, no one expects you to open the shop." Aubrey put her hands out in front of her, as if she was gifting this idea to Fiona. "Everybody understands."

"I understand." Fiona glanced at where her underwear had been the night before. They were not there. "You came here to fuck away your sorrow. Very romantic. Wearing my panties you took off the floor?"

Where was the binder? Carabiners, sunglasses, packets of electrolytes. Energy bars. Swiss Army knives. The bowl of chocolate kisses he kept at the counter.

"Where's the binder?"

Luke's cheeks went red. He straightened an inch or so. "You owe Aubrey an apology."

Fiona wanted to laugh. Aubrey would get no apology. There was nothing Fiona was sorry for. Aubrey stood well off to the side, red-cheeked and watching.

"I put those in the garbage," Aubrey said. "I didn't know how they got here. Or who they belonged to."

"It's not like I fucked the reporter," Fiona said. "I just took them off."

"Fiona!" Luke took Aubrey's hand. "Just shut up."

"Luke just didn't want to be at home right now," Aubrey said. "That's why we're here. Are you okay? You don't look very good. Can we take you home?"

"Am I okay?"

"You're totally acting strange," Aubrey said.

"She has a history of acting strange," Luke said. "She's crazy. Which is no excuse for treating you like this. Say you're sorry, Fiona."

"Luke." Fiona brought her hands together, as if in prayer. "I am so glad that you are out of the hospital and feeling well enough to fuck your girlfriend and take care of the store—"

"We weren't." Aubrey started to cry. "And he doesn't feel well!"

"I'm not opening the store," Luke said. "That's fucked up."

"Luke, I need the binder. That's all." Fiona kept her fingers steepled. "Could you please, please, please find the blue binder with the pre-trip checklists in it. It was right here." She put a hand on the shelf behind the cash register. There was the binder of special requests. The binder with his calendar in it. All of this should be on the computer. She wanted him to put all of this on the computer. Instead, he had highlighters and mechanical pencils and a stubby white eraser, as if he was a schoolboy. Making neat lists and sorting the details by colour.

"I guess it's missing." Luke said it too quickly. If he'd wanted her to believe his lie, he should've hesitated. He should've helped her look for it. *Gosh, Fiona. I don't know. Maybe Gus put it somewhere before he left. I'll keep looking. I'll let you know when I find it.*

"What did you do with it?"

"I didn't touch it." He looked at Aubrey when he said it. He should've looked at her. "I don't know where it is." And then he glanced behind him, at the storeroom.

"Is it back there? Where you two were fucking?" She laughed and said to Aubrey, "Did he fold you over the desk back there?"

She and Gus had sex like that once, when the store first opened. They hung the GRAND OPENING banner across the front window and then he pulled her back there and she wriggled her panties to her ankles and then kicked them off and they fucked fast and hard and he came inside her and then he pulled up his pants and zipped up his fly and smacked her ass and smiled as he went out to open the door. She straightened her dress and didn't put her panties back on. She brought out the champagne and orange juice and the sleeve of plastic cups and stood behind the till mixing mimosas, while his cum slid down her thigh.

Where was Ruby that night? She tried to remember. She stared at Luke and noticed for the first time the shadows under his eyes. Stitches above his brow, both ears with angry red tips to match his nose, two bandaged hands, one arm in a sling, the other around Aubrey. Where was Ruby? Where was Ruby when she and Gus were in the back, panting and grunting, his hands on her hips, holding her steady? She remembered now. Asleep on a sheepskin on the couch by the door. If someone had looked in, they would've seen her there, all alone, her arms flung over her head, her mouth a little moue. She was old enough to roll over. She'll be fine for five minutes, Fiona had said.

Is that all it will take? Gus kissed her. I want seven at least.

"I see now that you can't have been fucking," Fiona said. "Not with Luke in that state. Perhaps a blow job. Or just a bit of dry humping? That's always fun, in the right circumstance."

"I suggest you shut the fuck up," Luke said through gritted teeth.

"I won't."

"I'll tell you where the binder is—"

"Luke, don't." Aubrey put a hand on his shoulder.

"She's right." He scowled at her. "It's her store. She wants it, she can have it. It's on the shelf above the desk in the office. I hid it in a Bankers Box. I was going to shred it all, but I wanted to talk to you first. But screw that. You can deal with it yourself."

"Thank you, Luke."

Luke said nothing.

"I hope you feel better, Mrs. Tenner." Aubrey grabbed her coat from behind the counter and shoved her arms into it.

"Don't be nice to her, Aubs." Luke shook his head. "She doesn't care that Gus is dead. I can't even remember one nice thing she said to him in the last couple of years." To Fiona he added, "He was going to leave you. And he was taking Ruby with him. If I believed in witches, I'd bet you set that avalanche off. What are a few little kids as collateral damage, eh? Even your own kid."

Fiona dumped the banker's box onto the dirty carpet in front of the desk. There was the binder at last. Bright blue, *TRIPS* written in Gus's neat block printing on the front. He loved drafting in high school, and sometimes talked about it as the career the other Gus had.

She flipped through the pages.

She did like Gus. She *loved* him. And he loved her. If people were honest, anyone would admit that there were times in their marriage when they held both truths: that they loved their partner and they also wanted to leave their partner. Fiona didn't want to *leave*. He was leaving *her*. She just wanted to go to England.

But they both loved Ruby more. In some marriages, this still worked. Love the children more, but love each other too. Admit it, Fiona. Admit the thing that was different in your marriage.

No need. Over now. Move on.

No point in that, Fiona darling.

"I've been patient for a long time," Gus said.

When was that? When he suggested separation? Ruby was six, they were camping at Lil'wat Lake. Fiona wanted to kill herself, simply put. It sounds extreme, but it was the tail end of three

months of black inertia that she and her psychiatrist were trying to medicate. She was trying. He didn't see that, though. He
couldn't get past the eggshells at his feet. That's what he said.
He couldn't walk on them.

Fiona swam out into the ice water. It was chalky sky blue,
milky with glacial flour. Only the hardiest of children swam in
that lake, and even then, only in the shallows on the very hottest
days of the year. Ruby and Gus went on a hike, and from way up
high they spotted her a hundred metres away from shore.

"Fiona!"

Ruby screamed. Fists planted at her sides; eyes squeezed
shut. Screamed and screamed.

This would be the best way. He could tell her that she'd
drowned by accident.

But he called a friend who lived on the lake. He'd already
spotted her and was on his way to scoop her up, wrinkled, pale
and silent while he pestered her with questions.

"She insisted on coming back here," Gus's friend said.
"Instead of my place. I have spare clothes. A wood stove."

"She's a very strong swimmer," Gus said as he helped her
from the boat. "The wind just came up and caught her by surprise. Right?"

Fiona nodded. "We're good swimmers, Ruby. That's true,
isn't it?"

Ruby nodded.

"Go get Mommy's sleeping bag, okay, Rabbit?" After Ruby
left to collect it, and after Gus convinced his friend to leave them
by assuring him that they'd head home straight away, Gus squatted in front of Fiona and put his hands on her knees. "We can't
do this," he said. "It's too scary, and I don't know how to handle
it." He hugged Fiona, crying. "I can't. It's too scary."

Ruby delivered the sleeping bag. She arranged it over her mother, and then took the kettle down to the lake.

"Yes, thank you," Fiona said, as if Ruby had asked out loud whether she'd like tea or not. "I don't *want* to go," she said when Ruby was out of earshot. "It's just that in the moment it's the only thing I *can* do to make the pain stop and get out of the way so you two—my favourite people in all the world—can be happy."

"Not happy." Gus shook his head. "We wouldn't be happy. Ruby would be broken."

Ruby came up the bank, the kettle overflowing.

"Tip a little bit out, Rabbit," Gus said. To Fiona, "I'm glad you're okay. Let's get you warmed up and then we'll go home. We have to figure this out. Because I can't—"

"—do this anymore," Fiona cried. "As if *I* can either. That's the whole point, right?"

There was never any talk about taking her to the hospital. She'd made it clear when Ruby was newborn and she could not stop weeping that if Gus made her go into the hospital, she would get out and disappear with Ruby when he least expected it. When everything seems fine, she said. And then one day we just wouldn't be there anymore.

When they talked about divorce, he let her lay claim to Ruby too, as if she had just as much right to her as he did. She knew better, though. All it would take would be for a judge to look at her medical records.

Or maybe they would come and go from Ruby. Ruby would be with the house—a package deal. A porch. A chimney. The bathroom sink. A small, silent child; a part of the house. Of the house. Or not. There was so much more to say on the matter. Or not say. They weren't finished. Not in the way they needed to be. Fiona needed to keep him talking about it, and not acting on it.

He had the business. He made the money. His name was on the title of the house. He was the parent the entire village would vote for to keep Ruby. The one who carried her on his shoulders in the parades on Canada Day and Remembrance Day, the one who took her grocery shopping with him, and snowboarding, and to all the Cayoosh events. No one appreciates the parent at home, the one who does absolutely everything else.

She found the page for the old ladies. She put her finger on Helena's phone number. Gus and Helena joked that they had a May-December relationship. She reminds me of my mom, Gus said.

Fiona could see why. His mother, Muriel, and Helena were both wiry, more of a boyish shape. They both had very short hair, but still managed to look feminine and chic, despite the narrow hips and unlikely hair. Their difference was in the everyday. Helena was filthy rich, and had "lady friends" in Montreal, Los Angeles and New York. She'd never lived with anyone, not in any of her five homes. Muriel had followed her high school sweetheart into the woods to build the A-frame Gus grew up in, where Tim still lived. She gathered stinging nettles and fiddleheads in the spring. She could shoot, skin and butcher a deer. Helena was vegan, but a multi-millionaire thanks to a buffalo jerky empire. One time, Muriel made Ruby a set of stilts out of empty coffee cans and garden twine. One time, Helena brought Ruby a pendant made of actual mammoth tusk. Magically, those two things were worth the same to Ruby.

Fiona would call Helena. Right now.

The phone rang and rang.

"Hello?"

"Is this Helena Brooks?"

"Yes?"

"This is Fiona Tenner."

"Oh, my dear Fiona," Helena said. "I am so sorry for your loss. What a sad thing. How are you holding up, my dear?"

"You were going to go to Maui. Did you go?"

"I'm in Maui now, as a matter of fact."

"Is it nice there?"

"Well, it is." Fiona could hear the confusion in Helena's voice. "It is quite lovely. I'm looking to buy a condo here. On the beach."

"Can I ask you something?"

"Of course, my dear."

"How was he? On your trip?"

"I don't suppose it matters now. Does it, Fiona? Perhaps you'd do best to focus your attention on Ruby. She'll need you now. A little girl needs her mama at a time like this."

"She has me already," Fiona said. "Please, tell me."

"Fiona, I could lie to you. But I won't. He was very troubled about your marriage, as you know. Your health. He told me that you and he were discussing separating."

"He was discussing it."

"He was looking into custody law," Helena said. "He was trying to sort that out."

"He wanted Ruby all to himself."

"No, no, my dear. It's not like that. It's never as simple as that."

"Isn't it? When one parent is crazy?"

"He never used that word." Fiona could hear Helena thinking. "I'm not sure I want to share this, but he forgot our food."

As much as she wished Helena hadn't shared it, Fiona agreed that this was very out of character for Gus.

"What did you eat?"

"What was in our packs, and what was in the cache in the cabin."

"He's never done that," Fiona said. "Not that I know of."

"I know, dear, and it doesn't warrant mentioning to the authorities, but perhaps it does speak to his lack of focus as of late." Helena sighed. "Fiona, we always enjoyed our time with Gus. We always learned so much from him. We all respected him. And trusted him implicitly. And I would say as much—with confidence—in front of any inquiry. Even after what I've said just now, to you, in confidence."

How do you inquire of a dead man?

Fiona flipped through the pages until she found the page for the field trip with the kids.

This was what she was looking for.

Guide: GUS TENNER

All caps. Everything big. Always *big*.

Co-guide: LUKE

Customer Name(s):

NINO, SKYE, ANNA, TAG, SHANE, LIAM, RABBIT

Not even her proper name. None of the children's proper names. No birthdates, allergies, information. No route plans. No emergency contact numbers. No last names, even. Paper-clipped behind the form were all the signed permission slips from the school. And behind that, the waivers for Mount Casper Outfitters, all of them blank. Fiona flipped back to the page with the children's names. Halfway down the page was a tick box, empty. Beside it: CALL AVALANCHE CENTRE

And a space for notes below.

It was blank.

This must not be the finished form. There was another one somewhere. He just hadn't put all of it together. Maybe the complete form was in his backpack. No one would know until they found him. Or even just his pack. It was not possible that he was so distracted by—

By *her*.

So distracted by the ongoing mess of *her* that he hadn't checked things before he left with the children.

No.

The completed form was with him, or it was here. Somewhere.

Fiona opened the drawer, then another—pens, pencils, a length of paracord, business cards, screws and carabiners— and then she pawed through the loose papers on the shelf behind the counter. In the cupboard below she found a box of loose papers. Was this recycling? Or did these papers matter? She rifled through them, looking for something that would prove that he knew what he was doing. That he hadn't just set off distracted, because of what was going on between them. Without thinking. Without making just that one phone call, which would've postponed the trip. As she hunted, her anger grew. She would have to answer for this. She was the one left behind. Her and Mike. Was it more Mike's fault than hers? But it wasn't his, not really. He'd put the children in the care of Gus, who was more than fully qualified to shepherd them into the backcountry and home safely, without incident. Gus was meticulous with his clients' safety. And this trip included his own child.

She found a pamphlet for a restaurant in Whistler, and a note written on it with marker. A list.

Spare sleeping bag
Medication?
Camera

Was that for the trip with the kids? Was he going to check with the parents, see if any of the children were on medication that he'd need to take care of? No, no, that would've been the trip to his father's last summer, when she was on a higher dose of lithium, after swimming out into the lake.

Fiona dumped the box onto the floor and got on her knees and spread out the papers. She turned each one right side up. It did look like recycling. Flyers, catalogues, invoices, packing slips, envelopes, notes and notes and notes.

Phone M re: up top
Cucumbers, feta, tomatoes
Pick up R
Luke payroll
Call lawyer re: F. Custody. Separation agreement. Etc.

Etcetera? As if all the rest of it could fit under the category of *etcetera*?

And no question mark after *custody*. He was so certain. And who was the lawyer? Did he actually have one? There was no date on the note, which was maddening. Was this from last summer too?

On a full sheet of paper: *If I don't?* A phone number scribbled under that, some notes, with the name Emháka Joseph under-lined three times. *Bad idea to force her to stay. Shows lack of trust, suggests that I'm the bully. Reflects poorly. Risk that she will keep R there. But return tix=good thing. Assume the best. Be the good guy.*

Be the good guy.

Emháka Joseph. The social worker on call, for the clinic, the police and the Lil'wat Nation.

An arrow to another number. Fran Hills, Child Psychologist. *Make appointment. Ruby will choose parent.*

Which would seem generous to a stranger reading it. But not to her. It was a set-up. He was setting her up. As if it was an equal fight. As if Ruby wouldn't choose him. As if she would choose her. He just wanted his win to be sanctioned.

He was arming himself.

It had never occurred to Fiona to arm herself. She hadn't thought that far ahead.

Fiona had nothing.

No lawyer.

No social worker.

No child psychologist.

No money.

But Gus was dead now, right? Could she say that yet? He had no say anymore. He'd signed the travel permission papers, albeit reluctantly, and now she was so glad that he had, because with no body, when would a death certificate come? When do they decide that one of the world's most experienced back-country guides is really and truly dead? Long after she was on a plane to England. That was for certain. No one would even know as she made her way through customs. No one would know that he was dead. All they'd care about was that little piece of paper. Fiona—and probably everyone who knew him well—could imagine him up there, surviving in one of his snow caves.

The bell over the door rang and Fiona didn't even look up. She heard footsteps and it didn't matter. All these notes. He was trying so hard to organize things, but he was not an organized person. And then it didn't matter anyway. He'd been sideswiped by nature.

She laughed. It was so awful. *Sideswiped*. Sideswiped!

Mike's boots, damp with snow. Mike's boots, as big as Paul Bunyan's. From the floor looking up, he was Paul Bunyan, especially with that thick beard and tufty moustache under his big red nose. And bushy eyebrows, like squirrel tails.

"What is amazing," Fiona said, "is that he was going to leave me even without knowing about Sayulita. Luke went to get you, didn't he?" She folded the papers and slipped them into her pocket. Then she made a grid with the rest. Ten across, ten down, then another row, another row. Down the aisle that led from the front door to the backroom, backing up on her knees as she did. The words the logos the numbers black pen red pen assembly instructions for a backpacker stove a catalogue for climbing shoes, all of it hovering just above the papers, a low fog of nonsensical, essential information. She would find the completed form. She would put it together and find his plan. The mess at home was a mess, okay, she could admit that. But the mess at home did not kill those children.

"Fiona, get up."

"It will be in here. I bet he filled out one of his stupid paper forms and put it into the recycling instead of the binder. The one in the binder hardly has anything on it. Just the children's names. Just their names. Only their first names. Not even their last names. So he would've mixed them up—the completed one and the one he didn't finish."

"Fiona, stop."

"Don't you get it, Mike?" She looked up then. "He did fill it out. He did check the avalanche risk. He did do all the planning.

He did, and the proof is here. Or if it's not here, then it's with him. I just need to find it and show everyone that it was not his fault that those babies died."

Mike grabbed her arm and hauled her onto her feet. She twisted away and dropped to her knees again.

"You don't understand. You don't. Because if you did, you would be helping me!" This paper. What was this one? She brought it close to her face. Maybe if she really looked at it. Really looked. Really saw the truth. It was not just paper and black marks. It added up to something. It did and it had to and she would find it.

"Get up, Fiona."

"Did you know about us? Did you know what was happening? And don't flatter yourself, it had nothing to do with what you and I did. Once. Thousands of miles away. That didn't even matter." She sat back on her knees. "I can't. I have to do this."

"You have to get on your feet and go home. Now."

"No." She gathered up the papers instead, scooping them into a pile that she cradled in her arms as if it were a baby. Shuffling up the floor on her knees now, paper after paper.

"Fiona!"

She could turn now. She could afford to look. She could afford to speak to him. This could wait one minute. This could wait two minutes, or perhaps even five. There was Ruby standing just inside the door, staring at her. Why was she staring at her? That finger parked in the corner of her mouth. How many times had Fiona said stop sucking it, stop doing that, the noise is driving me mad, get your finger out of your mouth, what are you, a fucking baby?

"Fiona! Enough!" Mike grabbed her by both arms and lifted her to her feet. "You can't talk to her like that!"

"What? I didn't say it out loud. Did I?" Oh my god. Oh my god. She lunged towards Ruby. "Hey, I'm sorry. That was not okay, love. You know that, right? I didn't mean it."

"I'm taking you home." He knocked the papers out of her arms. They fluttered to the floor.

"No!" Fiona keened. "They were in order!"

Mike pulled her out of the store even as she was struggling against him.

"They were in a specific order!" she yelled, as he dragged her to his truck like some caveman joke, and Ruby was trailing behind and there was a satellite truck, the cameraman just getting out of the back with his camera on his shoulder. She kicked out at him. "What the fuck are you looking at?" Another satellite truck parked across the street. CBC. That one was empty.

Fiona twisted out of Mike's grasp. "Where the fuck are they?" He grabbed her again and wrestled her into the passenger side and shut the door and held it closed while Ruby got into the back seat and put her backpack between her and Liam, who was staring straight ahead. "Motherfuckers twisted my words!" Fiona screamed. "Motherfuckers!"

Ruby would not cry. Or she might, and that would be worse. To cry about her mother before she cried about her dad. Liam pushed her backpack to the floor and slid over until his shoulder was pressed against her and she was pressed against the window. He covered her ears. Ruby closed her eyes. She could still hear the swearing, and then the crying, which wasn't as bad. She pushed Liam's hands away from her ears, and held one instead. She had a finger in her mouth. When Fiona wrenched the door open and tried to jump out, Mike said, Oh no you don't, and tightened his grip on her wrist. Ruby was pretty sure she'd have a nasty red mark there. There was arnica cream in the bathroom cupboard. She could get it and put some on, like her dad did when Ruby's wrist was red like that. Remember that time? When my wrist was so red like that?

It's never okay, Rabbit. That is never okay.

Mike didn't let go until he pulled up in front of their small, dark house, with all the junk on the porch like so many trolls waiting to come to life. And the junk in the yard too, softened by snow, but waiting too. It wasn't a dead snowmobile or half a truck. It wasn't a stack of old tires or a pile of rotten lumber, Ruby knew. Trolls. Lots of trolls. They could all rear up and tear it all down with their sharp black teeth and gobble it all up, and then Ruby and her mother would have nowhere to live. She wanted to tell Liam about the trolls. They'd be so fast. They'd have claws like grizzly bears.

But she just kept holding his hand while Fiona flung open the door and made a dash for the road.

"I need to get the papers!"

Mike caught her and steered her towards the house and forced her up the stairs and opened the door and pushed her inside. He looked back at the truck and lifted a finger. Wait. Wait one minute. And then he disappeared inside.

It was more than a minute.

"Do you think he's tying her up?" Liam whispered.

Ruby shook her head. There could be a hundred trolls. Maybe two hundred.

"Do you think he's yelling at her?"

She shook her head again. Maybe there would be so many trolls that they'd gobble up the whole town.

"I think maybe he's tying her up. So she doesn't run away."

Hundreds and hundreds of trolls. A troll invasion. Gobble, gobble. Maybe they would eat up all the people and the dogs and the cats and everything. When they were done and sitting up on the mountains, fat-bellied and groaning with stomach aches, bits of bone between their ugly teeth, they'd look down on the town—polished off, nothing but an empty valley.

Mike gave Fiona a swig of whiskey, and then another and one more, and then told her to stay on the couch, but she followed him upstairs and watched him rifle through the medicine cabinet.

"What do you have that will knock you out?"

"I don't want to get knocked out."

"Look, NyQuil, Gravol?" He glanced at her. "Allergy pills? Melatonin? Anything? You need a long rest."

"Is that a euphemism?"

"No one else has become unhinged," Mike said. "That is what's amazing. So, let's deal with you and get you back on track, so you can mother your child."

In the back of a drawer full of makeup and creams was a line of pill bottles. Each one of them with Fiona's name on it.

He took out each bottle one at a time.

Lithium.

Lorazepam.

Tegretol.

Divalproex.

Quetiapine.

"Gus didn't say anything about this." Mike picked up a pill-box with a little door for each day of the week.

"I don't believe he never told you," Fiona said. "His best friend."

"We talked about you," Mike said. "What you did. *Do*. How hard it was on your marriage. On him. And Ruby. He never said you were on medication."

Fiona nodded, tears pressing at the back of her eyes.

"What's your diagnosis?"

"Guess."

"Bipolar." Fiona didn't say anything, but he nodded as if she had. "Okay. Yeah. This makes a lot of sense. He should've said. *You* should've said. And what about this, then?" All of the boxes were still full. "It's Wednesday."

The children were in the truck with the engine running. He put the bottles back and took the pillbox instead, and then the bottle of lorazepam too. He set them on the edge of the sink, dumped out the toothbrush cup, rinsed it and filled it with water, then turned to Fiona.

When she saw the pills, she shook her head and scrambled backwards, towards her bedroom. "No! I won't!"

He opened the Wednesday tab and tipped them into his hand. He added another two of the lorazepam.

"Back off, motherfucker!" And then she laughed. "You are a mother fucker. Ha!"

"Shut up, Fiona."

"Get the fuck out of my house."

"You're taking these first."

"The fuck I am."

"That's right, the fuck you are."

He wrestled her onto her back on the bed, straddled her, pulled down her jaw and dropped the pills in even as she was lifting her head to bite his finger. He poured in some water and she choked and spluttered as he clamped her jaw shut with one hand at her chin and the other on the top of her head. She had to swallow.

"That's how I get Ophelia to swallow pills," he said. "You want to be treated like a dog?"

He started to roll off, but she grabbed his shirt in her fists. "Stay with me."

He pushed her hands away and rolled off, nearly out of breath. "The kids are in the truck."

"That's the only reason?" Her words were slurred. "If they weren't, would you let me take your cock out of your jeans and sit on it?" Because when he'd straddled her, he did get hard.

"Don't leave the house, Fiona." He put his hands on his knees and shook his head. "Stay here and don't answer the door and don't answer the phone and don't do anything except eat and sleep and go to the bathroom. Tomorrow, take the pills for Thursday. You are fucking everything up."

"I have to go get the papers." But she wasn't speaking as fast anymore. He could hear the alcohol and the pills in her voice. "I have to sort them out. The answer is there. The answer is absolutely *there*."

"There's nothing in those papers."

"You don't know."

"There is no answer."

"There *is*. There has to be."

"It was a tragedy."

"There have to be reasons."

"Maybe we shouldn't look for them." He levelled a look at her.

Fiona said nothing. She slid a pillow under her head and closed her eyes.

Mike said, "There is nothing in those papers. I know it. Leave it alone, Fiona."

"Stay." Fiona reached for him, and he let her pull him closer. She draped her arms around his neck and lifted her face to his. "Please," she whispered in his ear. "Stay here."

"You stay here. Have a shower. Brush your teeth. Sleep." He got up, pointing at her as he backed out of the room. "Ruby is coming with us."

When he got back to the truck, Liam and Ruby were sitting in the front. Liam was pretending to drive. Ruby was fiddling with the stereo.

"Move over," Mike said, not unkindly. The children made room for him. "Where should we go, kids?"

He asked it playfully, inviting an answer like the moon, or Antarctica, or Timbuktu, because he longed for some silliness from them, some sign that they were still children, and not just survivors of a terrible thing.

Liam took Ruby's hand and held it, but not too tight. "Home," he said.

As they pulled out of the driveway, Ruby looked back at her yard. The trampoline had collapsed under the snow. The floor of it had split, and the legs had buckled. It looked like a dead spider.

When Ruby woke up, her body ached. She felt heavy and sore. Her finger throbbed. She must've been chewing it all night. The skin was raw and red and wrinkled, and there were specks of blood on Liam's pillowcase with the smiley basketball hoops all over it. Snowboard posters, lime-green walls, thick snow falling beyond the Lego figurines along the windowsill.

His pyjama bottoms were too big, so she bunched the waist in her fist when she went to the window. There was the school-yard, and the helicopter. No fresh footprints in the snow.

Was that the same helicopter that brought down the man SAR found in Stein Valley ten days after he got lost, two years ago? Her dad was on that search.

He did everything right, Rabbit. And he *survived*. Longer than anyone I've ever met. He'd dug a snow cave—just like yours—and made a snare for rabbits. He started a fire exactly how I taught you, with a notch in the wood and a stick and a bundle of tiny dry sticks he dug out from the base of a tree. He was almost comfortable. He just couldn't find his way home.

Like this, her dad said, shovelling down into the snow. Make your entrance as small as you can. Work the sides up. We don't have as much of a base layer as you'd want in the backcountry, but we can do it. Pile it up, and then we'll work on the inside.

Ruby loved it when he talked like that, a steady stream of words, every single one for her. And it was always interesting. How to catch a badger. Almost impossible! Those things are vicious. Did you know that you can make tea from pine needles? It's true.

How to build a snow cave. Step by step. They'd done it together. And it was still perfect and warm and hidden.

The streets were quiet. What day was it? Ruby tried to think. Thursday. And it was early. The fire hall bay doors were pulled down. The seniors' centre was dark. The Valley Lodge was lit up, like any hotel would be. The entrance glowed warm against the timber frame. Someone stood behind the desk, looking down. There was a TV on in the corner. The news.

Where were all the news vans?

Ruby cut through the schoolyard, skirting the field and the helicopter in the middle, that sleeping monster.

She stayed in the woods as she made her way to the cave. She moved the brush away from the entrance and slid inside. It was dark, and cool, but it would warm up soon. She found her headlamp and switched it on, and then took out a paper bag with five new candles in it. When she went to buy them at the hunting store, the man at the till smiled sadly at her. What was his name? Bob. Brad. Bud. It was Bud. Her dad didn't like him. She heard him talking to Luke about Bud once. I can't respect a man who kills for sport. He drinks out in the bush, you know. When he's on his ATV with all those other assholes. Someone is going to get killed that way, and he's going to wear it. People pay him to take them into the bush to hunt, not to get into a drunk driving accident with a cedar tree.

"I bet this is pretty hard on you," Bud said.

Ruby slid a five-dollar bill across the counter.

"It's more than five bucks, but don't worry about it. It's on the house."

The house? What house?

"That means it's free, honey."

Ruby took the money back.

"I liked your dad a lot, you know. Did you see me at that party at your place? For your dad's birthday? I was shoveling the trampoline off with the—" His cheeks turned red as she stood there, staring at him. "I watched you and him jumping."

Ruby chewed her finger.

"You know, if you need anything, I'd be happy to—" He glanced down at the candles. "Take them." He put them into a paper bag, and then threw in two more. "Good girl."

The candle lantern warmed up the cave soon enough. Ruby sat on the little ledge and took out the backcountry map book she'd slid into her pack when Bud wasn't looking. It was large, and had taken some shoving to get it in. He was selling a rifle to a man with a baby in his arms. They glanced at Ruby and spoke lower, and she knew they were talking about her.

The map book was the same as the ones her father sold in his store, but Ruby didn't want Luke to catch her there, or, worse, her mother. There were one or two in the basement. There was one in his truck too. She wanted this one. For herself. Maybe he had one of them with him? That would be even better. He could look for a good place. A safe place. The best place for a good snow cave. Near where rabbits would be. Too bad, dead little rabbits. This time it would be okay to eat them. Just this time.

When she brought her dad home, she would make him promise never to eat a rabbit again, not ever in his whole life.

She opened it to the index, and tried to figure out which section of the book the Tiffen Creek cabin would be in. The book was for the whole area, but it had sections, and one of them was the area around Mount Casper and Tiffen Lakes. She just had to find it, between all the pages and pages of places she'd never heard of.

"Ruby?" Liam said.

Startled, she dropped the book. How could she not have heard him coming? She had to be better in the bush. She had to hear animals coming. People, maybe even. This was not good. She blew out the candle, snapped off her headlamp and sat perfectly still.

"Can I come in?"

The cedar boughs lifted out of the way and flat midday winter light streamed in. Liam bent down and peered into the dark. Ruby turned on her headlamp so he could see. He slid in and then reached behind him to replace the boughs. He sat on the little snow bench across from hers. Her father's seat. Lower than hers, so her dad's head wouldn't hit the curved ceiling.

He'd brought a grocery bag, and he rooted through it now. He brought out two mandarin oranges and offered her one. She took it but didn't peel it. He peeled his, and then ate it in three sections, his chin dripping with juice. He reached for her orange, and she thought he was going to peel it and eat it himself, but when it was peeled, he carefully stripped off as much pith as he could and then broke it into individual pieces and held it out to her, the sections cupped in his hands. Ruby took a piece. "It's a really, really good secret spot. I won't tell anyone. Pinky swear." He stuck his out, and when she didn't, he grabbed her hand

and hooked their pinkies together. "Go ahead. I brought more." She put it in her mouth and bit down, and the sweet, tangy juice filled her mouth. All of a sudden she wanted all of it, at once, and so she stuffed in each piece until her cheeks bulged, and then she chewed and swallowed and could hardly believe that something so ordinary could taste so delicious.

"Want another one?"

Ruby nodded. Liam took the same care with the second one, and the third. He ate two more as well, until the cave was fragrant with citrus and bright-orange peels were scattered on the dirt floor.

"I followed you. I wrote a note."

Ruby looked at him, questioning.

"I said we went out to play. So they wouldn't worry about you. They would've freaked out, Ruby, if they woke up and you were just gone. That's why I left the note. Now no one is looking for us. That's better. See?"

"Thank you."

"What?" He stared at her with his mouth agape.

Ruby sat very still.

"Right," he said. "We're not supposed to make a big deal of it when you talk."

Ruby's cheeks burned with the idea of her parents and Liam's parents discussing her.

Ruby didn't say another word. Liam peeled another orange, but he held this one in his hand, not quite offering it to her, like he was waiting for her to ask for it, with actual words. But then he gave it to her, and she didn't say thank you again.

They ate ten oranges between them, and then they heard the helicopter wake up.

—

When Fiona woke, she was not at all surprised to find herself on the floor, halfway to the door, with one arm in her coat and the other bent at an awkward angle behind her. She'd been on her way to get Ruby. Now, she stuffed her other arm into the sleeve and climbed back upstairs on all fours. The toilet was bracingly cold, and the water had a thin layer of ice that her hot urine melted, sending a plume of steam up between her legs.

She considered calling the furnace repair place, but could not stand the thought of having a conversation. First, there was Gus to talk about. And then the other families with their beautiful children gone. Fiona considered her bed. She considered the couch. She considered Ruby, but she was too stoned on antipsychotics to go get her. Not yet. Not until she was sure that she wouldn't fuck it up.

She fetched a bottle of wine from the kitchen and had a glass and then slept for an hour or more on the couch until a car horn sounded three times in quick succession, almost cheerfully. Fiona tried to get up, but her limbs were still heavy, and her stomach roiled in protest as soon as she bent at the waist. The wine bottle, empty, lay on its side at her feet, a tiny spill of red on the dirty carpet. She sat up, and after what seemed like a truly stupid amount of time, she stood up and shuffled to the window, where she put one hand to her belly, to calm the churning, and pulled the drapes aside just enough to peek out, but not enough that Willy could see her from inside the shiny black Escalade.

Willy, who'd been trying every possible way of getting hold of her since it happened, including calling Sarah. Willy, who knew too much and therefore knew to come anyway, Fiona supposed. She would get her back on track. That was Willy's job. Only Fiona *was* on track. She did not need Willy at the moment.

The car idled, belching silently into the cold, while the driver attended to Willy. He opened the door and took her arm as she unfolded herself from the back seat. He walked her down the icy path and helped her up the steps. Willy knocked, and then clasped her hands together in front of her and waited. She was wearing one of those long down-filled coats, black, like a sleeping bag with arms and a hood, and sheepskin boots to mid-calf. Bright-purple leather gloves and a hat—the same purple— which was probably angora or cashmere. She looked like she should've stopped at Whistler instead, where the fancy hotels are. She didn't belong in Casper at all. This was a town ground to the nub.

The driver brought up Willy's two suitcases—both large— and there was an exchange. Did she want him to stay until someone was home?

"Oh no, she'll answer the door. She's here." She pulled her gloves off and knocked again. She knew not to bother with the buzzer. Long ago—last year?—Fiona had sent her a rambling email complaining about how Gus never fixed anything and that the house was falling apart and she had no means to fix it herself. The doorbell, for instance. Such an easy thing to fix and he wouldn't even do that.

Willy glanced around. What was she looking at? The broken dishwasher in the corner of the porch? The pieces of the bookshelf that Gus never built? Four buckets of de-icer, all empty. Three bags of the same, all full. What was that look on her face? What was it? Disdain? Pity? Or was it nothing, and she simply wanted to come in from the cold?

Fiona stood on the opposite side of the door, collecting herself. She belched and tasted wine and bile. It wasn't a question of if she would vomit very soon, but whether or not it would be right now. She would be fine, she decided, for the moment. She opened the door, a slip of snow sweeping in as she did.

"Not talking to me only proves that I had to come."

"I didn't call."

"You absolutely did not call." Willy embraced her, even as Fiona stiffened. "And you did not answer the phone. And you did not text me back, or email me, and so here I am. You cannot ignore me or my offer to help now. What a mess, love. What a terrible mess. Come on, Fiona. Hug me back. You can grieve all you want. You can go bonkers. But you may not shut me out."

Fiona hugged her back.

"Now," Willy said when she finally let her go, "where is Ruby?"

"At Mike and Sarah's."

"Well, let's go get her." She glanced into the house, the living room and the kitchen beyond, the stairs. "Or shall we put this place together a bit first? Clean it up for Ruby, and no doubt you will have company. People always want to come to the house when something awful happens."

"Not to my house."

"I came."

Fiona felt tears rise up and threw herself into Willy's arms and sobbed, drenching her coat with tears and snot. Willy opened her coat and wrapped it around Fiona too. When Fiona finally stopped crying, Willy whispered, "We look like a strange sort of cannoli."

"I'm so glad you're here." Fiona pulled away.

"Well, are you the stupid bitch for not realizing that sooner, so I didn't have to fly all the way here only to find out that you and Ruby had moved into a hotel off the Strip in Las Vegas."

"I wouldn't—"

"*I* might! Just to get out of this fucking cold house," she said. "For Christ's sake, Fiona, there is literally ice on the inside of the windows! This is not healthy. Poor Ruby. Where's the thermostat?"

"The furnace is broken."

"Then build a fire in the stove!"

Fiona shook her head.

"Fine, I will." Willy took her shoulders and steered Fiona to the couch. "Tell me how."

"They won't come."

"They *will*." She opened the stove door and threw in some paper. "This is how things work. A tragedy occurs, and people are devastated. And then they all want to *do* something. They want to reach out. They want to comfort and console and feed. And clean."

"Oh, don't."

"Is there someone I can call to come do it instead?"

There was, Fiona supposed, but a stranger coming to see the state of Gus's house would be even worse. "No."

"Then needs must." Willy struck a match. "Oh, look! It worked. Aren't I clever?"

Smoke billowed into the room while Fiona tidied a few library books into a pile, mostly Ruby's. *Volcanic Panic! What Do Spiders Eat for Supper? I'm Pooped: The Journey of Food through Your Body.* They went to the library once a week, she and Ruby. They hadn't been since before, but the books wouldn't be due for another two weeks. Fiona laughed at the thought of paying fines on those books. None of the librarians would make her pay. She was one of the broken families. There would be no library fines for the broken families. The library would forgive the fines, like they did for one week in the autumn if you brought a donation for the food bank. All your charges forgiven. No penalty. Amnesty Week, they called it.

"Fiona?" Willy stood in the doorway to the kitchen. "Where shall I put all the baking supplies? And where are the bin bags? You have made a very large mess, my dear."

It sounded like the helicopter was roaring right outside the cave's entrance. Ruby and Liam made their way to the edge of the forest behind the school and watched as it lifted off. There were the television trucks, lined up in the school drop-off zone, the little half-circle driveway between the front doors and the flagpole, the flag at half-mast.

"Where is it going?" Liam's words puffed out into the cold. He pulled his hat down over his ears. "You think they're going back?"

Ruby nodded. She felt her heart lift with the helicopter as it swayed to the north in the icy-blue sky. They were going to get her father, and Shane. They were bringing them home! He'd been looking after Shane this whole time, just waiting for the skies to clear so they could be brought home. What a hero! Everyone would be so impressed. Gus Tenner, hero! That's what the news people were there for. Her dad would lift Shane out of the helicopter himself and hold him up. Here he is! And he's not dead! And I'm not either. Ruby was right.

I was right.

Ruby tried to wait at the edge of the woods, but it was taking so long, and it was so cold, and she wasn't dressed for it. Her father would understand. Of course he would. If he was standing right there looking at her, he would tell her to get her butt to the cave. Or else go home.

She would not go home.

She could go back to the cave, though. She'd be able to hear the helicopter from there. She'd run back and be there before it landed. She would be the first one to see her father.

She sat at the edge of the little stool, with the cedar boughs separating her from the cold outside, and hardly moved, waiting to hear the helicopter return. Liam sat across from her, his knee bouncing. Ruby knew what he was thinking. Shane was dead. And they were bringing his body home. It would be really sad if Shane was dead and her father was bringing his body back for his parents. He would be so sad about what happened. He would be so sad about Anna and Tag and Skye and Nino, and Shane too. Her father would feel terrible, and he'd be so relieved to see Ruby. He would be so sad, and he would be so happy. He would be tired and cold and maybe all of his toes would have to be chopped off if he got frostbit. Maybe even his ears. But Ruby would never say he looked weird. She would never say that. She would be so happy that he came down from that stupid mountain. She would be so sad about the other kids. And happy that he was home. It was confusing, and it made her body hurt to even think about any of it except for being happy that her father was coming home. He would fix everything. He would make the town better. He would find some way to make it better for everyone. Even Anna and Tag and Skye and Nino. And Shane would be nicer, because he would've almost died. He would have to be nicer, and then everyone would like him and feel sorry for him and that would make him a nicer kid. When her father lifted him out of that helicopter, Shane would be a nicer kid. If he wasn't dead.

It wasn't long before they heard the *whop whop* of the helicopter coming back.

"That was really quick," Liam said.

Ruby agreed. What did that mean?

They put on all their layers this time and ran back to the edge of the field. The helicopter lowered squarely to the ground. The rotor wash kicked up the new snow, and when the doors opened, at first Ruby thought that the helicopter hadn't gone back to the mountain at all, because no one leapt out in a hurry. There were four people, still sitting on the benches facing each other. Four people in their orange SAR jackets. Four people just sitting there. They should be moving faster. And where was her dad? Were there seats behind those two benches? And what was that on the floor? That wasn't a person. That wasn't a body in a bag. That wasn't what she was looking at.

Two people came running towards the helicopter. Behind them, the news crews held back, but the cameras followed them.

"That's his moms," Liam whispered.

And so that was Shane on the floor by those men's boots. Shane in a white plastic bag. Was it plastic? It had to be heavier. Paper? Papery plastic?

Shane's mama slapped one of the men in the SAR jackets. His mom pulled her away. His mama shouted and screamed, "You let him go! You let him go!"

Even though his mama looked like she wouldn't have the muscles, she hauled the bag of Shane out of the helicopter and tried to carry it. Him? She tried to carry him in her arms, but he wasn't a baby. He wasn't a baby at all. She slipped and he toppled to the ground and then she was on her knees beside him and she was unzipping the bag and pulling him up so he was sitting, grey-faced, with wet hair, one arm of his parka ripped away, eyes blank and staring right in Ruby's direction. His mama was weeping and wailing and screaming at Shane's big mom. "I didn't want him to go! I said it would be too cold! And look! He's so cold now! He's so cold. He's so cold. He's so cold." She put her arms around him, her face against his. "He is so cold. You are so cold, baby. So cold."

Liam sobbed beside Ruby. "He still has my lucky arrowhead in his pocket. His left pocket." It was so close that one of them could make a run for it and snatch it back before they took him away from his mother.

"He's going to be buried with my arrowhead!" Liam turned and ran through the forest. Ruby watched Shane's moms for another moment, and then followed him.

Stupid helicopter. Stupid, dumb, empty helicopter.

Her father was not dead. Everyone would think he was now. But Ruby knew better. He was still up there, and it was her fault. He gave her his lucky rabbit, and Shawn took Liam's arrowhead. And then everything bad happened.

Leave no trace, Rabbit. Always pack out what you pack in.

That's what he was doing. He was looking for the backpacks and snowshoes and all the things scattered in the avalanche—the sled with the stoves and the food, all those hats and gloves. Anna's glasses. Luke said she wasn't wearing them. Luke said they were under the snow somewhere. Ruby held the little rabbit attached to her zipper. She held it tight. He was the only one cleaning up the mess. She held the rabbit so tight that when she finally let go, there were two deep indents from the ears. Ruby fit the rabbit's ears into the same angry red marks and squeezed and squeezed until the pain changed into something wet and hot, and when she pulled it away, there was blood. It oozed across her palm and over the edge and dripped tiny spots onto the snow, bright red and beautiful. And then her hand started throbbing, and hot streaks of pain shot up her arm. She stumbled back to the cave. She had a first aid kit in her backpack. A zippered, waterproof bag filled with all the things one person would need in the wilderness. There were Band-Aids in there, and one of those wipes. She should clean it first. It would sting, but she would do it anyway.

When Ruby crawled into the cave, she was surprised to see Liam curled on the floor, knees up to his chest, still crying. She thought he had gone home. She held out her hand to show him the blood, but he just kept crying as she used her one good hand to find the first aid kit. It was packed tightly and so she shook the contents onto the floor and picked out an antiseptic wipe and a Band-Aid. Liam sat up and wiped his face with his sleeve. He reached for the wipe and tore it open, still crying. He sniffed and wiped his face again with his other sleeve, leaving a long streak of snot on the cuff, and then he took Ruby's wrist and held it gently while he wiped at the two small wounds.

Now that Willy was there to take responsibility for Fiona, and the house had been resuscitated from its frozen state, she had retrieved Ruby from Mike and Sarah's. That evening, the three of them sat down to eat before going to the vigil that was being held at Cayoosh.

"You did not have a lot to work with," Willy said. "So I won't entertain any commentary about freezer-burnt naan or the fact that there is not enough Chef Boyardee to go around. I know neither of you care that there are no vegetables on the plate and are probably quietly celebrating that the biggest can in the cupboard was fruit cocktail." Willy took a bite of her naan. "Thank goodness your toaster is in good working order."

Ruby and Fiona didn't eat, except for a few bites of the bread.

Willy bundled everyone up and into the truck and lurched the complaining old thing towards the school, mostly staying on the correct side of the road.

"Very hard to tell," she said as she parked along the street, "what with the snow."

Ruby jumped out of the truck and scanned the crowd for Liam, then ran to catch up with him and his family. Fiona watched Sarah and Mike greet her with hugs and kisses.

"Her other family," she said with a catch in her throat.

Willy patted her shoulder. "It's good to have people. As many good ones as we can."

An old man approached Ruby and hugged her for a very long time.

"Hold on," Willy said. "Who is that and why is he hugging her so hard?"

"That's Gus's father, Tim." Fiona waved him over. She could see that he was taking a moment to decide if he would stay with Ruby or join Fiona. Eventually, he made his way to Fiona and took her hand, which was nice. Fiona appreciated his presence deeply, if only to buffer her like Willy was doing. No one spoke to her. They nodded when they caught her looking, but that was it. Some glances in her direction were filled with as much sympathy as the ones given to the other families, but other glances were hard.

Candles were passed around and lit. Mike and Sarah stood on the steps of the school, in front of pictures of the five children, enlarged and standing on easels. Luke and Liam stood beside them, and there was Ruby, tucked behind Liam with her finger in her mouth. When Mike started talking, she backed away and stuck her fingers in her ears, turning away from the lights. She took off at a run.

"Is she okay?" Tim let go of Fiona's hand.

"Do you want me to go get her?" Willy said.

Fiona shook her head. She desperately wanted to stick her fingers in her ears too, but that would get her flogged and banished, so she decided that she would fetch her daughter instead.

She held her candle in front of her, so as not to set anyone on fire.

"Excuse me," she murmured, and slowly people did, and then the rustle grew louder, because people realized that it was *her* and everyone wanted to get out of her way. Mike was talking about what a loss it was to the families, to the school, to the town, and even the province and country. And the *world*.

"These children were destined for such good things."

Past Liam and Luke, up the steps.

"The loss is extra profound because of the unique and giving nature of each one of these children."

Not Shane.

No mention of Gus?

Fiona found Ruby behind the shrubs. Before Ruby could bolt again, Fiona slid down to the hard-packed snow beside her and stuck her own fingers in her ears. She grinned at Ruby. Ruby leaned against her. The weight of her felt delicious. Nourishing. A reminder that this small child came from her. From her *body*.

Created by her and Gus. That was miracle enough, never mind the added mystery of the Universe that she'd been spared, unlike the other children.

The crowd was singing now.

"This little light of mine." Fiona pulled Ruby closer to her. "I'm going to let it shine."

Ruby dropped her fingers from her ears, not because she wanted to listen, but because she was fast asleep.

Tim carried Ruby to the truck and set her in the back seat.

"Meet you back at the house?"

"We're not really up for a visit," Fiona said.

"Thought I'd stay with you," he said. "Just for the night."

Fiona shook her head. She couldn't imagine him in the house with her. He was so big, and had such big eyes, always drinking in everything around him, collecting all of it for later, when he'd pull it out and bring it up. Never in a critical way—that was Muriel, when she was well—but just to roll it around and take up space. "I'm sorry, Tim. Willy's staying with us. It feels full."

"I can sleep on the couch," he said. "I just want to be close to you and Ruby."

"But Willy is on the couch." Not true. Willy was on Gus's side of the bed. "The motel is giving family members fifty percent off," she said.

"That's quite the discount," Tim said. "Pretty tacky, if you ask me." He patted the truck's roof. He stood there for another moment, stroking his beard, before he nodded. "All right. Motel it is. It's not a problem, Fiona. I'll come by in the morning."

"It's just not a good time—"

"No, it isn't." Tim shook his head. His cheeks reddened, and his eyes too. "It's a terrible time. But I am coming by in the morning. I have to leave after the service. Muriel will only eat for me now."

She hadn't asked about Muriel. Not once since he'd joined them.

"Tim, I'm so sorry." Fiona put her fingers to her cheeks. "I should've asked how she was. I should've been wondering how she was. But I *wasn't*, because of everything else. But I know she is your world. I should've asked—"

Willy gripped Fiona's arm and squeezed hard.

"Did you tell her?" Fiona asked Tim gently.

"I did not."

"That's kind of you."

"I told her I was going to see him," he said. "When she didn't answer, I showed her a picture of him with Ruby, when she was a baby and Muriel still knew him and loved that little girl so much, but then she asked what I had to do with a man that had so many tattoos." He choked back a sob. "She touched little Ruby's face and said to say hello to her. Give her a kiss for me, she said. Give that treasure a kiss from me."

The next morning, Fiona found herself flattened on the couch. Her head raged against the daylight slicing through the gap in the curtains. She heard Ruby padding to the bathroom in those pink felt slippers, the ones with the bells that tinkled. And then the toilet flushing. Another set of footsteps, heavier, but not as heavy as they should be. Not Gus, coming down into the tension that always followed her nights on the couch.

She closed her eyes and rolled onto her side. Two Mason jars lined up on the coffee table. The dregs of gin and tonic and melted ice at the bottom of each one. Her stomach churned. Fiona got up and took one of the jars into the kitchen. She emptied the jar and then tipped the rest of the bottle of gin into it. She heard Willy and Ruby coming down the stairs and took another moment to add a little tonic and a squeeze of lime. Fiona guzzled the entire concoction while she stood at the sink.

"Rehydrating," Willy said. "Smart girl."

"I was so thirsty," Fiona said as she filled it with tap water this time.

Willy stepped out onto the front porch with her coffee, like an ad for a mountain resort, before Fiona could tell her that it was the back porch that had the spectacular view of

Mount Casper. The front porch looked out on the hydro substation, and furthermore the couch out there was soaking with
damp, friable with rot and hosting a family of mice.

She came back in moments later. "Your porch is foul." She
tossed a stack of mail on Fiona's chest. "I'm guessing you haven't
checked that in a while."

It was all flyers, except for a sympathy card from the mayor
and another card, postmarked Maui. Inside was a cheque from
Helena.

To help, any way I can.
With utmost sympathy,
Helena

"Who is Helena?" Willy snatched it. "Is this your other
wealthy benefactor?"

"Gus's May-December."

"Ah, yes. I'll keep this safe." Willy folded the cheque for fifty
thousand dollars into her wallet. "This is not one for the fridge
and a macaroni-and-glue magnet Miss Ruby made in kinder-
garten. Now, there are also bags of food on the porch we need
to bring in."

All that food to absolve themselves for repudiating Gus. For
hating Fiona. Casserole dishes on the rotten couch. Boxes filled
with banana bread and bags of oranges, a block of cheese and a
package of hot dogs, a tin of cherry tarts. A plastic bag filled with
frozen burritos, individually wrapped. A tub of chili, still hot,
and a note. *I don't need the container back.* But no name.

Willy lined the food up on the counter.

"I don't know where we'll put all of this."

"The garbage."

"Fiona, don't be a brat."

Willy opened the fridge and started taking things out. Expired condiments. Mouldy leftovers from before. An empty milk container.

"I've brought a dress for Ruby. She'll love it."

"She won't."

"She will. Every single little girl in the world would want to wear this dress."

"Even if they are a small, silent, raging queer just waiting to happen?"

"You don't know that she's a lesbian."

"I didn't say *lesbian*," Fiona said. "But I know my child. Or, I know enough to know she's not a typical girl. Maybe she's not a girl at all. When she starts talking, she'll tell us all about herself. Or I hope she will. Gus and I were just waiting for the conversation. Any conversation. And we were ready. No dress."

"Does she have anything nice to wear?"

"We're not going to the memorial."

"You are," Willy said. "Because if you don't go, what you said on television will be even worse. You are going to represent Gus, for better or worse. Ruby can wear the dress for an hour."

"Everyone will know that I'm a fraud. Everyone knows that our marriage was falling apart. Half the town knew he was planning on leaving me. He brought those children up the mountain. *Those* people, those parents, they're the ones entitled to grief and anger. Not me."

"You are grieving," Willy said. "And sad and conflicted and bewildered and mad. And also angry that he got to the separation first?"

Fiona nodded.

"Go for Ruby. She's lost her father. She needs it. And the other families need to see her there. She'll give them hope."

"Or she's the ghost of their children."

"I can't pretend to imagine how they're feeling." Willy teared up. "If anything happened to Collette, I don't know what I'd do."

"That's right. You don't."

"But if anything did happen to Collette, I'd have to soldier on, for Kumar's sake. That's how it is, isn't it?"

"But your marriage is unique."

"They're all unique," Willy said. "Regardless, there are compelling reasons to keep going, and a child is the most compelling reason of all."

If all marriages were unique, then all children of them were too. Ruby most of all, perhaps. Quiet Ruby, sneaking around in the snow, knowing exactly what she was doing when she was out there, flat on her back in the powdered white, staring up at the sky and all the stars she knew how to name. What child has a secret snow cave that is actually *secret* from her mother? What child *can* tell her mother where it is but won't speak the words?

More than once Fiona had wondered if fairies came in through the window during those first weeks of Ruby's life, when Fiona was dutifully airing the baby, a suggestion from Sarah. She wondered if they took her baby and put this un-child, this changeling, in her place. Fiona loved this one, and she would never give it back, but sometimes she looked out across the white lakes of snow and wondered if she might see the other Ruby running home to her.

—

Late that afternoon, Fiona woke on the couch again. Her face came away with the imprint of the weave on it and left a dark spot of drool behind. Someone was opening the front door. She half sat up, grabbing the back of the couch to see who it was.

It was Ruby, with Mike behind her, a big hand on either side of her shoulders.

"Little thing, big thing," she said with a smile. "In come tall and small."

Her legs were heavy and disagreeable. She steadied herself on the wall and made her way to the door.

"Ruby," she said. "I thought we were all taking naps." Fiona pulled Ruby to her side. "Where did you go?"

Ruby stared at her boots.

"Do you know where she was, Mike?"

"Nope," Mike said. "She was with Liam. He won't say."

"Frustrating, isn't it?"

"Understandable, I suppose. Look, Fiona—"

"Thank you for bringing her home." Fiona pulled Ruby against her. "Willy is here too, in case you thought I might be unfit."

"Is she?" Mike glanced up the stairs. "Right now?"

"You can go check for yourself."

"That's okay." He glanced at Ruby. "Love you, kiddo."

Ruby kicked off her boots and hung up her parka and put her hat and gloves on the rack beside the wood stove. She went up the stairs and saw Willy curled up under the quilt on her mother's bed, still asleep. Ruby sat on the top stair, just out of sight.

"You are not the only one affected by this tragedy, Fiona," she heard Mike say.

"Says the one who sent them out there in the first place. Says the one who nobody seems to blame."

"What are you saying?"

"What is everyone saying?"

"You mean about Gus."

"But it's you too, right? You're the principal. Blame should fall on you too. Why isn't it falling on you? Why is everyone talking about Gus? Only Gus?"

"Because he was the one who was with them. He was in charge," Mike said. "Cayoosh does this trip every year. This was the first year Luke went. He's the only one who knows what really happened."

"Maybe it was unsafe every year."

Up the stairs, Ruby shook her head. It was not her father's fault. It was not his fault. It was *hers* because he gave her his lucky rabbit. It was not her dad's fault and it was not Mike's fault. It was her fault.

"You can't lay blame under circumstances like this."

"Oh, but people *do*. Have the lawyers showed up yet?"

Ruby didn't want to hear any more. She crawled down the hallway and into her room. She shut the door and kept crawling, over to her bed. She climbed under the covers and pulled them up over her head. She heard Willy get up and go downstairs, exclaiming about how cold it was. Ruby stayed under the warm covers and sucked her finger, well into the evening, but she didn't sleep. She listened to Willy and her mother talk and talk and talk. When they finally stumbled up the stairs together, bumping against the walls and even giggling,

Ruby waited for quiet. A long stretch of *quiet*. Then she tried to sleep.

But it was too cold. They'd let the wood stove go out. Ruby got up and went downstairs to rebuild the fire. It was stupid to let it go out. And it was stupid that no one had called to get the furnace fixed. It was stupid that her mom refused to touch the stove and Aunt Willy had no idea how to stoke it for the night. It was stupid to be this cold.

When Fiona woke that morning, she had no doubt at all about what day it was. Monday. The memorial. She slipped two lora-zepam under her tongue and went out the back door with the tin of pot and the little pipe. She smoked a full bowl, inhaling as deeply as she could. Pot is vulgar, Willy said. I realize that it has a different reputation here, but for goodness' sake, it smells foul. It's no better than sucking on a cigar or chewing tobacco. It's disgusting.

"But wine this early is perfectly acceptable?" Fiona said as she came back in.

"Utterly so, considering." Willy filled Fiona's tumbler and tipped the last of the bottle into hers. "Cheers."

"Cheers." They clinked glasses and did not smile.

"Here's to liquid fortification." Willy downed hers and then left to make sure that Ruby was ready to go. Fiona sat at the table and sipped at first, then gulped the rest, opened a new bottle and filled the glass again, nearly to the top.

"Finish up, Fi." Willy checked her watch as she came into the kitchen. "We'll deserve another glass when we get home. Time to go."

Fiona drank half of it. She set it down and made no move to get up.

"You have to go."

She drank the other half as she heard Ruby come down the stairs. Slowly, slowly, little feet. They stopped at the bottom of the stairs.

"Come see," Willy said.

Fiona tipped the last swallow into her mouth.

"You'll be impressed." Willy tilted her head towards the living room. "I got her into the dress."

"How?"

"Doesn't matter how. She looks beautiful."

"Twenty bucks?"

She shook her head.

"Fifty?"

"It might have been."

"Sixty?"

"I only had three twenties." Willy's cheeks coloured. "She wouldn't do it for two."

Ruby already had her winter coat on, so all Fiona could see was a crimson-red hem and black tulle squishing out from underneath. She was wearing tights too, which she never did. She hated the way the crotch always slid down to her knees. Fiona occasionally bullied her into knee-highs, but they fell down so quickly they looked messy by the time they got wherever they were going. And truly, she'd stopped caring about what Ruby wore. What did she care if Ruby wore pyjamas to the Remembrance Day ceremony at the cenotaph? What did she care if she wore a pair of filthy sweatpants to supper at Mike and Sarah's? It didn't matter. And it didn't matter now either, because Ruby was who she was, and seeing her in a beautiful dress—even covered by the coat—was like looking at a man wearing a ball gown. She looked uncomfortable and pained. She looked angry.

"You can take that off if you want, love."

Ruby shook her head.

"It's worth sixty dollars?"

Ruby nodded.

"What if I gave you sixty dollars to put your sweatpants back on?"

"Fiona!" Willy punched her in the arm. "It was a deal. Fair and square. Now, you go get dressed. Ruby and I will be waiting."

She stopped in the bathroom to do her makeup and take another pill, and then came back down in a black wrap dress that came together at her hip, a wide, deep V at her chest. She wore a necklace with a bird on it, flat silver, etched with detail. A swallow? A dove?

"That's what you're wearing?" Willy pulled on her coat.

"You think I should change?"

"No time. Let's go." Willy handed her the Liberty scarf. "Put this on. Cover up a bit."

Fiona held it in her hand. She should get changed. But into what?

"Exactly," Willy said. "The scarf will take care of the neckline. You look fine."

She'd lost track of the alcohol and the pills. This was not good. The best way to be crazy is to keep the curtains drawn against the sun, have a glass of water beside the bed and a bunch of pills in a tiny bowl.

Each night, she tipped them from the ugly plastic pill trough labelled with the days of the week and into the tiny porcelain dish on the table on her side of the bed. She would read for a while, while Gus had the TV on too loud downstairs. The bowl was shallow, about as big as a silver dollar. There was a little yellow bird painted on it, with green all around. It was easy to imagine that it was a nest with five little eggs. It was easy to imagine just not taking them at all.

You remind me of a bird, Fiona. He'd handed her the tiny dish in a tiny store filled with knick-knacks. They were in Park City, Utah. Fiona was pregnant. I'll get this for you. He was buying her things then. Clothes and jewellery, little treasures like the dish. He wanted her to stay. The pregnancy was a terrible mistake. A terrible, ignorant mistake. Those days and weeks after moving in with him, and not once did they use a condom. She loved him ejaculating in her. She told him she had an IUD, which she genuinely thought she did. When she went to the clinic in Whistler, the doctor said no, you do not have an IUD. And you are pregnant. She arranged for an abortion, but when she was supposed to get on the bus, she just didn't. She didn't want a baby, but she was afraid that if she left, everything behind her would disappear, and it wouldn't be there for her to come back to. She told Gus, who begged her to stay. Don't go back to London. Stay with me. I want to have this baby with you.

You remind me of a bird, Fiona. The dish in the palm of her hand, the small yellow bird. He meant, as graceful. Maybe he meant hard to catch. Maybe he meant way up high and far away and flighty. She was like a bird in all those ways and especially in the way that she could fly away any time she wanted. Any time she wanted. Any time, she told herself. I can go any time and take the baby with me. She put her hands to the necklace, the little bird etched in flight.

The memorial would start in twenty minutes. Fiona followed Willy to the truck. Ruby was already buckled up, red satin and black tulle bunched in her lap, big dirty winter boots dangling above the floor. The dress made Fiona inexplicably furious. Be that kid who would wear the dress, or don't be. But don't be both, not for sixty dollars.

The parking lot was full. Cars lined the street all around. "We should've walked," Willy said. "There's nowhere to park this horrible truck."

"Park here."

"Do you see a spot?" Willy leaned forward, looking.

Fiona's head felt fat and heavy now. She put her hands to the scarf at her throat. As delicate as it was, it was holding her head up, she was sure. If she unwound it, her head would roll away. "Just park right here. They all know it's Gus's truck. What are they going to do? Tow it?"

The sun was still working its way up the bright-blue sky, so light flooded the valley. How could anyone see anything with the glare bouncing off windows and melting snow?

Fiona steered Ruby towards the building, a hand on each shoulder. Fiona would not sit through the memorial if Ruby took off. Ruby was the whole reason.

Willy walked beside Fiona, whispering about what people were wearing. Jeans? Really? Doesn't anyone have a nice coat? How on earth are lumberjack shirts acceptable at a funeral?

"Memorial," Fiona said. She knew that Willy was doing this to try to distract her so she would feel better. But she felt worse, because she was thinking the same thing. And she was think-ing how it took a dead father and five dead children and sixty bucks to get Ruby out of sweatpants. It took all this awfulness to get her into a pretty dress. And it was sad that she looked so pretty on this terrible day, when no one would notice. Or would they? Did you see what Gus's girl was wearing? That little thing looked so sad, but she was pretty for once, wasn't she? And her mother too. What a bitch. But she was beautiful too. Oh, that poor little girl.

Ruby spotted her grandfather in a row about halfway to the front. She ran to him and pushed the chair next to him even closer. He smelled of cigarettes and man perfume. He put an arm around her and kissed the top of her head. Ruby leaned into him and held his arm with both of her hands. Willy and Fiona joined them.

"We didn't see you this morning," Willy said.

"I woke up to find that I didn't have it in me." Tim lifted his shoulders and let them drop. "It was hard enough getting myself here, to be honest." He patted Ruby's knee. "You think that's silly? An old grandpa who can't get out of bed?"

Ruby shook her head.

"We're glad you made it, Tim." Fiona kissed him on the cheek before looping her arm through his.

"As for you, Miss Ruby," Willy said as she took the seat on the other side of her, "you need to stay put." Willy put her hand on Ruby's other knee. "I will keep you in this seat myself. I will use brute force if necessary. And it will not be pleasant. Understood?"

Ruby nodded.

"She knows to sit still," her grandpa said. "Right, kiddo?"

Ruby lifted his arm and snugged herself under it. Now he smelled of old suit and dirty armpits. That was okay. It didn't matter. This was exactly who she wanted to sit beside, if she had to be here at all. She did not want to think about Skye and Anna and Nino and Tag. And definitely not Shane. She would think about her grandpa's smell, and how his long white beard tickled her cheek.

"Fiona?" Willy took her mother's cheeks in her hands like she was even littler than Ruby. "Look at me. This is entirely doable, Fi. You can do this. You know this, right?"

Her mother nodded, but it looked like she could've been nodding about anything. Are you wearing socks? Nod. Do you know how to spell your name, honey? Nod, nod.

"Good." Willy made a *tsk* sound. "Why we are not sitting up front with the families, I do not know."

Ruby did not want to sit up front. She'd have to spend the whole time plugging her ears in front of *everyone*.

"We were not invited to." Her mother's voice was slurry, like when she was drunk. But she only had one glass of wine before they came, right? "They don't want us up there."

"Maybe you're *expected* to sit up there," Willy said. "Of your own volition."

"The ushers know who Ruby is. Who I am." Fiona closed her eyes. "They all know who we are."

Ruby closed her eyes too. That was a way to plug her ears, sort of. When she had heard that the memorial would be at the ice rink, she thought that was very appropriate. It would be cold, and slippery, and everyone would be shivering. Their teeth should chatter, and their muscles should cramp, and they should slip and trip and fall and crash into each other on the way to the chairs.

But there was no ice. The floor was smooth. The building was warm, even, which was so odd, like ice cream that was warm but still looked like ice cream.

Ruby stared straight ahead, her grandfather's arm and cigarettes and stink too heavy on her now. She searched for Liam. He was in the second row, with his parents on one side of him and Aubrey and Luke on the other. She found his bright-yellow toque. She stared and stared and stared, willing him to turn around. Finally, he did, when everyone turned to watch the families come in. Everyone stood, like it was a wedding on TV.

Along came Skye's parents. To Ruby's horror, Skye's father leaned past her grandfather and grabbed her hand.

"Did she say anything? Just before?"

"Ruby, I'm sorry." Skye's mother tugged on his arm, tears streaming down her face as she did. "Come away, please."

Freed, Ruby cradled her hand to her chest. It had happened so fast that her grandpa, Willy and Fiona hadn't had a chance to act. They all touched her now, murmuring assurances. Ruby shook her head. She wanted everyone to leave her alone, and this was the very terrible opposite of that.

As the lights dimmed, Willy gripped that same hand, at the wrist. She whispered, "I know what you're thinking." And then she held tighter. "I am a very, very nice aunt, but make a scene and there will be hell to pay, small child. Hell, payment demanded in full."

There was so much crying, it sounded like the Zamboni. A loud, scraping drone that went on and on as pictures of the kids slid by on a gigantic screen above the stage. Tag and Anna building a snowman, Shane riding an ATV up a dirt road, Nino and his dog,

Skye on a beach somewhere, palm trees in the background. So many happy times, someone said. So many more never to be had.

The Zamboni got louder.

Ruby thought of the picture Shane brought to school once. It was of his penis, stiff and sticking straight out.

"It's a woody. Usually you have to be older."

"Good for you," Skye had said. She grabbed it, and everybody chased each other around the school with it. When Mike stepped out of his office to see what was going on, Shane grabbed it back. Mike said go outside and make snow angels instead of whatever they were up to. As they all trailed outside, Shane hid the photo somewhere in the foyer. It was probably still there. His penis, under the couch or behind the poster of the waterfall at Yosemite. His penis, hiding in the school. Even after he was dead.

It was dim and warm, and there was music playing. That dripping ukulele version of "Somewhere Over the Rainbow" that had become a modern-day dirge.

"Fi?" Willy touched Fiona's arm. "It's time to go."

How on earth did she find herself here? How could she be here, where five families were putting their grief on show, even when they were crippled by it?

Tim left the aisle of folding chairs first. He was going to find Mike to say hello. Willy took Fiona's hand, and Ruby's too. The three of them stepped into the slow-moving river of mourners leaving the rink.

Outside, the sky was bright and the sun shone on the roofs of all the cars and trucks. Everything looked so sparkly and colourful.

The media people were a tangled gauntlet at the bottom of the stairs.

Fiona stared out across the glistening parking lot and up to the dignified, frozen fortress that was Mount Casper beyond. The sun had lifted itself higher, in exaltation. Clouds too, rising up and setting themselves atop only the highest peaks. The sky was a lighter blue up there, as if it was giving the rest of it to the sky below. In honour of those babies.

"Isn't that spectacular?" she marvelled.

Just steps below her, every reporter had their camera and microphone trained on her, and her alone.

"Don't say a fucking word," Willy growled. She tightened her grip on both Fiona and Ruby. "Unless it's to say 'no comment.' That is the only acceptable thing to say. 'No comment.' 'I have no comment.' Understood? These people are dogs."

"Mrs. Tenner! Tell us about the service?"

Mrs. Tenner was Muriel, sat in a plastic-covered easy chair in a home meant to look like a hotel, to keep the patients from wandering off. A hotel with shitty murals and a pretend shop, where they could buy a juice box with play money.

She was not Mrs. Tenner.

Fiona's fingers were numb. Willy was not her mother. Fiona was not a child. She was a grown woman, a widow and a mother. This was ridiculous. As mourners streamed around her, she twisted away suddenly.

"Fiona!" Willy reached for her.

"I'm fine." She held on to the railing and stepped gingerly down the steps. The stairs were salted, but her heels were high, and everything was at a slight, ever-changing slant. "Come with me, Ruby."

Ruby hesitated.

"Ruby." Fiona held out a hand. "Let's go, love."

—

Ruby was not going anywhere with her mother. Not when she looked like she was barely even there, swaying just enough that Ruby could tell that even a very slight wind would sweep her away. Ruby tried to pull away from Willy, but Willy was too strong. Ruby pulled harder, grimacing, until it looked like Willy was violently restraining someone else's grieving child. Gus's poor little girl. Willy let go. Ruby's wrist was red, and there was Willy's thumbprint, and four red fingertips.

Ruby stood on the steps for a moment, calculating how long it would take her to run across the parking lot. In that time, the clouds parted, and her mother smiled a crystal-clear smile. Sunshine poured over her shoulders. She was so beautiful when she smiled like that.

"Come to me, Ruby love."

She was so perfect when she said Ruby's name like that.

Fiona beamed at the cameras, her arm holding Ruby close.

"How are you coping since the tragedy?"

Who asked that? A man, a man, a woman, more and more, faces caked with powder, wide, encouraging gazes. Trust me. Sympathetic eyes. We understand.

"So kind of you to ask." Fiona held Ruby's shoulders. "This is my daughter, Ruby. She survived the avalanche. She is a very lucky girl."

"We have no comment." Willy was beside Fiona again. "Let's go, Fiona."

"But, Willy, they want to know what I have to say." All of the reporters were so beautiful. When they first arrived in town, they dressed down, playing to the aesthetic of the locals: Gore-Tex jackets and expensive hiking boots, warm hats flattening their usually carefully coiffed hair. But now they were dressed for a funeral, in their shiniest black shoes and best suits, the women in conservative dresses under their long, puffy coats. Even the people behind the cameras were dressed up. They all glowed in the severe and glorious sunshine, even with all the black and grey. If only they would step out of the light, it wouldn't be so hard to behold their stunning good looks. The light and the heat waves lit them, and within the flames they shuffled, this one stepping forward, that one back, scurry, scurry. Fiona could hardly focus on them. "If you would all just stop moving and stand still."

"Excuse us," Willy said. "We're all grieving. This is not a suitable time. I politely demand that you not use anything you've recorded here today, with the not-so-polite threat of legal action should you choose to disregard our request. I am confident that you will do the right thing." She put a hand over one camera, but there were ten more. "Please, leave us alone. Come, Fiona. It's time to go home."

"Maybe your daughter would like to say something about her dad?"

"Who asked that?" Fiona said. "Who would ask such a thing?"

"Or her classmates?" a reporter called from the back. "Her friends?"

The cameras all shifted downward, focusing on Ruby, even if they didn't have the guts to ask her anything themselves.

"She doesn't talk," Fiona said. "Not even to me, hardly. Even though her father is dead. Up there somewhere." She threw up an arm, gesturing vaguely northeast. "Under the snow. And no one is looking for him. That's your story. Not harassing a little girl. Her heart is broken. It's *broken*. If you cut into her chest and had a look, you'd see bloody shards. Is that what you want? To see the blood?" She pushed Ruby in front of her, into the blazing, wicked sun.

"Fiona," Willy said. "Please stop talking."

Ruby yanked her hand away and lunged forward. The reporters let her through.

"See the blood trailing behind her?" Fiona shouted. "Her heart is *broken*."

Ruby ran across the parking lot and into the forest.

"Aren't you going after her?" a reporter asked.

"She'll be fine. She's practically feral," Fiona said, and excused her way through the scrum.

When she got to the truck, she saw someone had left a note under the wiper. *How dare you?*

How dare she what?

Which one? There were so many to choose from.

When Ruby finally came home, it was nearly dark and there was a fire in the stove. Her mother lifted a hand in greeting, from where she and Willy lay on opposite ends of the couch, their legs a jumble in the middle.

"Are you impressed?" Willy said. "I made the fire all by myself."

"I told her how," Fiona said.

"And did not lift a finger," Willy said. "You were at your snow cave, right?"

Ruby nodded.

"I wish you'd draw me a map," Fiona said. "And that you'd tell me when you go. Then I wouldn't worry so much."

"What if we needed to find you?" Willy said.

"What if someone came and wanted to know where you were and I couldn't tell them?" Fiona sat up. "This is a genuine possibility. Will you make me a map?"

"No maps."

Fiona raised an eyebrow at Willy. See? She can talk.

"Come on, then." Fiona rolled off the couch. "I'll draw you a bath."

The bath was full to the top with bubbles, and smelled of roses.

"I added some of those nice salts. Off with your clothes."

Fiona unzipped the dress and Ruby pulled it off. It sat crimson red at her feet, bloated with tulle. She worked the tights down and kicked them off before picking them up and shoving them into the little garbage can beside the toilet.

"Fair enough," Fiona said. "Get in, you."

Ruby put in one leg, but the bath was too hot and her cold foot felt like it was on fire. She gasped and pulled it out quickly.

"It'll cool down soon enough."

Ruby nodded.

"Will you be all right while I go sit with Aunt Willy?"

Ruby covered herself with a towel and perched on the edge of the tub.

Fiona kissed her forehead. "This will get better."

The bathwater? The dead kids?

Or missing her father? That would get better, because she was going to get him. She was going to bring him home and he could say what happened. That there was nothing he could do. He could say sorry. He was so sorry. Ruby was frozen now, so she let the towel drop to the floor and slid into the bathtub and right underwater, even though it was still too hot. When she came up for a breath, she was red all over and steaming. She was too hot. The bath was stupid. She got out and dried herself off. She put on Gus's T-shirt and tiptoed to the top of the stairs.

"What are these?" Her mother's words sounded strung together, like the bunting above Ruby's bed.

"Your flight itineraries."

Ruby slid down another couple of steps so she could see. Willy handed Fiona two sets of papers, folded into thirds.

"Yours. Ruby's. I printed them at the pharmacy," she said. "Your printer isn't working."

Her name in bold letters at the top. YVR to LHR.

"I leave day after tomorrow. The car comes around lunchtime. My flight is at eight o'clock or so."

"Why can't you fly with us?"

"Kumar is leaving for Jakarta the day after next."

"The nanny could take care of Collette?"

"She's going home to Slovakia for a few weeks. I've already changed her ticket twice."

A pause.

"You and Ruby will be fine. I'll see you at the airport on the twenty-eighth. Well, the twenty-ninth, by the time you get there, London time."

"Don't you think Ruby and I should stay here?"

"For what?"

There was a silence and then her mother said, "His body."

"Listen to me," Willy said. "No. And I'll tell you why."

Ruby slid down another step. If they glanced up, they'd see her. But they were knee to knee, Willy's hands on her mother's shoulders. They were not going to look up.

"No one is going back up for his body. They've looked everywhere. He's buried somewhere too deep. He's buried up there. That's his final resting place, Fiona."

"Someone will find him."

"Why should they?" Willy said. "Don't you think that mountain is a pretty good final resting place for Gus Tenner?"

"They'll look again, in the spring."

"Then you'll be here for it," Willy said. "*If* they find his body."

He's not dead. Ruby would find him. *That* would be the story of all time. Daughter goes up the mountain in the dead of winter and finds her father alive, when no one else could! *That* is something only a daughter can do for a dad, or a dad for a daughter. He would do the same. He would've gone already. He wouldn't be stuck trying to figure out how to get up there and where he might be, based on the extent of the avalanche.

She'd have to find him before January 28.

Ruby tiptoed into her room to find her school calendar.

That was only three days away, and one of them was her birthday. Tomorrow. She wasn't sure if she was going to pretend it wasn't her birthday or celebrate it by herself. Either way, she didn't want anyone else to celebrate it, not if her dad wasn't here. She planned to spend it figuring out how to get up the mountain.

Ruby woke up to a cold blue morning. She got dressed in her favourite pair of pants. You could wear them red plaid flannel out or black fleece out. She wore them flannel out, in honour of her birthday. She was nine now, even if she didn't feel any different. She had to pull her favourite top out of the dryer, which was better than pulling it out of the washing machine or dirty laundry basket. The turquoise shirt had the Mount Casper Outfitters logo on it—a compass, with the outline of Mount Casper in the background. She made sure the key to the store was attached to the loop in the flap of her pack before she stoked the stove for Aunt Willy and her mom, who were still fast asleep upstairs.

Her dad told her that he'd gotten her present the last time he was in Squamish, and she knew exactly where it would be. She'd get the present, and the few supplies she needed to go get her dad.

After the store, she'd stop and buy a cupcake and candle, and then she'd go to the cave and open her present. That way, when she found her dad, she could honestly tell him that she'd had a birthday party. Because he would want her to. If you don't celebrate your birthday, Rabbit, you end up staying that age forever. Never forget a birthday.

If she didn't blow out a candle, she'd be eight for her whole life, in the same way that Anna and Nino and Skye and Tag and Shane would always be nine years old.

The store smelled so good. There was a wood stove in the corner, and drying racks all around where he and Luke hung wet jackets and hats and gloves and long underwear. The stove was cold, but the smell lingered. Smoky clothes, damp wool. The smell of his jackets, with his sweat, and his laundry soap, so different from Luke's. She pulled down all her father's things, still hanging on the racks from the trip before. Long underwear, wool socks, silk undershirt, wool sweater, waterproof jacket, balaclava, toque, gloves. She piled them on the floor and made a nest of them. Curled up in the middle, she squeezed her eyes shut and waited for a message. *I'm over here, Ruby! Look for the tallest pine beside the biggest rock. I love you. Come for me.*

She took down the framed business association picture of him, set it on the floor, and then she dressed him. Long underwear first, snow pants, undershirt, sweater, jacket, toque, gloves, but not the balaclava. She didn't like him wearing that. It made him look like a bank robber.

The present was wrapped in a brochure from a snowshoe company. She tucked it in her pocket, grabbed another emergency candle, a whistle and a probe. She'd never had to carry a probe before, just a shovel. She picked the one that folded down the smallest and secured it into a webbed pocket on the outside for easy access. She helped herself to a couple of hand warmers, two energy gel packs and a bar of chocolate. Her dad kept them by the till, beside the Kisses. The chocolate bars were all dark chocolate, organic, with either orange, mint or salted caramel. Or plain. He'd hidden a plain one in her pack that day. Was it good luck or bad luck to choose the same kind? It was good luck, Ruby decided, so she took one of those, and then, on second thought, she took one for Liam too.

"I'll see you in a bit," she said to the dad shape on the floor, and then locked the store behind her.

When she got to the snow cave, she was so surprised to see Liam there that she fell backwards into the snowbank. He'd brought a helium balloon that took up most of the space. *Happy Birthday!* with a bunny holding a bouquet of flowers.

"My mom told me." Liam gave her the balloon as she crawled in. "Well, she didn't tell me. She was talking to my dad and they said how they felt really sorry for you. My mom is going to come by your house later with a cake, I think. I got you this balloon. With my own money. The woman asked me who it was for, but I didn't tell her."

Ruby smiled. She pulled out the cupcake and stuck the candle in it. She found the lighter her dad had taken the safety off of, because she couldn't start the ones that had one.

"Is that from Mexico?"

She shook her head.

"Remember they didn't have safeties on them there?" Liam said. "That was cool. I liked it there. Kinda hot, though. Are you going to sing?"

Ruby shook her head.

"I won't either. Only if you are."

She lit the candle and the ice cave was quiet for a moment, and then Liam did sing after all.

"Seems weird if we don't," he said when he was done.

Ruby cut the cupcake in half with her pocket knife and handed a piece to him. He took it and ate it in two big bites. When he was finished, he yawned.

"I don't think I sleep anymore," he said. "Or maybe I do, but I don't notice. Do you sleep?"

Ruby shook her head.

"I keep hearing the cracking and rumbling and screaming," Liam said. "I keep thinking about my arrowhead. I miss it a lot."

Ruby unzipped her pack. She lit an emergency candle to take off the chill.

"That's better." Liam took off his gloves and held his hands near the flame. "What did you get for your birthday?"

She showed him the package from her father.

"Open it," he said.

She picked at the tape. She unfolded the paper to find a little box. Inside the box was a paracord bracelet that also had a whistle and compass. There was something else, wrapped in tissue. It was a necklace, with a rabbit pendant.

She held one in each hand and stared at them.

"You already have a bunch of those bracelets."

Ruby was surprised that he knew that. She didn't have one with a whistle, though.

"But it's always good to have a few," Liam said in a hurry. "I have two. Luke got us them for Christmas, but I already bought one with my own money. You can use it in a bunch of ways if you get stranded." His face scrunched up. "Didn't help us much, did they?"

Liam plucked the necklace from her palm and unfastened it. Ruby bowed her head, waiting patiently while he struggled to close the clasp.

Ruby lifted her head. "Thanks."

"You're welcome."

She dug in her pack and handed him the chocolate bar, and an orange.

"That's funny." Liam handed her an orange from his own pack. "And look at this." He brought out an emergency candle. "I bought it with my allowance too."

She took the candle. It was fatter and smelled good.

"I need your help," she said.

"Okay," Liam said.

She told him everything. And not once did he shake his head no, no, no, Ruby. You can't. She knew he wouldn't. She knew he would understand. If no one else was going to go get her father, she would.

"I know how to get you up there," he said. "You know Cherise who works at the gas station?"

Ruby nodded.

"She told my dad that her house is close enough to the cabin that she can hike there in an hour. She said she wouldn't be surprised if your dad rolled right into her backyard and asked for a ride back to town. My dad told her Gus wasn't a log or a boulder, he was a dad and a father, and to respect the dead."

"My dad is not dead."

"Yes, he is," Liam said plainly. "My parents said so."

He was not dead. He made a snow cave and a fire and a snare to catch rabbits. This is *the* Gus Tenner.

"Ruby?"

She stared at him.

"I just really think he's dead. I'm really, really, really sorry."

"He's alive." Ruby peeled the orange and broke it in half. She stuck the whole half in her mouth. She picked up the wooden peg Gus and the wooden peg Ruby and sat them together in the little room where the Mom peg doll was already sitting at a tiny wooden table, on seats carved in the snow. She set the apple pie eraser between them, and three impossibly tiny forks.

Fiona's armpits were damp with sweat. The house was too warm and smoky. Willy kept opening the stove door and adding little sticks of wood. That defeats the purpose, Gus would say. Load it up, control it, let it burn slow. Instead, Willy had the flue wide open all the time, with smoke billowing out the chimney and the wood burning down too fast. That didn't matter, though, because she liked getting bundled up to go outside and get more wood from the woodpile that was quickly disappearing. And even the amount of wood left didn't matter, considering.

There was a knock at the door.

"Shall I get that?" Willy said.

It was Sarah, holding a cake box.

"What can I do for you?" Willy said.

"I thought I'd bring a cake in case you didn't get around to making one," she said. "Or picking one up."

"Oh, thank you. That is so thoughtful. But we have so much lovely food," Willy said. "Please, enjoy the cake with your family. Or maybe take it to the fire hall?"

Cake. Why would Fiona want a fucking cake? She strode towards the door. "Willy, just take the food and say thank you. Thank you, Sarah. We appreciate it so much."

Willy put her hand on Fiona's arm. "I can handle this."

"Handling it is taking the food and saying thank you." She reached for the cake, but Sarah—bewildered—took a step back.

"The cake is for Ruby's birthday," Sarah said. "Liam said there was no celebration planned. He spent the day with her at the snow cave."

"*Liam* knows where it is?" Fiona laughed.

"Oh, Fiona. Don't tell me that it was Ruby's birthday," Willy said. "Tell me that the children were playing a joke. They were having a bit of fun."

"It's not her birthday," Fiona said.

Ruby was upstairs, asleep. It was not her birthday.

"It *is*, Fiona." Sarah held the cake close to her now. "But you know what? Tell her to come over tomorrow and we'll do our own little celebration. I'm sure that you have your own plans."

"That's right," Fiona said. "We do. Because it is *still* her birthday." Fiona could smell vanilla, too much of it, and strawberry jam wafting from the box. Strawberry shortcake. Ruby's favourite.

"All right, then," Willy said. "We're letting all the warmth out. Let's get the door closed. Are we inviting you in, Sarah?"

"No, thank you," Sarah said. "I've got to get home."

"To your family," Fiona drawled. "To your husband. To your two boys. And Aubrey. Everything is still as it should be, isn't it? When you line them all up, no one is missing."

"True. And I am so thankful."

"Everyone should hate you even more than they hate me. One of mine is missing. You've still got all yours." Fiona held up three fingers on one hand and four on the other. "It was this. Mine. Yours. Now it's this." Two fingers on one hand. Four on the other. "So everybody should hate Mike and you just as much as they hate Gus and me. Maybe even one more for you." She added a finger. "We should count Aubrey. She practically lives there."

"She's lived with us for over a year," Sarah said. "For the record, Fiona, no one hates anyone."

"Everyone hates someone," Fiona said. "It's only natural."

"I'm sorry, Sarah." Willy pulled Fiona inside so she could close the door. "Good night."

"Good night," Sarah said, with a catch in her voice.

Willy returned to her wine. Fiona was about to join her, but then she spun around and was out the door and down the steps in her slippers before Willy could even put her glass down.

"Fiona! Where are you going?" Willy ran after her, but stopped when she saw her and Sarah talking, inside Sarah's car. That would be okay.

Sarah hadn't let her in. Fiona had just managed to open the door before she could lock it and got in.

"You came to my house to humiliate me?"

"I brought a gift for your child," Sarah said. "Who I adore."

"You were being cute."

"You forgot your own daughter's birthday!"

"I didn't forget it!" Fiona's feet were damp and cold. She shivered. Sarah turned up the heat. "You might not know that you want to humiliate me. Or shame me. Or make me look bad. Or privately smile because no one ever thought I was good enough for Gus. They think the deaths of those five children are all his fault. They think he didn't do something, or he *did* do something, to make it happen. Like he had the power to bring that snow down and bury them. Like he had some kind of premonition and sent his child ahead. Like he saved her at the expense of another child, one that he could've sent forward instead. You want to make me feel bad, so you will feel better. And you probably aren't aware of any of it."

Fiona paused. She could say more, or she could stop there. She should stop there. The best part of her said to stop. Stop, Fiona. That's enough. You've already said far, far too much. Don't drop the last marble you've got in your hand *again*. You and Mike and a couch in Mexico. What does it matter anymore? It was a long time ago. So many things have happened. It didn't matter.

"It did matter," Fiona suddenly said into the tense, hot quiet.

"Yes, it did." Sarah reached behind her for the cake box. "Just take the cake. You can tell her you made it."

"I'm not talking about Ruby's birthday, which we already have plans for."

"I suppose that you'll tell me what mattered." Sarah sighed. "And then after, could you please get out of my car?"

"I had sex with Mike," Fiona said. "In Mexico. On Boxing Day. Night. When you were all at the pub."

The expression on Sarah's face didn't change. Fiona mimicked what she'd expected to see; she contorted her own face into an exaggerated mask of disgust. When that didn't make any difference, Fiona tried sadness, twisting her mouth into a clownish frown, willing tears to come.

"Get out of my car, now."

"Did you hear what I said? Do you want to know any specifics?"

"Get out."

"Guess your marriage isn't so great either."

"I swear to God, Fiona." Sarah spoke through gritted teeth. There it was, the anger. "If you don't get out of this car, I will come around to your door and physically remove you."

"Wait a minute," Fiona said. "Are you mad because of what Mike and I did? Or are you actually just mad that I won't get out of your car?"

"You will get out of my car."

"I wasn't ever going to tell you about Sayulita." Fiona opened the door. "But then you brought that fucking cake."

Fiona watched her pull away. After a conversation like that, the other person takes off in a hurry. Spinning tires. Engines revving. Fishtailing on the ice. But Sarah drove so slowly that the brake lights didn't even come on at the stop sign. She idled there for so long that Fiona wondered if she'd stalled. But no, she pulled into the quiet intersection, rolled down her window and tossed out the cake. It slid out of the box on the way down, and landed jam down on the compact snow.

Fiona burst through the door and grabbed her purse and the keys to the truck. Willy leapt up from the couch. "Where are you going now?"

"The store."

"I'll come." Willy scrambled for her socks and boots, her coat. But she took too long. Fiona was down the walk and in the truck and the engine was running, cold and belching, and then the truck was lurching down the street. "Fuck," Willy said. "Fuck!" And she couldn't go anyway, of course. She wouldn't leave Ruby alone. Of course she wouldn't, now that she thought of it.

—

Fiona needed a cart. There were a lot of things to get.

Her slippers were soaked, so she had to walk slowly. Step carefully. Don't slip. Party section. Exactly the right things. And noisemakers too. Step carefully. Don't slip. This struck her as hilarious, and so she was laughing out loud as she turned into the baking aisle. A man glanced up from the flour section when he heard her. Fiona didn't recognize him. Wouldn't that be nice? Someone who didn't know who she was? *Slippers, slipping.* So funny. He stared at her for far too long. What? What's so funny? That's him talking. That's him saying that to her. She needed a cake mix. There they were. Vanilla. Chocolate. Vanilla and chocolate swirl. Maple fudge. Rainbow sparkle cake, red velvet, brownies, angel food. What to choose? Who needs to choose? She pulled one of each off the shelf and did the same with the icing. Butter cream, caramel, coconut pecan, milk chocolate, whipped vanilla.

She grabbed sprinkles and coloured sugar and those tiny silver balls that could break a tooth. She grabbed tubes of icing too. Ten colours! Snap off the tip and get writing! Swirl and curl. A tray of sugar flowers. A roll of ready-made fondant. No, two rolls! Striped candles, rainbow candles, tall, curly ones with polka dots, a fat number 8. Sparklers too.

Just before she got to the till, she remembered that she needed a 9 candle. Not an 8! She hurried back to the baking aisle, where the same man stared at her again. How long does it take you to buy a bag of flour? She guffawed and spun on her heel in her slippers and ended up on her ass. He helped her up.

"Big party," he said.

"You bet," she said. If he took her hand and led her anywhere, she would go. She would go with him. She would unzip his fly. She would sit on his cock.

Instead, he dropped her hand. "You should have boots on," he said.

"Would you believe that I didn't even think of it?" Fiona smiled. "No matter. Not far to go. I park in a nice warm garage at home, so that's something."

"Look, I don't know what to say right now," he said. "Except that I'm so sorry for your loss."

"Thank you." So he knew exactly where she lived. Of course. Didn't everyone? No garage. No heat at all. How about that? Fiona would never go anywhere with that man. His paunch covered his belt buckle, and his sideburns were unkempt. He was as old as her father. Candles, candles, where are the candles? Ah! She grabbed a 9. And then she had a great thought and grabbed a 1, 2, 3, 4, 5, 6, 7 and 8 too. She'd line them all up.

She passed the bakery on the way out, the sheet cakes lined up behind the glass with their airbrushed clouds and gelatinous ponds, *Happy Birthday* piped at a wobbly angle, little plastic hockey players and princesses and bears driving tractors. Who needs one of those crap cakes when a mother can make a better one? The mother always makes a better cake.

Willy followed her into the kitchen, arms folded across her chest as Fiona tipped everything out of the bags onto the counter.

"Where the hell did you go?"

"To the store," Fiona said. "Obviously."

"In your slippers?"

"It's not like I walked all the way there."

"We have to talk about this, Fi. You're in a spin. You might not think so, but you *are*. I am contractually obliged to point it out and feed you your nines."

"I'm not twenty-three. We're not roommates. You don't know how hard I work to manage now. This is not a 999 situation."

"You call this managing?" Willy picked up a box of cake mix from the floor.

"I'm making a cake now," Fiona said. "I'll apologize for everything in the morning. Profusely, and with great sincerity."

"This is not about cake."

"It's late," Fiona said. "You should go to bed. You'll have a long day tomorrow, getting home."

"You need to go to bed too," Willy said. "Very much so. Very much right now."

"I am making a cake."

"You're not taking your pills."

"I am fine."

"You are not fine. Where are your 999 pills?"

"Please, Will. Let's talk about this in the morning."

Fiona pulled down a mixing bowl, a cake pan, the measuring cups. She gave the stand mixer a quick dusting with a tea towel and then plugged it in.

"Do you even have any quetiapine, Fiona?"

"I don't have any 999 pills because I do not need any 999 pills."

"The nines are for in case of emergency. You need to come down—"

"Fuck off, Will! Leave me alone."

"That's not you talking to me like that."

"This is absolutely me. Look, I promise I will go to bed when I am done making this cake. Give me an hour. I might even take a quetiapine then. To help me sleep." She would not. They made her feel like a drugged giantess, drowsy and daft. Fiona tied on an apron. Daisies, with a delicate ruffle along the top. She opened a carton of eggs. "There. All set."

Ruby dreamed of snow. A big white plastic bag full of it, with all the kids inside. And then they were tobogganing down the hill behind Cayoosh. All the students, the dead kids too. Only, they were still dead. They were naked and blue, and Skye was missing two teeth. Anna had her one glove on, the one with the snowflake. They were all covered in bruises. They had no vaginas or penises. This was what Ruby remembered when Fiona woke her up. No vaginas or penises. Just cold blue skin, like dolls who never had to pee or poo.

"Wake up, love." Fiona turned on the light beside her bed. Ruby's eyes ached. Then the overhead light, and the room was ablaze. "It's your birthday!"

Ruby sat up, confused. Yesterday was her birthday. In the snow cave, with Liam.

It didn't matter that her mother forgot. She didn't mind. She really didn't mind. She didn't cry about it. She didn't miss whatever present she would give her.

"Get up! Get up!" Fiona searched through Ruby's closet. "Where is that dress? That beautiful red dress? I'll give you sixty bucks, just like Aunt Noreen."

She meant Aunt Willy. But Ruby had thrown out the dress. She'd stuffed it behind the dumpster at the gas station when she went to spy on Cherise. It was behind there somewhere, covered in grease and spilled pop and expired egg salad sandwiches and mouldy bread.

Downstairs, there were streamers and balloons and party hats and Willy, in tears.

"Let her go back to sleep, Fi."

"It's her birthday for another six minutes!" Fiona held out a small present. "I had this. I bought it ages ago. I was thinking of you." A pair of earrings. Little smiling rabbit faces. "Aren't they so sweet? We can get your ears pierced. We could do it right now. With half a potato and a boiled sewing needle. Remember, Will? We did that, Ruby. At school, when we thought we were in love with each other."

Ruby could run. She could grab her jacket and her boots and her father's big coat and she could run to the cave. She could sleep there. The coat would be like a sleeping bag.

"I have cake!" Her mother clapped her hands. "Come, come!" She disappeared into the kitchen.

Willy took Ruby's hand. "And then you can go back to bed, okay?"

Three cakes with nine candles apiece, one with candles 1 through 9 in a nifty grid, and two more with more random arrangements. The counter and floor were covered in flour and sprinkles and empty tubes of icing, and a stick of butter had slipped right off the plate when she went to put it in the microwave to soften it.

Fiona sang. She handed Ruby a plate piled with slices of the different cakes, all still so warm that the icing slid off. They stank of sugar. She took a bite of chocolate cake and it stuck in her mouth, dry and too sweet. If she could get to the cave, she could light an emergency candle to keep herself warm, and when it burnt out, she could light another one. Then it would be morning. The morning of the only day that mattered.

Cherise said it was about an hour hike up to the cabin, but Ruby didn't think that was true. Cherise didn't look like the type of person who would hike anywhere, so Liam and Ruby figured Ruby should double it. After getting out of the car, Ruby had to put on her snowshoes, because just past the clearing the snow was up to her shoulders. As she wrestled to secure them to her boots, she turned back to see if she could see Cherise's house. There it was, dark except for the porch light. It was nice to be able to see the light and know she was there, with her baby and her mom. A few steps later, Ruby turned back again. No house. No car. No little playhouse capped with snow.

Ruby glanced up at the moon. Her dad said you could tell the time by it, and so she'd thought she would too, but the only thing she could remember was that you had to know where the sun had been exactly twelve hours earlier. She and her father had to be back at Cherise's car before she left for work in the morning. She'd be the guide this time. *This way, Daddy! Hurry, before she drives away!* She dug out the GPS and hung it around her neck, dismayed to find that it was set to a 24-hour clock. She wasn't sure what all those numbers meant.

The trail was straight and steep. She had the coordinates to the cabin on the GPS, still on the screen from the field trip. It pointed her north. That made sense, she supposed, because the plateau should be directly above her. The creek bed was to her right, which she knew because the snow slumped along it, and there were spindly pine trees lining the bank on each side.

The air crackled and snapped with cold. The moonlight sliced in narrow ribbons between the trees. The *kick-slide, kick-slide* of her snowshoes sounded like someone sawing blocks for an igloo. Her pack was too heavy, and her shoulders were already sore, but she wanted all of it for when she found her dad. Her dad would shake his head that her pack was so big.

Had it been an hour? She looked at the moon. Was it higher now? She'd probably hiked at least an hour. But no, the GPS said the cabin was still forty-six minutes away. She could tell that much. She really had to pee. Never do your business on the trail, Rabbit. That's like peeing in the hallway of your house. So she took a few paces into the woods. It was much darker among the trees. She turned on her headlamp, but the bright light cast long, dangerous shadows wherever she turned, so she switched it off. Moonlit darkness was better. She took her pack off and hooked it onto a low knob of a nearby tree. She took off her gloves and jacket and undid the bib of her snow pants. She pushed her snow pants to her ankles and then her long under-wear and panties too. She wanted to pee quickly—it was so cold! She squatted, holding all her bunched layers away from her as best she could. It took a very long time to get her muscles to relax enough that her urine finally made a hissing sound as it melted the snow. She wished she had something to wipe with, but anything she could use was in her backpack, out of reach. She bounced, getting rid of the last drops.

As she was doing up her jacket, she heard a crack, then a rustle, a low huff. A growl, and then a very quiet—but unmistakable—*whoof.* Ruby froze for just a moment, and then she ran over the uneven terrain as fast as she could in her snowshoes, kicking them out to the side, stumbling and panting until she had to stop because she was suddenly teetering dangerously close to the edge of a cliff. She fell backwards and scrambled away from the edge. It was such a long way down that all she could see was black. The other birthday girl in the sleeping bag at the bottom, is that what she saw before she was smashed up? It was daytime for her, stupid. It was probably like a really long toboggan ride that ended with such a crash that she didn't even have a second to know she was dying. And then dead, broken up in her sleeping bag so search and rescue could just cinch up the hood and carry her out like a sack of bones. And blood. Probably a trail of it on the white snow. A bright-red birthday ribbon. No one would find Ruby if she fell here. And she wouldn't find her father. And he'd never know what happened to her. He'd just wander the mountain forever, growing a beard down to his knees, calling her name until he was hoarse and then using the orange whistle that matched hers.

Ruby crawled a safe distance and stood up. She didn't know which way to turn. She didn't hear the huffing anymore, only her own quick breaths, freezing hot in her throat.

Where was the trail from here?

Had she run in a straight line?

Had she taken a turn? Two?

She was so thirsty, and her throat burned from the cold. She reached behind her to get the water bottle from the outside pouch of her backpack. Which wasn't there.

Her stomach roiled, and she tasted bile. Her backpack was still hanging on the tree. Where had she put her gloves? But there were wolves. Snarling, terrible wolves behind her, and a

black gully in front of her, and a rocky bluff ahead. Think, Rabbit.
What do you do when you get in trouble? What do you do when
you don't know what to do next?

STOP.

Stop, Rabbit.

Stop. Think. Observe. Plan.

She checked the GPS. According to it, the cabin was thirty-
seven minutes away. Her father would be there, or nearby. He'd
get her warmed up. He'd layer her up with all the extra clothes
from the other kids' backpacks. She might even eat some rabbit,
if he had it on a spit over a fire. She was that hungry. She would
apologize before the first bite, and she would apologize after the
last bite, and then she'd give the bones a proper burial, marked
with a wooden cross, even though she and her dad did not
believe in God. They were atheists, unlike her mother, who said
she'd like to be an atheist, but she had invested too many years
of bruised knees on the prayer benches in Anglican churches,
and besides, it's nice to think an artist created the universe, and
not a bunch of gases thirteen billion years ago.

Fiona wanted to ignore the knocking on the door, because she didn't want to see anyone, and also because of any potential bad news that might be delivered. But Ruby was out somewhere with Liam, and what if it was about them? She got up, and the knocking stopped. Deciding it couldn't have been urgent after all, she returned to the couch, topped up her wine and found her spot in her book. She was reading the ones from Gus's side of the bed. She was nearly at the end of *Into the Wild*, where McCandless is stranded in the snowy spring on the far side of a river that has suddenly swollen so much that it won't let him cross. All he has to eat are wild potato seeds, which turn out to be toxic. A man, alone in the wilderness. Found dead. The story was far too close to home, but it felt good too, like pressing on a bruise.

There were suddenly two sharp knocks in quick succession. Had the person just been standing out there *thinking*? Then the door opened, and Sarah walked right in.

"What makes you think that you can just come in?"

"It's a small town, Fiona. Try locking your door. Are you alone?"

"You know she's with Liam somewhere." Fiona stood. "And the lock doesn't work."

Sarah shrugged. "You get away with all kinds of crazy shit. Excuse me this one wild and wacky thing."

"Fair enough. What are you doing here?"

"Willy's gone?"

"Yes."

"All right." Sarah sat down on the couch. "We'll do this without her, then." She patted the cushion. "Sit with me."

"No, thank you."

"Fiona, sit the fuck down and listen."

Of course, she knew what was coming. This was about Mexico. The question was, how much of Sarah's shit would Fiona take? Fiona looked at her hands as she sat. She shaped them like a bowl, a wide open one. This much? No, no. She made the ball smaller and smaller until her hands could only hold an espresso shot.

"I'm willing to take this much." She showed Sarah her narrowly separated hands.

"You'll take what I'm giving," Sarah said. "I don't care what you do with it."

Fiona lifted her espresso cup hands up to Sarah's face. "This much."

Sarah took Fiona's hands in hers. She lowered them to Fiona's lap with such gentleness that Fiona left them there.

"When Liam was two, I slept with another paramedic," Sarah said. "We'd never worked together before, but I could tell he wanted to. We were on standby for a fire for hours. We did it in the back of the ambulance. You're surprised, right?"

"I don't—"

"You don't believe it because you think you're the only fuckable woman in this town. Because you just assume that

someone fucking you is such a big deal that it would ruin everything. As if you hold that much power."

"Mike told you."

"I knew, Fiona. I knew that *night*." Sarah laughed. "Our marriage isn't like that."

"Well, good for you." Something was being swept away. The
last vestiges of that night in Mexico. Sarah was sitting there in
front of her, erasing something that was not hers to erase.

"You're ripped up because *you* don't matter to him. All this
time you thought you had something. Something you could
hold over Gus or Mike. Or me. Even Luke. I've seen you look at
him sometimes. He's a *child*."

"He and Aubrey are not children," Fiona said. "I caught them
fucking in the store just a couple of days ago."

"I just came to tell you that you don't hold anything over any
of us." Sarah stood. "It would've broken Gus and Mike, though,
so I'm glad you kept quiet about it long enough that Gus never
knew. Even if your marriage was over before Sayulita."

"It wasn't."

"It was." Sarah's voice thickened with either sympathy or grief.
"It was over when you didn't jump off the bridge that September.
Which, now, makes more sense."

So Gus had told them about that. And Mike had told Sarah
about her diagnosis. She hadn't even ended up in the hospital!
She'd just stood on the Lions Gate Bridge at four in the morning
while he and Ruby were asleep at his friend's place. She was at
the darkest, coldest, deepest point of a terrible spiral that told
her that Ruby and Gus would be better off without her. She
would be doing a good thing. It would be hard for them at first,
and it would become Ruby's legacy, just like her mother's death
was hers. But she understood how her mother simply *had* to go.

There was no choice involved. In that moment, Fiona was out of options to deal with the excruciating blackness that threatened to swallow her.

She'd put her hands on the fat green rail and leaned, lifting her feet off the ground. A cyclist with blinking lights crested the bridge, so she planted her feet back on the ground and pretended to be taking pictures. The second photo made her pause; blurry bridge lights slung away and up into the dark, foggy dawn in four illuminated arcs. She counted on a moment like this, each time, a tiny shift that would make her take one step away from the bridge, and then another. Absurdly small, when you'd think that all it should take is not wanting her daughter to go through what she went though. That was not enough, in those dark moments when she *knew* that her child would be better off without her.

Fiona showed Gus the photo after she walked the half-hour back to the apartment with the view of the orange shipping cranes in the harbour. He was horrified that she'd been intending to jump. He had appreciated that she'd stayed. That's what the point was. It was a *good* story. She'd managed to *stay.*

"I'm surprised Gus told you that."

"He couldn't do it all by himself."

"But did he show you the photo?"

"The picture doesn't matter," Sarah said as she headed for the door. "The fact that you were going to jump mattered."

"But I didn't jump." Fiona leapt up. "Right? Look, I want to show you something." She took the stairs two at a time, up to her room to get the framed photo she kept hidden under a stack of sweaters in the closet. She brought the picture down to Sarah, wiping the dust off it as she did. "I wanted to put it up on the wall. It means a lot to me. But Gus hated it."

Sarah took the photo. She gazed at it, shaking her head. "I don't see what you do," she finally said, and handed it back. "It's just sad, that's all."

Fiona held the frame to her chest. She knew it was beautiful. Sarah just suffered from that common small-town inability to appreciate depth.

"When you come back from England, we're happy to help with Ruby." Sarah put a hand on Fiona's shoulder. "But you have to get your own supports. We're not going to do what Gus did for you and cover it all up, like cats kicking dirt over their shit."

"I'm not shit." Fiona twisted away from Sarah's touch.

"That's not what I meant," Sarah said. "We're setting boundaries, that's all. The fact is, we would never have been friends with you if it weren't for Gus. And even then, it was reluctantly. You always said that you thought we didn't think you were good enough for him, and it's true we wanted better for him. We wanted him to be happy in his marriage, and not just as a dad."

"You won't have to see us again," Fiona said.

"We'll be seeing Ruby," Sarah said. "Because you *will* bring her back."

"I don't have to."

"Emháka is writing up a set of parental requirements that you'll need to complete," Sarah said. "And formalizing us as Ruby's respite care. Three nights a week. For the next few months."

"I'll take my pills."

Which worked for a while, until she was high enough to tell herself that she wasn't crazy at all. And then go on to run away from Harrogate and throw the cups off the Pont Neuf. Crashing her father's car—filled to the roof with pink plush hearts bought with stolen money—into the gate where the boy who had just dumped her lived. Staying up for a week doing speed before being pulled down off the bridge over the M2 by a constable who was not one bit sympathetic. You could kill someone down there, you stupid twat. That same constable talked her down two weeks later, when everything was black again and the only option was a quick exit. Pet, please. I don't want to go home to my family with your blood on my hands.

"You've hit Ruby," Sarah said. "More than once. You haven't made her a meal since it happened—"

"My husband just died!"

"Gus died, yes. But you can't pretend that it wasn't over before. That's not fair." Sarah listed the offences on her fingers. "You never know where she is. There was ice on the insides of your windows because you couldn't be bothered to make a fire in the stove or get the furnace fixed. You're stoned or drunk half the time. This house is falling down—"

"That's Gus's fault too."

"Ruby needs us more than ever now. She needs Liam. She needs Mike and me. She needs Luke and Aubrey. Aubrey adores her, you know. They have a special connection."

"You don't know what my daughter needs."

"I do. Better than you, right now. Get your shit together, Fiona. Or you will lose Ruby. Let us help her while you do. Emháka won't stop you going to England to be with your family. So long as you bring Ruby back and then start making things better for you both."

After she left, Fiona realized that Sarah hadn't taken off her boots, or her parka, or her hat. It was always going to be that brief. Or she was just that cold. The house was frigid again, now that Willy was gone. Ruby hadn't built a fire since the morning.

It was true that Fiona still hadn't called anyone about the furnace. It was true that Fiona had hit Ruby. More than once. A girl needs a mother. A child needs a good mother. She was not a good mother. She was unravelled. But that was okay, because on the plane ride to London she and Ruby would be knit back together. Mother and daughter, above the clouds, belted in beside each other, holding hands, breathing the same recycled air.

In this case, leaving was the easiest thing.

Ruby trudged along without her backpack. It wasn't that stupid to have lost it. It wouldn't take her long to get up there, and once she was there, she'd find him pretty quick, and then they'd head straight down to Cherise's. Right? Quick enough?

Was it colder all of a sudden? Or was it because her sweat was making her cold? How did it go? What would her dad do?

Survival isn't about what tools you have, Rabbit. Survival is a state of mind.

Have a piece of chocolate.

But she didn't have any chocolate. It was in the backpack's side pocket, zippered in snugly with a bag of roasted peanuts, one of the homemade granola bars, and an entire package of pepperoni sticks Liam bought her at the gas station.

She did not need chocolate. She just needed *tenacity*. Her dad said that if she ever joined a roller derby team when she was older, her name should be *Tenacious Tenner.*

She would find him. He would hear her calling and come out of the snow cave that was so warm he wouldn't even have a jacket on. He'd have a beard by now, and it would have caught bits of moss and twigs. She didn't need her backpack. She would be quick. Plus, she had an energy bar in her pocket, and she could eat snow for water.

Eating snow is a bad idea, Rabbit. It lowers your core temperature.

So she would melt it first, if she didn't find him right away. At the cabin. On the wood stove. She would make her way there. It wasn't far. Her father was probably just past that, up on the hill. Or maybe he'd be at the cabin by now? He should be. Unless. Maybe he had a broken leg? Maybe he had two broken legs?

Ruby tasted panic.

Her dad never panicked and neither would she. She scooped just a little snow into her mouth. Just to take away that terrible sour taste.

Once she got back onto the trail, she'd find the cabin. The GPS said she was forty-five minutes away. That couldn't be right. That was stupid. Well, if there was a good thing about losing her backpack, it was that she should be able to move faster. Ruby snowshoed away from the bluff, in a straight line through the trees, until she came to the trail and the snow-covered creek bed beside it.

If there were more wolves, she would scream at them and get ready to hit their snarly snouts with a stick. She grabbed the first solid one she could find, with a pelt of lichen to give it a good grip. She might not be able to outrun them, but she could beat them to death if she had to. She was no Red Riding Hood, no dummy in a red cape with a basket over her arm, wide-eyed and stupid. Whatever you say, Mr. Wolf.

There was the clearing—crumpled, and strewn with giant boulders of snow, all of it covered in so much new snow that it looked like a sleeping zoo, the animals with their humps and bumps and big heads under a soft white quilt, as if they might rise from their slumber and slough off the snow and amble away into the night. It didn't look anything like it did on that terrible night, with trees scattered like matchsticks and torn branches and clumps of earth and bushes sticking out like pompoms. The long divot of the creek bed had even filled in since then, but she could still tell where it was because of the long, narrow slump of it. This was where he would be. In the cabin if he could make it there, or a snow cave he built, or, if he was injured, in the care of a mama rabbit, in her warren deep under the snow.

"Daddy!" Her call was muffled, swallowed by the snow. "Daddy!" She turned in a slow circle, scanning the buried, snow-covered zoo. The pines were a tall fence at the edge. A rustle in the forest. A flutter, a low, questioning *who?* An owl swept across, wings outspread, its flat, round face turned to Ruby. Its big yellow eyes blinking.

"Daddy? I'm here!"

There was so much snow. Everywhere. All around. She turned on her transceiver and set it to *search*. The steady beeping was the worst thing. That meant either her dad's wasn't turned on or that he wasn't anywhere near her. Even if he was, she had no shovel. She had no probe. She had no gloves. She had the GPS, the half of an energy bar she'd saved for her dad, but no water. She had a stupid plastic rabbit that was nothing but unlucky, the paracord bracelet and necklace and her pocket knife. She found the plastic rabbit in her pocket and didn't even look at it before she threw the stupid thing with all her might. It landed somewhere in the dark, and she didn't care. Dumb rabbit. She threw the wooden Ruby peg doll too.

But then she suddenly wanted the rabbit back. Her dad had given it to her. She stumbled in the direction she had thrown it. She was crying, her tears were cold by the time they hit her chin. She was too cold. And where was the rabbit?

She fell to her knees. She couldn't find her father, and now she couldn't find the rabbit either.

"Daddy!"

She could stay in the clearing, calling and waiting. But her fingertips were numb, and her tears burned in two hot lines down her cheeks.

There was the rabbit! Tiny, almost black against the snow, its ears sticking up. Ruby crawled over and picked it up. It was just a torn bit of root.

"Daddy? Where are you?"

She could tell that she was close. Liam told her that she'd know it. He's your father, he said. You're connected. You love him and he loves you and you can probably even smell each other like animals in the forest. My dad says he'll always find me. It works the other way too. A kid can find a dad. It's animal science.

Ruby sniffed the air. Did she smell him? She did. Did she?

You'll sense him, Liam said. That's how you'll know where to look. Only you can find him.

Only me.

Hey, Rabbit.

She spun. "Daddy?"

No one was there.

Maybe he'd called to her from the cabin?

Had anyone even checked there again since they stopped searching? Maybe he had a broken leg and couldn't get down the mountain, but that didn't mean that he wasn't sitting by the fire, staying warm and wishing someone would bring him a burger.

Ruby made her way towards Tiffen Creek. She wished she had a burger for him. He wouldn't care if it was cold. And if he wasn't there? She'd light the fire and he'd see the smoke and come to her, if he could. Or she'd just warm up and go out again, hollering for him. Her voice was louder in the moonlight somehow. He'd hear her. And when she found him, she'd climb into that snow cave beside him and tell him how sad everyone was, but that they'd be happy once he came home. She was going to go to England, but not now. She'd stay with him. Even if it meant staying on the mountain and telling each other stories until they got so cold that they felt warm, and then fell asleep like that and turned to bones inside their snow pants and ski jackets. Even if he wasn't at the cabin and she had to find the rabbit warren under the snow. Maybe the chimney would be sticking out, with smoke drifting up, and it wouldn't be hard to find him at all.

There was no cabin.

Ruby's thoughts were as foggy as her breaths in the cold air. Her thoughts were grey and soupy and not in the right order. Cabin. There. Supposed to be. What? I don't get it. Check the GPS. The screen was a blur, no matter how many times she blinked. Which tree had her backpack? A fireplace underground and a rabbit. A plate of tiny cookies. Her father lifting a tiny mug of hot chocolate. She had it wrong. He was definitely in a rabbit warren. Magically shrunk so the mama rabbit could take care of him, letting him rest on a bed of the softest rabbit fur.

Her steps slowed. Her snowshoes slid along. There should be that big fallen tree where she dropped the crate, but over here the trees were all standing at attention, as if they didn't want her to enter the forest at all.

Stay out, they said.

You're tired.

Sit down.

Have a nap. Don't you want to sleep? It's the middle of the night, Rabbit. You must be so tired.

She was. She did want to sleep. She wanted her backpack for a pillow. She wanted a drink of cold water. Or tea. A grape juice box. Hot chocolate from the gas station. A tall glass of milk.

She wanted to light the emergency candle and look at the flame and take off her gloves and hold her hands over that magic little piece of hot light.

But wait. She didn't have her gloves on? And where was her jacket? She wasn't shivering. She knew what this meant.

When you stop shivering, you're in big trouble, Rabbit. When you're not shivering, it's heading straight to game over, and pretty fast.

But she hadn't found him! Even worse, he hadn't found her. She had to find him! But she was too cold. She had to go back. She had to go back and try again when she was warmer. If she died on the mountain, stripping off her clothes until she was just a naked little girl in a snowbank, she could not try again. She had one more night before they left for England. Resupply and go again. And *fast*.

Her father didn't believe in heaven, and so she didn't either, even if it was nice to think of the kids up there, together. If it was heaven, Shane would be nice. If her father was dead, he was just dead, because atheists don't go to heaven no matter how badly people want them to.

He's with God now, Grandpa Tim said. As hard as it is for us, it was his time.

It was *not* his time.

His time was with her!

She found her jacket, and with numb white fingers she struggled to make the zipper work. She couldn't, though, so she followed her tracks back as fast as she could, dragging her lichen-covered stick behind her to mark her path that way too. No stupid mistakes, Rabbit.

Wolves howled all around her, but now she didn't mind. They were singing to her, and she was howling back. Crying too, with hardly any tears now, because she was so, so thirsty, and a small voice, because she was so tired. But she heard herself howling, and it was loud and furious and mournful. They were following her, thank goodness. They would take her all the way back to the trailer, the empty rabbit hutch, the car.

There, at last, was the beautiful, glowing porch light, spread out across the mucky yard like arms waiting to fold her into an embrace. The sun eased up the back side of Mount Casper, turning the sky from black to deepest blue, even while the stars still hung high overhead. There were no lights on inside the trailer. Ruby tried to open the car door, but she couldn't feel her numb white fingers. She used her thumbs, both of them, and finally got it open. She kicked her snowshoes off and crawled in the front. The keys were still in the ignition, so she used the same thumbs to turn the engine on and flick the heat switch to high.

Ruby lay down. She stared at the jumble of key chains—an eight ball, a smiling cupcake and a glittery letter *c*. And a rabbit. Flat and pink and with big, sad eyes, holding a glittery red heart in its paws. She'd seen that rabbit key chain at the drugstore, on the spinner by the register. Her dad offered to get it for her, but she'd curled up her lip at it because it made no sense. Why was it so sad if it was holding such a big heart? Now she wished she'd let him get it for her. When she fell asleep, that sad rabbit fell into her dreams, bouncing bright pink against nothing but snow. The heart was nowhere to be seen.

—

"Hey!" Ruby woke to furious banging on the window. It was Cherise, yelling at her. "Get the heck out of my car!"

Ruby had been dreaming of a rabbit warren with so many tunnels that she couldn't find her dad, and when she gave up, she couldn't find her way out.

"What the hell are you even doing in there?" Cherise said as she flung open the door.

Ruby sat up, trembling with cold and fatigue.

"You're just a kid." She leaned into the car, her big boobs almost falling out of her stretched-out sweatshirt. "You're *that* kid. The one from the avalanche."

Ruby nodded.

"Why are you in my car?"

Ruby looked away.

"Right. You don't talk. You were probably cold. You want me to call your mom?"

Ruby shook her head.

"The police?"

Ruby shook her head violently. She started to cry.

"All right, all right. Stop it." The girl tossed her purse into the back. "You want a ride, is that it? I wasn't supposed to see you there? My warm car is a miracle? I'm not supposed to ask you where you've been or what you're doing? I'm supposed to be all whatever, because your daddy is dead?"

Ruby stopped crying. She wrestled with the seatbelt.

"Well, your daddy killed those kids." Cherise got into the car and shut the door.

"He didn't," Ruby whispered.

"She talks." She turned down the heat. "I'm Cherise."

Ruby stayed silent.

"You're Ruby Tenner. Now we know each other, right? You're

going to make me late for work. I'll take you, but I'm going to drop you off before town and you can walk the rest of the way. I don't want to get involved, got it? And I don't want anyone to see you, so stay low. And don't you dare tell anyone you used me and my car. Pinky swear?"

She held out a pinky, but Ruby didn't dare try to hook hers. Most of her fingers were throbbing and hot, but she couldn't feel her pinkies at all. She offered a thumb instead.

"That'll have to do," Cherise said as she did up Ruby's belt for her.

Relieved, Ruby curled up on the seat, the belt digging into her hip. The engine rumbled and the radio mumbled and the heat felt mostly good, except her fingers were being stabbed with so many hot needles. She was shivering so hard that her muscles ached. She fell asleep and dreamed of pulses of light in the snow, hot white probes stabbing down and down and never, ever finding her father.

A rap on the window. Cherise stood outside, the snow falling gently behind her.

"Get up."

Ruby tried to sit up, but she couldn't. She had to arrange each bone in order and drape the skin and clothes accordingly. Until she was the shape of Ruby again.

"You okay?" Cherise said.

Ruby nodded.

"Fine, then. Time to get out of my car."

Ruby sat up. Her fingertips and toes were burning. Where was she? Dumpsters, a mound of dirty ploughed snow at the edge of a parking lot. The propane tank like a big pill a giant could swallow. The gas station. A flash of red—that dress behind the garbage.

Did she ever leave? Was this last night? Or today? Which end of it was she on?

And then she remembered the wolves and the moon and the stars strung so low and bright. The slick, shiny snow and the sound of her snowshoes, *kick-slide, kick-slide.*

Ruby pressed the button to undo the seatbelt, but couldn't do it, even with two thumbs. She saw herself pressing the button, but she didn't feel it. She tried harder, and hot pain shot through her hands. She yelped.

"Never mind. I got it." Cherise undid it for her. "You sure you're okay?"

Ruby turned onto her knees and backed out of the car. She stood and wobbled. Her legs trembled. Her side hurt. She reached into the car for her backpack, but she didn't see it. She couldn't remember when she had it last. Before the car? A night forest. Moonlit snow. Terrible cold. No Dad. Not anywhere. Her snowshoes, she now realized, were back at Cherise's house, in the middle of the driveway.

"I've got to get to work," the girl said. "You want a hot chocolate or something from the machine?"

It would burn her hands. It would burn her throat. Ruby shook her head.

"You hungry?"

She was. She was so hungry, but she couldn't eat. Everything would slice her throat going down. Her stomach would be cut to shreds. She shook her head. No.

"You'll get home okay?" Cherise said. "I don't want to hear that you didn't make it."

Ruby nodded. "Thank you."

"You're welcome."

Ruby nodded again. She started walking. At the edge of the highway, she didn't even check for cars. She stepped onto the salty asphalt and plodded across. A truck stopped for her, then another. No one honked. They felt so sorry for her. Everyone felt so sorry for her. Too sorry to hit her with their trucks. Sorry enough to stop in the middle of the road and stare at her.

Just as she was about to slip into the forest on the narrow path between high banks of snow, she heard someone calling.

"Ruby!" It was Mike. Ruby wanted to run away, but her toes were pounding in her boots and her fingers were two bouquets of heavy hammers banging away at nothing. "Ruby, stop!"

Three steps at a run and she couldn't take another one. That was all she had.

She could hear him running up behind her. She didn't want to turn and see him, so she stared straight ahead. She didn't want Liam to get in trouble. She failed. She got lost. She didn't find her father. She didn't find anything. Not even the cabin.

He lifted her and carried her like that night. He slid her onto the bench and tucked a greasy old blanket over her. He took his jacket off and snugged it in over her shoulders, like a giant warm beard that smelled of BO. He lifted her wrists and inspected her fingers.

"These are in trouble, you know."

Ruby nodded.

"You're not going to run?"

"No."

"Good." He leaned in and cupped the back of her head with his hand and pulled her head to his lips. He kissed her. Ruby heard the wetness of tears in his voice and felt those tears on her brow. He stood back, wiped his face with both hands and then crossed around the front of the truck on the way to his side. He stopped halfway, though, spreading his arms on the dirty hood and bowing his head, just for a moment. After he got in, he spun his wheels in the sanded snow on the shoulder and then pulled onto the highway. He honked his horn over and over and over, passing on the wrong side, racing past the people who knew his truck and got out of the way.

He pulled up to the clinic, right where the ambulances park. He lifted Ruby out and carried her straight in, right past an old lady sitting up with an oxygen tank between her legs and her purse on her lap.

Ruby was tired. She was tired, and her toes and fingers were poker-hot hammers banging at nothing at all. There was the same nurse that let her go with her mother after the avalanche. A doctor. A police officer strode forward, accompanied by a woman with a long black braid and a laptop under her arm. There was her mother, finally, running for her, her jacket flapping like wings.

"Ruby!" She was a crying mess of snot and tears. "I didn't know you were gone! Were you at your cave? You have to tell me."

"I went to find Daddy." The lights were bright. The nurse rolled a machine over. "I didn't find him. But I'm going back up tonight."

"I'm here, love." Fiona kissed her softly on the cheek. "You can't go back up. He's gone, love. He's dead."

The doctor and nurse warmed her up and examined each finger and toe. There was concern. Significant concern, the doctor said. "It takes some time to know. We'll hope the situation improves.

I'll see her in three days and make a decision then. Hopefully, the tissue will recover on the two little fingers. If not, we will have to send her to the city for further assessment."

"I know what that means," Fiona said.

Ruby turned her face away. She was listening and she was not listening. It made no difference either way. When the nurse gave her a tetanus shot, she said, "I'm so glad that you're here." Ruby wasn't sure if she meant right now, in the clinic again, and not up on the mountain all by herself, or *here*, as in not up the mountain with her father and the rabbits, or dug out dead like the other children. "God has a plan for you." She glanced at Ruby's chart. "Now you are one of His very special children, Ruby Cathleen Tenner. Pray to Him, and He will give you comfort."

By the time Fiona was allowed to take Ruby home, it was dark again. The next morning they had their tickets for England, where decidely more expert doctors would be pleased to treat a precocious little adventurer with a tragic and compelling back-story. She'd sat with Emháka Joseph in her office for more than two hours, with one of the officers witnessing the conversation. She'd signed the parenting agreement that Sarah had men-tioned, only now it was two pages longer. Ruby would stay with Mike and Sarah five nights of the week; they were both still cer-tified from when they became legal guardians to Aubrey after she moved in.

"That's rich." Fiona laughed.

Emháka looked up from her tablet and did not smile.

There was more. Provided Fiona took her medication as prescribed, met with her psychiatrist monthly, maintained an appropriate home environment, enrolled Ruby in the elementary school, arranged for speech therapy once a week (and attended each time), took the Nobody's Perfect parenting program, attended AA and/or NA meetings, found a sponsor, and knew where Ruby was at all times, then Ruby could be at home four days a week, including weekends.

Fiona sat beside Ruby's bed while she slept, the quilt pulled up under her chin, her stuffed rabbit wedged under one arm. Ruby's cheeks were chafed, and it looked like the tip of her nose had been dipped in boiling water. She had been sleeping for three hours. When she woke, maybe Fiona would tell her about the parenting agreement. Just thinking the words made a shovel of shame dig deep into her gut.

"Ruby?"

Her eyes blinked open.

"Are you okay?"

Ruby nodded.

"Will you say so?" Fiona gently lifted Ruby's bandaged hand. When Ruby didn't say anything more, she said, "You talked to me in the hospital. Do you remember? Tell me about the mountain? How did you get there?"

Ruby shook her head.

Fiona took Ruby's other hand too. She held them so gently, but she could tell that she was making Ruby nervous. She set the fat white paws down and touched the necklace with the rabbit pendant.

"Where did you get this? Did Sarah give it to you?"

Ruby didn't answer, and she didn't shake her head either.

"Liam? Someone in town? Who gave it to you?"

Ruby lay very still in the bed. Rigid. Holding her breath. Staring at the ceiling.

"I love hearing you talk so much," Fiona said. "I miss your voice." She took her hand away from Ruby's throat. "I just want to know who gave it to you. That's all."

Ruby covered the rabbit with a bandaged hand.

"Okay. Okay, love. I love you. That's the most important thing to know. I loved you from the moment you were born. I've loved you every single day since, and I'll love you for every single day left on earth." Ruby blinked and her chest rose and fell, but otherwise, she was as still as a photograph. "You need to know that. Do you know that? Can you look at me? So I know you hear me?" Ruby kept her gaze on the ceiling. "It's okay. I know you hear me. You know how much I love you. I'll go. I'll leave you alone. I'll just go check my suitcase." Fiona stopped at the door before she left the room. "I see that you haven't packed yet. I wrote you a list. It's in the outside pocket. If you need help, because of your hands, let me know."

She'd brought Ruby's suitcase up from the basement when Willy had bought the tickets. It sat at the top of the stairs. Fiona lifted a foot and kicked it hard. It clattered and banged all the way to the bottom. When the silence was ringing again, Fiona waited for Ruby to call out.

Mommy!

Mommy, are you okay? Did you fall?

"I'm fine!" Fiona shouted. "Your suitcase just fell."

Fiona stomped down the stairs. The suitcase was pink with big purple polka dots, and a deep scrape along the front from when Fiona's father had flung it into the boot of his car after he picked them up at the airport the last time the three of them had gone to visit. Fiona left it where it landed.

—

When she heard her mother rummaging in the kitchen, Ruby sat up and wrestled herself into a pair of fleece pants over her pyjama bottoms, and into her thick fleece housecoat. She pulled the hood up. She gently tucked her feet into her roomiest slippers and made her way downstairs to collect the suitcase, which she hugged in her arms and hauled back upstairs. She set it on the bed beside her, then fumbled to open the clasps with her bandaged hands. The inside smelled of Aunt Noreen's flowery laundry soap. There was a pound coin, and a Tesco bag with a receipt in it, and a pair of socks in a mesh pocket. Ruby liked those socks. They had little bunnies on the side, and colourful Easter eggs. They'd be too small now. She'd have to wear her mom's while her feet were bandaged. Maybe even a pair of her mom's boots.

Those are socks for babies, Collette said. And your pants are for boys. Which of course makes sense. Because you *look* like a boy. A very, very, very *quiet* little boy.

Collette would have to be nice to her now, like everyone else.

Grandad would be loud and pretend nothing had happened. Come in, Ruby Cathleen! I'll make cinnamon toast! And Aunt Noreen would say all the things from all the cards. Time of need. Sorry for your loss. A dark time. In our hearts. And then she'd let Ruby choose a candy from the jar she kept beside her chair in front of the TV. Don't knock over my crochet basket, dearie. And do not change the channel until my programmes are done, love.

She had to pack this suitcase fast, because as soon as her mom was asleep, she had to sneak out and get back up the mountain.

Ruby's breath caught suddenly in the ice-cold house.

She couldn't go up the mountain until her feet and hands were better.

Thank goodness for the rabbit warren, then. The rabbits would take care of him until she got back from England and was all better and could go get him. She wouldn't be afraid of the wolves this time. And she would not put down her pack. Not even to pee.

He'd be cozy down in the warren, sitting with the mama rabbit in a matching rocking chair. A little carved table between them, with a game of backgammon going and two mugs of hot chocolate. If some people got to believe in God, then she could believe in this. He would be okay until she got home. He would understand that she had to go with her mother.

Ignoring the list, Ruby used her wrists and forearms to pile in leggings, sweatpants, T-shirts—plain, all the collars stretched, oh well—and underwear, all of which had frayed elastics at the waist, but nobody would see that. Not even Collette. She'd lock her door at Willy's house this time. She packed the picture of her and her dad mid-air, jumping off the dock into the lake. And her swimsuit and goggles because Aunt Noreen liked her to come do laps with her. A notebook, pencils, her father's *Pocket Book of Essential Knots*, along with a piece of paracord, her pocket knife—not allowed on the plane—a pair of running shoes and all of her favourite socks. She'd put her slippers in at the very last minute.

After her mother went to bed, Ruby hugged her suitcase in her lap and bumped down the stairs on her bum as quietly as she could. She parked it beside her mother's, which sat beside the door, her good winter coat neatly draped over it. There was another bag that Ruby didn't recognize. A duffle bag with a flowered print, pink-and-yellow roses. Ruby unzipped it. A book of short stories by Alice Munro. Fancy chocolate, a satin nightgown. A brand new pair of sheepskin slippers. Fuzzy socks with the tags still on, a bar of soap. Two bars of soap. A soft shawl.

A compact covered in rhinestones. New makeup still in packages. A bottle of hand cream, still sealed. At the very bottom, folded into a knit blanket, was an outfit for a baby. A sleeper with grey-and-cream stripes, knitted booties, and a bonnet that was as soft as rabbit fur, and a sweater to match, with pearly buttons. In another bag, a dozen tiny diapers. And an index card dated nine years earlier in Gus's squished printing.

BABY NAMES:

GIRL	BOY
Stella	Ethan
Ruby	Noah
Muriel	Tim

Muriel? Ruby laughed. She loved Grandma Far Away, but it was bad enough to have Cathleen as a middle name. It was so old-fashioned. Ruby hated it. She folded the card and outfit back into the blanket. She took the bundle upstairs and hid it under her bed. Those were meant for her, and so she got to keep them.

She couldn't brush her teeth, so she squirted some toothpaste in her mouth and swished with water, like she'd seen her dad do sometimes. She got into bed, dressed as she was. She had no idea what time it was. It was dark out, but it could be morning or night. It was always dark. Either way, her mother would get her up before it was time to catch the bus. Oh! Ruby remembered suddenly that Aunt Willy was sending a fancy black car to take them all the way to the airport, which was hours and hours away. Almost a limo, but not quite. Even still, it had heated seats.

When Ruby woke up, she couldn't feel her frostbitten fingers at all, and the house was freezing. It was too early to get up, but she couldn't get back to sleep. When she lay down, something felt wrong in her body. Did she have to pee? Or poo? Was she sick? Was it her fingers? Were they turning into ghosts? She couldn't feel her pinkies at all. Maybe they would just fall off, and she wouldn't have to have surgery. She could just put the bones in a bucket of lye. That's how her dad got his frostbite bones clean.

Best way to clean a bone, Rabbit. If you can get past the smell.

It was dark out, and snowing. The clock said that it was just after 5 a.m. Ruby wanted to see her ghost fingers, so she got up and went to the bathroom. She peed, then wound toilet paper around and around the bandage and then her whole hand, so she could wipe.

What about washing her hands after? Some people drink their pee, her father said once. Supposedly it's sterile. Should we try it? He disappeared into the kitchen and came back with a glass full of clear amber liquid.

Apple juice, of course.

Is it? He handed her the glass. It was warm. He took it back and downed the whole thing.

Ruby stared at him.

Okay, so I warmed it up, he said. But Ruby already knew that. She'd heard the microwave beeping.

She wanted to wash her face, though, so she ran the hot water until it steamed. How would she do this? She didn't want to get her mother to help. She wanted to do it herself. She left the hot water running—she wanted it to be super hot—and ran downstairs to get a couple of plastic sandwich bags. She slipped one over each hand and ran back upstairs and put the face cloth under the water. The heat rang a bell in her fingers and now they throbbed. She squeezed out as much water as she could without wringing it, and then leaned over the sink and wiped her face, even as her fingers banged and banged. Her forehead, her eyelids, cheeks, chin, nose, neck, up to and behind her ears. The air in the bathroom was humid, and her nose dripped.

When she was done, she went back to check the time. It was nearly six o'clock. They would be leaving for the airport in half an hour. She could go downstairs and find something to eat. The fridge was half-full of cake, plus all the containers and tubs and bags of food that didn't smell like their house at all. Capers and red pepper, too much garlic. She didn't want any of it. She just wanted a peanut butter and jam sandwich. And an orange.

The door to her parents' room was open and the bed was made. Her mother never made the bed. Her father didn't either, unless they were leaving on a trip. I like to come back to a bed like that and wonder what neat person lives here. This made her laugh, because their house was always messy. Maybe now her mother was going to do that too, which was a very nice thing. Ruby had forgotten to make her bed. She always made her bed. Ruby always liked to look at the messy house and think one thing, and then look at her own tidy room and her made-up bed and think another. She wasn't sure what the two things were, but she liked the feeling when she was thinking them one after the other. Her mother thought the opposite. She'd come stand in the doorway of Ruby's room—smelling of outside cold and cigarettes—with a frown on her face.

Ruby ran back to her room and tidied her own bed. Ten past six. Her stomach rumbled. She didn't smell coffee or toast or anything like that, so maybe her mother was planning to stop along the way. Muffins or doughnuts or a breakfast wrap. No, probably a croissant from the bakery in Squamish. Willy was sending a limo. Ruby's mother would get the driver to stop. She'd get him one too, and she'd probably tell the story of when she went on a date with a French boy one summer when she was a teenager and the next day they ran away to Paris and lived on the streets for two weeks, stealing croissants and cups of espresso from sidewalk tables at a run. We had so many little cups by the time we left, she said. Can you imagine? We lined them up on the railing of the Pont Neuf and took a picture, and then we tossed them in, one by one.

Croissants always left Ruby hungry. She better go get a granola bar. And one for the plane. And another apple and the entire bag of raisins, because her mother wouldn't notice, and it'd be nice to be able to offer them to her when they were in the sky, flying through the clouds. She'd hold open the bag and Fiona would take a few.

Just a few.

But she'd be so hungry because the croissant would be ages ago. She'd eat the raisins.

There was only one light on downstairs, and that was the back porch light. Her mother was probably having a cigarette. Ruby's suitcase sat by the front door, all alone. Before she went to bed last night, she'd put her suitcase right beside her mother's and that duffle bag. Were they on the porch? Was she having a smoke? She opened the door to see if the fancy black car was waiting at the curb. It wasn't. She thought back. Had her mother woken her up? Did she touch her arm, or call her name from the door, with the hallway light too bright behind her? How had Ruby woken up?

All on her own. Her mother hadn't woken her up at all.

Ruby's whole body suddenly felt like her fingers. She was a hot, throbbing ghost. She walked very slowly to the back door. The worst thing to see would be the big dark morning, with the indigo sky sparkling with stars and no mother as far as she could see.

She opened the door just to not see her mother and then she pulled the door shut so hard that the kitchen window rattled.

She ran back to the front door, shoved on her mother's old boots and took a few steps outside. The same dark, terrible morning, knotted around the ugly pipes of the hydro substation. Two sets of footprints decorated the fresh skiff of snow on the walk. One smaller set leading to the street. And a larger set coming from the street and going back to the street. Her mother. The driver. And no tracks for the suitcase wheels. He was strong. He'd lifted it above the fresh snow.

It was almost noon when Ruby started out for Liam's house. She'd eaten a granola bar and the whole bag of raisins hours ago, and she was hungry again even though she had a terrible, terrible tummy ache and might actually vomit, but she didn't want to be in the house anymore, staring at her pink suitcase parked by the door. She needed someone to open her pill bottle. She tried to get the lid off, but she couldn't. The label said one every four hours, and it was a whole night and half a day more than four hours now and her fingers really, really hurt. She bet Liam could get it off. She put the pill bottle into the outside pocket of her suitcase. She would bring her suitcase. There was no telling.

She should not bring her suitcase.

She should bring her suitcase, because she would not be coming back here. There was no one to look after her. She wasn't stupid. She knew what that meant.

She would not bring her suitcase because her mother was coming back. And when she did, Ruby would talk to her, if that's what she wanted. She would tell her about everything. She would talk and talk and talk, and when they went to the grocery store, her mother would say, Can you believe there was a time when this child didn't talk? And now listen to her! You can't shut the girl up. Come along, Ruby, let's go get a croissant. But the only croissants in Casper were in the deli section at the grocery store, in clear plastic boxes. Oily and flat, the croissants sat very sadly atop a square of red-and-white checked paper. As if that makes them special, her mother said. As if that's a tablecloth at a café on the Seine. It's worse than if there were no paper at all. Let's drive down to Squamish and get some. It'll be fun!

Maybe she would take her suitcase after all. She wanted her things. Even just a pair of underwear if her mom didn't come back until tomorrow. Pyjamas, toothbrush, her stuffed rabbit. Ruby tied a rope around her waist and attached it to the suitcase so she could pull it behind her, her stuffed rabbit under one arm.

The suitcase twisted and fell over, and when she did manage to get it rolling, the wheels crunched and bumped on the hard-packed snow. A truck slowed. Need a hand, Ruby? She didn't look up. All righty, then, you take care, sweetheart. And then a car. Where you off to in such a hurry? Are you okay, honey?

She ignored them, and eventually they drove off.

Another truck pulled up behind her and honked. It was Mike. Ruby's shoulders slumped with relief. He hopped out, took her suitcase and threw it in the back. He took her arm and led her around to the passenger side and lifted her up.

"Seat belt." He did it for her, reaching across her lap and clicking it into place. He was going to take her back home. And then she would have to show him. Her mother was gone. The suitcase. And the footprints in the snow.

But he wasn't driving to her house. He drove to his. When he parked, he left the truck running.

"I know she left," he said. "She called a few minutes ago."

Ruby looked at him, her eyes brimming with tears, despite her trying to hold them back.

"She said she was sorry. She said you could stay with us for a little while," he said. "You can't fly with your hands and feet like that. The doctor has to keep an eye on you. She was going to change her flights. Did she tell you that?"

Ruby shook her head.

"It's okay to cry, kiddo." He opened his arms. "One thing is for absolutely sure. She's doing what she thinks is best for you." Ruby scrambled across the seat and climbed into his lap, not caring one bit that the steering wheel was digging into her back.

Ruby did not want to cry, but that didn't matter. She wept and wept until Mike ran out of napkins from the glovebox. He let her wipe her face on his flannel sleeves, until both were soaked and snotty.

I want you all to take something away, Mike had said that morning before the children piled into the van. Some nugget of understanding of yourself that you didn't have before. That excellent feeling of having accomplished something hard. The exhilaration and challenge of the experience while it's happening, and the sense of accomplishment afterwards. You'll be cold. Your muscles will ache. Your nose will drip. And you will be so glad to see the cabin, and you will be so amazed when you build the caves. When you get back, you will feel different. You'll be more *you* than you ever were before, with the memories and deepened friendships to prove it.

Everyone sat around the table, eating lunch, but Ruby only wanted cereal. No one was talking about her mother. Aubrey sat beside her and kept stroking her hair, which felt good, and heavy, like it was helping her stay in her seat. Liam kept sneaking glances at her. He was grounded for a month because of keeping Ruby's secret, but he didn't look mad. Mike and Sarah spoke quietly to each other at the head of the table, a notepad between them.

When she finished her cereal, she poured herself another bowl. When she was done that one, she went for a third.

"Hey," Aubrey said. "Maybe later, okay?"

Ruby nodded.

"You want me to read to you?"

"Me too," Liam said.

Aubrey had been reading them *The Giver* for about a month.

Liam and Ruby sat on either side of her while she read, all of them under an enormous down quilt Aubrey tucked in all around them. It was the king-sized white one from Mike and Sarah's room. Of course, Ruby thought of snow.

—

Fiona asked the driver to stop at the bakery in Squamish. She bought two croissants. When she took the warm bag from the young woman, the smell made her gag. She swallowed bile. Outside, the car idled. The driver hadn't spoken to her since saying hello and just the bag and the suitcase and mind your head, ma'am.

He honked the horn twice. Not aggressive. Just informing. Airports. Check-in times. Traffic. *Beep-beep.*

The girl said, "Is something wrong with the croissants?"

"It's better this way," Fiona said. "It's the right thing to do."

"Sorry?"

"She's perfect. They're perfect." Fiona held the bag to her chest and patted it. "Thank you."

She clutched the greasy paper bag on her lap the entire way to the airport. She checked her suitcase and the duffle and got her boarding pass and endured a very long line at security.

She put her purse and her boots in the tray.

"Other bag too," the man said.

"What bag?"

"That paper bag. In the tray."

"Do I have to?"

"Yes, you have to."

She beeped when she went through, and so she stood with her arms outstretched while he drew the wand up one side and down the other and between her legs. Was it her bird necklace?

"You can go."

Permission, at last.

She collected the bag with the croissants and walked towards her gate. The airport was alive. Breathing and coursing with blood, full of thoughts. Synapses. Lights flashing. Electronic noise and announcements and children in strollers, screaming. A fountain in the middle of the departure lounge, with coins scattered in the chlorinated water. Deep fryers. Perfume in the duty-free. Alcohol.

Two bottles of gin. That's all she could afford.

She heard her flight number announced. Last call. She'd missed the boarding announcements. What time was it? Where was Ruby? Was that her flight? Where was she going? She didn't have time to check. She should run. But she could not. If she missed it, she would take the next one. She was the last one to the gate. She handed over the boarding pass, and the man handed her her purse.

You left it at security, he said. Lucky to get it back.

Yes, Fiona said. Very lucky. Thank you.

Where's the minor traveling with you? He checked his screen. Ruby Tenner?

Not coming, Fiona said.

She was seated between an elderly woman who smelled of rosewater and a young man who worked in forensic accounting. She let him talk, while she blinked and blinked, trying to get rid of images of Ruby and the others at the breakfast table at Mike and Sarah's. Dishes clattering, arguing over boxes of cereal and turns with the milk. The hiss of their ancient coffee maker that seemed to be a point of pride. Ruby, sitting there, wanting her mother, and not understanding that this was the best she could do for her. For now. There was nothing Fiona could do except make more of a mess for her if she stayed. And if she'd brought her along, Willy would take over, and Fiona knew that's not what Ruby would ever want.

White-collar guys, her seatmate said. That's where the crime is. Fraud. Embezzlement. Extortion. We track the numbers. No one can hide in the numbers.

The elderly woman watched two movies. Dinner was served. Fiona didn't eat it. The croissants were squashed in the pocket of the seatback in front of her. She kept her eye on the croissants for the entire flight. She did not sleep, even as her eyes burned in the dry, dim cabin. She did not leave her seat. When the man finally asked her name, she didn't answer.

When the plane landed, Fiona was still staring at the croissants. She knew she had to leave them. She knew that she was sick and that those croissants held some power, some connection to Ruby being with her. Acknowledging the absurdity of this and leaving them would make her just the tiniest bit better, wouldn't it? Taking them with her would make her worse. Everyone else got off the plane until it was only her, staring at the croissants.

"Ma'am?" The attendant put a hand on her shoulder. Slender fingers. Baby-pink nail polish. "Do you need assistance?"

"No." Fiona grabbed the croissants and stood up. "Thank you, no."

She saw the accountant coming out of the men's washroom. Without a word, she took his hand and led him to the parents' toilet. She locked the door behind them and then backed him up until he was sitting in the chair meant for nursing. Fiona lifted her skirt and pulled down her panties while he raised his hips and pushed his jeans to his ankles.

—

There was Willy with a dozen roses. Collette stood beside her, even more coltish now. She moved her head, looking for Ruby. She clutched a big teddy bear and an even bigger balloon covered with butterflies. Willy rushed forward, clearly stricken.

"Where is she?"

"I didn't bring her."

"Oh, Fi." Willy pulled Fiona into a tight hug. Fiona was nauseous for a moment, smelling the forensic accountant on her face, the waft of the stale croissants, and now Willy's perfume.

"What have you *done*?"

"Where is she?" Collette whined.

Fiona said, "She is where it's best for her right now. This is me, being the best mother I can be right now."

"It isn't, Fi. She needs her mother. She's already enduring a terrible loss."

"You know what it came right down to?" Fiona threw the croissants into the garbage. She grabbed the bear and the balloon. "She did not want to come, that's what." She thrust both at the first child she saw, insisted that the parent let them keep them. "She said she hates England and that you don't like her and so she'd rather stay with her friends."

"I never said I didn't like her," Collette said. "I just—"

"What friends?" Willy said.

"Friends!" Fiona yelled. "You know exactly who!"

"Fiona," Willy said. "What is this? Do I have to take you up to Noreen right away? Or do you think we might have a nice visit for a day or two? Maybe we could fly Ruby over as an unaccompanied minor. We can get you stabilized while she makes her way here. I can call—"

"I do not want Noreen. Or her doctors," Fiona said. She took hold of her suitcase and duffle and walked ahead of Willy and Collette out of the airport into the grey drizzle, the dark clouds so low that she was sure, if she stretched her arms up, her fingers would get lost in the gloom.

Across the road, the child she gave the balloon to let it go, and was now screaming as it drifted up, up, up, all the way to the dark, ducted ceiling of the car park.

They shared a bottle of wine, during which Fiona calmed down considerably. Willy didn't bother asking any more questions. She knew Fiona, and persistence made no difference. When Fiona could hardly keep her eyes open, Willy steered her to the guest room.

"Do I need to lock the door?" She said it lightly, but Fiona heard only sadness behind the words. "Or will you stay put?"

"Yes."

An hour later, she came upon a narrow, gated garden between two stately buildings. She scaled the fence and explored the garden until dawn. She found a tiny, sun-bleached hummingbird skull, half buried in icy mud. Impossibly fragile, but intact. Fiona folded it into her handkerchief. That afternoon she cleaned it and took it to the post office, where she nestled the skull and handkerchief in a small box and sent it across the ocean and into the mountains.

After the hummingbird skull came a magnifying glass with a carved ivory handle, then a stuffed shrew, nailed to a board, its jumble of tiny teeth forcing a grimace. When her mother started walking the shore of the Thames, she sent things like a section of bone pipe, a clasp from a Victorian shoe and a miniature teacup, no bigger than a thimble, chipped and stained, with a map of cracks decorating it inside and out, but not broken. *It's called mud larking*, she wrote to Ruby. *You would be very, very good at it. Sometimes people even find gold, or a human skull. Or things so precious and rare they turn them over to the museums.* That letter came with an old key that looked like it could open a castle or a dungeon. Then came half a locket, so worn that only a tiny patch of etching remained.

"You don't have to keep that stuff," Liam said.

But she did, lined up neatly on her half of the windowsill in their room.

Ruby and Liam didn't go to Cayoosh now. No one did. There was no Cayoosh anymore. Just five dead children marking its place. And that roof between the buildings, which did collapse when no one was there to clear the snow. Caution tape. Dusty rooms.

Children's art curling on the walls. The books in the little library, swelling with damp.

Sometimes Ruby has to wait for the bathroom, but she doesn't mind. She stands in the hall, tugging on her rabbit necklace or the small leather bag hanging from a cord around her neck. Mike made the bag for the bones from her pinky fingers. She likes to listen to the house talking: clanging water pipes, the squeak of the wood stove door. *Chunk, chunk* as Mike loads the stove with logs. The blender droning in the kitchen. Sarah is all about smoothies lately. Green ones, with apple and spinach and a scoop of awful, bitter powder. Music thumps up from Luke and Aubrey's room downstairs. The whir of the remote-control monster truck in her and Liam's room. They've built an elaborate track that reaches from the floor and all the way around and up—in steps—to the ceiling. Sometimes she hears Sarah's blow-dryer, or Mike coughing and spitting into the sink. Or Luke, peeing and peeing and peeing, and then the slam of the toilet seat because if any of them don't put it down, Sarah charges them a dollar.

Once Ruby hears Aubrey throwing up, and then the tap running and the sound of her brushing her teeth. When she comes out, she puts her lips to Ruby's ear.

"I have a secret," she says. "We're going to have a baby."

Ruby already has the perfect present for the baby, the tiny, soft sleeper, the impossibly small sweater and bonnet that were meant for her. She's going to give the baby the blanket too, once she's washed it enough to get the smell of her old house—cigarettes and mildew—out of it.

There's almost always someone at the house, and no matter who it is who sees them off to school each morning, they all say the same thing.

Take care of each other.

Liam takes Ruby's hand and they walk to the public school together like that, every single day. The kids laugh at them and sing the kissing song. They call them married, or boyfriend and girlfriend. The older kids call them the Hoppy Humpers because every day at lunch Liam and Ruby take their lunch boxes to the fence and wait for the rabbits. They always come to Ruby first. Liam says maybe these are the ones from Cayoosh.

"Maybe they come across town just for you."

"Maybe," Ruby says.

They bring parsley and kale that they buy with their allowance, and which the rabbits like best. Sometimes kids will dare each other to sneak up and scare the rabbits away. Other times a kid—always one of the younger ones—will ask if they can feed them too. Ruby gives them the best piece of greens and puts a hand on their back to remind them to stay very, very still.

The rabbits stop coming as winter slowly takes shape. The trees shiver naked in the cold air. The first snow is late, but when it comes, it falls in a sudden soft curtain, folding and piling on the ground.

Way up the highway, in the belly of a tight s-curve below Tiffen Creek, there is a rest stop with two outhouses and a garbage bin. The outhouses are nearly buried, and even though Highways doesn't dig them out, the cross-country skiers and truck drivers do. The doors are just clear enough to open halfway. A backpack leans up against one of the outhouses. An older man emerges from the outhouse and fastens his worn leather belt. He grabs the pack and puts it in his truck. He found it in the narrow, still-snowless lee of a looming basalt rock face. It belongs to Gus Tenner. It's soggy and everything inside is ruined. He plans to drop it off at Mike and Sarah's on his way home. It's hard for a little girl to lose her father. He's still out there somewhere. Every time the older man comes up here, he wonders if he's going to find Tenner's body. All summer long, people were out looking for him. He could tell people where he found the pack. He took a waypoint on his GPS, so it'd be exact. Maybe Tenner himself was nearby too. He'd be bones now. Or a soupy mess inside all his fancy backcountry gear, maybe.

Or maybe he is still under the snow that hadn't melted on one half of that meadow, even at the height of summer, kept cool in the shade of the forest. All those tattoos. Does that kind of ink stay in the skin after death? He looks at the backpack. Maybe the little girl is better off without it. Maybe all the rot and ruin will make her think of her father not in a good way.

He drives down the highway, losing a little more of his determination to hand over the pack with each mile. When he crosses the Lil'wat River, he sees a construction waste bin at the lumberyard and pulls over. He tosses the pack into the bin, and immediately knows it's the right thing to do. A backpack and a body would be one thing, but a ruined backpack on its own is another.

A little girl should not be pulled back into it like that. A little girl should be able to let go.

A town should be able to let go.

CARRIE MAC was born and raised in small-town British Columbia. She lived and worked as a paramedic in Pemberton, which is the inspiration for the location of *Last Winter*. She quit the ambulance service to homeschool her two children. Mac is the author of several award-winning novels for teen readers, and as a queer author, proudly writes for marginalized youth. She's won the CBC Non-Fiction prize, as well as a BC Book Prize. While *Last Winter* is entirely fiction, she does bring her lived experience as a paramedic, as a widow, and as a parent living with Bipolar 1 to the story. She has taught creative writing across ages and venues for two decades, and has recently completed her MFA from UBC's School of Creative Writing. She lives in East Vancouver.